The Collected Shorter
Supernatural & Weird
Fiction of
Algernon Blackwood
Volume 4

ALGERNON BLACKWOOD

The Collected Shorter Supernatural & Weird Fiction of Algernon Blackwood Volume 4

Twenty-Nine Short Stories of the Strange and Unusual Including 'Confession', 'If the Cap Fits', 'The Destruction of Smith', 'The Man Who Found Out' and 'The Wings of Horus'

Algernon Blackwood

LEONAUR

The Collected Shorter Supernatural & Weird Fiction of
Algernon Blackwood
Volume 4
Twenty-Nine Short Stories of the Strange and Unusual Including 'Confession', 'If the
Cap Fits', 'The Destruction of Smith', 'The Man Who Found Out' and 'The Wings
of Horus'
by Algernon Blackwood

Leonaur is an imprint of Oakpast Ltd

ISBN: 978-1-916535-12-1 (hardcover)
ISBN: 978-1-916535-13-8 (softcover)

http://www.leonaur.com

Publisher's Notes

Contents

Confession

The fog swirled slowly round him, driven by a heavy movement of its own, for of course there was no wind. It hung in poisonous thick coils and loops; it rose and sank; no light penetrated it directly from street lamp or motor-car, though here and there some big shop-window shed a glimmering patch upon its ever-shifting curtain.

O'Reilly's eyes ached and smarted with the incessant effort to see a foot beyond his face. The optic nerve grew tired, and sight, accordingly, less accurate. He coughed as he shuffled forward cautiously through the choking gloom. Only the stifled rumble of crawling traffic persuaded him he was in a crowded city at all—this, and the vague outlines of groping figures, hugely magnified, emerging suddenly and disappearing again, as they fumbled along inch by inch towards uncertain destinations.

The figures, however were human beings; they were real. That much he knew. He heard their muffled voices, now close, now distant, strangely smothered always. He also heard the tapping of innumerable sticks, feeling for iron railings or the kerb. These phantom outlines represented living people. He was not alone.

It was the dread of finding himself *quite* alone that haunted him, for he was still unable to cross an open space without assistance. He had the physical strength, it was the mind that failed him. Midway the panic terror might descend upon him, he would shake all over, his will dissolve, he would shriek for help, run wildly—into the traffic probably—or, as they called it in his North Ontario home, "throw a fit" in the street before advancing wheels. He was not yet entirely cured, although under ordinary conditions he was safe enough, as Dr. Henry had assured him.

When he left Regent's Park by Tube an hour ago the air was clear, the November sun shone brightly, the pale blue sky was cloudless, and the assumption that he could manage the journey across London Town alone was justified. The following day he was to leave for Brighton for the week of final convalescence: this little preliminary test of his powers on a bright November afternoon was all to the good. Doctor Henry furnished minute instructions: "You change at Piccadilly Circus—without leaving the underground station, mind—and get out at South Kensington. You know the address of your V.A.D. friend. Have your cup of tea with her, then come back the same way to Regent's Park. Come back before dark—say six o'clock at latest. It's better." He had described exactly what turns to take after leaving the station, so many to the right, so many to the left; it was a little confusing, but the distance was short. "You can always ask. You can't possibly go wrong."

The unexpected fog, however, now blurred these instructions in a confused jumble in his mind. The failure of outer sight reacted upon memory. The V.A.D. besides had warned him her address was "not easy to find the first time. The house lies in a backwater. But with your 'backwoods' instincts you'll probably manage it better than any Londoner!" She, too, had not calculated upon the fog.

When O'Reilly came up the stairs at South Kensington Station, he emerged into such murky darkness that he thought he was still underground. An impenetrable world lay round him. Only a raw bite in the damp atmosphere told him he stood beneath an open sky. For some little time, he stood and stared—a Canadian soldier, his home among clear brilliant spaces, now face to face for the first time in his life with that thing he had so often read about—a bad London fog. With keenest interest and surprise, he "enjoyed" the novel spectacle for perhaps ten minutes, watching the people arrive and vanish, and wondering why the station lights stopped dead the instant they touched the street—then, with a sense of adventure—it cost an effort—he left the covered building and plunged into the opaque sea beyond.

Repeating to himself the directions he had received—first to the right, second to the left, once more to the left, and so forth—he checked each turn, assuring himself it was impossible to go wrong. He made correct if slow progress, until someone blundered into him with an abrupt and startling question: "Is this right, do you know, for South Kensington Station?"

It was the suddenness that startled him; one moment there was no one, the next they were face to face, another, and the stranger had vanished into the gloom with a courteous word of grateful thanks. But the little shock of interruption had put memory out of gear. Had he already turned twice to the right, or had he not? O'Reilly realised sharply he had forgotten his memorized instructions. He stood still, making strenuous efforts at recovery, but each effort left him more uncertain than before. Five minutes later he was lost as hopelessly as any townsman who leaves his tent in the backwoods without blazing the trees to ensure finding his way back again. Even the sense of direction, so strong in him among his native forests, was completely gone. There were no stars, there was no wind, no smell, no sound of running water. There was nothing anywhere to guide him, nothing but occasional dim outlines, groping, shuffling, emerging and disappearing in the eddying fog, but rarely coming within actual speaking, much less touching, distance. He was lost utterly; more, he was alone.

Yet not *quite* alone—the thing he dreaded most. There were figures still in his immediate neighbourhood. They emerged, vanished, reappeared, dissolved. No, he was not quite alone. He saw these thickenings of the fog, he heard their voices, the tapping of their cautious sticks, their shuffling feet as well. They were real. They moved, it seemed, about him in a circle, never coming very close.

"But they're real," he said to himself aloud, betraying the weak point in his armour. "They're human beings right enough. I'm positive of that."

He had never argued with Dr. Henry—he wanted to get well; he had obeyed implicitly, believing everything the doctor told him—up to a point. But he had always had his own idea about these "figures," because, among them, were often enough his own pals from the Somme, Gallipoli, the Mespot horror, too. And he ought to know his own pals when he saw them! At the same time, he knew quite well he had been "shocked," his being dislocated; half dissolved as it were, his system pushed into some lopsided condition that meant inaccurate registration. True. He grasped that perfectly. But, in that shock and dislocation, had he not possibly picked up another gear? Were there not gaps and broken edges, pieces that no longer dovetailed, fitted as usual, interstices, in a word? Yes, that was the word—interstices. Cracks, so to speak, between his perception of the outside world and his inner interpretation of these? Between memory and recognition? Between the various states of consciousness that usually dovetailed so neatly that the joints were normally imperceptible?

His state, he well knew, was abnormal, but were his symptoms on that account unreal? Could not these "interstices" be used by—others? When he saw his "figures," he used to ask himself: "Are not these the real ones, and the others—the human beings—unreal?"

This question now revived in him with a new intensity. Were these figures in the fog real or unreal? The man who had asked the way to the station, was he not, after all, a shadow merely?

By the use of his cane and foot and what of sight was left to him he knew that he was on an island. A lamppost stood up solid and straight beside him, shedding its faint patch of glimmering light. Yet there were railings, however, that puzzled him, for his stick hit the metal rods distinctly in a series. And there should be no railings round an island. Yet he had most certainly crossed a dreadful open space to get where he was. His confusion and bewilderment increased with dangerous rapidity. Panic was not far away.

He was no longer on an omnibus route. A rare taxi crawled past occasionally, a whitish patch at the window indicating an anxious human face; now and again came a van or cart, the driver holding a lantern as he led the stumbling horse. These comforted him, rare though they were. But it was the figures that drew his attention most. He was quite sure they were real. They were human beings like himself.

For all that, he decided he might as well be positive on the point. He tried one accordingly—a big man who rose suddenly before him out of the very earth.

"Can you give me the trail to Morley Place?" he asked.

But his question was drowned by the other's simultaneous inquiry in a voice much louder than his own.

"I say, is this right for the Tube station, d'you know? I'm utterly lost. I want South Ken."

And by the time O'Reilly had pointed the direction whence he himself had just come, the man was gone again, obliterated, swallowed up, not so much as his footsteps audible, almost as if—it seemed again—he never had been there at all.

This left an acute unpleasantness in him, a sense of bewilderment greater than before. He waited five minutes, not daring to move a step, then tried another figure, a woman this time who, luckily, knew the immediate neighbourhood intimately. She gave him elaborate instructions in the kindest possible way, then vanished with incredible swiftness and ease into the sea of gloom beyond. The instantaneous way she vanished was disheartening, upsetting; it was so uncannily abrupt and sudden. Yet she comforted him. Morley Place, according to her version, was not two hundred yards from where he stood. He felt his way forward, step by step, using his cane, crossing a giddy open space kicking the kerb with each boot alternately, coughing and choking all the time as he did so.

"They were real, I guess, anyway," he said aloud. "They were both real enough all right. And it may lift a bit soon!" He was making a great effort to hold himself in hand. He was already fighting, that is. He realized this perfectly. The only point was—the reality of the figures. "It may lift now any minute," he repeated louder. In spite of the cold, his skin was sweating profusely.

But, of course, it did not lift. The figures, too, became fewer. No carts were audible. He had followed the woman's directions carefully, but now found himself in some by-way, evidently, where pedestrians at the best of times were rare. There was dull silence all about him. His foot lost the kerb, his cane swept the empty air, striking nothing solid, and panic rose upon him with its shuddering, icy grip. He was alone, he knew himself alone, worse still—he was in another open space.

It took him fifteen minutes to cross that open space, most of the way upon his hands and knees, oblivious of the icy slime that stained his trousers, froze his fingers, intent only upon feeling solid support against his back and spine again. It was an endless period. The moment of collapse was close, the shriek already rising in his throat, the shaking of the whole body uncontrollable, when—his outstretched fingers struck a friendly kerb, and he saw a glimmering patch of diffused radiance overhead. With a great, quick effort he stood upright, and an instant later his stick rattled along an area railing. He leaned against it, breathless, panting, his heart beating painfully while the street lamp gave him the further comfort of its feeble gleam, the actual flame, however, invisible. He looked this way and that; the pavement was deserted. He was engulfed in the dark silence of the fog.

But Morley Place, he knew, must be very close by now. He thought of the friendly little V.A.D. he had known in France, of a warm bright fire, a cup of tea and a cigarette. One more effort, he reflected, and all these would be his. He pluckily groped his way forward again, crawling slowly by the area railings. If things got really bad again, he would ring a bell and ask for help, much as he shrank from the idea. Provided he had no more open spaces to cross, provided he saw no more figures emerging and vanishing like creatures born of the fog and dwelling within it as within their native element—it was the figures he now dreaded more than anything else, more even than the loneliness—provided the panic sense——

A faint darkening of the fog beneath the next lamp caught his eye and made him start. He stopped. It was not a figure this time, it was the shadow of the pole grotesquely magnified. No, it moved. It moved towards him. A flame of fire followed by ice flowed through him. It was a figure—close against his face. It was a woman.

The doctor's advice came suddenly back to him, the counsel that had cured him of a hundred phantoms:

"Do not ignore them. Treat them as real. Speak and go with them. You will soon prove their unreality then. And they will leave you. . .."

He made a brave, tremendous effort. He was shaking. One hand clutched the damp and icy area railing.

"Lost your way like myself, haven't you, ma'am?" he said in a voice that trembled. "Do you know where we are at all? Morley Place I'm looking for——"

He stopped dead. The woman moved nearer and for the first time he saw her face clearly. Its ghastly pallor, the bright, frightened eyes that stared with a kind of dazed bewilderment into his own, the beauty above all, arrested his speech midway. The woman was young, her tall figure wrapped in a dark fur coat.

"Can I help you?" he asked impulsively, forgetting his own terror for the moment. He was more than startled. Her air of distress and pain stirred a peculiar anguish in him. For a moment she made no answer, thrusting her white face closer as if examining him, so close, indeed, that he controlled with difficulty his instinct to shrink back a little.

"Where am I?" she asked at length, searching his eyes intently. "I'm lost—I've lost myself. I can't find my way back." Her voice was low, a curious wailing in it that touched his pity oddly. He felt his own distress merging in one that was greater.

"Same here," he replied more confidently. "I'm terrified of being alone, too. I've had shell-shock, you know. Let's go together. We'll find a way together——"

"Who are you!" the woman murmured, still staring at him with her big bright eyes, their distress, however, no whit lessened. She gazed at him as though aware suddenly of his presence.

He told her briefly. "And I'm going to tea with a V.A.D. friend in Morley Place. What's your address? Do you know the name of the street?"

She appeared not to hear him, or not to understand exactly; it was as if she was not listening again.

"I came out so suddenly, so unexpectedly," he heard the low voice with pain in every syllable; "I can't find my home again. Just when I was expecting him too——" She looked about her with a distraught expression that made O'Reilly long to carry her in his arms to safety then and there. "He may be there now—waiting for me at this very moment—and I can't get back." And so sad was her voice that only by an effort did O'Reilly prevent himself putting out his hand to touch her. More and more he forgot himself in his desire to help her. Her beauty, the wonder of her strange bright eyes in the pallid face, made an immense appeal. He became calmer. This woman was real enough. He asked again the address, the street and number, the distance she thought it was. "Have you any idea of the direction, ma'am, any idea at all? We'll go together and——"

She suddenly cut him short. She turned her head as if to listen, so that he saw her profile a moment, the outline of the slender neck, a glimpse of jewels just below the fur.

"Hark! I hear him calling! I remember...!" And she was gone from his side into the swirling fog.

Without an instant's hesitation O'Reilly followed her, not only because he wished to help, but because he dared not be left alone. The presence of this strange, lost woman comforted him; he must not lose sight of her, whatever happened. He had to run, she went so rapidly, ever just in front, moving with confidence and certainty, turning right and left, crossing the street, but never stopping, never hesitating, her companion always at her heels in breathless haste, and with a growing terror that he might lose her any minute. The way she found her direction through the dense fog was marvellous enough, but O'Reilly's only thought was to keep her in sight, lest his own panic redescend upon him with its inevitable collapse in the dark and lonely street.

It was a wild and panting pursuit, and he kept her in view with difficulty, a dim fleeting outline always a few yards ahead of him. She did not once turn her head, she uttered no sound, no cry; she hurried forward with unfaltering instinct. Nor did the chase occur to him once as singular; she was his safety, and that was all he realised.

One thing, however, he remembered afterwards, though at the actual time he no more than registered the detail, paying no attention to it—a definite perfume she left upon the atmosphere, one, moreover, that he knew, although he could not find its name as he ran. It was associated vaguely, for him, with something unpleasant, something disagreeable. He connected it with misery and pain. It gave him a feeling of uneasiness. More than that he did not notice at the moment, nor could he remember—he certainly did not try—where he had known this particular scent before.

Then suddenly the woman stopped, opened a gate and passed into a small private garden—so suddenly that O'Reilly, close upon her heels, only just avoided tumbling into her. "You've found it?" he cried. "May I come in a moment with you? Perhaps you'll let me telephone to the doctor."

She turned instantly. Her face close against his own, was livid.

"Doctor!" she repeated in an awful whisper. The word meant terror to her. O'Reilly stood amazed. For a second or two neither of them moved. The woman seemed petrified.

"Dr. Henry, you know," he stammered, finding his tongue again. "I'm in his care. He's in Harley Street."

Her face cleared as suddenly as it had darkened, though the original expression of bewilderment and pain still hung in her great eyes. But the terror left them, as though she suddenly forgot some association that had revived it.

"My home," she murmured. "My home is somewhere here. I'm near it. I must get back—in time—for him. I must. He's coming to me." And with these extraordinary words she turned, walked up the narrow path, and stood upon the porch of a two-storey house before her companion had recovered from his astonishment sufficiently to move or utter a syllable in reply. The front door, he saw, was ajar. It had been left open.

For five seconds, perhaps for ten, he hesitated; it was the fear that the door would close and shut him out that brought the decision to his will and muscles. He ran up the steps and followed the woman into a dark hall where she had already preceded him, and amid whose blackness she now had finally vanished. He closed the door, not knowing exactly why he did so, and knew at once by an instinctive feeling that the house he now found himself in with this unknown woman was empty and unoccupied. In a house, however, he felt safe. It was the open streets that were his danger. He stood waiting, listening a moment before he spoke; and he heard the woman moving down the passage from door to door, repeating to herself in her low voice of unhappy wailing some words he could not understand:

"Where is it? Oh, where is it? I must get back. . . ."

O'Reilly then found himself abruptly stricken with dumbness, as though, with these strange words, a haunting terror came up and breathed against him in the darkness.

"Is she after all a figure?" ran in letters of fire across his numbed brain. "Is she unreal—or real?"

Seeking relief in action of some kind, he put out a hand automatically, feeling along the wall for an electric switch, and though he found it by some miraculous chance, no answering glow responded to the click.

And the woman's voice from the darkness: "Ah! Ah! At last, I've found it. I'm home again—at last. . .!" He heard a door open and close upstairs. He was on the ground-floor now—alone. Complete silence followed.

In the conflict of various emotions—fear for himself lest his panic should return, fear for the woman who had led him into this empty house and now deserted him upon some mysterious errand of her own that made him think of madness—in this conflict that held him a moment spell-bound, there was a yet bigger ingredient demanding instant explanation, but an explanation that he could not find. Was the woman real or was she unreal? Was she a human being or a "figure"? The horror of doubt obsessed him with an acute uneasiness that betrayed itself in a return of that unwelcome inner trembling he knew was dangerous.

What saved him from a *crise* that must have had most dangerous results for his mind and nervous system generally, seems to have been the outstanding fact that he felt more for the woman than for himself. His sympathy and pity had been deeply moved; her voice, her beauty, her anguish and bewilderment, all uncommon, inexplicable, mysterious, formed together a claim that drove self into the background. Added to this was the detail that she had left him, gone to another floor without a word, and now, behind a closed door in a room upstairs, found herself face to face at last with the unknown object of her frantic search—with "it," whatever "it" might be. Real or unreal, figure or human being, the overmastering impulse of his being was that he must go to her.

It was this clear impulse that gave him decision and energy to do what he then did. He struck a match, he found a stump of candle, he made his way by means of this flickering light along the passage and up the carpetless stairs. He moved cautiously, stealthily, though not knowing why he did so. The house, he now saw, was indeed untenanted; dust-sheets covered the piled-up furniture; he glimpsed through doors ajar, pictures were screened upon the walls, brackets draped to look like hooded heads. He went on slowly, steadily, moving on tiptoe

15

as though conscious of being watched, noting the well of darkness in the hall below, the grotesque shadows that his movements cast on walls and ceiling.

The silence was unpleasant, yet, remembering that the woman was "expecting" someone, he did not wish it broken. He reached the landing and stood still. Closed doors on both sides of a corridor met his sight, as he shaded the candle to examine the scene. Behind which of these doors, he asked himself, was the woman, figure or human being, now alone with "it"?

There was nothing to guide him, but an instinct that he must not delay sent him forward again upon his search. He tried a door on the right—an empty room, with the furniture hidden by dust-sheets, and the mattress rolled up on the bed. He tried a second door, leaving the first one open behind him, and it was, similarly, an empty bedroom. Coming out into the corridor again he stood a moment waiting, then called aloud in a low voice that yet woke echoes unpleasantly in the hall below: "Where are you? I want to help—which room are you in?"

There was no answer; he was almost glad he heard no sound, for he knew quite well that he was waiting really for another sound—the steps of him who was "expected." And the idea of meeting with this unknown third sent a shudder through him, as though related to an interview he dreaded with his whole heart, and must at all costs avoid. Waiting another moment or two, he noted that his candle-stump was burning low, then crossed the landing with a feeling, at once of hesitation and determination, towards a door opposite to him. He opened it; he did not halt on the threshold. Holding the candle at arm's length, he went boldly in.

And instantly his nostrils told him he was right at last, for a whiff of the strange perfume, though this time much stronger than before, greeted him, sending a new quiver along his nerves. He knew now why it was associated with unpleasantness, with pain, with misery, for he recognised it—the odour of a hospital. In this room a powerful anaesthetic had been used—and recently.

Simultaneously with smell, sight brought its message too. On the large double bed behind the door on his right lay, to his amazement, the woman in the dark fur coat. He saw the jewels on the slender neck; but the eyes he did not see, for they were closed—closed, too, he grasped at once, in death. The body lay stretched at full length, quite motionless. He approached. A dark thin streak that came from the parted lips and passed downwards over the chin, losing itself then

16

in the fur collar, was a trickle of blood. It was hardly dry. It glistened.

Strange it was perhaps that, while imaginary fears had the power to paralyse him, mind and body, this sight of something real had the effect of restoring confidence. The sight of blood and death, amid conditions often ghastly and even monstrous, was no new thing to him. He went up quietly, and with steady hand he felt the woman's cheek, the warmth of recent life still in its softness. The final cold had not yet mastered this empty form whose beauty, in its perfect stillness, had taken on the new strange sweetness of an unearthly bloom. Pallid, silent, untenanted, it lay before him, lit by the flicker of his guttering candle. He lifted the fur coat to feel for the unbeating heart. A couple of hours ago at most, he judged, this heart was working busily, the breath came through those parted lips, the eyes were shining in full beauty. His hand encountered a hard knob—the head of a long steel hat-pin driven through the heart up to its hilt.

He knew then which was the figure—which was the real and which the unreal. He knew also what had been meant by "it."

But before he could think or reflect what action he must take, before he could straighten himself even from his bent position over the body on the bed, there sounded through the empty house below the loud clang of the front door being closed. And instantly rushed over him that other fear he had so long forgotten—fear for himself. The panic of his own shaken nerves descended with irresistible onslaught. He turned, extinguishing the candle in the violent trembling of his hand, and tore headlong from the room.

The following ten minutes seemed a nightmare in which he was not master of himself and knew not exactly what he did. All he realized was that steps already sounded on the stairs, coming quickly nearer. The flicker of an electric torch played on the banisters, whose shadows ran swiftly sideways along the wall as the hand that held the light ascended. He thought in a frenzied second of police, of his presence in the house, of the murdered woman. It was a sinister combination. Whatever happened, he must escape without being so much as even seen. His heart raced madly. He darted across the landing into the room opposite, whose door he had luckily left open. And by some incredible chance, apparently, he was neither seen nor heard by the man who, a moment later, reached the landing, entered the room where the body of the woman lay, and closed the door carefully behind him.

Shaking, scarcely daring to breathe lest his breath be audible, O'Reilly, in the grip of his own personal terror, remnant of his uncured shock of war, had no thought of what duty might demand or not demand of him. He thought only of himself. He realised one clear issue—that he must get out of the house without being heard or seen. Who the newcomer was he did not know, beyond an uncanny assurance that it was *not* him whom the woman had "expected," but the murderer himself, and that it was the murderer, in his turn, who was expecting this third person. In that room with death at his elbow, a death he had himself brought about but an hour or two ago, the murderer now hid in waiting for his second victim. And the door was closed.

Yet any minute it might open again, cutting off retreat.

O'Reilly crept out, stole across the landing, reached the head of the stairs, and began, with the utmost caution, the perilous descent. Each time the bare boards creaked beneath his weight, no matter how stealthily this weight was adjusted, his heart missed a beat. He tested each step before he pressed upon it, distributing as much of his weight as he dared upon the banisters. It was a little more than half-way down that, to his horror, his foot caught in a projecting carpet tack; he slipped on the polished wood, and only saved himself from falling headlong by a wild clutch at the railing, making an uproar that seemed to him like the explosion of a hand-grenade in the forgotten trenches. His nerves gave way then, and panic seized him. In the silence that followed the resounding echoes he heard the bedroom door opening on the floor above.

Concealment was now useless. It was impossible, too. He took the last flight of stairs in a series of leaps, four steps at a time, reached the hall, flew across it, and opened the front door, just as his pursuer, electric torch in hand, covered half the stairs behind him. Slamming the door, he plunged headlong into the welcome, all-obscuring fog outside.

The fog had now no terrors for him, he welcomed its conceal-ing mantle; nor did it matter in which direction he ran so long as he put distance between him and the house of death. The pursuer had, of course, not followed him into the street. He crossed open spaces without a tremor. He ran in a circle nevertheless, though without be-ing aware he did so. No people were about, no single groping shadow passed him; no boom of traffic reached his ears, when he paused for breath at length against an area railing.

Then for the first time he made the discovery that he had no hat. He remembered now. In examining the body, partly out of respect, partly perhaps unconsciously, he had taken it off and laid it—on the very bed.

It was there, a tell-tale bit of damning evidence, in the house of death. And a series of probable consequences flashed through his mind like lightning. It was a new hat fortunately; more fortunate still, he had not yet written name or initials in it; but the maker's mark was there for all to read, and the police would go immediately to the shop where he had bought it only two days before. Would the shop-people remember his appearance? Would his visit, the date, the conversation be recalled? He thought it was unlikely; he resembled dozens of men; he had no outstanding peculiarity. He tried to think, but his mind was confused and troubled, his heart was beating dreadfully, he felt desperately ill. He sought vainly for some story to account for his being out in the fog and far from home without a hat. No single idea presented itself. He clung to the icy railings, hardly able to keep upright, collapse very near—when suddenly a figure emerged from the fog, paused a moment to stare at him, put out a hand and caught him, and then spoke:

"You're ill, my dear sir," said a man's kindly voice. "Can I be of any assistance? Come, let me help you." He had seen at once that it was not a case of drunkenness. "Come, take my arm, won't you? I'm a physician. Luckily, too, you are just outside my very house. Come in." And he half dragged, half pushed O'Reilly, now bordering on collapse, up the steps and opened the door with his latch-key.

"Felt ill suddenly—lost in the fog . . . terrified, but be all right soon, thanks awfully——" the Canadian stammered his gratitude, but already feeling better. He sank into a chair in the hall, while the other put down a paper parcel he had been carrying, and led him presently into a comfortable room; a fire burned brightly; the electric lamps were pleasantly shaded; a decanter of whisky and a siphon stood on a small table beside a big arm-chair; and before O'Reilly could find another word to say the other had poured him out a glass and bade him sip it slowly, without troubling to talk till he felt better.

"That will revive you. Better drink it slowly. You should never have been out a night like this. If you've far to go, better let me put you up——"

"Very kind, very kind, indeed," mumbled O'Reilly, recovering rapidly in the comfort of a presence he already liked and felt even drawn to.

"No trouble at all," returned the doctor. "I've been at the front, you know. I can see what your trouble is—shell-shock, I'll be bound."

The Canadian, much impressed by the other's quick diagnosis, noted also his tact and kindness. He had made no reference to the absence of a hat, for instance.

"Quite true," he said. "I'm with Dr. Henry, in Harley Street," and he added a few words about his case. The whisky worked its effect, he revived more and more, feeling better every minute. The other handed him a cigarette; they began to talk about his symptoms and recovery; confidence returned in a measure, though he still felt badly frightened. The doctor's manner and personality did much to help, for there was strength and gentleness in the face, though the features showed unusual determination, softened occasionally by a sudden hint as of suffering in the bright, compelling eyes. It was the face, thought O'Reilly, of a man who had seen much and probably been through hell, but of a man who was simple, good, sincere. Yet not a man to trifle with; behind his gentleness lay something very stern. This effect of character and personality woke the other's respect in addition to his gratitude. His sympathy was stirred.

"You encourage me to make another guess," the man was saying, after a successful reading of the impromptu patient's state, "that you have had, namely, a severe shock quite recently, and"—he hesitated for the merest fraction of a second—"that it would be a relief to you," he went on, the skilful suggestion in the voice unnoticed by his companion, "it would be wise as well, if you could unburden yourself to—someone—who would understand." He looked at O'Reilly with a kindly and very pleasant smile. "Am I not right, perhaps?" he asked in his gentle tone.

"Someone who would understand," repeated the Canadian. "That's my trouble exactly. You've hit it. It's all so incredible."

The other smiled. "The more incredible," he suggested, "the greater your need for expression. Suppression, as you may know, is dangerous in cases like this. You think you have hidden it, but it bides its time and comes up later, causing a lot of trouble. Confession, you know"—he emphasised the word—"confession is good for the soul!"

"You're dead right," agreed the other.

"Now if you can, bring yourself to tell it to someone who will listen and believe—to myself, for instance. I am a doctor, familiar with such things. I shall regard all you say as a professional confidence, of course; and, as we are strangers, my belief or disbelief is of no particular consequence. I may tell you in advance of your story, however—I think I can promise it—that I shall believe all you have to say."

O'Reilly told his story without more ado, for the suggestion of the skilled physician had found easy soil to work in. During the recital his host's eyes never once left his own. He moved no single muscle of his body. His interest seemed intense.

"A bit tall, isn't it?" said the Canadian, when his tale was finished. "And the question is——" he continued with a threat of volubility which the other checked instantly.

"Strange, yes, but incredible, no," the doctor interrupted. "I see no reason to disbelieve a single detail of what you have just told me. Things equally remarkable, equally incredible, happen in all large towns, as I know from personal experience. I could give you instances." He paused a moment, but his companion, staring into his eyes with interest and curiosity, made no comment. "Some years ago, in fact," continued the other, "I knew of a very similar case—strangely similar."

"Really! I should be immensely interested——"

"So similar that it seems almost a coincidence. *You* may find it hard, in your turn, to credit it." He paused again, while O'Reilly sat forward in his chair to listen. "Yes," pursued the doctor slowly, "I think everyone connected with it is now dead. There is no reason why I should not tell it, for one confidence deserves another, you know. It happened during the Boer War—as long ago as that," he added with emphasis. "It is really a very commonplace story in one way, though very dreadful in another, but a man who has served at the front will understand and—I'm sure—will sympathize."

"I'm sure of that," offered the other readily.

"A colleague of mine, now dead, as I mentioned—a surgeon, with a big practice, married a young and charming girl. They lived happily together for several years. His wealth made her very comfortable. His consulting-room, I must tell you, was some distance from his house—just as this might be—so that she was never bothered with any of his cases. Then came the war. Like many others, though much over age, he volunteered. He gave up his lucrative practice and went to South Africa.

"His income, of course, stopped; the big house was closed; his wife found her life of enjoyment considerably curtailed. This she considered a great hardship, it seems. She felt a bitter grievance against him. Devoid of imagination, without any power of sacrifice, a selfish type, she was yet a beautiful, attractive woman—and young. The inevitable lover came upon the scene to console her. They planned to run away together. He was rich. Japan, they thought would suit them. Only, by some ill luck, the husband got wind of it and arrived in London just in the nick of time."

"Well rid of her," put in O'Reilly, "*I* think."

The doctor waited a moment. He sipped his glass. Then his eyes fixed upon his companion's face somewhat sternly.

"Well rid of her, yes," he continued, "only he determined to make that riddance final. He decided to kill her—and her lover. You see, he loved her."

O'Reilly made no comment. In his own country this method with a faithless woman was not unknown. His interest was very concentrated. But he was thinking, too, as he listened, thinking hard.

"He planned the time and place with care," resumed the other in a lower voice, as though he might possibly be overheard. "They met, he knew, in the big house, now closed, the house where he and his young wife had passed such happy years during their prosperity. The plan failed, however, in an important detail—the woman came at the appointed hour, but without her lover. She found death waiting for her—it was a painless death. Then her lover, who was to arrive half an hour later, did not come at all. The door had been left open for him purposely. The house was dark, its rooms shut up, deserted; there was no caretaker even. It was a foggy night, just like this."

"And the other?" asked O'Reilly in a failing voice. "The lover——"

"A man did come in," the doctor went on calmly, "but it was not the lover. It was a stranger."

"A stranger?" the other whispered. "And the surgeon—where was he all this time?"

"Waiting outside to see him enter—concealed in the fog. He saw the man go in. Five minutes later he followed, meaning to complete his vengeance, his act of justice, whatever you like to call it. But the man who had come in was a stranger—he came in by chance—just as you might have done—to shelter from the fog—or——"

O'Reilly, though with a great effort, rose abruptly to his feet. He had an appalling feeling that the man facing him was mad. He had a keen desire to get outside, fog or no fog, to leave this room, to escape from the calm accents of this insistent voice. The effect of the whisky was still in his blood. He felt no lack of confidence. But words came to him with difficulty.

"I think I'd better be pushing off now, doctor," he said clumsily. "But I feel I must thank you very much for all your kindness and help." He turned and looked hard into the keen eyes facing him. "Your friend," he asked in a whisper, "the surgeon—I hope—I mean, was he ever caught?"

"No," was the grave reply, the doctor standing up in front of him, "he was never caught."

O'Reilly waited a moment before he made another remark. "Well," he said at length, but in a louder tone than before, "I think—I'm glad." He went to the door without shaking hands.

"You have no hat," mentioned the voice behind him. "If you'll wait a moment, I'll get you one of mine. You need not trouble to return it." And the doctor passed him, going into the hall. There was a sound of tearing paper, O'Reilly left the house a moment later with a hat upon his head, but it was not till he reached the Tube station half an hour afterwards that he realised it was his own.

Egyptian Sorcery

1

Sanfield paused as he was about to leave the Underground station at Victoria, and cursed the weather. When he left the City, it was fine; now it was pouring with rain, and he had neither overcoat nor umbrella. Not a taxi was discoverable in the dripping gloom. He would get soaked before he reached his rooms in Sloane Street.

He stood for some minutes, thinking how vile London was in February, and how depressing life was in general. He stood also, in that moment, though he knew it not, upon the edge of a singular adventure. Looking back upon it in later years, he often remembered this particularly wretched moment of a pouring wet February evening, when everything seemed wrong, and Fate had loaded the dice against him, even in the matter of weather and umbrellas.

Fate, however, without betraying her presence, was watching him through the rain and murk; and Fate, that night, had strange, mysterious eyes. Fantastic cards lay up her sleeve. The rain, his weariness and depression, his physical fatigue especially, seemed the conditions she required before she played these curious cards. Something new and wonderful fluttered close. Romance flashed by him across the driving rain and touched his cheek. He was too exasperated to be aware of it.

Things had gone badly that day at the office, where he was junior partner in a small firm of engineers. Threatened trouble at the works had come to a head. A strike seemed imminent. To add to his annoyance, a new client, whose custom was of supreme importance, had just complained bitterly of the delay in the delivery of his machinery. The senior partners had left the matter in Sanfield's hands; he had not succeeded. The angry customer swore he would hold the firm to its contract. They could deliver or pay up—whichever suited them. The junior partner had made a mess of things.

The final words on the telephone still rang in his ears as he stood

25

sheltering under the arcade, watching the downpour, and wondering whether he should make a dash for it or wait on the chance of its clearing up—when a further blow was dealt him as the rain-soaked poster of an evening paper caught his eye: "Riots in Egypt. Heavy Fall in Egyptian Securities," he read with blank dismay. Buying a paper, he turned feverishly to the City article—to find his worst fears confirmed. Delta Lands, in which nearly all his small capital was invested, had declined a quarter on the news, and would evidently decline further still. The riots were going on in the towns nearest to their property. Banks had been looted, crops destroyed; the trouble was deep-seated.

So grave was the situation that mere weather seemed suddenly of no account at all. He walked home doggedly in the drenching rain, paying less attention to it than if it had been Scotch mist. The water streamed from his hat, dripped down his back and neck, splashed him with mud and grime from head to foot. He was soaked to the skin. He hardly noticed it. His capital had depreciated by half, at least, and possibly was altogether lost; his position at the office was insecure. How could mere weather matter?

Sitting, eventually, before his fire in dry clothes, after an apology for a dinner he had no heart to eat, he reviewed the situation. He faced a possible total loss of his private capital. Next, the position of his firm caused him grave uneasiness, since, apart from his own mishandling of the new customer, the threatened strike might ruin it completely; a long strain on its limited finances was out of the question. George Sanfield certainly saw things at their worst. He was now thirty-five. A fresh start—the mere idea of it made him shudder—occurred as a possibility in the near future. Vitality, indeed, was at a low ebb, it seemed. Mental depression, great physical fatigue, weariness of life in general made his spirits droop alarmingly, so that almost he felt tired of living. His tie with existence, at any rate, just then was dangerously weak.

Thought turned next to the man on whose advice he had staked his all in Delta Lands. Morris had important Egyptian interests in various big companies and enterprises along the Nile. He had first come to the firm with a letter of introduction upon some business matter, which the junior partner had handled so successfully that acquaintance thus formed had ripened into a more personal tie. The two men had much in common; their temperaments were suited; understanding grew between them; they felt at home and comfortable with one another. They became friends; they felt a mutual confidence. When Morris paid his rare visits to England, they spent much time together; and it was on one of these occasions that the matter of the Egyptian shares was mentioned, Morris urgently advising their purchase.

Sanfield explained his own position clearly enough, but his friend was so confident and optimistic that the purchase eventually had been made. There had been, moreover, Sanfield now remembered, the flavour of a peculiarly intimate and personal kind about the deal. He had remarked it, with a touch of surprise, at the moment, though really it seemed natural enough. Morris was very earnest, holding his friend's interest at heart; he was affectionate almost.

"I'd like to do you this good turn, old man," he said. "I have the strong feeling, somehow, that I owe you this, though heaven alone knows why!" After a pause he added, half shyly: "It may be one of those old memories we hear about nowadays cropping up out of some previous life together." Before the other could reply, he went on to explain that only three men were in the parent syndicate, the shares being unobtainable. "I'll set some of my own aside for you—four thousand or so, if you like."

They laughed together; Sanfield thanked him warmly; the deal was carried out. But the recipient of the favour had wondered a little at the sudden increase of intimacy even while he liked it and responded.

Had he been a fool, he now asked himself, to swallow the advice, putting all his eggs into a single basket? He knew very little about Morris after all. . . . Yes, while reflection showed him that the advice was honest, and the present riots no fault of the adviser's, he found his thoughts turning in a steady stream towards the man. The affairs of the firm took second place. It was Morris, with his deep-set eyes, his curious ways, his dark skin burnt brick-red by a fierce Eastern sun; it was Morris, looking almost like an Egyptian, who stood before him as he sat thinking gloomily over his dying fire.

He longed to talk with him, to ask him questions, to seek advice. He saw him very vividly against the screen of thought; Morris stood beside him now, gazing out across the limitless expanse of tawny sand. He had in his eyes the "distance" that sailors share with men whose life has been spent amid great trackless wastes. Morris, moreover, now he came to think of it, seemed always a little out of place in England. He had few relatives and, apparently, no friends; he was always intensely pleased when the time came to return to his beloved Nile. He had once mentioned casually a sister who kept house for him when duty detained him in Cairo, but, even here, he was something of an Oriental, rarely speaking of his women folk. Egypt, however, plainly drew him like a magnet. Resistance involved disturbance in his being, even ill-health. Egypt was "home" to him, and his friend, though he had never been there, felt himself its potent spell.

Another curious trait Sanfield remembered, too—his friend's childish superstition; his belief, or half-belief, in magic and the super-natural. Sanfield, amused, had ascribed it to the long sojourn in a land where anything unusual is at once ascribed to spiritual agencies. Morris owed his entire fortune, if his tale could be believed, to the magical apparition of an unearthly kind in some lonely *wadi* among the Bedouins. A sand-diviner had influenced another successful speculation. . . . He was a picturesque figure, whichever way one took him: yet a successful business man into the bargain.

These reflections and memories, on the other hand, brought small comfort to the man who had tempted Fate by following his advice. It was only a little strange how Morris now dominated his thoughts, directing them towards himself. Morris was in Egypt at the moment.

He went to bed at length, filled with uneasy misgivings, but for a long time he could not sleep. He tossed restlessly, his mind still running on the subject of his long reflections. He ached with tiredness. He dropped off at last. Then came a nightmare dream, in which the firm's works were sold for nearly nothing to an old Arab *sheikh* who wished to pay for them—in goats. He woke up in a cold perspiration. He had uneasy thoughts. His fancy was travelling. He could not rest.

To distract his mind, he turned on the light and tried to read, and, eventually, towards morning, fell into a sleep of sheer exhaustion. And his final thought—he knew not exactly why—was a sentence Morris had made use of long ago: "I feel I owe you a good turn; I'd like to do something for you. . . ."

This was the memory in his mind as he slipped off into unconsciousness.

But what happens when the mind is unconscious and the tired body lies submerged in deep sleep, no man, they say, can really tell.

2

The next thing he knew he was walking along a sun-baked street in some foreign town that was familiar, although, at first, its name escaped him. Colour, softness, and warmth pervaded it; there was sparkle and lightness in the exhilarating air; it was an Eastern town.

Though early morning, a number of people were already stirring; strings of camels passed him, loaded with clover, bales of merchandise, and firewood. Gracefully-draped women went by silently, carrying water jars of burnt clay upon their heads. Rude wooden shutters were being taken down in the bazaars; the smoke of cooking-fires rose in the blue spirals through the quiet air. He felt strangely at home and happy. The light, the radiance stirred him. He passed a mosque from which the worshippers came pouring in a stream of colour.

Yet, though an Eastern town, it was not wholly Oriental, for he saw that many of the buildings were of semi-European design, and that the natives sometimes wore European dress, except for the *fez* upon the head. Among them were Europeans, too. Staring into the faces of the passers-by he found, to his vexation, that he could not focus sight as usual, and that the nearer he approached, the less clearly, he discerned the features. The faces, upon close attention, at once grew shadowy, merged into each other, or, in some odd fashion, melted into the dazzling sunshine that was their background. All his attempts in this direction failed; impatience seized him; of surprise, however, he was not conscious. Yet this mingled vagueness and intensity seemed perfectly natural.

Filled with a stirring curiosity, he made a strong effort to concentrate his attention, only to discover that this vagueness, this difficulty of focus, lay in his own being, too. He wandered on, unaware exactly where he was going, yet not much perturbed, since there was an objective in view, he knew, and this objective *must* eventually be reached. Its nature, however, for the moment entirely eluded him.

The sense of familiarity, meanwhile, increased; he had been in this town before, although not quite within recoverable memory. It seemed, perhaps, the general atmosphere, rather than the actual streets, he knew; a certain perfume in the air, a tang of indefinable sweetness, a vitality in the radiant sunshine. The dark faces that he could not focus, he yet knew; the flowing garments of blue and red and yellow, the softly-slippered feet, the slouching camels, the burning human eyes that faded ere he fully caught them—the entire picture in this blazing sunlight lay half-hidden, half-revealed. And an extraordinary sense of happiness and well-being flooded him as he walked; he felt at home; comfort and bliss stole over him. Almost he knew his way about. This was a place he loved and knew.

The complete silence, moreover, did not strike him as peculiar until, suddenly, it was broken in a startling fashion. He heard his own name spoken. It sounded close beside his ear.

"George Sanfield!" The voice was familiar. Morris called him. He realized then the truth. He was, of course, in Cairo.

Yet, instead of turning to discover the speaker at his side, he hurried forward, as though he knew that the voice had come through distance. His consciousness cleared and lightened; he felt more alive; his eyes now focused the passers-by without difficulty. He was there to find Morris, and Morris was directing him. All was explained and natural again. He hastened. But even while he hastened, he knew that his personal desire to speak with his friend about Egyptian shares and Delta Lands was not his single object. Behind it, further in among as yet unstirring shadows, lay another deeper purpose. Yet he did not trouble about it, nor make a conscious effort at discovery. Morris was doing him that "good turn I feel I owe you." This conviction filled him overwhelmingly. The question of how and why did not once occur to him. A strange, great happiness rose in him.

Upon the outskirts of the town now, he found himself approaching a large building in the European style, with wide verandas and a cultivated garden filled with palm trees. A well-kept drive of yellow sand led to its chief entrance, and the man in khaki drill and riding-breeches walking along this drive, not ten yards in front of him, was— Morris. He overtook him, but his cry of welcome recognition was not answered. Morris, walking with bowed head and stooping shoulders, seemed intensely preoccupied; he had not heard the call.

"Here I am, old fellow!" exclaimed his friend, holding out a hand. "I've come, you see. . .!" then paused aghast before the altered face. Morris paid no attention. He walked straight on as though he had not heard. It was the distraught and anguished expression on the drawn and haggard features that impressed the other most. The silence he took without surprise.

It was the pain and suffering in his friend that occupied him. The dark rims beneath heavy eyes, the evidence of sleepless nights, of long anxiety and ceaseless dread, afflicted him with their too-plain story. The man was overwhelmed with some great sorrow. Sanfield forgot his personal trouble; this larger, deeper grief usurped its place entirely.

"Morris! Morris!" he cried yet more eagerly than before. "I've come, you see. Tell me what's the matter. I believe—that I can—help you. . .!"

The other turned, looking past him through the air. He made no answer. The eyes went through him. He walked straight on, and Sanfield walked at his side in silence. Through the large door they passed together, Morris paying as little attention to him as though he were not there, and in the small chamber they now entered, evidently a waiting-room, an Egyptian servant approached, uttered some inaudible words, and then withdrew, leaving them alone together.

It seemed that time leaped forward, yet stood still; the passage of minutes, that is to say, was irregular, almost fanciful. Whether the interval was long or short, however, Morris spent it pacing up and down the little room, his hands thrust deep into his pockets, his mind oblivious of all else but his absorbing anxiety and grief. To his friend, who watched him by the wall with intense desire to help, he paid no attention. The latter's spoken words went by him, entirely unnoticed; he gave no sign of seeing him; his eyes, as he paced up and down, muttering inaudibly to himself, were fixed every few seconds on an inner door. Beyond that door, Sanfield now divined, lay someone who hesitated on the narrow frontier between life and death.

It opened suddenly and a man, in overall and rubber gloves, came out, his face grave yet with faint signs of hope about it—a doctor, clearly, straight from the operating table. Morris, standing rigid in his tracks, listened to something spoken, for the lips were in movement, though no words were audible. The operation, Sanfield divined, had been successful, though danger was still present. The two men passed out, then, into the hall and climbed a wide staircase to the floor above, Sanfield following noiselessly, though so close that he could touch them. Entering a large, airy room where French windows, carefully shaded with green blinds opened on to a veranda, they approached a bed. Two nurses bent over it. The occupant was at first invisible.

Events had moved with curious rapidity. All this had happened, it seemed, in a single moment, yet with the irregular effect already mentioned which made Sanfield feel it might, equally, have lasted hours. But, as he stood behind Morris and the surgeon at the bed, the deeps in him opened suddenly, and he trembled under a shock of intense emotion that he could not understand. As with a stroke of lightning some heavenly fire set his heart aflame with yearning. The very soul in him broke loose with passionate longing that *must* find satisfaction. It came to him in a single instant with the certain knowledge of an unconquerable conviction. Hidden, yet ever waiting, among the broken centuries, there now leaped upon him this flash of memory—the memory of some sweet and ancient love Time might veil yet could not kill.

He ran forward, past the surgeon and the nurses, past Morris who bent above the bed with a face ghastly from anxiety. He gazed down upon the fair girl lying there, her unbound hair streaming over the pillow. He saw, and he remembered. And an uncontrollable cry of recognition left his lips. . . .

The irregularity of the passing minutes became so marked then, that he might well have passed outside their measure altogether, beyond what men call Time; duration, interval, both escaped. Alone and free with his eternal love, he was safe from all confinement, free, it seemed, either of time or space. His friend, however, was vaguely with him during the amazing instant. He felt acutely aware of the need each had, respectively, for the other, born of a heritage the Past had hidden over-long. Each, it was clear, could do the other a good turn. . . .Sanfield, though unable to describe or disentangle later, knew, while it lasted, this joy of full, delicious understanding. . . .

The strange, swift instant of recognition passed and disappeared. The cry, Sanfield realized, on coming back to the Present, had been soundless and inaudible as before. No one observed him; no one stirred. The girl, on that bed beside the opened windows, lay evidently dying. Her breath came in gasps, her chest heaved convulsively, each attempt at recovery was slower and more painful than the one before. She was unconscious. Sometimes her breathing seemed to stop. It grew weaker, as the pulse grew fainter. And Sanfield, transfixed as with paralysis, stood watching, waiting, an intolerable yearning in his heart to help. It seemed to him that he waited with a purpose.

This purpose suddenly became clear. He knew why he waited. There was help to be given. He was the one to give it.

The girl's vitality and ebbing nerves, her entire physical organism now fading so quickly towards that final extinction which meant death—could these but be stimulated by a new tide of life, the danger-point now fast approaching might be passed, and recovery must follow. This impetus, he knew suddenly, he could supply. How, he could not tell. It flashed upon him from beyond the stars, as from ancient store of long-forgotten, long-neglected knowledge. It was enough that he felt confident and sure. His soul burned within him; the strength of an ancient and unconquerable love rose through his being. He would try.

The doctor, he saw, was in the act of giving his last aid in the form of a hypodermic injection, Morris and the nurses looking on. Sanfield observed the sharp quick rally, only too faint, too slight; he saw the collapse that followed. The doctor, shrugging his shoulders, turned with a look that could not express itself in words, and Morris, burying his face in his hands, knelt by the bed, shaken with convulsive sobbing. It was the end.

In which moment, precisely, the strange paralysis that had bound Sanfield momentarily, was lifted from his being, and an impelling force, obeying his immense desire, invaded him. He knew how to act. His will, taught long ago, yet long-forgotten, was set free.

"You have come back to me at last," he cried in his anguish and his power, though the voice was, as ever, inaudible and soundless, "*I shall not let you go!* . . . ."

Drawn forward nearer and nearer to the bed, he leaned down, as if to kiss the pale lips and streaming hair. But his knowledge operated better than he knew. In the tremendous grip of that power which spins the stars and suns, while drawing souls into manifestation upon a dozen planets, he raced, he dived, he plunged, helpless, yet driven by the creative stress of love and sacrifice towards some eternal purpose. Caught in what seemed a vortex of amazing force, he sank away, as a straw is caught and sunk within the suction of a mighty whirlpool. His memory of Morris, of the doctor, of the girl herself, passed utterly. His entire personality became merged, lost, obliterated. He was aware of nothing; not even aware of nothingness. He lost consciousness....

3

The reappearance was as sudden as the obliteration. He emerged. There had been interval, duration, time. He was not aware of them. A spasm of blinding pain shot through him. He opened his eyes. His whole body was a single devouring pain. He felt cramped, confined, uncomfortable. He must escape. He thrashed about. Someone seized his arm and held it. With a snarl he easily wrenched it free.

He was in bed. How had he come to this? An accident? He saw the faces of nurse and doctor bending over him, eager, amazed, surprised, a trifle frightened. Vague memories floated to him. Who was he? Where had he come from? And where was. . . .where was. . . .someone. . . .who was dearer to him than life itself? He looked about him: the room, the faces, the French windows. . . .but in vain. . . .

A spasm of violent pain burned through his body like a fire, and he shut his eyes. He groaned. A voice sounded just above him: "Take this, dear. Try and swallow a little. It will relieve you. Your brother will be back in a moment. You are much better already."

He looked up at the nurse; he drank what she gave him.

"My brother!" he murmured. "I don't understand. I have no brother." Thirst came over him; he drained the glass. The nurse, wearing a startled look, moved away. He watched her go. He pointed at her with his hand, meaning to say something that he instantly forgot—as he saw his own bare arm. Its dreadful thinness shocked him. He must have been ill for months. The arm, wasted almost to nothing, showed the bone. He sank back exhausted, the sleeping draught began to take effect. The nurse returned quietly to a chair beside the bed, from which she watched him without ceasing as the long minutes passed. . . .

He found it difficult to collect his thoughts, to keep them in his mind when caught. There floated before him a series of odd scenes like coloured pictures in an endless flow. He was unable to catch them. Morris was with him always. They were doing quite absurd, impossible things. They rode together across the desert in the dawn, they wandered through old massive temples, they saw the sun set behind mud villages mid wavering palms, they drifted down a river in a sailing boat of quaint design. It had an enormous single sail. Together they visited tombs cut in the solid rock, hot airless corridors, and huge, dim, vaulted chambers underground. There was an icy wind by night, fierce burning sun by day. They watched vast troops of stars pass down a stupendous sky. . . . They knew delight and tasted wonder. Strange memories touched them. . . .

"Nurse!" he called aloud, returning to himself again, and remembering that he must speak with his friend about something—he failed to recall exactly what. "Please ask Mr. Morris to come to me."

"At once, dear. He's only in the next room waiting for you to wake." She went out quickly, and he heard her voice in the passage. It sank to a whisper as she came back with Morris, yet every syllable reached him distinctly:

". . . .and pay no attention if she wanders a little; just ignore it. She's turned the corner, thank God, and that's the chief thing." Each word he heard with wonder and perplexity, with increasing irritability too.

"I'm a hell of a wreck," he said, as Morris came, beaming, to the bedside. "Have I been ill long? It's frightfully decent of you to come, old man."

But Morris, staggered at this greeting, stopped abruptly, half turning to the nurse for guidance. He seemed unable to find words. Sanfield was extremely annoyed; he showed his feeling. "I'm *not* balmy, you old ass!" he shouted. "I'm all right again, though very weak. But I wanted to ask you—oh, I remember now—I wanted to ask you about my—er—*Deltas*."

"My poor dear Maggie," stammered Morris, fumbling with his voice. "Don't worry about your few shares, darling. Deltas are all right—it's *you* we——"

"Why, the devil, do you call me Maggie?" snapped the other viciously. "And 'darling'!" He felt furious, exasperated. "Have *you* gone balmy, or have I? What in the world are you two up to?" His fury tired him. He lay back upon his pillows, fuming. Morris took a chair beside the bed; he put a hand gently on his wasted arm.

"My darling girl," he said, in what was intended to be a soothing voice, though it stirred the sick man again to fury beyond expression, "you must really keep quiet for a bit. You've had a very severe operation"—his voice shook a little—"but, thank God, you've pulled through and are now on the way to recovery. You are my sister Maggie. It will all come back to you when you're rested——"

"Maggie, indeed!" interrupted the other, trying to sit up again, but too weak to compass it. "Your sister! You bally idiot! Don't you know me? I wish to God the nurse wouldn't 'dear' me in that senseless way. And you, with your atrocious 'darling,' I'm not your precious sister Maggie. I'm—I'm George San——"

But even as he said it, there passed over him some dim lost fragment of a wild, delicious memory he could not seize. Intense pleasure lay in it, could he but recover it. He knew a sweet, forgotten joy. His broken, troubled mind lay searching frantically but without success. It dazzled him. It shook him with an indescribable emotion—of joy, of wonder, of deep sweet confusion. A rapt happiness rose in him, yet pain, like a black awful shutter, closed in upon the happiness at once. He remembered a girl. But he remembered, too, that he had seen her die. Who was she? Had he lost her....again....!

"My dear fellow," he faltered in a weaker voice to Morris, "my brain's in a whirl. I'm sorry. I suppose I've had some blasted concussion—haven't I?"

But the man beside his bed, he saw, was startled. An extraordinary look came into his face, though he tried to hide it with a smile.

"My shares!" cried Sanfield, with a half scream. "Four thousand of them!"

Whereupon Morris blanched. "George Sanfield!" he muttered, half to himself, half to the nurse who hurried up. "That voice! The very number too!" He looked white and terrified, as if he had seen a ghost. A whispered colloquy ensued between him and the nurse. It was inaudible.

"Now, dearest Maggie," he said at length, making evidently a tremendous effort, "do try and lie quiet for a bit. Don't bother about George Sanfield, my London friend. His shares are quite safe. You've heard me speak of him. It's all right, my darling, quite all right. Oh, believe me! I'm your brother."

"Maggie. . . .!" whispered the man to himself upon the bed, whereupon Morris stooped, and, to his intense horror, kissed him on the cheek. But his horror seemed merged at once in another personality that surged through and over his entire being, drowning memory and recognition hopelessly. "Darling," he murmured. He realised that he was mad, of course. It seemed he fainted. . . .

The momentary unconsciousness soon passed, at any rate. He opened his eyes again. He saw a palm tree out of the window. He knew positively he was *not* mad, whatever else he might be. Dead perhaps? He felt the sheets, the mattress, the skin upon his face. No, he was alive all right. The dull pains where the tight bandages oppressed him were also real. He was among substantial, earthly things. The nurse, he noticed, regarded him anxiously. She was a pleasant-looking young woman. He smiled; and, with an expression of affectionate, even tender pleasure, she smiled back at him.

"You feel better now, a little stronger," she said softly. "You've had a sleep, Miss Margaret." She said "Miss Margaret" with a conscious effort. It was better, perhaps, than "dear"; but his anger rose at once. He was too tired, however, to express his feelings. There stole over him, besides, the afflicting consciousness of an alien personality that was familiar, and yet not his. It strove to dominate him. Only by a great effort could he continue to think his own thoughts. This other being kept trying to intrude, to oust him, to take full possession. It resented his presence with a kind of violence.

He sighed. So strong was the feeling of another personality trying to foist itself upon his own, upon his mind, his body, even upon his very face, that he turned instinctively to the nurse, though unaware exactly what he meant to ask her for.

"My hand-glass, please," he heard himself saying—with horror. The phrase was not his own. Glass or mirror were the words *he* would have used.

A moment later he was staring with acute and ghastly terror at a reflection that was not his own. It was the face of the dead girl he saw within the silver-handled, woman's hand-glass he held up.

36

★★★★★★★★★★

The dream with its amazing, vivid detail haunted him for days, even coming between him and his work. It seemed far more real, more vivid than the commonplace events of life that followed. The occurrences of the day were pale compared to its overpowering intensity. And a cable, received the very next afternoon, increased this sense of actual truth—of something that had really happened.

"Hold shares writing Morris."

Its brevity added a convincing touch. He was aware of Egypt even in Throgmorton Street. Yet it was the face of the dead, or dying, girl that chiefly haunted him. She remained in his thoughts, alive and sweet and exquisite. Without her he felt incomplete, his life a failure. He thought of nothing else.

The affairs at the office, meanwhile, went well; unexpected success attended them; there was no strike; the angry customer was pacified. And when the promised letter came from Morris, Sanfield's hands trembled so violently that he could hardly tear it open. Nor could he read it calmly. The assurance about his precious shares scarcely interested him. It was the final paragraph that set his heart beating against his ribs as though a hammer lay inside him:

". . . .I've had great trouble and anxiety, though, thank God, the danger is over now. I forget if I ever mentioned my sister, Margaret, to you. She keeps house for me in Cairo, when I'm there. She is my only tie in life. Well, a severe operation she had to undergo, all but finished her. To tell you the truth, she very nearly died, for the doctor gave her up. You'll smile when I tell you that odd things happened—at the very last moment. I can't explain it, nor can the doctor. It rather terrified me. But at the very moment when we thought her gone, something revived in her. She became full of unexpected life and vigour. She was even violent—whereas, a moment before, she had not the strength to speak, much less to move. It was rather wonderful, but it was terrible too.

"You don't believe in these things, I know, but I must tell you, because, when she recovered consciousness, she began to babble about yourself, using your name, though she has rarely, if ever, heard it, and even speaking—you won't believe this, of course!—of your shares in Deltas, giving the *exact* number that you hold. When you write, please tell me if you were very anxious about these? Also, whether your thoughts were directed particularly to me? I thought a good deal about you, knowing you might be uneasy, but my mind was pretty full, as you will understand, of her operation at the time. The climax, when all this happened, was about 11 a. m. on February 13th.

"Don't fail to tell me this, as I'm particularly interested in what you may have to say."

"And, now, I want to ask a great favour of you. The doctor forbids Margaret to stay here during the hot weather, so I'm sending her home to some cousins in Yorkshire, as soon as she is fit to travel. It would be most awfully kind—I know how women bore you—if you could manage to meet the boat and help her on her way through London. I'll let you know dates and particulars later, when I hear that you will do this for me. . . ."

Sanfield hardly read the remainder of the letter, which dealt with shares and business matters. But a month later he stood on the dock-pier at Tilbury, watching the approach of the tender from the *Egyptian Mail*.

He saw it make fast; he saw the stream of passengers pour down the gangway; and he saw among them the tall, fair woman of his dream. With a beating heart he went to meet her. . . .

Faith Cure on the Channel

A letter from my vague friend was always a source of difficulty: it allowed of so many interpretations—contradictory often. But this one was comparatively plain sailing:—

> You said you were going abroad about this time. So am I. Let's go as far as Paris together. Send me a line to above address at once. Thursday or Friday would suit me.—Yours, X.Y. Z.
> P.S.—I enclose P.O. for that 10s. I owe you.

I received this letter on a Wednesday morning.

It was written from the Club, but the Club address was carefully scored out and no other given.

The "P.O." was not enclosed.

In spite of these obstacles, however, we somehow met and arranged to start on Saturday; and the night before we dined together in that excellent little Soho restaurant—"there's nothing," my friend always said, "between its cooking and the Ritz, except prices"—and discussed our prospects, he going to finish a book at a Barbizon inn, I to inspect certain machinery in various Continental dairies.

His heart, it was plain, however, was neither in the cooking nor the book, nor in my wonderful machinery. Like a boy with a secret, he was mysterious about something hitherto unshared Happy, too, for he kept smiling at nothing.

"The fact is," he observed at last over coffee, "I'm really a vile, simply a vile sailor."

"I remember," I said, for we had once been companions on the same yacht.

"And you," he added, holding the black eyebrows steady, "you—are another." When dealing with simple truths he was often brutally frank.

"What's the good of talking about it?"

"This," he replied, paying the bill and giving me the amount of the "P.O.," "I'll show you."

He conducted me into a little box of a place bearing the legend outside "Foreign Chemist," and proceeded first to buy the most curious assortment of strange medicines I ever heard of. Weird indeed must have been his ailments. I had no time for reflection, however, on the point, for suddenly turning to me by way of introduction, and allowing the eyebrow next the chemist to dance and bristle so as to attract his attention, he mumbled, "This is my seasick friend. We're off tomorrow. If you've got the stuff ready, we might take it now." And, before I had time to ask or argue, he had pocketed a little package and we were in the street again.

Never had I known him so brisk and practical. "It's a new seasick cure," he explained darkly as we went home; "something quite new—just invented, in fact; and that chap's asking a few of his special customers to try it and give their honest opinions. So, I told him we were pretty bad—vile, in fact—and I've got this for nothing. He only wants vile sailors, you see, otherwise there's no test—"

"Know what's in it?"

He shook his head so violently that I was afraid for the eyebrows.

"But I believe in it. It's simply wonderful stuff; no bromide, he assured me, and no harmful drugs. Just a seasick cure; that's all!"

"I'll take it if you will," I laughed. "I could take poison with impunity before going on the Channel!"

He gave me one bottle. "Take a dose tonight," he explained, "another after breakfast in the morning, another in the train, and another the moment you go on board."

I gave my promise and we separated on his doorstep. It was a lot to promise, but as I have explained, I could drink tar or prussic acid before going on a steamer, and neither would have the time to work injury. I marvelled greatly, however, at my vague friend's fit of abnormal lucidity, and in the night, I dreamed of him surrounded by all the medicine bottles he had bought to take abroad with him, swallowing their contents one by one, and smiling while he did so, with eyebrows grown to the size of hedges.

I took my doses faithfully, with the immediate result that in the train I became aware of symptoms that usually had the decency to wait for the steamer. My friend took his too. He was in excellent spirits, eyes bright, full of confidence. The bottles were wrapped in neat white paper, only the necks visible; and we drank our allotted quantity from the mouths, without glasses.

"Not much taste," I remarked.

"Wonderful stuff," he replied. "I believe in it absolutely. It's good for other things, too; it made me sleep like a top, and I had the appetite of a horse for breakfast. That chemist'll make his fortune when he brings it out. People will pay a pound a bottle, lots of 'em."

At Newhaven the sea was agitated—hideously so; even in the harbour the steamers rose and fell absurdly. Not all the fresh, salt winds in the world, nor all the jolly sunshine and sparkling waves, nor all that strong beauty that comes with the first glimpse of the sea and long horizons, could lessen the sinking dread that was in my—my heart. Truth to tell, I had no more belief in the elixir than if it had been chopped hay and treacle.

My friend, however, was confidence personified. "The fact is," he said, laughing at the wind and sea, "the real fact is *I believe in that chemist*. He told me this stuff was infallible; and I believe it is. The trouble with you is funk—sheer blue funk."

We stuck to our guns and swallowed the last prescribed dose just before the syren announced our departure—and fifteen minutes later—.

It was a degrading three hours; and the sting of it was that my friend, with a hideous cap tied down about his ears, a smile that was in the worst possible taste, and a jaunty confidence that was even more insulting than he intended it to be, walked up and down that loathsome, sliding, switchback deck the entire way. Not the entire way, though, for half-way across he disappeared into the dining-room, and returned in due course with that brown beard of his charged with breadcrumbs, and between his lips actually—a pipe. And, without so much as speaking to me, he paced to and fro before my chair, when a little of that imagination he put so delightfully into his books would have led him discreetly to pace the other deck where I could not see him.

I thought out endless revenges, but the fact was I never had time to think out any single revenge properly to its conclusion. Something— something unspeakably vile—always came to interfere; and the sight of my friend, balancing up and down the rolling deck chatting to sailors, admiring the sea and sky, and puffing hard at his pipe all the time, was, I think, the most abominable thing I have ever seen.

"Simply marvellous, I call it," he told me in the *douane* at Dieppe. "The stuff is a revolutionary discovery. It's the first time I ever ate a meal on a steamer in my life. Sorry you suffered so. Can't understand it," he added, with a complacency that was insufferable. I was positively delighted to see the Customs officer open *all* his bags and litter his things about in glorious confusion. . .

In Paris that night our little hotel was rather full, and we had to share a big two-bedded room. My friend groaned a good deal between two and three in the morning and kept me awake; and once, somewhere about five a.m., I saw him with a lighted candle fumbling at the table among a lot of little white paper packages which I recognised as his purchases from that criminal London chemist who had concocted the seasick cure.

It was at nine o'clock, however, while he was down at his bath, that I noticed something on the table by his bed that instantly arrested my attention. Regardless of morals, I investigated. It was unmistakable. It was his own bottle of the seasick cure. He had never taken it at all!

Then, just as his step sounded in the passage, it flashed across me. He had made one of his usual muddles. He had mistaken the bottle He had swallowed the contents of some other phial instead.

Revenge is sweet; but I felt well again, and no longer harboured any spite. There was just time to hide the bottle in my hand when he entered.

"Awful headache I've got," he said. "Can't make out what's wrong with me. Such funny pains, too."

"After-effects of the seasick cure, probably. They'll pass in time," I suggested. But he remained in bed for a day and a night with all the symptoms of *mal de mer* on land.

It was many weeks later when I told him the truth, and showed the bottle to prove it—just in time to prevent his telling the chemist, "I have tried your seasick cure and found it absolutely efficacious," etc.

"What cured you," I said, "was far more wonderful than anything one can buy in bottles. It was faith, sheer faith!"

"I believe you're right," he replied meekly. "I believed in that stuff *absolutely*." Then he added, "But, you know, I should like to find out what it was I *did* take."

First Hate

They had been shooting all day; the weather had been perfect and the powder straight, so that when they assembled in the smoking-room after dinner, they were well pleased with themselves. From discussing the day's sport and the weather outlook, the conversation drifted to other, though still cognate, fields. Lawson, the crack shot of the party, mentioned the instinctive recognition all animals feel for their natural enemies, and gave several instances in which he had tested it—tame rats with a ferret, birds with a snake, and so forth.

"Even after being domesticated for generations," he said, "they recognise their natural enemy at once by instinct, an enemy they can never even have seen before. It's infallible. They know instantly."

"Undoubtedly," said a voice from the corner chair; "and so do we."

The speaker was Ericssen, their host, a great hunter before the Lord, generally uncommunicative but a good listener, leaving the talk to others. For this latter reason, as well as for a certain note of challenge in his voice, his abrupt statement gained attention.

"What do you mean exactly by 'so do we'?" asked three men together, after waiting some seconds to see whether he meant to elaborate, which he evidently did not.

"We belong to the animal kingdom, of course," put in a fourth, for behind the challenge there obviously lay a story, though a story that might be difficult to drag out of him. It was.

Ericssen, who had leaned forward a moment so that his strong, humorous face was in clear light, now sank back again into his chair, his expression concealed by the red lampshade at his side. The light played tricks, obliterating the humorous, almost tender lines, while emphasizing the strength of the jaw and nose. The red glare lent to the whole a rather grim expression.

Lawson, man of authority among them, broke the little pause.

"You're dead right," he observed, "but how do you know it?"—for

John Ericssen never made a positive statement without a good reason for it. That good reason, he felt sure, involved a personal proof, but a story Ericssen would never tell before a general audience. He would tell it later, however, when the others had left. "There's such a thing as instinctive antipathy, of course," he added, with a laugh, looking around him. "That's what you mean probably."

"I meant exactly what I said," replied the host bluntly. "There's first love. There's first hate, too."

"Hate's a strong word," remarked Lawson.

"So is love," put in another.

"Hate's strongest," said Ericssen grimly. "In the animal kingdom, at least," he added suggestively, and then kept his lips closed, except to sip his liquor, for the rest of the evening—until the party at length broke up, leaving Lawson and one other man, both old trusted friends of many years' standing.

"It's not a tale I'd tell to everybody," he began, when they were alone. "It's true, for one thing; for another, you see, some of those good fellows"—he indicated the empty chairs with an expressive nod of his great head—"some of 'em knew him. You both knew him too, probably."

"The man you hated," said the understanding Lawson.

"And who hated me," came the quiet confirmation. "My other reason," he went on, "for keeping quiet was that the tale involves my wife."

The two listeners said nothing, but each remembered the curiously long courtship that had been the prelude to his marriage. No engagement had been announced, the pair were devoted to one another, there was no known rival on either side; yet the courtship continued without coming to its expected conclusion. Many stories were afloat in consequence. It was a social mystery that intrigued the gossips.

"I may tell you two," Ericssen continued, "the reason my wife refused for so long to marry me. It is hard to believe, perhaps, but it is true. Another man wished to make her his wife, and she would not consent to marry me until that other man was dead. Quixotic, absurd, unreasonable? If you like. I'll tell you what she said." He looked up with a significant expression in his face which proved that he, at least, did not now judge her reason foolish. "'Because it would be murder,' she told me. 'Another man who wants to marry me would kill you.'"

"She had some proof for the assertion, no doubt?" suggested Lawson.

44

"None whatever," was the reply. "Merely her woman's instinct. Moreover, I did not know who the other man was, nor would she ever tell me."

"Otherwise, you might have murdered him instead?" said Baynes, the second listener.

"I did," said Ericssen grimly. "But without knowing he was the man." He sipped his whisky and relit his pipe. The others waited.

"Our marriage took place two months later—just after Hazel's disappearance."

"Hazel?" exclaimed Lawson and Baynes in a single breath. "Hazel! Member of the Hunters!" His mysterious disappearance had been a nine days' wonder some ten years ago. It had never been explained. They had all been members of the Hunters' Club together.

"That's the chap," Ericssen said. "Now I'll tell you the tale, if you care to hear it." They settled back in their chairs to listen, and Ericssen, who had evidently never told the affair to another living soul except his own wife, doubtless, seemed glad this time to tell it to two men.

"It began some dozen years ago when my brother Jack and I came home from a shooting trip in China. I've often told you about our adventures there, and you see the heads hanging up here in the smoking-room—some of 'em." He glanced round proudly at the walls. "We were glad to be in town again after two years' roughing it, and we looked forward to our first good dinner at the club, to make up for the rotten cooking we had endured so long. We had ordered that dinner in anticipatory detail many a time together. Well, we had it and enjoyed it up to a point—the point of the *entrée*, to be exact.

"Up to that point it was delicious, and we let ourselves go, I can tell you. We had ordered the very wine we had planned months before when we were snowbound and half starving in the mountains." He smacked his lips as he mentioned it. "I was just starting on a beautifully cooked grouse," he went on, "when a figure went by our table, and Jack looked up and nodded. The two exchanged a brief word of greeting and explanation, and the other man passed on. Evidently, they knew each other just enough to make a word or two necessary, but enough.

"'Who's that?' I asked.

"'A new member, named Hazel,' Jack told me. 'A great shot.' He knew him slightly, he explained; he had once been a client of his— Jack was a barrister, you remember—and had defended him in some financial case or other. Rather an unpleasant case, he added. Jack did not 'care about' the fellow, he told me, as he went on with his tender wing of grouse."

Ericssen paused to relight his pipe a moment.

"Not care about him!" he continued. "It didn't surprise me, for my own feeling, the instant I set eyes on the fellow, was one of violent, instinctive dislike that amounted to loathing. Loathing! No. I'll give it the right word—hatred. I simply couldn't help myself; I hated the man from the very first go off. A wave of repulsion swept over me as I followed him down the room a moment with my eyes, till he took his seat at a distant table and was out of sight. Ugh! He was a big, fat-faced man, with an eyeglass glued into one of his pale-blue cod-like eyes—out of condition, ugly as a toad, with a smug expression of intense self-satisfaction on his jowl that made me long to——

"I leave it to you to guess what I would have liked to do to him. But the instinctive loathing he inspired in me had another aspect, too. Jack had not introduced us during the momentary pause beside our table, but as I looked up, I caught the fellow's eye on mine—he was glaring at me instead of at Jack, to whom he was talking—with an expression of malignant dislike, as keen evidently as my own. That's the other aspect I meant. He hated me as violently as I hated him. We were instinctive enemies, just as the rat and ferret are instinctive enemies. Each recognized a mortal foe. It was a case—I swear it—of whoever got first chance."

"Bad as that!" exclaimed Baynes. "I knew him by sight. He wasn't pretty, I'll admit."

"I knew him to nod to," Lawson mentioned. "I never heard anything particular against him." He shrugged his shoulders.

Ericssen went on. "It was not his character or qualities I hated," he said. "I didn't even know them. That's the whole point. There's no reason you fellows should have disliked him. *My* hatred—our mutual hatred—was instinctive, as instinctive as first love. A man knows his natural mate; also, he knows his natural enemy. I did, at any rate, both with him and with my wife. Given the chance, Hazel would have done me in; just as surely, given the chance, I would have done him in. No blame to either of us, what's more, in my opinion."

"I've felt dislike, but never hatred like that," Baynes mentioned. "I came across it in a book once, though. The writer did not mention the instinctive fear of the human animal for its natural enemy, or anything of that sort. He thought it was a continuance of a bitter feud begun in an earlier existence. He called it memory."

46

"Possibly," said Ericssen briefly. "My mind is not speculative. But I'm glad you spoke of fear. I left that out. The truth is, I feared the fellow, too, in a way; and had we ever met face to face in some wild country without witnesses I should have felt justified in drawing on him at sight, and he would have felt the same. Murder? If you like. I should call it self-defence. Anyhow, the fellow polluted the room for me. He spoilt the enjoyment of that dinner we had ordered months before in China."

"But you saw him again, of course, later?"

"Lots of times. Not that night, because we went on to a theatre. But in the club, we were always running across one another—in the houses of friends at lunch or dinner; at race meetings; all over the place; in fact, I even had some trouble to avoid being introduced to him. And every time we met our eyes betrayed us. He felt in his heart what I felt in mine. Ugh! He was as loathsome to me as leprosy, and as dangerous. Odd, isn't it? The most intense feeling, except love, I've ever known. I remember"—he laughed gruffly—"I used to feel quite sorry for him. If he felt what I felt, and I'm convinced he did, he must have suffered. His one object—to get me out of the way for good—was so impossible. Then Fate played a hand in the game. I'll tell you how.

"My brother died a year or two later, and I went abroad to try and forget it. I went salmon fishing in Canada. But though the sport was good, it was not like the old times with Jack. The camp never felt the same without him. I missed him badly. But I forgot Hazel for the time; hating did not seem worthwhile, somehow.

"When the best of the fishing was over on the Atlantic side, I took a run back to Vancouver and fished there for a bit. I went up the Campbell River, which was not so crowded then as it is now, and had some rattling sport. Then I grew tired of the rod and decided to go after wapiti for a change. I came back to Victoria and learned what I could about the best places, and decided finally to go up the west coast of the island. By luck I happened to pick up a good guide, who was in the town at the moment on business, and we started off together in one of the little Canadian Pacific Railway boats that ply along that coast.

"Outfitting two days later at a small place the steamer stopped at, the guide said we needed another man to help pack our kit over portages, and so forth, but the only fellow available was a Siwash of whom he disapproved. My guide would not have him at any price; he was lazy, a drunkard, a liar, and even worse, for on one occasion he came back without the sportsman he had taken up country on a shooting trip, and his story was not convincing, to say the least. These disappearances are always awkward, of course, as you both know. We preferred, anyhow, to go without the Siwash, and off we started.

"At first our luck was bad. I saw many wapiti, but no good heads; only after a fortnight's hunting did I manage to get a decent head, though even that was not so good as I should have liked.

"We were then near the head waters of a little river that ran down into the Inlet; heavy rains had made the river rise; running downstream was a risky job, what with old log-jams shifting and new ones forming; and, after many narrow escapes, we upset one afternoon and had the misfortune to lose a lot of our kit, amongst it most of our cartridges. We could only muster a few between us. The guide had a dozen; I had two—just enough, we considered, to take us out all right. Still, it was an infernal nuisance. We camped at once to dry out our soaked things in front of a big fire, and while this laundry work was going on, the guide suggested my filling in the time by taking a look at the next little valley, which ran parallel to ours. He had seen some good heads over there a few weeks ago. Possibly I might come upon the herd. I started at once, taking my two cartridges with me.

"It was the devil of a job getting over the divide, for it was a badly bushed-up place, and where there were no bushes there were boulders and fallen trees, and the going was slow and tiring. But I got across at last and came out upon another stream at the bottom of the new valley. Signs of wapiti were plentiful, though I never came up with a single beast all the afternoon. Blacktail deer were everywhere, but the wapiti remained invisible. Providence, or whatever you like to call that which there is no escaping in our lives, made me save my two cartridges."

Ericssen stopped a minute then. It was not to light his pipe or sip his whisky. Nor was it because the remainder of his story failed in the recollection of any vivid detail. He paused a moment to think.

"Tell us the lot," pleaded Lawson. "Don't leave out anything."

Ericssen looked up. His friend's remark had helped him to make up his mind apparently. He *had* hesitated about something or other, but the hesitation passed. He glanced at both his listeners.

"Right," he said. "I'll tell you everything. I'm not imaginative, as you know, and my amount of superstition, I should judge, is microscopic." He took a longer breath, then lowered his voice a trifle. "Anyhow," he went on, "it's true, so I don't see why I should feel shy about admitting it—but as I stood there in that lonely valley, where only the noises of wind and water were audible, and no human being, except my guide, some miles away, was within reach, a curious feeling came over me I find difficult to describe. I felt"—obviously he made an effort to get the word out—"I felt creepy."

"You," murmured Lawson, with an incredulous smile—"you creepy?" he repeated under his breath.

"I felt creepy and afraid," continued the other, with conviction. "I had the sensation of being seen by someone—as if someone, I mean, was watching me. It was so unlikely that anyone was near me in that Godforsaken bit of wilderness, that I simply couldn't believe it at first. But the feeling persisted. I felt absolutely positive somebody was not far away among the red maples, behind a boulder, across the little stream, perhaps, somewhere, at any rate, so near that I was plainly visible to him. It was not an animal. It was human. Also, it was hostile.

"I was in danger.

"You may laugh, both of you, but I assure you the feeling was so positive that I crouched down instinctively to hide myself behind a rock. My first thought, that the guide had followed me for some reason or other, I at once discarded. It was not the guide. It was an enemy.

"No, no, I thought of no one in particular. No name, no face occurred to me. Merely that an enemy was on my trail, that he saw me, and I did not see him, and that he was near enough to me to—well, to take instant action. This deep instinctive feeling of danger, of fear, of anything you like to call it, was simply overwhelming.

"Another curious detail I must also mention. About half an hour before, having given up all hope of seeing wapiti, I had decided to kill a blacktail deer for meat. A good shot offered itself, not thirty yards away. I aimed. But just as I was going to pull the trigger a queer emotion touched me, and I lowered the rifle. It was exactly as though a voice said, 'Don't!' I heard no voice, mind you; it was an emotion only, a feeling, a sudden inexplicable change of mind—a warning, if you like. I didn't fire, anyhow.

"But now, as I crouched behind that rock, I remembered this curious little incident, and was glad I had not used up my last two cartridges. More than that I cannot tell you. Things of that kind are new to me. They're difficult enough to tell, let alone to explain. But they were *real*.

"I crouched there, wondering what on earth was happening to me, and, feeling a bit of a fool, if you want to know, when suddenly, over the top of the boulder, I saw something moving. It was a man's hat. I peered cautiously. Some sixty yards away the bushes parted, and two men came out on to the river's bank, and I knew them both. One was the Siwash I had seen at the store. The other was Hazel. Before I had time to think I cocked my rifle."

"Hazel. Good Lord!" exclaimed the listeners.

"For a moment I was too surprised to do anything but cock that rifle. I waited, for what puzzled me was that, after all, Hazel had *not* seen me. It was only the feeling of his beastly proximity that had made me feel I was seen and watched by him. There was something else, too, that made me pause before—er—doing anything. Two other things, in fact. One was that I was so intensely interested in watching the fellow's actions. Obviously, he had the same uneasy sensation that I had. He shared with me the nasty feeling that danger was about. His rifle, I saw, was cocked and ready; he kept looking behind him, over his shoulder, peering this way and that, and sometimes addressing a remark to the Siwash at his side. I caught the laughter of the latter. The Siwash evidently did not think there was danger anywhere. It was, of course, unlikely enough——"

"And the other thing that stopped you?" urged Lawson, impatiently interrupting.

Ericssen turned with a look of grim humour on his face.

"Some confounded or perverted sense of chivalry in me, I suppose," he said, "that made it impossible to shoot him down in cold blood, or, rather, without letting him have a chance. For my blood, as a matter of fact, was far from cold at the moment. Perhaps, too, I wanted the added satisfaction of letting him know who fired the shot that was to end his vile existence."

He laughed again. "It was rat and ferret in the human kingdom," he went on, "but I wanted my rat to have a chance, I suppose. Anyhow, though I had a perfect shot in front of me at easy distance, I did not fire. Instead, I got up, holding my cocked rifle ready, finger on trigger, and came out of my hiding place. I called to him. 'Hazel, you beast! So, there you are—at last!'

"He turned, but turned away from me, offering his horrid back. The direction of the voice he misjudged. He pointed downstream, and the Siwash turned to look. Neither of them had seen me yet. There was a big log-jam below them. The roar of the water in their ears concealed my footsteps. I was, perhaps, twenty paces from them when Hazel, with a jerk of his whole body, abruptly turned clean round and faced me. We stared into each other's eyes.

"The amazement on his face changed instantly to hatred and resolve. He acted with incredible rapidity. I think the unexpected suddenness of his turn made me lose a precious second or two. Anyhow he was ahead of me. He flung his rifle to his shoulder. 'You devil!' I heard his voice. 'I've got you at last!' His rifle cracked, for he let drive the same instant. The hair stirred just above my ear.

"He had missed!

"Before he could draw back his bolt for another shot, I had acted.

"'You're not fit to live!' I shouted, as my bullet crashed into his temple. I had the satisfaction, too, of knowing that he heard my words. I saw the swift expression of frustrated loathing in his eyes.

"He fell like an ox, his face splashing in the stream. I shoved the body out. I saw it sucked beneath the log-jam instantly. It disappeared. There could be no inquest on him, I reflected comfortably. Hazel was gone—gone from this earth, from my life, our mutual hatred over at last."

The speaker paused a moment. "Odd," he continued presently— "very odd indeed." He turned to the others. "I felt quite sorry for him suddenly. I suppose," he added, "the philosophers are right when they gas about hate being very close to love."

His friends contributed no remark.

"Then I came away," he resumed shortly. "My wife—well, you know the rest, don't you? I told her the whole thing. She—she said nothing. But she married me, you see."

There was a moment's silence. Baynes was the first to break it. "But—the Siwash?" he asked. "The witness?"

Lawson turned upon him with something of contemptuous impatience.

"He told you he had *two* cartridges."

Ericssen, smiling grimly, said nothing at all.

Her Birthday

It was her birthday on the morrow, and I set forth to find a suitable and worthy present. My means, judged by the standards of the big merchants, seemed trivial; yet, could I but discover the right gift, no matter how insignificant, I felt sure that it would please her, and so make me doubly happy. And the kind of gift I already knew, for I had a specimen of it in my humble lodgings; only of so poor a type that I was ashamed to offer it. I must find somewhere a much, much better one, if possible, perfect and without a single flaw. I went, therefore, into the great shops and saw a thousand wonderful and lovely things. . . . .

So particular was I, however, and so difficult to suit, that I wearied the salesfolk, and began to feel despondent. All that they showed me was so wrong—so cheap. In the matter of actual expense there was no disagreement, for I mentioned plainly beforehand the price that I would pay, or, rather, that I was prepared to pay. But in the nature and quality of the goods there was no satisfying me at all.

Everything that they spread before my eyes seemed ordinary, trifling, even spurious. Marvellously fashioned, and of the most costly description, they yet seemed somewhere counterfeit. The goods were sham. Already she possessed far better. There was nowhere—and I went to the very best emporiums where the rich and favoured of the world bought their offerings—there was nowhere the little genuine thing I sought. The finest that was set before me seemed unworthy. I compared one and all with the specimen, broken yet authentic, that I had at home. And even the cleverest of the salesfolk was unable to deceive me, because I *knew*.

"And this, for instance?" I asked at length, far from content, yet thinking it might just do perhaps in place of anything better I could find. "How much is this magnificent, jewelled thing, with its ingenious little surprise for each day in the entire year You mentioned—?"

"Ten million pounds, sir," said the man obsequiously, while he eyed me with a close and questioning glance.

"Ten million only!" And I laughed in his face.

"That was the price you named, sir," he murmured.

I drew myself up, looking disdainfully, pityingly at him. And, though he met my eye, he hesitated. Over his tired features there stole a soft and marvellous expression. Something more tender than starlight shone in his little eyes. And, as he answered in a gentle voice that was almost a whisper, I saw him smile as a man may smile when he understands a divine, unutterable thing. Glory touched him for an instant with high radiance, and a hint of delicious awe hid shyly in his voice. I barely caught the words, so low he murmured them:

"I fear, sir, that what you want is not to be had at all—in our establishment. You will hardly find it. It is not in the market." He seemed to bow his head in reverence a moment. "It is not—for sale."

And so I went back to my dingy lodgings, having made no single purchase. I looked fondly at my own little specimen, trying to imagine it had somehow gained in value, in beauty, almost in splendour. At least, I said to myself, it is not spurious. It is real. . . .

And, sitting down to my table, I dipped my broken pen into a penny bottle of inferior ink, and began my birthday letter:—

"This is your birthday, dear, and I send you *all my love*—" Being young, I underlined the words describing my little present, thinking to increase its value thus.

But I did not complete the sentence, for there was another thing that I must find to send her, or she would be disappointed. And a birthday comes but once a year. But, again, though I already possessed a tiny specimen of this other thing I sought, it did not seem to me nearly good enough to offer. Though genuine, it was worn by frequent use. Its lustre had dimmed a little, for I touched it daily. It seemed too ordinary and common for a special present. I was ashamed to send it.

So, I set out again and searched . . . and searched . . . in every likely and unlikely place, even groping in the dark about the altars of the churches where I found by chance the doors ajar, and penetrating to those secret shrines where those who seek truth, it is said, go in to pray. For I knew that there was this other little present from me that she would look for—because she had need of it. . .

And my search was wonderful and full of high adventure, yet so long that the moon had drawn the hood over the door of her silver tent, and the stars were fading in the east behind the towers of the night, before I returned home, footsore, aching, empty-handed, and very humble in my heart. For nowhere had I been able to find this other little thing she would be pleased to have from me. To my amazement, yet to my secret joy, I found nothing better than what I had at home—nothing, that is, indubitably genuine. In quantity it was not anywhere for sale. It was more rare than I had guessed—and I felt delicious triumph in me.

I sat down, humble, reverent, but incommunicably proud and happy, to my unfinished letter. Unless I posted it immediately, she would not get it when she woke upon her birthday morning. I finished it. I posted it just as it was—brief, the writing a little shaky, the paper cheap, blot, smudge, and all:

"... *and my worship.*"

And then, like a scrap of paper that enclosed the other gifts, yet need not be noticed unless she wished it, I added (above the little foolish name she knew me by) another tiny present—all that I had brought into the world or could take out with me again when I left it:

I wrote: "Yours ever faithfully."

H. S. H.

In the mountain Club Hut, to which he had escaped after weeks of gaiety in the capital, Delane, young travelling Englishman, sat alone, and listened to the wind that beat the pines with violence. The firelight danced over the bare stone floor and raftered ceiling, giving the room an air of movement, and though the solid walls held steady against the wild spring hurricane, the cannonading of the wind seemed to threaten the foundations. For the mountain shook, the forest roared, and the shadows had a way of running everywhere as though the little building trembled. Delane watched and listened. He piled the logs on. From time to time he glanced nervously over his shoulder, restless, half uneasy, as a burst of spray from the branches dashed against the window, or a gust of unusual vehemence shook the door.

Over-wearied with his long day's climb among impossible conditions, he now realised, in this mountain refuge, his utter loneliness; for his mind gave birth to that unwelcome symptom of true loneliness—that he was not, after all, alone. Continually he heard steps and voices in the storm. Another wanderer, another climber out of season like himself, would presently arrive, and sleep was out of the question until first he heard that knocking on the door. Almost—he expected someone.

He went for the tenth time to the little window. He peered forth into the thick darkness of the dropping night, shading his eyes against the streaming pane to screen the firelight in an attempt to see if another climber—perhaps a climber in distress—were visible. The surroundings were desolate and savage, well named the Devil's Saddle. Black-faced precipices, streaked with melting snow, rose towering to the north, where the heights were hidden in seas of vapour; waterfalls poured into abysses on two sides; a wall of impenetrable forest pressed up from the south; and the dangerous ridge he had climbed all day slid off wickedly into a sky of surging cloud.

But no human figure was, of course, distinguishable, for both the lateness of the hour and the elemental fury of the night rendered it most unlikely. He turned away with a start, as the tempest delivered a blow with massive impact against his very face. Then, clearing the remnants of his frugal supper from the table, he hung his soaking clothes at a new angle before the fire, made sure the door was fastened on the inside, climbed into the bunk where white pillows and thick Austrian blankets looked so inviting, and prepared finally for sleep.

"I must be over-tired," he sighed, after half an hour's weary tossing, and went back to make up the sinking fire. Wood is plentiful in these climbers' huts; he heaped it on. But this time he lit the little oil lamp as well, realising—though unwilling to acknowledge it—that it was not over-fatigue that banished sleep, but this unwelcome sense of expecting someone, of being not quite alone. For the feeling persisted and increased. He drew the wooden bench close up to the fire, turned the lamp as high as it would go, and wished unaccountably for the morning. Light was a very pleasant thing; and darkness now, for the first time since childhood, troubled him. It was outside; but it might so easily come in and swamp, obliterate, extinguish. The darkness seemed a positive thing. Already, somehow, it was established in his mind—this sense of enormous, aggressive darkness that veiled an undesirable hint of personality. Some shadow from the peaks or from the forest, immense and threatening, pervaded all his thought.

"This can't be entirely nerves," he whispered to himself. "I'm not so tired as all that!" And he made the fire roar. He shivered and drew closer to the blaze. "I'm out of condition; that's part of it," he realised, and remembered with loathing the weeks of luxurious indulgence just behind him.

For Delane had rather wasted his year of educational travel. Straight from Oxford, and well supplied with money, he had first saturated his mind in the latest Continental thought—the science of France, the metaphysics and philosophy of Germany—and had then been caught aside by the gaiety of capitals where the lights are not turned out at midnight by a Sunday School police. He had been surfeited, physically, emotionally, and intellectually, till his mind and body longed hungrily for simple living again and simple teaching—above all, the latter. The Road of Excess leads to the Palace of Wisdom—for certain temperaments (as Blake forgot to add), of which Delane was one. For there was stuff in the youth, and the reaction had set in with violent abruptness. His system rebelled.

He cut loose energetically from all soft delights, and craved for severity, pure air, solitude and hardship. Clean and simple conditions he must have without delay, and the tonic of physical battling. It was too early in the year to climb seriously, for the snow was still dangerous and the weather wild, but he had chosen this most isolated of all the mountain huts in order to make sure of solitude, and had come, without guide or companion, for a week's strenuous life in wild surroundings, and to take stock of himself with a view to full recovery.

And all day long as he climbed the desolate, unsafe ridge, his mind—good, wholesome, natural symptom—had reverted to his childhood days, to the solid worldly wisdom of his church-going father, and to the early teaching (oh, how sweet and refreshing in its literal spirit!) at his mother's knee. Now, as he watched the blazing logs, it came back to him again with redoubled force; the simple, precious, old-world stories of heaven and hell, of a paternal Deity, and of a daring, subtle, personal devil——

The interruption to his thoughts came with startling suddenness, as the roaring night descended against the windows with a thundering violence that shook the walls and sucked the flame half-way up the wide stone chimney. The oil lamp flickered and went out. Darkness invaded the room for a second, and Delane sprang from his bench, thinking the wet snow had loosened far above and was about to sweep the hut into the depths. And he was still standing, trembling and uncertain, in the middle of the room, when a deep and sighing hush followed sharp upon the elemental outburst, and in the hush, like a whisper after thunder, he heard a curious steady sound that, at first, he thought must be a footstep by the door. It was then instantly repeated. But it was not a step. It was someone knocking on the heavy oaken panels—a firm, authoritative sound, as though the new arrival had the right to enter and was already impatient at the delay.

The Englishman recovered himself instantly, realising with keen relief the new arrival—at last.

"Another climber like myself, of course," he said, "or perhaps the man who comes to prepare the hut for others. The season has begun." And he went over quickly, without a further qualm, to unbolt the door.

"Forgive!" he exclaimed in German, as he threw it wide, "I was half asleep before the fire. It is a terrible night. Come in to food and shelter, for both are here, and you shall share such supper as I possess."

And a tall, cloaked figure passed him swiftly with a gust of angry wind from the impenetrable blackness of the world beyond. On the threshold, for a second, his outline stood full in the blaze of firelight with the sheet of darkness behind it, stately, erect, commanding, his cloak torn fiercely by the wind, but the face hidden by a low-brimmed hat; and an instant later the door shut with resounding clamour upon the hurricane, and the two men turned to confront one another in the little room.

Delane then realised two things sharply, both of them fleeting impressions, but acutely vivid: First, that the outside darkness seemed to have entered and established itself between him and the new arrival; and, secondly, that the stranger's face was difficult to focus for clear sight, although the covering hat was now removed. There was a blur upon it somewhere. And this the Englishman ascribed partly to the flickering effect of firelight, and partly to the lightning glare of the man's masterful and terrific eyes, which made his own sight waver in some curious fashion as he gazed upon him.

These impressions, however, were but momentary and passing, due doubtless to the condition of his nerves and to the semi-shock of the dramatic, even theatrical entrance. Delane's senses, in this wild setting, were guilty of exaggeration. For now, while helping the man remove his cloak, speaking naturally of shelter, food, and the savage weather, he lost this first distortion and his mind recovered sane proportion. The stranger, after all, though striking, was not of appearance so uncommon as to cause alarm; the light and the low doorway had touched his stature with illusion. He dwindled. And the great eyes, upon calmer subsequent inspection, lost their original fierce lightning. The entering darkness, moreover, was but an effect of the upheaving night behind him as he strode across the threshold. The closed door proved it.

And yet, as Delane continued his quieter examination, there remained, he saw, the startling quality which had caused that first magnifying in his mind. His senses, while reporting accurately, insisted upon this arresting and uncommon touch: there was, about this late wanderer of the night, some evasive, lofty strangeness that set him utterly apart from ordinary men.

The Englishman examined him searchingly, surreptitiously, but with a touch of passionate curiosity he could not in the least account for nor explain. There were contradictions of perplexing character about him. For the first presentment had been of splendid youth, while on the face, though vigorous and gloriously handsome, he now discerned the stamp of tremendous age. It was worn and tired. While radiant with strength and health and power, it wore as well this certain signature of deep exhaustion that great experience rather than physical experience brings. Moreover, he discovered in it, in some way he could not hope to describe, man, woman, and child. There was a big, sad earnestness about it, yet a touch of humour too; patience, tenderness, and sweetness held the mouth; and behind the high pale forehead intellect sat enthroned and watchful. In it were both love and hatred, longing and despair; an expression of being ever on the defensive, yet hugely mutinous; an air both hunted and beseeching; great knowledge and great woe.

Delane gave up the search, aware that something unalterably splendid stood before him. Solemnity and beauty swept him too. His was never the grotesque assumption that man must be the highest being in the universe, nor that a thing is a miracle merely because it has never happened before. He groped, while explanation and analysis both halted. "A great teacher," thought fluttered through him, "or a mighty rebel! A distinguished personality beyond all question! Who can he be?" There was something regal that put respect upon his imagination instantly. And he remembered the legend of the country-side that Ludwig of Bavaria was said to be about when nights were very wild. He wondered. Into his speech and manner crept unawares an attitude of deference that was almost reverence, and with it—whence came this other quality?—a searching pity.

"You must be wearied out," he said respectfully, busying himself about the room, "as well as cold and wet. This fire will dry you, sir, and meanwhile I will prepare quickly such food as there is, if you will eat it." For the other carried no knapsack, nor was he clothed for the severity of mountain travel.

"I have already eaten," said the stranger courteously, "and, with my thanks to you, I am neither wet nor tired. The afflictions that I bear are of another kind, though ones that you shall more easily, I am sure, relieve."

He spoke as a man whose words set troops in action, and Delane glanced at him, deeply moved by the surprising phrase, yet hardly marvelling that it should be so. He found no ready answer. But there was evidently question in his look, for the other continued, and this time with a smile that betrayed sheer winning beauty as of a tender woman:

"I saw the light and came to it. It is unusual—at this time."

His voice was resonant, yet not deep. There was a ringing quality about it that the bare room emphasised. It charmed the young Englishman inexplicably. Also, it woke in him a sense of infinite pathos.

"You are a climber, sir, like myself," Delane resumed, lifting his eyes a moment uneasily from the coffee he brewed over a corner of the fire. "You know this neighbourhood, perhaps? Better, at any rate, than I can know it?" His German halted rather. He chose his words with difficulty. There was uncommon trouble in his mind.

"I know all wild and desolate places," replied the other, in perfect English, but with a wintry mournfulness in his voice and eyes, "for I feel at home in them, and their stern companionship my nature craves as solace. But, unlike yourself, I am no climber."

"The heights have no attraction for you?" asked Delane, as he mingled steaming milk and coffee in the wooden bowl, marvelling what brought him then so high above the valleys. "It is their difficulty and danger that fascinate me always. I find the loneliness of the summits intoxicating in a sense."

And, regardless of refusal, he set the bread and meat before him, the apple and the tiny packet of salt, then turned away to place the coffee pot beside the fire again. But as he did so a singular gesture of the other caught his eyes. Before touching bowl or plate, the stranger took the fruit and brushed his lips with it. He kissed it, then set it on the ground and crushed it into pulp beneath his heel.

And, seeing this, the young Englishman knew something dreadfully arrested in his mind, for, as he looked away, pretending the act was unobserved, a thing of ice and darkness moved past him through the room, so that the pot trembled in his hand, rattling sharply against the hearthstone where he stooped. He could only interpret it as an act of madness, and the myth of the sad, drowned monarch wandering through this enchanted region, pressed into him again unsought and urgent. It was a full minute before he had control of his heart and hand again.

The bowl was half emptied, and the man was smiling—this time the smile of a child who implores the comfort of enveloping and understanding arms.

"I am a wanderer rather than a climber," he was saying, as though there had been no interval, "for, though the lonely summits suit me well, I now find in them only—terror. My feet lose their sureness, and my head its steady balance. I prefer the hidden gorges of these mountains, and the shadows of the covering forests. My days"—his voice drew the loneliness of uttermost space into its piteous accents—"are passed in darkness. I can never climb again."

He spoke this time, indeed, as a man whose nerve was gone for ever. It was pitiable almost to tears. And Delane, unable to explain the amazing contradictions, felt recklessly, furiously drawn to this trapped wanderer with the mien of a king yet the air and speech sometimes of a woman and sometimes of an outcast child.

"Ah, then you have known accidents," Delane replied with outer calmness, as he lit his pipe, trying in vain to keep his hand as steady as his voice. "You have been in one perhaps. The effect, I have been told, is——"

The power and sweetness in that resonant voice took his breath away as he heard it break in upon his own uncertain accents:

"I have—fallen," the stranger replied impressively, as the rain and wind wailed past the building mournfully, "yet a fall that was no part of any accident. For it was no common fall," the man added with a magnificent gesture of disdain, "while yet it broke my heart in two." He stooped a little as he uttered the next words with a crying pathos that an outcast woman might have used. "I am," he said, "engulfed in intolerable loneliness. I can never climb again."

With a shiver impossible to control, half of terror, half of pity, Delane moved a step nearer to the marvellous stranger. The spirit of Ludwig, exiled and distraught, had gripped his soul with a weakening terror; but now sheer beauty lifted him above all personal shrinking. There seemed some echo of lost divinity, worn, wild yet grandiose, through which this significant language strained towards a personal message—for himself.

"In loneliness?" he faltered, sympathy rising in a flood.

"For my Kingdom that is lost to me for ever," met him in deep, throbbing tones that set the air on fire. "For my imperial ancient heights that jealousy took from me——"

The stranger paused, with an indescribable air of broken dignity and pain.

Outside the tempest paused a moment before the awful elemental crash that followed. A bellowing of many winds descended like artillery upon the world. A burst of smoke rushed from the fireplace about them both, shrouding the stranger momentarily in a flying veil. And Delane stood up, uncomfortable in his very bones. "What can it be?" he asked himself sharply. "Who is this being that he should use such language?" He watched alarm chase pity, aware that the conversation held something beyond experience.

But the pity returned in greater and ever greater flood. And love surged through him too. It was significant, he remembered afterwards, that he felt it incumbent upon himself to stand. Curious, too, how the thought of that mad, drowned monarch haunted memory with such persistence. Some vast emotion that he could not name drove out his subsequent words. The smoke had cleared, and a strange, high stillness held the world. The rain streamed down in torrents, isolating these two somehow from the haunts of men. And the Englishman stared then into a countenance grown mighty with woe and loneliness. There stood darkly in it this incommunicable magnificence of pain that mingled awe with the pity he had felt. The kingly eyes looked clear into his own, completing his subjugation out of time. "I would follow you," ran his thought upon its knees, "follow you with obedience for ever and ever, even into a last damnation. For you are sublime. You shall come again into your Kingdom, if my own small worship——"

Then blackness sponged the reckless thought away. He spoke in its place a more guarded, careful thing:

"I am aware," he faltered, yet conscious that he bowed, "of standing before a Great One of some world unknown to me. Who he may be I have but the privilege of wondering. He has spoken darkly of a Kingdom that is lost. Yet he is still, I see, a Monarch." And he lowered his head and shoulders involuntarily.

For an instant, then, as he said it, the eyes before him flashed their original terrific lightnings. The darkness of the common world faded before the entrance of an Outer Darkness. From gulfs of terror at his feet rose shadows out of the night of time, and a passionate anguish as of sudden madness seized his heart and shook it.

He listened breathlessly for the words that followed. It seemed some wind of unutterable despair passed in the breath from those non-human lips:

"I am still a Monarch, yes; but my Kingdom is taken from me, for I have no single subject. Lost in a loneliness that lies out of space and time, I am become a throneless Ruler, and my hopelessness is more than I can bear." The beseeching pathos of the voice tore him in two. The Deity himself, it seemed, stood there accused of jealousy, of sin and cruelty. The stranger rose. The power about him brought the picture of a planet, throned in mid-heaven and poised beyond assault. "Not otherwise," boomed the startling words as though an avalanche found syllables, "could I now show myself to—you."

Delane was trembling horribly. He felt the next words slip off his tongue unconsciously. The shattering truth had dawned upon his soul at last.

"Then the light you saw, and came to——?" he whispered.

"Was the light in your heart that guided me," came the answer, sweet, beguiling as the music in a woman's tones, "the light of your instant, brief desire that held love in it." He made an opening movement with his arms as he continued, smiling like stars in summer. "For you summoned me; summoned me by your dear and precious belief: how dear, how precious, none can know but I who stand before you."

His figure drew up with an imperial air of proud dominion. His feet were set among the constellations. The opening movement of his arms continued slowly. And the music in his tones seemed merged in distant thunder.

"For your single, brief belief," he smiled with the grandeur of a condescending emperor, "shall give my vanished Kingdom back to me."

And with an air of native majesty he held his hand out—to be kissed.

The black hurricane of night, the terror of frozen peaks, the yawning horror of the great abyss outside—all three crowded into the Englishman's mind with a slashing impact that blocked delivery of any word or action. It was not that he refused, it was not that he withdrew, but that Life stood paralysed and rigid. The flow stopped dead for the first time since he had left his mother's womb. The God in him was turned to stone and rendered ineffective. For an appalling instant God was *not*.

He realised the stupendous moment. Before him, drinking his little soul out merely by his Presence, stood one whose habit of mind, not alone his external accidents, was imperial with black prerogative before the first man drew the breath of life. August procedure was native to his inner process of existence The stars and confines of the universe owned his sway before he fell, to trifle away the dreary little centuries by haunting the minds of feeble men and women, by hiding himself in nursery cupboards, and by grinning with stained gargoyles from the roofs of city churches. . . .

And the lad's life stammered, flickered, threatened to go out before the enveloping terror of the revelation.

"I called to you ... but called to you in play," thought whispered somewhere deep below the level of any speech, yet not so low that the audacious sound of it did not crash above the elements outside; "for . . . till now ... you have been to me but a ... coated bogy ... that my brain disowned with laughter . . . and my heart thought picturesque. If you are here . . . *alive!* May God forgive me for my . . ."

It seemed as though tears—the tears of love and profound commiseration—drowned the very seed of thought itself.

A sound stopped him that was like a collapse in heaven. Some crashing, as of a ruined world, passed splintering through his little timid heart. He did not yield, but he understood—with an understanding which seemed the delicate first sign of yielding—the seductiveness of evil, the sweet delight of surrendering the Will with utter recklessness to those swelling forces which disintegrate the heroic soul in man. He remembered. It was true. In the reaction from excess, he *had* definitely called upon his childhood's teaching with a passing moment of genuine belief. And now that yearning of a fraction of a second bore its awful fruit.

The luscious Capitals where he had rioted passed in a coloured stream before his eyes; the Wine, the Woman, and the Song stood there before him, clothed in that Power which lies insinuatingly disguised behind their little passing show of innocence. Their glamour donned this domino of regal and virile grandeur. He felt entangled beyond recovery. The idea of God seemed sterile and without reality. The one real thing, the one desirable thing, the one possible, strong and beautiful thing—was to bend his head and kiss those imperial fingers. He moved noiselessly towards the Hand. He raised his own to take it and lift it towards his mouth——

When there rose in his mind with startling vividness a small, soft picture of a child's nursery, a picture of a little boy, kneeling in scanty nightgown with pink upturned soles, and asking ridiculous, audacious things of a shining Figure seated on a summer cloud above the kitchen-garden walnut tree.

The tiny symbol flashed and went its way, yet not before it had lit the entire world with glory. For there came an absolutely routing power with it. In that half-forgotten instant's craving for the simple teaching of his childhood days, Belief had conjured with two immense traditions. This was the second of them. The appearance of the one had inevitably produced the passage of its opposite . . .

And the Hand that floated in the air before him to be kissed sank slowly down below the possible level of his lips. He shrank away. Though laughter tempted something in his brain, there still clung about his heart the first aching, pitying terror. But size retreated, dwindling somehow as it went. The wind and rain obliterated every other sound; yet in that bare, unfurnished room of a climber's mountain hut, there was a silence, above the roar, that drank in everything and broke the back of speech. In opposition to this masquerading splendour Delane had set up a personal, paternal Deity.

"I thought of you, perhaps," cried the voice of self-defence, "but I did not call to you with real belief. And, by the name of God, I did not summon you. For your sweetness, as your power, sickens me; and your hand is black with the curses of all the mothers in the world, whose prayers and tears——"

He stopped dead, overwhelmed by the cruelty of his reckless utterance.

And the Other moved towards him slowly. It was like the summit of some peaked and terrible height that moved. He spoke. He changed appallingly.

"But *I* claim," he roared, "your heart. I claim you by that instant of belief you felt. For by that alone you shall restore to me my vanished Kingdom. You shall worship me."

In the countenance was a sudden awful power; but behind the stupefying roar there was weakness in the voice as of an imploring and beseeching child. Again, deep love and searching pity seared the Englishman's heart as he replied in the gentlest accents he could find to master:

"And I claim *you*," he said, "by my understanding sympathy, and by my sorrow for your Godforsaken loneliness, and by my love. For no Kingdom built on hate can stand against the love you would deny——"

Words failed him then, as he saw the majesty fade slowly from the face, grown small and shadowy. One last expression of desperate energy in the eyes struck lightnings from the smoky air, as with an abandoned movement of the entire figure, he drew back, it seemed, towards the door behind him.

Delane moved slowly after him opening his arms. Tenderness and big compassion flung wide the gates of love within him. He found strange language, too, although actual, spoken words did not produce them further than his entrails where they had their birth.

"Toys in the world are plentiful, Sire, and you may have them for your masterpiece of play. But you must seek them where they still survive; in the churches, and in isolated lands where thought lies unawakened. For they are the children's blocks of make-believe whose palaces, like your once tremendous kingdom, have no true existence for the thinking mind."

And he stretched his hands towards him with the gesture of one who sought to help and save, then paused as he realised that his arms enclosed sheer blackness, with the emptiness of wind and driving rain.

For the door of the hut stood open, and Delane balanced on the threshold, facing the sheet of night above the abyss. He heard the waterfalls in the valley far below. The forest flapped and tossed its myriad branches. Cold draughts swept down from spectral fields of melting snow above; and the blackness turned momentarily into the semblance of towers and bastions of thick beaten gloom. Above one soaring turret, then, a space of sky appeared, swept naked by a violent, lost wind—an opening of purple into limitless distance. For one second, amid the vapours, it was visible, empty and untenanted. The next, there sailed across its small diameter a falling Star. With an air of slow and endless leisure, yet at the same time with terrific speed, it dived behind the ragged curtain of the clouds, and the space closed up again. Blackness returned upon the heavens.

And through this blackness, plunging into that abyss of woe whence he had momentarily risen, the figure of the marvellous stranger melted utterly away. Delane, for a fleeting second, was aware of the earnestness in the sad, imploring countenance; of its sweetness and its power so strangely mingled; of its mysterious grandeur; and of its pathetic childishness.

But, already, it was sunk into interminable distance. A star that would be baleful, yet was merely glorious, passed on its endless wandering among the teeming systems of the universe. Behind the fixed and steady stars, secure in their appointed places, it set. It vanished into the pit of unknown emptiness. It was gone.

"God help you!" sighed across the sea of wailing branches, echoing down the dark abyss below. "God give you rest at last!"

For he saw a princely, nay, an Imperial Being, homeless for ever, and for ever wandering, hunted as by keen remorseless winds about a universe that held no corner for his feet, his majesty unworshipped, his reign a mockery, his Court unfurnished, and his courtiers mere shadows of deep space . . .

And a thin, grey dawn, stealing up behind clearing summits in the east, crept then against the windows of the mountain hut. It brought with it a treacherous, sharp air that made the sleeper draw another blanket near to shelter him from the sudden cold. For the fire had died out, and an icy draught sucked steadily beneath the doorway.

If the Cap Fits

Field-Martin, the naturalist, sat in his corner armchair at the Club and watched them—this group of men that had drifted together round the table just opposite and begun to talk. He did not wish to listen, but was too near to help himself. The newspaper over which he had dozed lay at his feet, and he bent forward to pick it up and make it crackle with a pretence of reading.

"Then what *is* psychometry?" was the question that first caught his attention. It was Slopkins who asked it, the man with the runaway chin and over-weighted, hooked nose, that seemed to bring forward all the top of his face and made him resemble a large codfish for ever in the act of rising to some invisible bait.

"Something to do with soul measuring, I suppose, unless my Greek has gone utterly to pot," said the jovial man beside him, pouring out his tea from a height, as a waiter pours out flat beer when he wants to force it to froth in the glass.

"Like those Yankee doctors, don't you remember," put in someone else, with the irrelevance of casual conversation," who weighed a human body just before it died and just after, and made an affidavit that the difference in ounces represented the weight of the soul."

Several laughed. Field-Martin wheeled up his chair with vigorous strokes of his heels and joined the group, accepting the offer of an extra cup out of that soaring teapot. The particular subject under discussion bored him, but he liked to sit and watch men talking, just as he liked to sit and watch birds or animals in the open air, studying their movements, learning their little habits, and the rest. The conversation flowed on in desultory fashion in the way conversations usually do flow on, one or two talkers putting in occasional real thoughts, the majority merely repeating what they have heard others say.

"Yes, but what *is* psychometry really?" repeated the codfish man, after an interval during which the talk had drifted into an American story that grew apparently out of the reference to American doctors. For that particular invisible bait still hovered above the surface of his slow mental stream, and he was making a second shot at it, after the manner of his ilk.

The question was so obviously intended to be answered seriously that this time no one guffawed or exercised his wit. For a moment, indeed, no one answered at all. Then a man at the back of the group, a man with a deep voice and a rather theatrical and enthusiastic manner, spoke.

"Psychometry, I take it," he said with conviction," is the quality possessed by everything, even by inanimate objects, of sending out vibrations which—which can put certain sensitive persons *en rapport*, pictorially as it were, with all the events that have ever happened within the ken of such objects—"

"Persons known as psychometrists, I suppose?" from the codfish man, who seemed to like things labelled carefully.

The other nodded. "Psychometrist, I believe," he continued, "is the name of that very psychical and imaginative type that can such infinitely delicate vibrations. In reality, I suppose, they are receptive folk who correspond to the sensitive photographic plate that records vibrations of light in a similar way and results in a visible picture."

A man dropped his teaspoon with a clatter; another splashed noisily in his cup, stirring it; a third plunged at the buttered toast of his neighbour; and Field-Martin, the naturalist, gave an impatient kick with his leg against the armchair opposite. He loathed this kind of talk. The speaker evidently was one of those who knew by heart the "patter" of psychical research, or what passes for it among credulous and untrained minds—master of that peculiar jargon, quasi-scientific, about vibrations and the rest, that such persons affect. But he was too lazy to interrupt or disagree. Wondering vaguely who the speaker might be, he drank his tea, and listened with laughter and disgust about equally mingled in his mind. Others, besides the codfish, were asking questions. Answers were not behindhand.

"You remember Denton's experiments—Professor Denton, of Cambridge, Mass.," the enthusiastic man was saying, "who found that his wife was a psychometrist, and how she had only to hold a thing in her hand, with eyes blindfolded, to get pictures of scenes that had passed before it. A bit of stone he gave her brought vivid and gorgeous pictures of processions and pageants before her inner eye, I remember, and at the end of the experiment her husband told her what the stone was."

"By Jove! And what was it?" asked codfish.

"A fragment from an old temple at Thebes," was the reply.

"Telepathy," suggested someone.

"Quite possible," was the reply. "But, another time, when he gave her something wrapped up in a bit of paper, taken from a tray covered with objects similarly wrapped up so that he could not know what particular one he held at the moment, she took it for a second, then screamed out that she was rushing, tearing, falling through space, and let it drop with a gasp of breathless excitement—"

"And?" asked one or two.

"It was a piece of meteorite," was the answer. "You see, she had psychometrised the sensations of the falling star. I know, for instance, another woman who is so sensitive to the atmospheres of things and people, that she can tell you every blessed thing about a stranger whose just-vacated chair she sits down in. I've known her leave a bus, too, when certain people have got in and sat next to her, because—"

Field-Martin paid for his neighbour's tea by mistake and moved away, hoping his contempt was not too clearly marked for politeness.

"—everything, you see, has an atmosphere charged with its own individual associations. An object can communicate an emotion it has borrowed by contact with someone living—" was a fragment of the last sentence he heard as he left the room and went downstairs, spitting fire internally against the speaker and all his kidney.

He seized his hat and hurried away. He walked home to his Chelsea flat, fuming inwardly, wondering vaguely if there was any other club he could join where he could have his tea without being obliged to listen to such stuff. . . He walked through the park, meaning to cut through *via* Queensgate, and as he went he followed his usual custom of thinking out details of his work: the next day, for instance, he was to lecture upon "English Birds of Prey," and in his mind he reviewed carefully the form and substance of what he would say.

He skirted the Serpentine, watching the seagulls wheeling through the graceful figures of their evening dance against the saffron sky. The exquisite tilt and balance of their bodies fascinated him as usual. He stopped a moment to watch it. To a mind like his it was full of suggestion, and instinctively he began comparing the method of flight with that of the hawks; one or two points occurred to him that he could make good use of in his lecture . . . when he became aware that something drew his attention down from the sky to the water, and that the interest he felt in the birds was being usurped by thoughts of another kind. Without apparent reason, reflections of a very different order passed into the stream of his consciousness—somewhat urgently.

Seagulls, hawks, birds of prey, and the rest faded from his mental vision; wings and details of flight departed; his eye, and with it his thought, dropped from the sky to the surface of the water, shimmering there beneath the last tints of the sunset. The emotion of the naturalist," stirred into activity by the least symbol of his lifelong study—a bird, an animal, an insect—had been curiously replaced; and the transition was abrupt enough to touch him with a sense of surprise—almost, perhaps, of shock.

Now, vigorous imagination, the kind that creates out of next to nothing, was not an ingredient of his logical and "scientific" cast of mind, and Field-Martin, slightly puzzled, was at a loss to explain this irregular behaviour of his usually methodical system. He stepped back farther from the brink where the little waves splashed . . . yet, even as he did so, he realised that the force dictating the impulse was of a protective character, guiding, directing, almost warning. In words, had he been a writer, he might have transposed it thus: "Be careful of that water!" For the truth was it had suddenly made him *shrink*.

He continued his way, puzzled and disturbed. Of the mutinous forces that lie so thinly screened behind life, dropping from time to time their faint, wireless messages upon the soul, Field-Martin hardly discerned the existence. And this passing menace of the water was disquieting—all the more so because his temperament furnished him with no possible instrument of measurement. A sense of deep water, cold, airless, still, invaded his mind; he thought of its suffocating mass lying over mouth and ears; he realised something of the struggle for breath, and the frantic efforts to reach the surface and keep afloat that a drowning man—

"But what nonsense is this? Where do these thoughts suddenly come from?" he exclaimed, hurrying along. He had crossed the road now, so as to put a greater distance, and a stretch of wholesome human traffic, between him and that sheet of water lying like painted glass beneath the fading sky. Yet it pulled and drew him back again to the shore, inviting him with a curious, soft insistence that rendered necessary a distinct effort of will to resist it successfully. Birds were utterly forgotten. His very being was steeped in water—to the neck, to the eyes, his lungs filled, his ears charged with the rushing noises of singing and drumming that come to complete the dread bewilderment of the drowning man.

Field-Martin shook and trembled as he crossed the bridge by Kensington Gardens. That impulse to throw himself over the parapet was the most outrageous and unaccountable thing that had ever come upon him . . . and as he hurried down Queensgate, he tried to calculate whether there was time for him to see his doctor that very night before dinner, or whether he must postpone it to the first thing in the morning. For, assuredly, this passing disorder of his brain must have immediate attention; such results of overwork could not be seen to quickly enough. If necessary, he would take a holiday at once. . . .

He decided to say nothing to his wife and yet the odd thing was that before dinner was half over the whole mood had vanished so completely, and his normal wholesome balance of mind recovered such perfect control, that he could afford to laugh at the whole thing, and *did* laugh at it—what was more, even made his wife laugh at it too. The fact remained to puzzle and perplex, but the reality of it was gone.

But that night, when he went to the Club, the hall-porter stopped him:

"Beg pardon, sir, but Mr. Finsen thought you might have taken his hat by mistake last night?"

"His hat?" The name "Finsen" was unknown to him.

"He wears a green felt hat like yours, sir, and they were on adjoining pegs."

Field-Martin took off his head-covering and discovered his mistake. Finsen's name was inside in small gold letters. He explained matters with the porter, and left the necessary directions for the exchange to be effected. Upstairs he ran into Slopkins.

"That chap Finsen was asking for you," he remarked; it seems you exchanged hats last night by mistake, and the porter thought possibly—"

"Who is Finsen?"

"You remember, he was talking so wonderfully last night about psychometry—"

"Oh, is *that* Finsen?"

"Yes," replied the other. "Interesting man, but a bit queer, you know. Gets melancholia and that sort of thing, I believe. It was only a week or two ago, don't you remember, that he tried to drown himself?"

"Indeed," said Field-Martin dryly, and went upstairs to look at the evening papers.

Imagination

Having dined upon a beefsteak and a pint of bitter, Jones went home to work. The trouble with Jones—his first name William—was that he possessed creative imagination: that luggage upon which excess charges have to be paid all through life—to the critic, the stupid, the orthodox, the slower minds without the" flash." He was alone in his brother's flat. It was after nine o'clock. He was half-way into a story, and had—stuck! Sad to relate, the machinery that carries on the details of an original inspiration had blocked. And to invent he knew not how. Unless the imagination "produced" he would not allow his brain to devise mere episodes—dull and lifeless substitutes. Jones, poor fool, was also artist.

And the reason he had stuck was not surprising, for his story was of a kind that might well tax the imagination of any sane man. He was writing at the moment about a being who had survived his age—a study of one of those rare and primitive souls who walk the earth today in a man's twentieth-century body, while yet the spirit belongs to the Golden Age of the world's history. You may come across them sometimes, rare, ingenuous, delightful beings, the primal dews still upon their eyelids, the rush and glow of earth's pristine fires pulsing in their veins, careless of gain, indifferent to success, lost, homeless, exiled—*dépaysés*.

The idea had seized him. He had met such folk. He burned to describe their exile, the pathos of their loneliness, their yearnings and their wanderings-rejected by a world they had outlived. And for his type, thus representing some power of unexpended mythological values strayed back into modern life to find itself denied and ridiculed— he had chosen a Centaur! For he wished it to symbolise what he believed was to be the next stage in human evolution: Intuition no longer neglected, but developed equally with Reason. His Centaur was to stand for instinct (the animal body close to Nature) combined with, yet not dominated by, the upright stature moving towards deity. The conception was true and pregnant.

And—he had stuck. The detail that blocked him was the man's *appearance*. How would such a being look? In what details would he betray that, though outwardly a man, he was inwardly this survival of the Golden Age, escaped from some fair Eden, splendid, immense, simple, and beneficent, yet—a Centaur?

Perhaps it was just as well he had "stuck," for his brother would shortly be in, and his brother was a successful business man with the money-sense and commercial instincts strongly developed. He dealt in rice and sugar. With his brother in the flat no Centaur could possibly survive for a single moment. "It'll come to me when I'm not thinking about it," he sighed, knowing well the waywardness of his particular genius. He threw the reins upon the subconscious self and moved into an armchair to read in the evening paper the things the public loved—that public who refused to buy his books, pleading they were "queer."

He waded down the list of immoralities, murders and assaults with a dreamy eye, and had just reached the witness's description of finding the bloody head in the faithless wife's bedroom, when there came a hurried, pelting knock at the door, and William Jones, glad of the relief, went to open it. There, facing him, stood the bore from the flat below. Horrors!

It was not, however, a visit after all. "Jones," he faltered, "there's an odd sort of chap here asking for you or your brother. Rang my bell by mistake."

Jones murmured some reply or other, and as the bore vanished with a hurry unusual to him, there passed into the flat a queer shape, born surely of the night and stars and desolate places. He seemed in some undefinable way bent, humpbacked, very large. With him came a touch of open spaces, winds, forests, long clean hills and dew-drenched fields.

"Come in, please. . . ." said Jones, instantly aware that the man was not for his brother. "You have something to—er—" he was going to use the word "ask," then changed it instinctively—"*say* to me, haven't you?"

The man was ragged, poor, outcast. Clearly it was a begging episode; and yet he trembled violently, while in his veins ran fire. The caller refused a seat, but moved over to the curtains by the window, drawing them slightly aside so that he could see out. And the window was high above old smoky London—open. It felt cold. Jones bent down, always keeping his caller in view, and lit the gas-stove. "You wish to see me," he said, rising again to an upright position. Then he added more hurriedly, stepping back a little towards the rack where the walking-sticks were, "Please let me know what I can do for you!"

Bearded, unkempt, with massive shoulders and huge neck, the caller stood a moment and stared. "Your name and address," he said at length, were given to me"—he hesitated a moment, then added— "you know by whom." His voice was deep and windy and echoing. It made the stretched cords of the upright piano ring against the wall. "He told me to call," the man concluded.

"Ah yes; of course," Jones stammered, forgetting for the moment who or where he was. "Let me see—where are you"—the word did not want to come out—"staying?" The caller made an awful and curious movement; it seemed so much bigger than his body. "In what way—er—can I be of assistance?" Jones hardly knew what he said. The other volunteered so little. He was frightened.

Then, before the man could answer, he caught a dreadful glimpse, as of something behind the outline. It moved. Was it shadow that thus extended his form? Was it the glare of that ugly gas-stove that played tricks with the folds of the curtain, driving bodily outline forth into mere vacancy? For the figure of his strange caller seemed to carry with it the idea of projections, extensions, growths, in themselves not monstrous, fine and comely, rather—yet awful.

The man left the window and moved towards him. It was was a movement both swift and enormous. It was instantaneous.

"Who are you—*really*?" asked Jones, his breath catching, while he went pluckily out to meet him, irresistibly drawn. "And what is it you *really* want of me?" He went very close to the shrouded form, caught the keen air from the open window behind, sniffed a wind that was not London's stale and weary wind, then stopped abruptly, frozen with terror and delight. The man facing him was splendid and terrific, exhaling something that overwhelmed.

"What can I . . . do . . . for . . . you?" whispered Jones, shaking like a leaf. A delight of racing clouds was in him.

The answer came in a singular roaring voice that yet sounded far away, as though among mountains. Wind might have brought it down.

"There is nothing you can do for me! But, by Chiron, there is something I can do for you!"

"And that is?" asked Jones faintly, feeling something sweep against his feet and legs like the current of a river in flood.

The man eyed him appallingly a moment.

"Let you see me!" he roared, while his voice set the piano singing again, and his outline seemed to swim over the chairs and tables like a fluid mass. "Show myself to you!"

The figure stretched out what looked like arms, reared gigantically aloft towards the ceiling, and swept towards him. Jones saw the great visage close to his own. He smelt the odour of caves, river-beds, hillsides—space. In another second he would have been lost—

His brother made a great rattling as he opened the door. The atmosphere of rice and sugar and office desks came in with him.

"Why, Billy, old man, you look as if you'd seen a ghost. You're white!"

William Jones mopped his forehead. "I've been working rather hard," he answered. "Feel tired. Fact is—I got stuck in a story for a bit."

"Too bad. Got it straightened out at last, I hope?"

"Yes, thanks. *It came to me*—in the end."

The other looked at him. "Good," he said shortly. "Rum thing, imagination, isn't it?" And then he began talking about his day's business—in tons and tons of food.

Jimbo's Longest Day

The Longest Day has in it for children a strange, incommunicable thrill. It begins so early in the morning, for one thing, that half of it—the first half—belongs to the mystery of night. It steals upon the world as though from Fairyland, a thing apart from the rush and scurry of ordinary days; it is so it is so long that nothing happens quickly in it; there is a delicious leisure throughout its shining hours that makes it possible to carry out a hundred schemes unhurried.

No voice can call "Time's up!"; no one can urge "Be quick!"; it passes, true, yet passes like a dream that flows in a circle, having neither proper beginning nor definite end. Christmas Day and Easter Day seem short and sharp by comparison. They are measurable. The Longest Day brims with a happy, endless wonder from dawn to sunset. Exceptional happenings are its prerogative.

All this, and something more no elder can quite grasp, lay stealthily in Jimbo's question: "Uncle, tomorrow's the Longest Day. What shall we do?" He glanced across the room at his mother, prepared for a prohibitive remark of some sort. But mother, deep in a stolen book, paid no attention. He looked back at me. "It's all right; she's not listening; but we can go outside to discuss it, if you prefer," his expression said. I beckoned him over to me, however, for safety's sake. My position was fairly strong, I knew, because the stolen book was mine, and had been taken from my worktable.

Jimbo's mother has this way with books, her passion almost unmoral. If a book comes to me for review, if a friend makes me a present of a book, if I buy or borrow one—the instant it comes into the house she knows it. "I just looked in to see if your room had been dusted," she says; I'm sorry to disturb you," and is gone again. But she has seen the new book. Her instinct is curious. I used to think she bribed the postman. She smells a new arrival, and goes straight for it. "Were you looking for *this*?" she will ask innocently an hour later when I catch her with it, household account-books neglected by her side. "I'm so sorry. I was just peeping into it." And she is incorrigible, as unashamed. No book is ever lost, at any rate. "Mother's got it," indicates its hiding-place infallibly.

So, I felt safe enough discussing plans for the Longest Day with Jimbo, and talked openly with him, while I watched her turn the pages.

"It's the *very* beginning I like," he said. "I want to see it start. The sun rises at 3.44, you see. That's a quarter to four—three hours and a quarter before I usually get up. How shall we manage it, d'you think?" He had worked it all out.

"There's hardly any night either," I said, "for the sun sets at 8.18, and that leaves very little time for darkness. It's light at two, remember."

He stared into my face. "Maria has an alarum clock. She wakes with that. It's by her bed in the attic room, you know."

Mother turned a page noisily, but did not look up. There was no cause for alarm, though we instinctively lowered our voices at once. I cannot say how it was so swiftly, so deftly arranged between us that *I* was to steal the clock, set it accurately for two in the morning, rise, dress, and come to fetch Jimbo. But the result was clear beyond equivocation, and I had accepted the duty as a man should. Generously he left this exciting thing to me.

"And suppose it doesn't go off and wake you," he inquired anxiously, "will you be sure to get up and *make* it go off? Because we might miss the beginning of the day unless you do."

I explained something about the mechanism of the mind and the mechanism of an alarum clock that seemed to satisfy him, and then he asked another vital question: "What is exactly the Longest Day, uncle? I thought all days were about the same—like that," and he stretched an imaginary line in the air with one hand, so that Mac, the terrier, thought he wanted to play a moment. I explained that too, to his satisfaction, whereupon he nestled much closer to me, glancing first over his shoulder at his mother, and inquired whether "everything knew it was the Longest Day—birds, cows, and out-of-door things all over the world—rabbits, I mean—like that? They know, I suppose?"

"They certainly must find it longer than other days, ordinary days, just common days," I said. I'm sure of that." And then I cleared my throat so loudly that mother looked up from her book with an unmistakable start.

"Oh, I'm so sorry," she exclaimed, with unblushing mendacity, "but d'you want your book? Were you looking for it? I just took a peep—" And when I turned to leave the room with it beneath my arm Jimbo had vanished, leaving no trace behind him.

That night he went to bed without a murmur at half-past eight. He trusted me implicitly. There were no questions: "Have you got the clock?" or " How did you get it?" or anything of the kind—just his absolute confidence that I *had* got it and that I *would* wake him. At the stairs, however, he turned and made a sign. Leading me through the back door of the Sussex cottage, we found ourselves a moment in the orchard together. And then, saying no word, he pointed. He pointed everywhere; he stared about him, listening; he looked up into my face, and then at the orchard, and then back into my face again. His whole little person stood on tiptoe, observing, watching, listening.

And at first, I was disappointed, for I noticed nothing unusual anywhere. "Well, what is it?" my manner probably expressed. But neither of us said a word. The saffron sky shone between the trunks of the apple trees; swallows darted to and fro; a blackbird whistled out of sight; and over the hedge a big cow thrust her head towards us, her body concealed. In the foreground were beehives. The air was very still and scented. My pipe smoke hung almost motionless. I moved from one foot to the other.

"Aha!" I said mysteriously below my breath, aha!"

And that was sufficient for him. He knew I had seen and understood. He came a step nearer to me, his face solemn and expectant.

"It's begun already, you see. Isn't it wonderful? Everything knows."

"And is getting ready," I added, "for its coming."

"The Longest Day," he whispered, looking about him with suppressed excitement and ready, if necessary, to believe the earth would presently stop turning. He gave one curious look at the sky, shuddered an instant with intense delight, gave my hand a secret squeeze, and disappeared like a goblin into the cottage. But behind him lingered something his little presence had evoked. Wonder and expectation are true words of power, and anticipation constructs the mould along which Imagination later shall lead her fairy band. I realised what he had seen. The orchard, the cow, the beehives *did* look different. They were inviting, as though something was on the way.

The very sky, as the summer dusk spread down it, wore colouring no ordinary June evening knew. Midsummer Eve set free the fairies, and Jimbo knew it. The roses seemed to flutter everywhere on wings.

. .The very lilac blooms had eyes. . . . I heard a rustle as of skirts high up among the peeping stars. . . .

How it came about is more than I can say, for I went to bed with a whirr of wings and flowers in my head. The stillness of the night was magical, four short hours of transparent darkness that seemed to gleam and glimmer without hiding anything. Maria's alarum clock was not beside my bed, for the simple reason that I had not asked for it. Jimbo and the Longest Day between them had cast a glamour over me that had nothing to do with hours, minutes, seconds. It was delicious and inexplicable. Yet at other times I am an ordinary person, who knows that time is money and money is difficult to come by without uncommon effort. All this came for nothing. Jimbo did it.

And what did I do for Jimbo? I cannot say. His is the grand old magical secret. He believed and wondered; he waited and asked no futile questions; time and space obeyed his imperious little will; waking or sleeping he dreamed, creating the world anew. I shut no eye that night. I watched the wheeling constellations rise and pass. The whole, clear summer night was rich with the silence of the gods. dreamed, perhaps, beside my open window, where the roses and the clematis climbed, shining like lamps of starry beauty above the tiny lawn. And at half-past one, when the east began to whisper stealthily that Someone was on the way, I left my chair and stole quietly down the narrow passage-way to Jimbo's room. . . . I was clever in my wickedness.

I knew that if I waked him, whispering that the Longest Day was about to break, he would open half an eye, turn over in his thick childhood sleep, and murmur, as in dream, "Then let it come." And so, a little weary, if the truth be told, I did all this, and—to my intense surprise—discovered Jimbo perched, wide awake and staring, at the casement window. He had never closed an eye, nor half an eye. He was watchful and alert, but undeniably tired out, as I was.

"Jimbo," I whispered, stealing in upon him, "the Longest Day is very near. It's so close in can hear it coming down the sky. It's softer than any dream you ever dreamed in your life. Come out—if you will—we'll see it from the orchard."

He turned towards me in his little nightshirt like a goblin. His eyes were very big, but the eyelids held open with an effort.

"Uncle," he said in a tiny voice," do you think it's really come at last? It's been terribly slow, but I suppose that's because it's such an awful length. Wasn't it *wonderful?*"

And I tucked him up. Before the sheet was round his shoulder, he was asleep. . . and next morning when we met at breakfast, he just asked me slyly, "Do you think mother guessed or saw anything of what *we* saw?" We glanced across the table, full of secret signs, together. Mother's letters were piled beside her plate, a book beneath them. It was my stolen book. She had clearly sat up half the night devouring it.

"No," I whispered, "I don't think mother guesses anything at all. Besides," I added, today is the Longest Day, so in any case she'd be a very long time finding out." And, as he seemed satisfied, I felt my conscience clear, and said no more about it.

Strange Disappearance of a Baronet

His intrinsic value before the Eternities was exceedingly small, but he possessed most things the world sets store by—presence, name, wealth—and, above all, that high opinion of himself which saves it the bother of a separate and troublesome valuation. Outside these possessions he owned nothing of permanent value, or that could decently claim to be worthy of immortality. The fact was he had never even experienced that expansion of self commonly known as generosity. No apology, however, is necessary for his amazing adventure, for these same Eternities who judged him have made their affidavit that it was They who stripped him bare and showed himself—to himself.

It all began with the receipt of that shattering letter from his solicitors. He read and re-read it in his comfortable first-class compartment as the express hurried him to town, exceedingly comfortable among his rugs and furs, exceedingly distressed and ill at ease in his mind. And in his private sitting-room of the big hotel that same evening Mr. Smirles, more odious even than his letter, informed him plainly that this new and unexpected claimant to his title and estates was likely to be exceedingly troublesome—"even dangerous, Sir Timothy! I am bound to say, since you ask me that it might be wise to regard the future—er—with a different scale of vision than the one you have been accustomed to."

Sir Timothy practically collapsed. Instinctively he perceived that the lawyer's manner already held less respect: the reflection was a shock to his vain and fatuous personality. "After all, then, it wasn't me he worshipped, but my position, and so forth. . .!" If this nonsense continued, he would be no longer "Sir Timothy," but simply "Mister" Puffe, poor, a nobody. He seemed to shrink in size as he gazed at himself in the mirror of the gorgeous, flamboyantly decorated room. "It's too preposterous and absurd! There's nothing in it! Why, the whole County would go to pieces without me!" He even thought of making his secretary draft a letter to the *Times*—a letter of violent, indignant protest.

He was a handsome, portly man, with a full-blown vanity justified by no single item of soul or mind; not unkind, so much as empty; created and kept alive by the small conventions and the ceaseless contemplation of himself, the withdrawal of which might be expected to leave him flat as a popped balloon.... Such a mass of pompous conceit obscured his vision that he only slowly took in the fact that his very existence was at stake. His thoughts rumbled on without direction, the sense of loss, however, dreadfully sharp and painful all the time, till at length he sought relief in something he could *really* understand. He changed for dinner!

He would dine in his sitting-room alone. And, meanwhile, he rang for the remainder of his voluminous luggage. But it was vastly annoying to his diminishing pride to discover that the gorgeous Head Porter (he remembered now having vaguely recognised him in the hall) was the same poor relation to whom he had denied help a year ago. The vicissitudes of life were indeed preposterous. He ought to have been protected from so ridiculous an encounter. For the moment, of course, he merely pretended not to see him—certainly he did not commend the excellently quick delivery of the luggage. And to praise the young fellow's pluck never occurred to him for one single instant.

"The house valet, please," he asked of the waiter who answered the bell soon afterwards—and then directed somewhat helplessly the unpacking of his emporium of exquisite clothes. "Yes, take everything out—everything," he said in reply to the man's question—rather an extraordinary, almost insolent question when he came to reflect upon it, surely: "Is it worthwhile, perhaps, sir ...?" It flashed across his dazed mind that the head porter had made the very same remark to his subordinate in the passage when he asked if "everything" was to come in. With a shrug of his gold-braided shoulders that poor relation had replied, "Seems hardly worthwhile, but they may as well all go in, yes."

And, with the double rejoinder perplexingly in his mind, Sir Timothy turned sharply upon the valet.

But the thing he was going to say faded on his lips. The man, holding out in his arms a heap of clothes, suits and what not, seemed so much taller than before. Sir Timothy had looked down upon him a moment ago, whereas now their eyes stared level. It was passing strange.

"Will you want these, sir?"

"Not tonight, of course."

"Want them at all, I meant, sir?"

Sir Timothy gasped. "Want them at all? Of course! What in the world are you talking about?"

"Beg pardon, sir. Didn't know if it was worthwhile now," the man said, with a quick flush. And, before the pompous and amazed baronet could get any words between his quivering lips, the man was gone. The waiter, head waiter it was, answered the bell almost immediately, and Sir Timothy found consolation for his injured feelings in discussing food and wine. He ordered an absurdly sumptuous meal for a man dining alone. He did so with a vague feeling that it would spite somebody, perhaps; he hardly knew whom. "The Pol Roger well iced, mind," he added with a false importance as the clever servant withdrew. But at the door the man paused and turned, as though he had not heard. "*Large* bottle, I said," repeated the other.

The head waiter made an extraordinary gesture of indifference. "As you wish, Sir Timothy, as you wish!" And he was gone in his turn.

But it was only the man's adroitness that had chosen the words instead of those others: " Is it really worthwhile?"

And at that very moment, while Sir Timothy stood there fuming inwardly over the extraordinary words and ways of these people—veiled insolence, *he* called it—the door opened, and a tall young woman poked her head inside, then followed it with her person. She was dignified, smart even for a hotel like this, and uncommonly pretty. It was the upper housemaid. Full in the eye she looked at him. In her face was a kind of swift sympathy and kindness; but her whole presentment betrayed more than anything else—terror.

"Make an effort, make an effort!" she whispered earnestly. "Before it's too late, make an effort!" And *she* was gone. Sir Timothy, hardly knowing what he meant to do, opened the door to dash after her and make her explain this latest insolence. But the passage was dark, and he heard the swish of skirts far away—too far away to overtake; while running along the walls, as in a whispering gallery, came the words, "Make an effort, make an effort!"

"Confound it all, then, I will!" he exclaimed to himself, as he stumbled back into the room, feeling horribly bewildered. "I will make an effort." And he dressed to go downstairs and show himself in the halls and drawing-rooms, give a few pompous orders, assert himself, and fuss about generally. But that process of dressing without his valet was chiefly and weirdly distressing because he had so amazingly—

dwindled. His sight was, of course, awry; disordered nerves had played tricks with vision, proportion, perspective; something of the sort must explain why he seemed so small to himself in the reflection. The pier-glass, which showed him full length, he turned to the wall. But, none the less, to complete his toilet, he had to stand upon a footstool before the other mirror above the mantelpiece.

And go downstairs he did, his heart working with a strange and increasing perplexity. Yet, wherever he went, there came that poor relation, the head porter, to face him. Always big, he now looked bigger than ever. Sir Timothy Puffe felt somehow ridiculous in his presence. The young fellow had character, pluck, some touch of intrinsic value. For all his failure in life, the Eternities considered him *real*. He towered rather dreadfully in his gold braid and smart uniform—towered in his great height all about the hall, like some giant in his own palace. The other's head scarcely came up to his great black belt where the keys swung and jangled.

The baronet went upstairs again to his room, strangely disconcerted. The first thing he did as he left the lift was to stumble over the step. The liftman picked him up as though he were a boy. Down the passage, now well lighted, he went quickly, his feet almost pattering, his tread light, and—so oddly short. His importance had gone. A voice behind each door he passed whispered to him through the narrow crack as it cautiously opened, "Make an effort, make an effort! Be yourself, be real, be alive before it's too late!"

But he saw no one, and the first thing he did on entering his room was to hide the smaller mirror by turning it against the wall, just as he had done to the pier-glass. He was so painfully little and insignificant now. As the externals and the possessions dropped away one by one in his thoughts, the revelation of the tiny little centre of activity within was horrible. He puffed himself out in thought as of old, but there was no response. It was degrading.

The fact was—he began to understand it now—his mind had been pursuing possible results of his loss of title and estates to their logical conclusion. The idea in all its brutal nakedness, success. of course, hardly reached him—namely, that, without possessions, he was practically—nil! All he grasped was that he was—*less*. Still, the notion did prey upon him atrociously. He followed the advice of the strange housemaid and "made an effort," but without marked So empty, indeed, was his life that, once stripped of the possessions, he would stand there as useless and insignificant as an ownerless street dog.

And the thought appalled him. He had not even enough real interest in others to hold him upright, and certainly not enough sufficiency of self, good or evil, to stand alone before any tribunal. The discovery shocked him inexpressibly. But what distressed him still more was to find a fixed mirror in his sitting-room that he could *not* take down, for in its depths he saw himself shrunken and dwindled to the proportions of a . . .

The knock at the door and the arrival of his dinner broke the appalling train of thought, but rather than be seen in his present diminutive appearance—later, of course, he would surely grow again—he ran into the bedroom. And when he came out again after the waiter's departure, he found that his dinner shared the same abominable change. The food upon the dishes was reduced to the minutest proportions— the toast like children's, the soup an egg-cupful, the tenderloin a little slice the size of a visiting-card, and the bird not much larger than a black beetle. And yet more than he could eat; more than sufficient! He sat in the big chair positively lost, his feet dangling. Then, mortified, frightened, and angry beyond expression, he undressed and concealed himself beneath the sheets and blankets of his bed.

"Of course, I'm going mad—that's what it all means," he exclaimed. "I'm no longer of any account in the world. I could never go into my Club, for instance, *like this!*"—and he surveyed the small outline that made a little lump beneath the surface of the bedclothes—"or read the lessons having to stand upon a chair to reach the lectern." And tears of bleeding vanity and futile wrath mingled upon his pillow. . . . . The humiliation was agonising.

In the middle of which the door opened and in came the hotel valet, bearing before him upon a silver salver what at first appeared to be small, striped sandwiches, darkish in hue, but upon closer inspection were seen to be several wee suits of clothes, neatly pressed and folded for wearing. Glancing round the room and perceiving no one, the man proceeded to put them away in the chest of drawers, soliloquising from time to time as he did so.

"So, the old buffer did go out after all!" he reflected, as he smoothed the tiny trousers in the drawer. "'E's nothing but a gas-bag, anyway! Close with the coin, too—always was that!" He whistled, spat in the grate, hunted about for a cigarette, and again found relief in speech. My little dawg's worth two of 'im all the time, and lots to spare. Tim's *real* . . .!" And other things, too, he said in similar vein. He was utterly oblivious of Sir Timothy's presence—serenely unconscious that the

89

thin, fading line beneath the sheets *was* the very individual he was talking about.

"Even hides his cigarettes, does he? He's right, though. Take away what he's got and there wouldn't be enough left over to stand upright at a poultry show!" And he guffawed merrily to himself. But what brought the final horror into that vanishing Personality on the bed was the singular fact that the valet made no remark about the absurd and horrible size of those tiny clothes. *This, then, was how others—even a hotel valet—saw him!*

All night long, it seemed, he lay in atrocious pain, the darkness mercifully hiding him, though never from himself, and only towards daylight did he pass off into a condition of unconsciousness. He must have slept very late indeed, too, for he woke to find sunlight in the room, and the housemaid—that tall, dignified girl who had tried to be kind—dusting and sweeping energetically. He screamed to her, but his voice was too feeble to make itself heard above the sweeping. The high-pitched squeak was scarcely audible even to himself. Presently she approached the bed and flung the sheets back. "That's funny,' she observed, "could've sworn I saw something move!"

She gave a hurried look, then went on sweeping. But in the process, she had tossed his person, now no larger than a starved mouse, out on to the carpet. He cried aloud in his anguish, but the squeak was too faint to be audible. "Ugh!" exclaimed the girl, jumping to one side, "there's that 'orrid mouse again! Dead, too, I do declare!" And then, without being aware of the fact, she swept him up with the dust and bits of paper into her pan.

Whereupon Sir Timothy awoke with a bad start, and perceived that his train was running somewhat uneasily into King's Cross, and that he had slept nearly the whole way.

The Attic

The forest-girdled village upon the Jura slopes slept soundly, although it was not yet many minutes after ten o'clock. The clang of the *couvre-feu* had indeed just ceased, its notes swept far into the woods by a wind that shook the mountains. This wind now rushed down the deserted street. It howled about the old rambling building called La Citadelle, whose roof towered gaunt and humped above the smaller houses—*château* left unfinished long ago by Lord Wemyss, the exiled Jacobite. The families who occupied the various apartments listened to the storm and felt the building tremble. 'It's the mountain wind. It will bring the snow,' the mother said, without looking up from her knitting. 'And how sad it sounds.'

But it was not the wind that brought sadness as we sat round the open fire of peat. It was the wind of memories. The lamplight slanted along the narrow room towards the table where breakfast things lay ready for the morning. The double windows were fastened. At the far end stood a door ajar, and on the other side of it the two elder children lay asleep in the big bed. But beside the window was a smaller unused bed, that had been empty now a year. And tonight was the anniversary. . . .

And so, the wind brought sadness and long thoughts. The little chap that used to lie there was already twelve months gone, far, far beyond the Hole where the Winds came from, as he called it; yet it seemed only yesterday that I went to tell him a tuck-up story, to stroke Riquette, the old motherly cat that cuddled against his back and laid a paw beside his pillow like a human being, and to hear his funny little earnest whisper say, '*Oncle, tu sais, j'ai prié pour Petavel.*' For La Citadelle had its unhappy ghost—of Petavel, the usurer, who had hanged himself in the attic a century gone by, and was known to walk its dreary corridors in search of peace and this wise Irish mother, calming the boy's fears with wisdom, had told him, 'If you pray for Petavel, you'll save his soul and make him happy, and he'll only love you.'

And, thereafter, this little imaginative boy had done so every night. With a passionate seriousness he did it. He had wonderful, delicate ways like that. In all our hearts he made his fairy nests of wonder. In my own, I know, he lay closer than any joy imaginable, with his big blue eyes, his queer soft questionings, and his splendid child's unself-ishness—a sun-kissed flower of innocence that, had he lived, might have sweetened half a world.

'Let's put more peat on,' the mother said, as a handful of rain like stones came flinging against the windows; 'that must be hail.' And she went on tiptoe to the inner room. 'They're sleeping like two pud-dings,' she whispered, coming presently back. But it struck me she had taken longer than to notice merely that; and her face wore an odd expression that made me uncomfortable. I thought she was some-how just about to laugh or cry. By the table a second she hesitated. I caught the flash of indecision as it passed. 'Pan,' she said suddenly—it was a nickname, stolen from my tuck-up stories, he had given me—'I wonder how Riquette got in.' She looked hard at me. 'It wasn't you, was it? 'For we never let her come at night since he had gone. It was too poignant.

The beastie always went cuddling and nestling into that empty bed. But this time it was not my doing, and I offered plausible expla-nations. 'But she's on the bed. Pan, *would* you be so kind—' She left the sentence unfinished, but I easily understood, for a lump had somehow risen in my own throat too, and I remembered now that she had come out from the inner room so quickly—with a kind of hurried rush almost. I put 'Mère Riquette' out into the corridor. A lamp stood on the chair outside the door of another occupant further down, and I urged her gently towards it.

She turned and looked at me—straight up into my face; but, in-stead of going down as I suggested, she went slowly in the opposite direction. She stepped softly towards a door in the wall that led up broken stairs into the attics. There she sat down and waited. And so, I left her, and came back hastily to the peat fire and companionship. The wind rushed in behind me and slammed the door.

And we talked then somewhat busily of cheerful things; of the chil-dren's future, the excellence of the cheap Swiss schools, of Christmas presents, skiing, snow, tobogganing. I led the talk away from mourn-fulness; and when these subjects were exhausted, I told stories of my own adventures in distant parts of the world. But 'mother' listened the whole time—not to me. Her thoughts were all elsewhere. And her air of intently, secretly listening, bordered, I felt, upon the uncanny. For she often stopped her knitting and sat with her eyes fixed upon the air before her; she stared blankly at the wall, her head slightly on one side, her figure tense, attention strained—elsewhere. Or, when my talk positively demanded it, her nod was oddly mechanical and her eyes looked through and past me.

The wind continued very loud and roaring; but the fire glowed, the room was warm and cosy. Yet she shivered, and when I drew attention to it, her reply, 'I do feel cold, but I didn't know I shivered,' was given as though she spoke across the air to someone else. But what impressed me even more uncomfortably were her repeated questions about Riquette. When a pause in my tales permitted, she would look up with 'I wonder where Riquette went?' or, thinking of the inclement night, 'I hope Mère Riquette's not out of doors. Perhaps Madame Favre has taken her in?' I offered to go and see. Indeed, I was already half-way across the room when there came the heavy bang at the door that rooted me to the ground where I stood.

It was not wind. It was something alive that made it rattle. There was a second blow. A thud on the corridor boards followed, and then a high, odd voice that at first was as human as the cry of a child.

It is undeniable that we both started, and for myself I can answer truthfully that a chill ran down my spine; but what frightened me more than the sudden noise and the eerie cry was the way 'mother' supplied the immediate explanation. For behind the words 'It's only Riquette; she sometimes springs at the door like that; perhaps we'd better let her in,' was a certain touch of uncanny quiet that made me feel she had known the cat would come, and knew also why she came. One cannot explain such impressions further. They leave their vital touch, then go their way.

Into the little room, however, in that moment there came between us this uncomfortable sense that the night held other purposes than our own—and that my companion was aware of them. There was something going on far, far removed from the routine of life as we were accustomed to it. Moreover, our usual routine was the eddy, while this was the main stream. It felt big, I mean.

And so, it was that the entrance of the familiar, friendly creature brought this thing both itself and 'mother' knew, but whereof I as yet was ignorant. I held the door wide. The draught rushed through behind her, and sent a shower of sparks about the fireplace. The lamp flickered and gave a little gulp. And Riquette marched slowly past, with all the impressive dignity of her kind, towards the other door that stood ajar. Turning the corner like a shadow, she disappeared into the room where the two children slept. We heard the soft thud with which she leaped upon the bed. Then, in a lull of the wind, she came back again and sat on the oilcloth, staring into 'mother's' face. She mewed and put a paw out, drawing the black dress softly with half-opened claws.

And it was all so horribly suggestive and pathetic, it revived such poignant memories, that I got up impulsively I think I had actually said the words, 'We'd better put her out, mother, after all' when my companion rose to her feet and forestalled me. She said another thing instead. It took my breath away to hear it. 'She wants us to go with her. Pan, will you come too?' The surprise on my face must have asked the question, for I do not remember saying anything. 'To the attic,' she said quietly.

She stood there by the table, a tall, grave figure dressed in black, and her face above the lampshade caught the full glare of light. Its expression positively stiffened me. She seemed so secure in her singular purpose. And her familiar appearance had so oddly given place to something wholly strange to me. She looked like another person—almost with the unwelcome transformation of the sleep-walker about her. Cold came over me as I watched her, for I remembered suddenly her Irish second-sight, her story years ago of meeting a figure on the attic stairs, the figure of Petavel. And the idea of this motherly, sedate, and wholesome woman, absorbed day and night in prosaic domestic duties, and yet 'seeing' things, touched the incongruous almost to the point of alarm. It was so distressingly convincing.

Yet she knew quite well that I would come. Indeed, following the excited animal, she was already by the door, and a moment later, still without answering or protesting, I was with them in the draughty corridor. There was something inevitable in her manner that made it impossible to refuse. She took the lamp from its nail on the wall, and following our four-footed guide, who ran with obvious pleasure just in front, she opened the door into the courtyard. The wind nearly put the lamp out, but a minute later we were safe inside the passage that led up flights of creaky wooden stairs towards the world of tenantless attics overhead.

And I shall never forget the way the excited Riquette first stood up and put her paws upon the various doors, trotted ahead, turned back to watch us coming, and then finally sat down and waited on the threshold of the empty, raftered space that occupied the entire length of the building underneath the roof. For her manner was more that of an intelligent dog than of a cat, and sometimes more like that of a human mind than either.

We had come up without a single word. The howling of the wind as we rose higher was like the roar of artillery. There were many broken stairs, and the narrow way was full of twists and turnings. It was a dreadful journey. I felt eyes watching us from all the yawning spaces of the darkness, and the noise of the storm smothered footsteps everywhere. Troops of shadows kept us company. But it was on the threshold of this big, chief attic, when 'mother' stopped abruptly to put down the lamp, that real fear took hold of me. For Riquette marched steadily forward into the middle of the dusty flooring, picking her way among the fallen tiles and mortar, as though she went towards—someone. She purred loudly and uttered little cries of excited pleasure. Her tail went up into the air, and she lowered her head with the unmistakable intention of being stroked.

Her lips opened and shut. Her green eyes smiled. She was being stroked.

It was an unforgettable performance. I would rather have witnessed an execution or a murder than watch that mysterious creature twist and turn about in the way she did. Her magnified shadow was as large as a pony on the floor and rafters. I wanted to hide the whole thing by extinguishing the lamp. For, even before the mysterious action began, I experienced the sudden rush of conviction that others besides ourselves were in this attic—and standing very close to us indeed. And, although there was ice in my blood, there was also a strange swelling of the heart that only love and tenderness could bring.

But whatever it was, my human companion, still silent, knew and understood. She saw. And her soft whisper that ran with the wind among the rafters, '*Il a prié pour Petavel et le bon Dieu l'a entendu,*' did not amaze me one quarter as much as the expression I then caught upon her radiant face. Tears ran down the cheeks, but they were tears of happiness. Her whole figure seemed lit up. She opened her arms—picture of great Motherhood, proud, blessed, and tender beyond words. I thought she was going to fall, for she took quick steps forward; but when I moved to catch her, she drew me aside instead with a sudden gesture that brought fear back in the place of wonder.

'Let them pass,' she whispered grandly. 'Pan, don't you see. . . . He's leading him into peace and safety ... by the hand!' And her joy seemed to kill the shadows and fill the entire attic with white light. Then, almost simultaneously with her words, she swayed. I was in time to catch her, but as I did so, across the very spot where we had just been standing—two figures, I swear, went past us like a flood of light.

There was a moment next of such confusion that I did not see what happened to Riquette, for the sight of my companion kneeling on the dusty boards and praying with a curious sort of passionate happiness, while tears pressed between her covering fingers—the strange wonder of this made me utterly oblivious to minor details. ...

We were sitting round the peat fire again, and 'mother' was saying to me in the gentlest, tenderest whisper I ever heard from human lips 'Pan, I think perhaps that's why God took him. ...'

And when a little later we went in to make Riquette cosy in the empty bed, ever since kept sacred to her use, the mournfulness had lifted; and in the place of resignation was proud peace and joy that knew no longer sad or selfish questionings.

The Destruction of Smith

Ten years ago, in the western States of America, I once met Smith. But he was no ordinary member of the clan: he was Ezekiel B. Smith of Smithville. He was Smithville, for he founded it and made it live.

It was in the oil region, where towns spring up on the map in a few days like mushrooms, and may be destroyed again in a single night by fire and earthquake. On a hunting expedition Smith stumbled upon a natural oil well, and instantly staked his claim; a few months later he was rich, grown into affluence as rapidly as that patch of wilderness grew into streets and houses where you could buy anything from an evening's gambling to a tin of Boston baked pork-and-beans. Smith was really a tremendous fellow, a sort of human dynamo of energy and pluck, with rare judgment in his great square head—the kind of judgment that in higher walks of life makes statesmen. His personality cut through the difficulties of life with the clean easy force of putting his whole life into anything he touched. 'God's own luck,' his comrades called it; but really it was sheer ability and character and personality. The man had power.

From the moment of that 'oil find' his rise was very rapid, but while his brains went into a dozen other big enterprises, his heart remained in little Smithville, the flimsy mushroom town he had created. His own life was in it. It was his baby. He spoke tenderly of its hideousness. Smithville was an intimate expression of his very self.

Ezekiel B. Smith I saw once only, for a few minutes; but I have never forgotten him. It was the moment of his death. And we came across him on a shooting trip where the forests melt away towards the vast plains of the Arizona desert. The personality of the man was singularly impressive. I caught myself thinking of a mountain, or of some elemental force of Nature so sure of itself that hurry is never necessary. And his gentleness was like the gentleness of women. Great strength often—the greatest always—has tenderness in it, a depth of tenderness

97

unknown to pettier life.

Our meeting was coincidence, for we were hunting in a region where distances are measured by hours and the chance of running across white men very rare. For many days our nightly camps were pitched in spots of beauty where the loneliness is akin to the loneliness of the Egyptian Desert. On one side the mountain slopes were smothered with dense forest, hiding wee meadows of sweet grass like English lawns; and on the other side, stretching for more miles than a man can count, ran the desolate alkali plains of Arizona where tufts of sage-brush are the only vegetation till you reach the lips of the Colorado Canyons.

Our horses were tethered for the night beneath the stars. Two backwoodsmen were cooking dinner. The smell of bacon over a wood fire mingled with the keen and fragrant air—when, suddenly, the horses neighed, signalling the approach of one of their own kind. Indians, white men—probably another hunting party—were within scenting distance, though it was long before my city ears caught any sound, and still longer before the cause itself entered the circle of our firelight.

I saw a square-faced man, tanned like an Indian, in a hunting shirt and a big *sombrero*, climb down slowly from his horse and move towards us, keenly searching with his eyes; and at the same moment Hank, looking up from the frying-pan where the bacon and venison spluttered in a pool of pork-fat, exclaimed, 'Why, it's Ezekiel B.!' The next words, addressed to Jake, who held the kettle, were below his breath: 'And if he ain't all broke up! Jest look at the eyes on him!' I saw what he meant—the face of a human being distraught by some extraordinary emotion, a soul in violent distress, yet betrayal well kept under. Once, as a newspaper man, I had seen a murderer walk to the electric chair. The expression was similar. Death was *behind* the eyes, not in them. Smith brought in with him—terror.

In a dozen words we learned he had been hunting for some weeks, but was now heading for Tranter, a 'stop-off' station where you could flag the daily train 140 miles south-west. He was making for Smithville, the little town that was the apple of his eye. Something 'was wrong' with Smithville. No one asked him what—it is the custom to wait till information is volunteered. But Hank, helping him presently to venison (which he hardly touched), said casually, 'Good hunting, Boss, your way?'; and the brief reply told much, and proved how eager he was to relieve his mind by speech. 'I'm glad to locate your camp, boys,' he said. 'That's luck. There's something going wrong'—and a catch came into his voice—'with Smithville.'

Behind the laconic statement emerged somehow the terror the man experienced. For Smith to confess cowardice and in the same breath admit mere 'luck,' was equivalent to the hysteria that makes city people laugh or cry. It was genuinely dramatic. I have seen nothing more impressive by way of human tragedy—though hard to explain why—than this square-jawed, dauntless man, sitting there with the firelight on his rugged features, and saying this simple thing. For how in the world could he know it——?

In the pause that followed, his Indians came gliding in, tethered the horses, and sat down without a word to eat what Hank distributed. But nothing was to be read on their impassive faces. Indisns, whatever they may feel, show little. Then Smith gave us another pregnant sentence. '*They* heard it too,' he said, in a lower voice, indicating his three men; 'they saw it jest as I did.' He looked up into the starry sky a second. 'It's hard upon our trail right now,' he added, as though he expected something to drop upon us from the heavens. And from that moment I swear we all felt creepy.

The darkness round our lonely camp hid terror in its folds; the wind that whispered through the dry sage-brush brought whispers and the shuffle of watching figures; and when the Indians went softly out to pitch the tents and get more wood for the fire, I remember feeling glad the duty was not mine. Yet this feeling of uneasiness is something one rarely experiences in the open. It belongs to houses overwrought imaginations, and the presence of evil men. Nature gives peace and security. That we all felt it proves how real it was. And Smith, who felt it most, of course, had brought it.

'There's something gone wrong with Smithville' was an ominous statement of disaster. He said it just as a man in civilised lands might say, 'My wife is dying; a telegram's just come. I must take the train.' But how he felt so sure of it, a thousand miles away in this uninhabited corner of the wilderness, made us feel curiously uneasy. For it was an incredible thing—yet true. We all felt *that*. Smith did not imagine things. A sense of gloomy apprehension settled over our lonely camp, as though things were about to happen. Already they stalked across the great black night, watching us with many eyes. The wind had risen, and there were sounds among the trees.

I, for one, felt no desire to go to bed. The way Smith sat there, watching the sky and peering into the sheet of darkness that veiled the desert, set my nerves all jangling. He expected something—but what?

It was following him. Across this tractless wilderness, apparently above him against the brilliant stars, Something was 'hard upon his trail.'

Then, in the middle of painful silences, Smith suddenly turned loquacious—further sign with him of deep mental disturbance. He asked questions like a schoolboy—asked them of me too, as being 'an edicated man.' But there were such queer things to talk about round an Arizona campfire that Hank clearly wondered for his sanity. He knew about the 'wilderness madness' that attacks some folks. He let his green cigar go out and flashed me signals to be cautious. He listened intently, with the eyes of a puzzled child, half cynical, half touched with superstitious dread.

For, briefly, Smith asked me what I knew about stories of dying men appearing at a distance to those who loved them much. He had read such tales, 'heard tell of 'em,' but 'are they dead true, or are they jest little feery tales?' I satisfied him as best I could with one or two authentic stories. Whether he believed or not I cannot say; but his swift mind jumped in a flash to the point.

'Then, if that kind o' stuff is true,' he asked, simply, 'it looks as though a feller had a dooplicate of himself—sperrit maybe—that gits loose and active at the time of death, and heads straight for the party it loves best. Ain't that so, Boss?' I admitted the theory was correct. And then he startled us with a final question that made Hank drop an oath below his breath—sure evidence of uneasy excitement in the old backwoodsman. Smith whispered it, looking over his shoulder into the night: 'Ain't it jest possible then,' he asked, 'seeing that men an' Nature is all made of a piece like, that places too have this dooplicate appearance of theirselves that gits loose when they go under?'

It was difficult, under the circumstances, to explain that such a theory *had* been held to account for visions of scenery people sometimes have, and that a city may have a definite personality made up of all its inhabitants—moods, thoughts, feelings, and passions of the multitude who go to compose its life and atmosphere, and that hence is due the odd changes in a man's individuality when he goes from one city to another. Nor was there any time to do so, for hardly had he asked his singular question when the horses whinnied, the Indians leaped to their feet as if ready for an attack, and Smith himself turned the colour of the ashes that lay in a circle of whitish-grey about the burning wood. There was an expression in his face of death, or, as the Irish peasants say, 'destroyed.'

'That's Smithville,' he cried, springing to his feet, then tottering so that I thought he must fall into the flame; 'that's my baby town—got loose and huntin' for me, who made it, and love it better'n anything on Gawd's green earth!' And then he added with a kind of gulp in his throat as of a man who wanted to cry but couldn't: 'And it's going to bits—it's dying—and I'm not thar to save it——!'

He staggered and I caught his arm. The sound of his frightened, anguished voice, and the shuffling of our many feet among the stones, died away into the night. We all stood, staring. The darkness came up closer. The horses ceased their whinnying. For a moment nothing happened. Then Smith turned slowly round and raised his head towards the stars as though he saw something. 'Hear that?' he whispered. 'It's coming up close. That's what I've bin hearing now, on and off, two days and nights. Listen!' His whispering voice broke horribly; the man was suffering atrociously. For a moment he became vastly, horribly animated—then stood still as death.

But in the hollow silence, broken only by the sighing of the wind among the spruces, we at first heard nothing. Then, most curiously, something like rapid driven mist came trooping down the sky, and veiled a group of stars. With it, as from an enormous distance, but growing swiftly nearer, came noises that were beyond all question the noises of a city rushing through the heavens. From all sides they came; and with them there shot a reddish, streaked appearance across the misty veil that swung so rapidly and softly between the stars and our eyes. Lurid it was, and in some way terrible.

A sense of helpless bewilderment came over me, scattering my faculties as in scenes of fire, when the mind struggles violently to possess itself and act for the best. Hank, holding his rifle ready to shoot, moved stupidly round the group, equally at a loss, and swearing incessantly below his breath. For this overwhelming certainty that Something living had come upon us from the sky possessed us all, and I, personally, felt as if a gigantic Being swept against me through the night, destructive and enveloping, and yet that it was not one, but many. Power of action left me. I could not even observe with accuracy what was going on. I stared, dizzy and bewildered, in all directions; but my power of movement was gone, and my feet refused to stir. Only I remember that the Indians stood like figures of stone, unmoved.

And the sounds about us grew into a roar. The distant murmur came past us like a sea. There was a babel of shouting. Here, in the deep old wilderness that knew no living human beings for hundreds of leagues, there was a tempest of voices calling, crying, shrieking;

men's hoarse clamouring, and the high screaming of women and children. Behind it ran a booming sound like thunder. Yet all of it, while apparently so close above our heads, seemed in some inexplicable way far off in the distance—muted, faint, thinning out among the quiet stars. More like a *memory* of turmoil and tumult it seemed than the actual uproar heard at first hand. And through it ran the crash of big things tumbling, breaking, falling in destruction with an awful detonating thunder of collapse. I thought the hills were toppling down upon us. A shrieking city, it seemed, fled past us through the sky.

How long it lasted it is impossible to say, for my power of measuring time had utterly vanished. A dreadful wild anguish summed up all the feelings I can remember. It seemed I watched, or read, or dreamed some desolating scene of disaster in which human life went overboard wholesale, as though one threw a hatful of insects into a blazing fire. This idea of burning, of thick suffocating smoke and savage flame, coloured the entire experience. And the next thing I knew was that it had passed away as completely as though it had never been at all; the stars shone down from an air of limpid clearness, and—there was a smell of burning leather in my nostrils. I just stepped back in time to save my feet. I had moved in my excitement against the circle of hot ashes. Hank pushed me back roughly with the barrel of his rifle.

But, strangest of all, I understood, as by some flash of divine intuition, the reason of this abrupt cessation of the horrible tumult. The Personality of the town, set free and loosened in the moment of death, had returned to him who gave it birth, who loved it, and of whose life it was actually an expression. The Being of Smithville was literally a projection, an emanation of the dynamic, vital personality of its puissant creator. And, in death, it had returned on him with the shock of an accumulated power impossible for a human being to resist. For years he had provided it with life—but *gradually*. It now rushed back to its source, thus concentrated, in a single terrific moment.

'That's him,' I heard a voice saying from a great distance as it seemed. 'He's fired his last shot!'—and saw Hank turning the body over with his rifle-butt. And, though the face itself was calm beneath the stars, there was an attitude of limbs and body that suggested the bursting of an enormous shell that had twisted every fibre by its awful force yet somehow left the body as a whole intact.

We carried 'it' to Tranter, and at the first real station along the line we got the news by telegraph:

'Smithville wiped out by fire. Burned two days and nights. Loss of life, 3,000.'

And all the way in my dreams I seemed still to hear that curious, dreadful cry of Smithville, the shrieking city rushing headlong through the sky.

The Goblin's Collection

Dutton accepted the invitation for the feeble reason that he was not quick enough at the moment to find a graceful excuse. He had none of that facile brilliance which is so useful at weekend parties; he was a big, shy, awkward man. Moreover, he disliked these great houses. They swallowed him. The solemn, formidable butlers oppressed him. He left on Sunday night when possible. This time, arriving with an hour to dress, he went upstairs to an enormous room, so full of precious things that he felt like an insignificant item in a museum corridor. He smiled disconsolately as the underling who brought up his bag began to fumble with the lock.

But, instead of the sepulchral utterance he dreaded, a delicious human voice with an unmistakable brogue proceeded from the stooping figure. It was positively comforting. "It 'ull be locked, sorr, but maybe ye have the key?" And they bent together over the disreputable kit-bag, looking like a pair of ants knitting antennae on the floor of some great cave. The giant four-poster watched them contemptuously; mahogany cupboards wore an air of grave surprise; the gaping, open fireplace alone could have swallowed all his easels—almost, indeed, his little studio. This human, Irish presence was distinctly consoling—some extra hand or other, thought Dutton, probably.

He talked a little with the lad; then, lighting a cigarette, he watched him put the clothes away in the capacious cupboards, noticing in particular how neat and careful he was with the little things. Nail-scissors, silver stud box, metal shoe-horn, and safety razor, even the bright cigar-cutter and pencil-sharpener collected loose from the bottom of the bag—all these he placed in a row upon the dressing-table with the glass top, and seemed never to have done with it. He kept coming back to rearrange and put a final touch, lingering over them absurdly.

Dutton watched him with amusement, then surprise, finally with exasperation. Would he never go? "Thank you," he said at last; "that will do. I'll dress now. What time is dinner?"

The lad told him, but still lingered, evidently anxious to say more. "Everything's out, I think," repeated Dutton impatiently; "all the loose things, I mean?"

The face at once turned eagerly. What mischievous Irish eyes he had, to be sure!" I've put thim all together in a row, sorr, so that ye'll not be missing annything at all," was the quick reply, as he pointed to the ridiculous collection of little articles, and even darted back to finger them again. He counted them one by one. And then suddenly he added, with a touch of personal interest that was *not* familiarity, "It's so easy, ye see, sorr, to lose thim small bright things in this great room." And he was gone.

Smiling a little to himself, Dutton began to dress, wondering how the lad had left the impression that his words meant more than they said. He almost wished he had encouraged him to talk. "The small bright things in this great room"—what an admirable description, almost a criticism! He felt like a prisoner of state in the Tower. He stared about him into the alcoves, recesses, deep embrasured windows; the tapestries and huge curtains oppressed him; next he fell to wondering who the other guests would be, whom he would take in to dinner, how early he could make an excuse and slip off to bed; then, midway in these desultory thoughts, became suddenly aware of a curiously sharp impression—that he was being watched.

Somebody, quite close, was looking at him. He dismissed the fancy as soon as it was born, putting it down to the size and mystery of the old-world chamber; but in spite of himself the idea persisted teasingly, and several times he caught himself turning nervously to look over his shoulder. It was not a ghostly feeling; his nature was not accessible to ghostly things. The strange idea, lodged securely in his brain, was traceable, he thought, to something the Irish lad had said—grew out, rather, of what he had left unsaid. He idly allowed his imagination to encourage it.

Someone, friendly but curious, with inquisitive, peeping eyes, was watching him. Someone very tiny was hiding in the enormous room. He laughed about it; but he felt different. A certain big, protective feeling came over him that he must go gently lest he tread on some diminutive living thing that was soft as a kitten and elusive as a baby mouse. Once, indeed, out of the corner of his eye, he fancied he saw a little thing with wings go fluttering past the great purple curtains at the other end. It was by a window.

"A bird, or something, outside," he told himself with a laugh, yet moved thenceforth more often than not on tiptoe. This cost him a certain effort: his proportions were elephantine. He felt a more friend-ly interest now in the stately, imposing chamber.

The dressing-gong brought him back to reality and stopped the flow of his imagining. He shaved, and laboriously went on dressing then; he was slow and leisurely in his movements, like many big men; very orderly, too. But when he was ready to put in his collar stud it was nowhere to be found. It was a worthless bit of brass, but most important; he had only one. Five minutes ago, it had been standing inside the ring of his collar on the marble slab; he had carefully placed it there. Now it had disappeared and left no trail. He grew warm and untidy in the search. It was something of a business for Dutton to go on all fours.

"Malicious little beast!" he grunted, rising from his knees, his hand sore where he had scraped it beneath the cupboard. His trouser-crease was ruined, his hair was tumbled. He knew too well the elusive activ-ity of similar small objects. "It will turn up again," he tried to laugh, "if I pay it no attention. Mal—" he abruptly changed the adjective, as though he had nearly said a dangerous thing—"naughty little imp!"

He went on dressing, leaving the collar to the last. He fastened the cigar-cutter to his chain, but the nail-scissors, he noticed now, had also gone. "Odd," he reflected, very odd!" He looked at the place where they had been a few minutes ago. "Odd!" he repeated. And finally, in desperation, he rang the bell. The heavy curtains swung inwards as he said, "Come in," in answer to the knock, and the Irish boy, with the merry, dancing eyes, stood in the room. He glanced half nervously, half expectantly, about him.

"It'll be something ye have lost, sorr?" he said at once, as though he knew.

"I rang," said Dutton, resenting it a little, "to ask you if you could get me a collar stud—for this evening. Anything will do." He did not say he had lost his own. Someone, he felt, who was listening, would chuckle and be pleased. It was an absurd position.

"And will it be a shtud like this, sorr, that yez wanting?" asked the boy, picking up the lost object from inside the collar on the marble slab.

"Like that, yes," stammered the other, utterly amazed. He had over-looked it, of course, yet it was in the identical place where he had left it. He felt mortified and foolish. It was so obvious that the boy grasped the situation—more, had expected it. It was as if the stud had been taken and replaced deliberately. "Thank you," he added, turning away to hide his face as the lad backed out—with a grin, he imagined, though he did not see it. Almost immediately, it seemed, then he was back again, holding out a little cardboard box containing an assortment of ugly bone studs. Dutton felt as if the whole thing had been prepared beforehand. How foolish it was! Yet behind it lay something real and true and—utterly incredible!

"*They* won't get taken, sorr," he heard the lad say from the doorway. "They're not nearly bright enough."

The other decided not to hear. "Thanks," he said curtly; "they'll do nicely."

There was a pause, but the boy did not go. Taking a deep breath, he said very quickly, as though greatly daring, "It's only the bright and little lovely things he takes, sorr, if ye plaze. He takes thim for his collection, and there's no stoppin' him at all." It came out with a rush, and Dutton, hearing it, let the human thing rise up in him. He turned and smiled.

"Oh, he takes these things for his collection, does he?" he asked more gently.

The boy looked dreadfully shame-faced, confession hanging on his lips. "The little bright and lovely things, sorr, yes. I've done me best, but there's things he can't resist at all. The bone ones is safe, though. He won't look at thim."

"I suppose he followed you across from Ireland, eh?" the other inquired.

The lad hung his head. "I told Father Madden," he said in a lower voice," but it's not the least bit of good in the wurrld." He looked as though he had been convicted of stealing and feared to lose his place. Suddenly, lifting his blue eyes, he added, "But if ye take no notice at all he ginrelly puts everything back in its place agin. He only borrows thim, just for a little bit of toime. Pretend ye're not wantin' thim at all, sorr, and back they'll come prisintly again, brighter than before maybe."

"I see," answered Dutton slowly. All right, then," he dismissed him, "and I won't say a word downstairs. You needn't be afraid," as the lad looked his gratitude and vanished like a flash, leaving the other with a queer and eerie feeling, staring at the ugly bone studs. He finished dressing hurriedly and went downstairs. He went on tiptoe out of the great room, moving delicately and with care, lest he might tread on something very soft and tiny, almost wounded, like a butterfly with a broken wing. And from the corners, he felt positive, something watched him go.

The ordeal of dinner passed off well enough; the rather heavy evening too. He found the opportunity to slip off early to bed. The nail-scissors were in their place again. He read till midnight; nothing happened. His hostess had told him the history of his room, inquiring kindly after his comfort.

"Some people feel rather lost in it," she said; "I hope you found all you want," and, tempted by her choice of words—the "lost" and "found"—he nearly told the story of the Irish lad whose goblin had followed him across the sea and "borrowed little bright and lovely things for his collection." But he kept his word; he told nothing; she would only have stared, for one thing. For another, he was bored, and therefore uncommunicative. He smiled inwardly. All that this giant mansion could produce for his comfort and amusement were ugly bone studs, a thieving goblin, and a vast bedroom where dead royalty had slept.

Next day, at intervals, when changing for tennis or back again for lunch, the "borrowing continued; the little things he needed at the moment had disappeared. They turned up later. To ignore their disappearance was the recipe for their recovery—invariably, too, just where he had seen them last. There was the lost object shining in his face, propped impishly on its end, just ready to fall upon the carpet, and ever with a quizzical, malicious air of innocence that was truly goblin. His collar stud was the favourite; next came the scissors and the silver pencil-sharpener.

Trains and motors combined to keep him Sunday night, but he arranged to leave on Monday before the other guests were up, and so got early to bed. He meant to watch. There was a merry, jolly feeling in him that he had established quasi-friendly relations with the little Borrower. He might even see an object go—catch it in the act of disappearing! He arranged the bright objects in a row upon the glass-topped dressing-table opposite the bed, and while reading kept an eye slyly on the array of tempting bait. But nothing happened. "It's the wrong way," he realised suddenly. What a blunderer I am!' He turned the light out then. Drowsiness crept over him. . . . Next day, of course, he told himself it was a dream.

The night was very still, and through the latticed windows stole faintly the summer moonlight. Outside the foliage rustled a little in the wind. A night-jar called from the fields, and a secret, furry owl made answer from the copse beyond. The body of the chamber lay in thick darkness, but a slanting ray of moonlight caught the dressing-table and shone temptingly upon the silver objects. "It's like setting a nightline," was the last definite thought he remembered—when the laughter that followed stopped suddenly, and his nerves gave a jerk that turned him keenly alert.

From the enormous open fireplace, gaping in darkness at the end of the room, issued a thread of delicate sound that was softer than a feather. A tiny flurry of excitement, furtive, tentative, passed shivering across the air. An exquisite, dainty flutter stirred the night, and through the heavy human brain upon the great four-poster fled this picture, as from very far away, picked out in black and silver—of a wee knight-errant crossing the frontiers of fairyland, high mischief in his tiny, beating heart. Pricking along over the big, thick carpet, he came towards the bed, towards the dressing table, intent upon bold plunder.

Dutton lay motionless as a stone, and watched and listened. The blood in his ears smothered the sound a little, but he never lost it altogether. The flicking of a mouse's tail, or whiskers could hardly have been more gentle than this sound, more wary, circumspect, discreet, certainly not half so artful. Yet the human being in the bed, so heavily breathing, heard it well Closer it came, and closer, oh, so elegant and tender, this bold attack of a wee Adventurer from another world. It shot swiftly past the bed. With a little flutter, delicious, almost musical, it rose in the air before his very face and entered the pool of moonlight on the dressing-table.

Something blurred it then; the human sight grew troubled and confused a moment; a mingling of moonlight with the reflections from the mirror, slab of glass, and shining objects obscured clear vision somehow. For a second Dutton lost the proper focus. There was a tiny rattle and a tiny click. He saw that the pencil-sharpener stood balanced on the table's very edge. It was in the act of vanishing.

But for his stupid blunder then, he might have witnessed more. He simply could not restrain himself, it seems. He sprang, and at the same instant the silver object fell upon the carpet. Of course, his elephantine leap made the entire table shake. But, anyhow, he was not quick enough. He saw the reflection of a slim and tiny hand slide down into the mirrored depths of the reflecting sheet of glass—deep, deep down, and swift as a flash of light. This he thinks he saw, though the light, he admits, was oddly confusing in that moment of violent and clumsy movement.

One thing, at any rate, was beyond all question: the pencil-sharpener had disappeared. He turned the light up; he searched for a dozen minutes, then gave it up in despair and went back to bed.

Next morning, he searched again. But, having overslept himself, he did not search as thoroughly as he might have done, for half-way through the tiresome operation the Irish lad came in to take his bag for the train.

"Will ut be something ye've lost, sorr? "he asked gravely.

"Oh, it's all right," Dutton answered from the floor. "You can take the bag—and my overcoat." And in town that day he bought another pencil-sharpener and hung it on his chain.

The Heath Fire

The men at luncheon in Rennie's Surrey cottage that September day were discussing, of course, the heat. All agreed it had been exceptional. But nothing unusual was said until O'Hara spoke of the heath fires. They had been rather terrific, several in a single day, devouring trees and bushes, endangering human life, and spreading with remarkable rapidity. The flames, too, had been extraordinarily high and vehement for heath fires. And O'Hara's tone had introduced into the commonplace talk something new—the element of mystery; it was nothing definite he said, but manner, eyes, hushed voice and the rest conveyed it. And it was genuine. What he *felt* reached the others rather than what he said.

The atmosphere in the little room, with the honeysuckle trailing sweetly across the open windows, changed; the talk became of a sudden less casual, frank, familiar; and the men glanced at one another across the table, laughing still, yet with an odd touch of constraint marking little awkward, unfilled pauses. Being a group of normal Englishmen, they disliked mystery; it made them feel uncomfortable; for the things O'Hara hinted at had touched that kind of elemental terror that lurks secretly in all human beings. Guarded by 'culture,' but never wholly concealed, the unwelcome thing made its presence known—the hint of primitive dread that, for instance, great thunderstorms, tidal waves, or violent conflagrations rouse.

And instinctively they fell at once to discussing the obvious causes of the fires. The stockbroker, scenting imagination, edged mentally away, sniffing. But the journalist was full of brisk information, 'simply given.'

'The sun starts them in Canada, using a dewdrop as a lens,' he said, 'and an engine's spark, remember, carries an immense distance without losing its heat.'

'But hardly miles,' said another, who had not been really listening.

'It's my belief,' put in the critic keenly, 'that a lot were done on purpose. Bits of live coal wrapped in cloth were found, you know.' He was a little, weasel-faced iconoclast, dropping the acid of doubt and disbelief wherever he went, but offering nothing in the place of what he destroyed. His head was turret-shaped, lips tight and thin, nose and chin running to points like gimlets, with which he bored into the unremunerative clays of life.

'The general unrest, yes,' the journalist supported him, and tried to draw the conversation on to labour questions. But their host preferred the fire talk. 'I must say,' he put in gravely, 'that some of the blazes hereabouts were uncommonly—er—queer. They started, I mean, so oddly. You remember, O'Hara, only last week that suspicious one over Kettlebury way?——'

It seemed he wished to draw the artist out, and that the artist, feeling the general opposition, declined.

'Why seek an unusual explanation at all?' the critic said at length, impatiently. 'It's all natural enough, if you ask me.'

'Natural! Oh yes!' broke in O'Hara, with a sudden vehemence that betrayed feeling none had as yet suspected; 'provided you don't limit the word to mean only what we understand. There's nothing anywhere—unnatural.'

A laugh cut short the threatened tirade, and the journalist expressed the general feeling with 'Oh *you*, Jim! You'd see a devil in a dust-storm, or a fairy in the tea-leaves of your cup!'

'And why not, pray? Devils and fairies are every bit as true as formulae.'

Someone tactfully guided them away from a profitless discussion, and they talked glibly of the damage done, the hideousness of the destroyed moors, the gaunt, black, ugly slopes, fifty-foot flames, roaring noises, and the splendour of the enormous smoke-clouds that had filled the skies. And Rennie, still hoping to coax O'Hara, repeated tales the beaters had brought in that crying, as though living things were caught, had been heard in places, and that some had seen tall shapes of fire passing headlong through the choking smoke.

For the note O'Hara had struck refused to be ignored. It went on sounding underneath the commonest remark; and the atmosphere to the end retained that curious tinge that he had given to it—of the strange, the ominous, the mysterious and unexplained. Until, at last, the artist, having added nothing further to the talk, got up with some abruptness and left the room. He complained briefly that the fever he had suffered from still bothered him and he would go and lie down a bit. The heat, he said, oppressed him.

A silence followed his departure. The broker drew a sigh as though the market had gone up. But Rennie, old, comprehending friend, looked anxious. 'Excitement,' he said, 'not oppression, is the word he meant. He's always a bit strung up when that Black Sea fever gets him. He brought it with him from Batoum.' And another brief silence followed.

'Been with you most of the summer, hasn't he?' enquired the journalist, on the trail of a 'par,' painting those wild things of his that no one understands.' And their host, weighing a moment how much he might in fairness tell, replied—among friends it was—'Yes; and this summer they have been more—er—wild and wonderful than usual—an extraordinary rush of colour—splendid schemes, "conceptions," I believe you critics call 'em, of fire, as though, in a way, the unusual heat had possessed him for interpretation.'

The group expressed its desultory interest by uninspired interjections.

'That was what he meant just now when he said the fires had been mysterious, required explanation, or something—the way they started, rather,' concluded Rennie.

Then he hesitated. He laughed a moment, and it was an uneasy, apologetic little laugh. How to continue he hardly knew. Also, he wished to protect his friend from the cheap jeering of miscomprehension. 'He is very imaginative, you know,' he went on, quietly, as no one spoke. 'You remember that glorious mad thing he did of the Fallen Lucifer—driving a star across the heavens till the heat of the descent set a light to half the planets, scorched the old moon to the white cinder that she now is, and passed close enough to earth to send our oceans up in a single jet of steam?

'Well, this time—he's been at something every bit as wild, only truer—finer. And what is it? Briefly, then, he's got the idea, it seems, that the unusual heat from the sun this year has penetrated deep enough—in places—especially on these unprotected heaths that retain their heat so cleverly—to reach another kindred expression—to waken a response—in sympathy, you see—from the central fires of the earth.'

He paused again a moment awkwardly, conscious how clumsily he expressed it. 'The parent getting into touch again with its lost child, eh? See the idea? Return of the Fire Prodigal, as it were?'

His listeners stared in silence, the broker looking his obvious relief that O'Hara was not on 'Change, the critic's eyes glancing sharply down that pointed, boring nose of his.

'And the central fires have felt it and risen in response,' continued Rennie in a lower voice. 'You see the idea? It's big, to say the least. The volcanoes have answered too—there's old Etna, the giant of 'em all, breaking out in fifty new mouths of flame. Heat is latent in everything, only waiting to be called out. That match you're striking, this coffee-pot, the warmth in our bodies, and so on—their heat comes first from the sun, and is therefore an actual part of the sun, the origin of all heat and life.

'And so, O'Hara, you know, who sees the universe as a single homogeneous One and—and—well, I give it up. Can't explain it, you see. You must get him to do that. But somehow this year—cloudless— the protecting armour of water all gone too—the sun's rays managed to sink in and reach their kind buried deep below. Perhaps, later, we may get him to show us the studies that he's made—whew!—the most—er—amazing things you ever saw!'

The 'superiority' of unimaginative minds was inevitable, making Rennie regret that he had told so much. It was almost as if he had been untrue to his friend. But at length the group broke up for the afternoon. They left messages for O'Hara. Two motored, and the journalist took the train. The critic followed his sharp nose to London, where he might ferret out the failures that his mind delighted in. And when they were gone the host slipped quickly upstairs to find his friend. The heat was unbearable to suffocation, the little bedroom like an oven. But Jim O'Hara was not in it.

★★★★★★★★★★

For, instead of lying down as he had said, a fierce revolt, stirred by the talk of those unvisioned minds below, had wakened, and the deep, sensitive, poet's soul in him had leaped suddenly to the acceptance of an impossible thing. He had escaped, driven forth by the secret call of wonder. He made full speed for the destroyed moors. Fever or no fever, he must see for himself. Did no one understand? Was he the only one? . . . Walking quickly, he passed the Frensham Ponds, came through that spot of loneliness and beauty, the Lion's Mouth, noting that even there the pool of water had dried up and the rushes waved in the hot air over a bed of hard, caked mud, and so reached within the hour the wide expanse of Thursley Common.

On every side the world stretched dark and burnt, a cemetery of cinders. Great thrills rushed through his heart; and with the power of a tide that yet came at flashing speed the truth rose up in him. . . . Half running now, he plunged forward another mile or two, and found himself, the only living thing, amid the great waste of heather-land. The blazing sunlight drenched it. It lay, a sheet of weird dark beauty, spreading like a black, enormous garden as far as the eye could reach.

Then, breathless, he paused and looked about him. Within his heart something, long smouldering, ran into sudden flame. Light blazed upon his inner world. For as the scorch of vehement passion may quicken tracts of human consciousness that lie ordinarily inert and unproductive, so here the surface of the earth had turned alive. He knew; he saw; he understood.

Here, in these open sun-traps that gathered and retained the heat, the fire of the Universe had dropped and lain, increasing week by week. These parched, dry months, the soil, free from rejecting and protective moisture, had let it all accumulate till at length it had sunk downwards, inwards, and the sister fires below, responding to the touch of their ancient parent source, too long unfelt, had answered with a swift uprising roar. They had come up with answering joy, and here and there had actually reached the surface, and had leaped out with dancing cry, wild to escape from an age-long prison back to their huge, eternal origin.

This sunshine, ah! what was it? These farthing dips of heat men complained about in their tiny, cage-like houses! It scorched the grass and fields, yes; but the surface never held it long enough to let it sink to union with its kindred of the darker fires beneath! These cried for it, but union was ever denied and stifled by the weight of cooled and cooling rock. And the ages of separation had almost cooled remembrance too—fire—the kiss and strength of fire—the flaming embrace and burning lips of the father sun himself. . . He could have cried with the fierce delight of it all, and the picture he would paint rose there before him, burnt gloriously into the canvas of the entire heavens. Was not his own heat and life also from the sun? . . .

He stared about him in the deep silence of the afternoon. The world was still. It basked in the windless heat. No living thing stirred, for the common forms of life had fled away. Earth waited. He, too, waited. And then some touch of intuition, blown to white heat, supplied the link the pedestrian intellect missed, and he knew that what he waited for was on the way. For he would *see*. The message he should paint would come before his outer eye as well, though not, as he had first stupidly expected, on some grand, enormous scale. Rather would it be the equivalent of that still, small voice that once had inspired an entire nation. . . .

The wind passed very softly across the unburnt patch of heather where he lay; he heard it rustling in the skeletons of scorched birch trees, and in the gorse and furze bushes that the flame had left so ghostly pale. Farther off it sang in the isolated pines, dying away like surf upon some far-off reef. He smelt the bitter perfume of burnt soil, the pungent, acrid odour of beaten ashes. The purple-black of the moors yawned like openings in the side of the earth. In all directions for miles stretched the deep emptiness of the heather-lands, an immense, dark, magic garden, still black with the feet of wonder that had flown across it and left it so beautifully scarred. The shadow of the terrible embrace still trailed and lingered as though Midnight had screened a time of passion with this curtain of her softest plumes.

And *they* had called it ugly, had spoken of its marred beauty, its hideousness! He laughed exultantly as he drank it in, for the weird and savage splendour everywhere broke loose and spread, passing from the earth into the receptive substance of his own mind. Even the roots of gorse and heather, like petrified, shadow-eating snakes, charged with the mystery of that eternal underworld whence they had risen, lay waiting for the return of the night of sleep whence Fire had wakened them. Lost ghosts of a salamander army that the flame had swept above the ground, they lay anguished and frightened in the glare of the unaccustomed sun. . .

And waiting, he stared about him in the deep silence of the afternoon. Hazy with distance he saw the peak of Crooksbury, dim in its sheet of pines, waving a blue-plumed crest into the sky for signal; and close about him rose the more sombre glory of the lesser knolls and boulders, still cloaked in the swarthy magic of the smoke. Amid pools of ashes in the nearer hollows he saw the blue beauty of the fire-weed that rushes instantly into life behind all conflagrations. It was blowing softly in the wind.

And here and there, set like emeralds upon some dusky bosom, lay the brilliant spires of young bracken that rose to clap a thousand tiny hands in the heart of exquisite desolation. In a cloud of green they rustled in the wind above the sea of black. . . . And so, within himself O'Hara realised the huge excitement of the flame this fragment of the earth had felt. For Fire, mysterious symbol of universal life, spirit that prodigally gives itself without itself diminishing, had passed in power across this ancient heather-land, leaving the soul of it all naked and unashamed. The sun had loved it. The fires below had risen up and answered. They had known that union with their source which some call death. . . .

And the fires were rising still. The poet's heart in him became suddenly and awfully aware. Ye stars of fire! This patch of unburnt heather where he lay had been untouched as yet, but now the flame in his soul had brought the little needed link and he would *see*. The thing of wonder that the Universe should teach him how to paint was already on the way. Called by the sun, tremendous, splendid parent, the central fires were still rising.

And he turned, weakness and exultation racing for possession of him. The wind passed softly over his face, and with it came a faint, dry sound. It was distant and yet close beside him. At the stir of it there rose also in himself a strange vast thing that was bigger than the bulk of the moon and wide as the extension of swept forests, yet small and gentle as a blade of grass that pricks the lawn in spring. And he realised then that 'within' and 'without' had turned one, and that over the entire moorland arrived this thing that was happening too in a white-hot point of his own heart. He was linked with the sun and the farthest star, and in his little finger glowed the heat and fire of the universe itself. In sympathy *his own fires were rising too*.

The sound was born—a faint, light noise of crackling in the heather at his feet. He bent his head and searched, and among the obscure and tiny underways of the roots he saw a tip of curling smoke rise slowly upwards. It moved in a thin, blue spiral past his face. Then terror took him that was like a terror of the mountains, yet with it at the same time a realisation of beauty that made the heart leap within him into dazzling radiance. For the incense of this fairy column of thin smoke drew his soul out with it—upwards towards its source. He rose to his feet, trembling. . . .

He watched the line rise slowly to the sky and vanish into blue. The whole expanse of blackened heather-land watched too. Wind sank away; the sunshine dropped to meet it. A sense of deep expectancy, profound and reverent, lay over all that sun-baked moor; and the entire sweep of burnt world about him knew with joy that what was taking place in that wee, isolated patch of Surrey heather was the thing the Hebrew mystic knew when the Soul of the Universe became manifest in the bush that burned, yet never was consumed. In that faint sound of crackling, as he stood aside to listen and to watch,

O'Hara knew a form of the eternal Voice of Ages.

There was no flame, but it seemed to him that all his inner being passed in fiery heat outwards towards its source. . . . He saw the little patch of dried-up heather sink to the level of the black surface all about it—a sifted pile of delicate, pale-blue ashes. The tiny spiral vanished; he watched it disappear, winding upwards out of sight in a little ghostly trail of beauty. So small and soft and simple was this wonder of the world. It was gone. And something in himself had broken, dropped in ashes, and passed also outwards like a tiny mounting flame.

★★★★★★★★★★

But the picture O'Hara had thought himself designed to paint was never done. It was not even begun. The great canvas of 'The Fire Worshipper' stood empty on the easel, for the artist had not strength to lift a brush. Within two days the final breath passed slowly from his lips. The strange fever that so perplexed the doctor by its rapid development and its fury took him so easily. His temperature was extraordinary. The heat, as of an internal fire, fairly devoured him, and the smile upon his face at the last—so Rennie declared—was the most perplexingly wonderful thing he had ever seen. 'It was like a great, white flame,' he said.

The Impulse

"My dear chap," cried Jones, throwing his hands out in a gesture of distress he thought was quite real," nothing would give me greater pleasure—if only I could manage it. But the fact is I'm as hard up as yourself!"

"The little pale-faced man of uncertain age opposite shrugged his shoulders ever slightly.

"In a month or so, perhaps"—Jones added, hedging instinctively, "If it's not too late then—I should be delighted—"

The other interrupted quickly, a swift flush emphasising momentarily the pallor of his strained and tired face. Overworked, overweary he looked.

"Oh, thanks, but it's really of no consequence. I felt sure you wouldn't mind my asking, though." And Jones replied heartily that he only wished he were flush "enough to lend it. They talked weather and politics then—after a pause, finished their drinks, Jones refusing the offer of another, and, presently, the elder man said goodnight and left the club. Jones, with a slight sigh of boredom, as though life went hard with him, passed upstairs to the card-room to find partners for a game.

Jones was not a bad fellow really; he was untaught. Experience had neglected him a little, so that his sympathies knew not those sweet though difficult routes by which interest travels away from self—towards others. He entirely lacked that acuter sense of life which only comes to those who have known genuine want and hardship. A fat income had always tumbled into his bank without effort on his part, the harvest of another's sweat; yet, as with many such, he imagined that he earned his thousand a year, and figured somehow to himself that he deserved it.

He was neither evil-liver nor extravagant; he knew not values, that was all—least of all money values; and at the moment when his cousin asked for twenty pounds to help his family to a holiday, he found that debts pressed a bit hard, that he owed still on his motorcar, and that some recent speculations seemed suddenly very doubtful. He was hard up, yes. . . . Perhaps, if the cards were lucky, he might do it after all. But the cards were not lucky. Soon after midnight he took a taxi home to his rooms in St. James's Street. And then it was he found a letter marked "Urgent" placed by his man upon the table by the door so that he could not miss it.

The letter kept him awake most of the night in keen distress—for himself. It was anonymous, signed "Your Well-wisher." It warned him, in words that proved the writer to be well informed, that the speculation in which he, Jones, had plunged so recklessly a week before would mean a total loss unless he instantly took certain steps to retrieve himself. Such steps, moreover, were just possible, provided he acted immediately.

Jones, as he read it, turned pale, if such a thing were possible, all over his body; then he turned hot and cold. He sweated, groaned, sighed, raged; sat down and wrote urgent instructions to solicitors and others; tore the letters up and wrote others. The loss of that money would reduce his income by at least half, alter his whole plan and scale of living, make him poor. He tried to reflect, but the calmness necessary to sound reflection lay far from him.

Action was what he needed, but action was just then out of the question, for all the machinery of the world slept-solicitors, company secretaries, influential friends, lawcourts. The telephone on the wall merely grinned at him uselessly. Sleep was as vain a remedy as the closed and silent banks. There was absolutely nothing he could do till the morning; and he realised that the letters he wrote were futile even while he wrote them—and tore them up the next minute. Personal as interviews the first thing in the morning, energetic talk and action based upon the best possible advice, were the only form relief could take, and these personal interviews he could obtain even before the letters would be delivered, or as soon.

For him that money seemed as good already lost . . . and tossing upon his sleepless bed he faced the change of life the loss involved—bitterly, savagely, with keen pain: the lowered scale of self-indulgence, the clipped selfishness, restricted pleasures, fewer clothes, cheaper rooms, difficult and closely calculated travelling, and all the rest. It bit him hard—this first grinding of the little wheels of possible development in an ordinary selfish, though not evil, heart.

And then it was, as the grey dawn-light crept past the blinds, that the sharpness of his pain and the keen flight of his stirred imagination, projecting itself as by these forced marches into new, untried conditions, produced a slight reaction. The swing of the weary pendulum went a little beyond himself. He fell to wondering vaguely, and with poor insight, yet genuinely, what other men might feel, and how they managed on smaller incomes than his own—smaller than his would be even with the loss. Gingerly, tentatively, he snatched fearful glimpses (fearful, they seemed, to him, at least) into the enclosures of these more restricted lives of others.

He knew a mild and weak extension of himself, as it were, that fringed the little maps of lives less happy and indulgent than his own. And the novel sensation brought a faint relief. The small, clogged wheels of sympathy acquired faster movement, almost impetus. It seemed as though the heat and fire of his pain, though selfish pain, generated some new energy that made them turn.

Jones, in all his useless life, had never *thought*; his mind had reflected images perhaps, but had never taken hold of a real idea and followed it by logical process to an end. His mind was heavy and confused, for his nature, as with so many, only moved to calculated action when a strong enough desire instinctively showed the quickest, easiest way by which two and two could be made into four. His reflections upon comparative poverty—the poverty he was convinced now faced him cruelly—were therefore obscure and trivial enough, while wholly honest. Wealth, he divined dimly, was relative, and money represented the value of what is wanted, perhaps of what is needed rather, and usually of what cannot be obtained.

Some folk are poor because they cannot afford a second motor-car, or spend more than £100 upon a trip abroad; others because the moors and sea are out of reach; others, again, because they are glad of cast-off clothing and only dare "the gods" one night a week or take the free standing-room at Sunday concerts. . . . He suddenly recalled the story of some little penniless, elderly governess in Switzerland who made her underskirts from the silk of old umbrellas because she liked the *frou-frou* sound. Again, and again this thought for others slipped past the network of his own distress, making his own selfish pain spread wider and therefore less acutely.

For even with a mere £500 his life, perhaps, need not be too hard and unhappy. . . . The little wheels moved faster. His pain struck sparks. He saw strange glimpses of a new, far country, a fairer land than he had ever dreamed of, with endless horizons, and flowers, small and very simple, yet so lovely that he would have liked to pick them for their perfume. A sense of joy came for a moment on some soft wind of beauty, fugitive, but sweet. It vanished instantly again, but the vision caught for a moment, too tiny to be measured even by a fraction of a second, had flamed like summer lightning through his heart. It almost seemed as though his grinding selfish pain had burned the dense barriers that hid another world, bringing a light that just flamed above those huge horizons before they died. For they did die—and quickly, yet left behind a touch of singular joy and peace that somehow glowed on through all his subsequent self-pity.

And then, abruptly, with a vividness of detail that shocked him, he saw the Club smoking-room, and the worn face of his cousin close before him—the overworked hack-writer, who had asked a temporary £20, a little sum he would assuredly have paid back before the end of the year, a sum he asked, not for himself, but that he might send his wife and children to the sea.

Impulse, usually deplored as weakness, may prove first seed of habit. Whether Jones afterwards regretted his unconsidered action may be left unrecorded—whether he *would* have regretted it, rather, if the saving of his dreaded loss had not subsequently been effected. As matters stand, he only knew a sense of flattering self-congratulation that he had slipped that letter—the only one he left untorn—into the pillar-box at the corner before the sun rose, and that it contained a pink bit of paper that should bring to another the relief he himself had, for the first time in his life, known imaginatively upon that sleepless bed.

Before the day was over the letter reached its destination, and his own affairs had been put right. And two days later, when they met in the club, and Jones noticed the obvious happiness in the other's eyes and manner, he only answered to his words of thanks:

"I wish I could have given it at once. The fact is I found letters on getting home that night which—er—made it possible, you!"

But in his heart, as he said it, flamed again see quite suddenly the memory of that fair land with endless horizons he had sighted for a second, and the sentence that ran unspoken through his mind was: "By Jove, that's something I must do again. It's worth it . . .!"

The Invitation

They bumped into one another by the swinging doors of the little Soho restaurant, and, recoiling sharply, each made a half-hearted pretence of lifting his hat (it was French manners, of course, inside). Then, discovering that they were English, and not strangers, they exclaimed, "Sorry!" and laughed.

"Hulloa! It's Smith!" cried the man with the breezy manner; "and when did *you* get back?" It sounded as though "Smith" and "*you*" were different persons. "I haven't seen you for months!" They shook hands cordially.

"Only last Saturday—on the *Rollitania*," answered the man with the *pince-nez*. They were acquaintances of some standing. Neither was aware of anything in the other he disliked. More positive cause for friendship there was none. They met, however, not infrequently.

"Last Saturday! Did you really?" exclaimed the breezy one; and after an imperceptible pause which suggested nothing more vital, he added, "And had a good time in America, eh?"

"Oh! not bad, thanks—not bad at all." He likewise was conscious of a rather barren pause. "Awful crossing, though," he threw in a few seconds later with a slight grimace.

"Ah! At this time of year, you know——" said Breezy, shaking his head knowingly; "though *sometimes*, of course, one has better trips in winter than in summer. I crossed once in December when it was like a mill-pond the whole blessed way."

They moved a little to one side to let a group of Frenchmen enter the swinging doors.

"It's a good line," he added, in a voice that settled the reputation of the steamship company for ever. "By Jove, it's a good line."

Oh! it's a good line, yes," agreed Pince-nez, gratified to find his choice approved. He shifted his glasses modestly. The discovery reflected glory upon his judgment. "*And* such an excellent table!"

Breezy agreed heartily. "I'd never cross now on any other," he declared, as though he meant the table. "You're right."

This happy little agreement about the food pleased them both; it showed their judgment to be sound; also, it established a ground of common interest—a link—something that gave point to their little chat, and made it seem worthwhile to have stopped and spoken. They rose in one another's estimation. The chance meeting ought to lead to something, perhaps. Yet neither found the expected inspiration; for neither *au fond* had anything to say to the other beyond passing the time of day.

"Well," said Pince-nez, lingeringly but very pleasantly, making a movement towards the doors; "I suppose I must be going in. You—er—you've had lunch, of course?"

"Thanks, yes, I have," Breezy replied with a certain air of disappointment, as though the question had been an invitation. He moved a few steps backwards down the pavement. "But, now you're back," he added more cheerfully, "we must try and see something of one another."

"By all means. Do let's," said Pince-nez. His manner somehow suggested that he too expected an invitation, perhaps. He hesitated a moment, as though about to add something, but in the end said nothing.

"We must lunch together one day," observed Breezy, with his jolly smile. He glanced up at the restaurant.

"By all means—let's," agreed the other again, with one foot on the steps. Any day you like. Next week, perhaps. You let me know." He nodded cordially, and half turned to enter.

"Lemme see, where are you staying?' called Breezy by way of afterthought.

"Oh! I'm at the X—" mentioning an obscure hostel in the W.C. district.

"Of course; yes, I remember. That's where you stopped before, isn't it? Up in Bloomsbury somewhere—?"

"Rooms ain't up to much, but the cooking's *quite* decent."

"Good. Then we'll lunch one day soon What sort of time, by the bye, suits you?" The breezy one, for some obscure reason, looked vigorously at his watch.

"Oh! any time; one o'clock onwards, sort of thing, I suppose?" with an air of "just let me know and I'll be there."

"Same here, yes," agreed the other, with slightly less enthusiasm.

"That's capital, then," from Pince-nez. He paused a moment, not

126

finding precisely the suitable farewell phrase. Then, to his own undoing, he added carelessly, "There are one or two things—er—I should like to tell you about—"

"And luncheon *is* the best time," Breezy suggested at once, "for busy men like us. You might bespeak a table, in fact." He jerked his head towards the restaurant.

The two acquaintances, one on the pavement, the other on the steps, stood and stared at each other. The onus of invitation had somehow shifted insensibly from Breezy to Pince-nez. The next remark would be vital. Neither thought it worthwhile to incur the slight expense of a luncheon that involved an hour in each other's company. Yet it was nothing stronger than a dread of possible boredom that dictated the hesitancy.

"Not a bad idea," agreed Pince-nez vaguely. "But I doubt if they'll keep a table after one o'clock, you know."

"Never mind, then. You're on the telephone, I suppose, aren't you?" called Breezy down the pavement, still moving slowly backwards.

"Yes, you'll find it under the name of the hotel," replied the other, putting his head back round the door-post in the act of going in.

"My number's not in the book!" Breezy cried back; "but it's 0417 Westminster. Then you'll ring me up one day? That'll be very jolly indeed. *Don't forget the number!*" This shifting of telephonic responsibility, he felt, was a master-stroke.

"Right-O. I'll remember. So long, then, for the present," Pince-nez answered more faintly, disappearing into the restaurant.

"Decent fellow, that. I shall go to lunch if he asks me," was the thought in the mind of each. It lasted for perhaps half a minute, and then—oblivion.

Ten days later they ran across one another again about luncheon-time in Piccadilly; nodded, smiled, hesitated a second too long—and turned back to shake hands.

"How's everything?" asked the breezy one with gusto.

"First-rate, thanks. And, how are *you?*"

"Jolly weather, isn't it?" Breezy said, looking about him generally. "this sunshine—by Jove—"

"Nothing like it," declared Pince-nez, shifting his glasses to look at the sun, and concealing his lack of something to say by catching at the hearty manner.

"Nothing," agreed Breezy.

"In the world," echoed Pince-nez,

Again, the topic was a link. The stream of pedestrians jostled them. They moved a few yards up Dover Street. Each was really on his way to luncheon. A pause followed the move.

"Still at—er—that hotel up there?" The name had escaped him. He jerked his head vaguely northwards.

"Yes; I thought you'd be looking in for lunch one day," a faint memory stirring in his brain.

"Delighted! Or—you'd better come to my club, eh? Less out of the way, you know," declared Breezy.

"Very jolly. Thanks; that'd be first-rate." Both paused a moment. Breezy looked down the street as though expecting someone or something. They ignored that it was luncheon hour.

"You'll find me in the telephone book," observed Pince-nez presently.

"Under X— Hotel, I suppose?" from Breezy. "All right."

"0995 Northern's the number, yes."

"And mine," said Breezy, "is 0417 Westminster; or the Club"—with an air of imparting valuable private information—"is 0866 Mayfair. Any day you like. Don't forget!"

"Rather not. Somewhere about one o'clock, eh?"

"Yes—or one-thirty." And off they went again—each to his solitary luncheon.

A fortnight passed, and once more they came together—this time in an A.B.C. shop

"Hulloa! There's Smith," thought Breezy "By Jove, I'll ask him to lunch with me."

"Why, there's that chap again," thought Pince-nez. "I'll invite him, I think."

They sat down at the same table. "But this is capital," exclaimed both; "you must lunch with me, of course!" And they laughed pleasantly. They talked of food and weather. They compared Soho with A.B.C. Each offered light excuses for being found in the latter.

"I was in a hurry today, and looked in by the merest chance for a cup of coffee," observed Breezy, ordering quite a lot of things at once, absent-mindedly, as it were.

"I like the butter here so awfully," mentioned Pince-nez later. "It's *quite* the best in London, and the freshest, I always think." As this was not *the* luncheon, they felt that only common-place things were in order. The special things they had to discuss must wait, of course.

The waitress got their paper checks muddled somehow. "I've put a 'alfpenny of yours on 'is," she explained cryptically to Pince-nez.

"Oh," laughed Breezy," that's nothing. This gentleman is lunching with me, anyhow."

"You'll 'ave to make it all right when you get outside, then," said the girl gravely.

They laughed over her reply. At the pay-desk both made vigorous search for money. Pince-nez, being nimbler, produced a florin first, "This is *my* lunch, of course. I asked you, remember," he said. Breezy demurred with a good grace.

"You can be host another time, if you insist," added Pince-nez, pocketing twopence change.

"Rather," said the other heartily. "You must come to the Club—any day you like, you know."

"I'll come tomorrow, then," said Pince-nez, quick as a flash. I've got the telephone number." "Do," cried Breezy, very, very heartily indeed. "I shall be delighted! One o'clock, remember."

The Lease

The other day I came across my vague friend again. Last time it was in an A.B.C. shop; this time it was in a bus. We always meet in humble places.

He was vaguer than ever, fuddled and distrait; but delightfully engaging. He had evidently not yet lunched, for he wore no crumb; but I had a shrewd suspicion that beneath his green Alpine hat there lurked a straw or two in his untidy hair. It would hardly have surprised me to see him turn with his childlike smile and say, "Would you mind *very much* taking them out for me? You know they *do* tickle so!"—half mumbled, half shouted.

Instead, he tried to shake hands, and his black eyebrows danced. He looked as loosely put together as a careless parcel. I imagined large bits of him tumbling out.

"You're off somewhere or other, I suppose?" he said; and the question was so characteristic it was impossible not to laugh.

I mentioned the City.

I'm going that way too," he said cheerfully. He had come to the conclusion that he could not shake hands with safety; there were too many odds and ends about him—gloves, newspapers, half-open umbrella, parcels. Evidently, he had left the house uncertain as to where he was going, and had brought all these things in case, like the White Knight, he might find a use for them on the way. His overcoat was wrongly buttoned, too, so that on one side the collar reached almost to his ear. From the pockets protruded large envelopes, white and blue. I marvelled again how he ever concentrated his mind enough to write plays and novels; for in both the action was quick and dramatic; the dialogue crisp, forcible, often witty.

"Going to the City!" I exclaimed. "*You?*" Museums, libraries, second-hand bookshops were his usual haunts—places where he could be vague and absent-minded without danger to anyone. I felt genuinely curious. "Copy of some kind? Local colour for something, eh?" I laughed, hoping to draw him out.

A considerable pause followed, during which he rearranged several of his parcels, and his eyebrows shot up and down like two black-beetles dancing a hornpipe.

"I'm helping a chap with his lease," he replied suddenly, in such a very loud voice that everybody in the bus heard and became interested.

He had this way of alternately mumbling and talking very loud—absurdly loud; picking out unimportant words with terrific emphasis. He also had this way of helping others. Indeed, it was difficult to meet him without suspecting an errand of kindness—rarely mentioned, however.

"Chap with his lease," he repeated in a kind of roar, as though he feared someone had not heard him—the driver, possibly!

We were in a white Putney bus, going East. The policeman just then held it up at Wellington Street.

"It's jolly stopping like this," he cried; "one can chat a bit without having to shout."

My curiosity about the lease, or rather about his part in it, prevented an immediate reply. How he could possibly help in such a complicated matter puzzled me exceedingly.

"Horrible things, leases!" I said at length. "Confusing, I mean, with their endless repetitions and absence of commas. Legal language seems so needlessly—"

"Oh, but this one is right enough," he interrupted. "You see, my pal hasn't signed it yet. He's in rather a muddle about it, to tell the truth, and I'm going to get it straightened out by my solicitor."

The bus started on with a lurch, and he rolled against me.

"It's a three-year lease," he roared," with an option to renew, you know—oh no, I'm wrong there, by the bye," and he tapped my knee and dropped a glove, and, when it was picked up and handed to him, tried to stuff it up his sleeve as though it was a handkerchief—"I'm wrong there—that's the house he's in at present, and his wife wants to break *that* lease because she doesn't like it, and they've got more children than they expected (these words whispered), and there's no bathroom, and the kitchen stairs are absurdly narrow—"

"But the lease—you were just saying—?"

"Quite so; I was," and both eyebrows dropped so that the eyes were almost completely hidden, "but *that* lease is all right. It's the other one

132

I was talking about just then—"" "

"The house he's in now, you mean, or—?" My head already swam. The attention of the people opposite had begun to wander.

My friend pulled himself together and clutched several parcels.

"No, no, no," he explained, smiling gently; "he likes *this* one. It's the other I meant—the one his wife doesn't approve of—the one with the narrow bathroom stairs and no kitchen I mean the narrow kitchen stairs and no bathroom. It has so few cupboards, too, and the nursery chimneys smoke every time the wind's in the east. (Poor man! How devotedly he must have listened while it was being drummed into his good-natured ears!) So, you see, Henry, my pal, thought of giving it up when the lease fell in and taking this other house—the one I was just talking about—and putting in a bathroom at his own expense, provided the landlord—"

A man opposite who had been listening intently got up to leave the bus with such a disappointed look that my friend thought it was the conductor asking for another fare, and fumbled for coppers. Seeing his mistake in time, he drew out instead a large blue envelope. Two other papers, feeling neglected, came out at the same time and dropped upon the floor. My friend and a working-man beside him stooped to pick them up and knocked their heads violently in the process.

"I *beg* your pardon," exclaimed the vague one, very loud, with a tremendous emphasis on the "beg."

"Oh, that's all right, guv'nor," said the working-man, handing over the papers. Might 'appen to anybody, that!"

"I beg your pardon?" repeated my friend, not hearing him quite.

"I said a thing like that might 'appen to anyone," repeated the other, louder.

He turned to me with his happy smile. "I suppose it might, yes," he said, very low. Then he opened the blue envelope and began to hunt.

"Oh no, that's the wrong envelope. It's the other," he observed vaguely. "What a bore, isn't it? This is merely a copy of his letters to—er—to—"

He looked distressingly about him through the windows, as though he hoped to find his words in the shop-letterings or among the advertisements.

"Where are we, I wonder? Oh yes; there's St. Paul's. Good!" His mind returned to the subject in hand. Several people got out, and swept the papers from his knee to the ground; and the next few minutes he spent gathering them up, stooping, clutching his coat, stuffing envelopes into his pockets, and exclaiming "I *beg* your pardon!" to the various folk he collided with in the process.

At last, some sort of order was restored.

"—merely the letters," he resumed where he had left off, and in a voice that might suitably have addressed a public meeting, "the letters to his tenant. There's a tenant in the other house. I forgot to mention *that*, I think—"

"I think you did. But, I say, look here, my dear chap," I burst out, at length, in sheer self-preservation, "why in the world don't you let the fellow manage his own leases? It's giving you a dreadful lot of trouble. It's the most muddled-up thing I ever heard."

"That's because you've got no head for business," he whispered sweetly. "Besides, it's really a pleasure to me to help him. That's the best part of life, after all—helping people who get into muddles." He looked at me with his kindly smile. Then he turned and smiled at everybody in the bus—vaguely, happily, his black eyebrows very fierce. Several people, I fancied, smiled back at him.

"Let's see," he said, after a pause; "where was I?"

"You were saying something about a lease," I told him; but, honestly, old man, I'm afraid I haven't quite followed it."

"That's my fault," he said; all my fault. I feel a bit stupid today. I've got the 'flue, you know, and a touch of fever with it. But I promised Henry I would see to it for him, because he's awfully busy—"

"Is he really!" I wished I knew Henry. I felt a strong desire to say something to him.

"—packing up for a trip to Mexico, you know, or something; so, of course, he finds it difficult to—er—to—" He looked gently about him. "Where the deuce am I?" he asked in a very loud voice indeed.

Several people, myself among them, mentioned the Mansion House.

"Dear me!" he exclaimed, gathering up parcels, envelopes, and various loose parts of his body—his aching body, I'm afraid—"I must be getting out. I'm in the wrong bus. I wanted Essex Street—up there by the Law Courts, you know."

But I really couldn't stand it any longer. I took him by the arm and planted him, parcels, papers, and all, by my side in a taxi. We whizzed back along Queen Victoria Street, and on the way, I sorted him out, buttoned his overcoat so that it no longer tickled his ear, rolled up his umbrella so that the points no longer got caught, and made him put on both gloves, so that he could not drop them anymore. And I kept tight hold of him until we reached Essex Street. He talked leases the whole way.

"Thanks awfully," he said at the end, smiling; "you're always kind if a little rough. But I'll keep on the taxi, I think, now. The fact is, I find I've left the right lease at home after all—you know, the one about the house without the—"

I heard the rest, alternately mumbled and shouted at me, as the taxi whirred off into the Strand, bound for some unknown destination in Chelsea. It was impossible to help him more. But I should like to have heard what he said to (a) the chauffeur at the end of his journey, (b) to the solicitor. I should also like to swear that when he got back to his rooms, he found the right lease had been in his pocket all the time.

I met him again the following day, but I had not the courage to ask him anything.

The Man Who Found Out

(A Nightmare)

1

Professor Mark Ebor, the scientist, led a double life, and the only persons who knew it were his assistant, Dr. Laidlaw, and his publishers. But a double life need not always be a bad one, and, as Dr. Laidlaw and the gratified publishers well knew, the parallel lives of this particular man were equally good, and indefinitely produced would certainly have ended in a heaven somewhere that can suitably contain such strangely opposite characteristics as his remarkable personality combined.

For Mark Ebor, F.R.S., etc., etc., was that unique combination hardly ever met with in actual life, a man of science and a mystic.

As the first, his name stood in the gallery of the great, and as the second—but there came the mystery! For under the pseudonym of "Pilgrim" (the author of that brilliant series of books that appealed to so many), his identity was as well concealed as that of the anonymous writer of the weather reports in a daily newspaper. Thousands read the sanguine, optimistic, stimulating little books that issued annually from the pen of "Pilgrim," and thousands bore their daily burdens better for having read; while the Press generally agreed that the author, besides being an incorrigible enthusiast and optimist, was also—a woman; but no one ever succeeded in penetrating the veil of anonymity and discovering that "Pilgrim" and the biologist were one and the same person.

Mark Ebor, as Dr. Laidlaw knew him in his laboratory, was one man; but Mark Ebor, as he sometimes saw him after work was over, with rapt eyes and ecstatic face, discussing the possibilities of "union with God" and the future of the human race, was quite another.

"I have always held, as you know," he was saying one evening as he sat in the little study beyond the laboratory with his assistant and intimate, "that Vision should play a large part in the life of the awakened man—not to be regarded as infallible, of course, but to be observed and made use of as a guide-post to possibilities——"

"I am aware of your peculiar views, sir," the young doctor put in deferentially, yet with a certain impatience.

"For Visions come from a region of the consciousness where observation and experiment are out of the question," pursued the other with enthusiasm, not noticing the interruption, "and, while they should be checked by reason afterwards, they should not be laughed at or ignored. All inspiration, I hold, is of the nature of interior Vision, and all our best knowledge has come—such is my confirmed belief—as a sudden revelation to the brain prepared to receive it——"

"Prepared by hard work first, by concentration, by the closest possible study of ordinary phenomena," Dr. Laidlaw allowed himself to observe.

"Perhaps," sighed the other; "but by a process, none the less, of spiritual illumination. The best match in the world will not light a candle unless the wick be first suitably prepared."

It was Laidlaw's turn to sigh. He knew so well the impossibility of arguing with his chief when he was in the regions of the mystic, but at the same time the respect he felt for his tremendous attainments was so sincere that he always listened with attention and deference, wondering how far the great man would go and to what end this curious combination of logic and "illumination" would eventually lead him.

"Only last night," continued the elder man, a sort of light coming into his rugged features, "the vision came to me again—the one that has haunted me at intervals ever since my youth, and that will not be denied."

Dr. Laidlaw fidgeted in his chair.

"About the Tablets of the Gods, you mean—and that they lie somewhere hidden in the sands," he said patiently. A sudden gleam of interest came into his face as he turned to catch the professor's reply.

"And that I am to be the one to find them, to decipher them, and to give the great knowledge to the world——"

"Who will not believe," laughed Laidlaw shortly, yet interested in spite of his thinly-veiled contempt.

"Because even the keenest minds, in the right sense of the word, are hopelessly—unscientific," replied the other gently, his face positively aglow with the memory of his vision. "Yet what is more likely," he continued after a moment's pause, peering into space with rapt eyes that saw things too wonderful for exact language to describe, "than that there should have been given to man in the first ages of the world some record of the purpose and problem that had been set him to solve? In a word," he cried, fixing his shining eyes upon the face of his perplexed assistant, "that God's messengers in the far-off ages should have given to His creatures some full statement of the secret of the world, of the secret of the soul, of the meaning of life and death—the explanation of our being here, and to what great end we are destined in the ultimate fullness of things?"

Dr. Laidlaw sat speechless. These outbursts of mystical enthusiasm he had witnessed before. With any other man he would not have listened to a single sentence, but to Professor Ebor, man of knowledge and profound investigator, he listened with respect, because he regarded this condition as temporary and pathological, and in some sense a reaction from the intense strain of the prolonged mental concentration of many days.

He smiled, with something between sympathy and resignation as he met the other's rapt gaze.

"But you have said, sir, at other times, that you consider the ultimate secrets to be screened from all possible——"

"The *ultimate* secrets, yes," came the unperturbed reply; "but that there lies buried somewhere an indestructible record of the secret meaning of life, originally known to men in the days of their pristine innocence, I am convinced. And, by this strange vision so often vouchsafed to me, I am equally sure that one day it shall be given to me to announce to a weary world this glorious and terrific message."

And he continued at great length and in glowing language to describe the species of vivid dream that had come to him at intervals since earliest childhood, showing in detail how he discovered these very Tablets of the Gods, and proclaimed their splendid contents— whose precise nature was always, however, withheld from him in the vision—to a patient and suffering humanity.

"The *Scrutator*, sir, well described 'Pilgrim' as the Apostle of Hope," said the young doctor gently, when he had finished; "and now, if that reviewer could hear you speak and realise from what strange depths comes your simple faith——"

The professor held up his hand, and the smile of a little child broke over his face like sunshine in the morning.

"Half the good my books do would be instantly destroyed," he said sadly; "they would say that I wrote with my tongue in my cheek

But wait," he added significantly; "wait till I find these Tablets of the Gods! Wait till I hold the solutions of the old world-problems in my hands! Wait till the light of this new revelation breaks upon confused humanity, and it wakes to find its bravest hopes justified! Ah, then, my dear Laidlaw——"

He broke off suddenly; but the doctor, cleverly guessing the thought in his mind, caught him up immediately.

"Perhaps this very summer," he said, trying hard to make the suggestion keep pace with honesty; "in your explorations in Assyria—your digging in the remote civilization of what was once Chaldea, you may find—what you dream of——"

The professor held up his hand, and the smile of a fine old face.

"Perhaps," he murmured softly, "perhaps!"

And the young doctor, thanking the gods of science that his leader's aberrations were of so harmless a character, went home strong in the certitude of his knowledge of externals, proud that he was able to refer his visions to self-suggestion, and wondering complaisantly whether in his old age he might not after all suffer himself from visitations of the very kind that afflicted his respected chief.

And as he got into bed and thought again of his master's rugged face, and finely shaped head, and the deep lines traced by years of work and self-discipline, he turned over on his pillow and fell asleep with a sigh that was half of wonder, half of regret.

2

It was in February, nine months later, when Dr. Laidlaw made his way to Charing Cross to meet his chief after his long absence of travel and exploration. The vision about the so-called Tablets of the Gods had meanwhile passed almost entirely from his memory.

There were few people in the train, for the stream of traffic was now running the other way, and he had no difficulty in finding the man he had come to meet. The shock of white hair beneath the low-crowned felt hat was alone enough to distinguish him by easily.

"Here I am at last!" exclaimed the professor, somewhat wearily, clasping his friend's hand as he listened to the young doctor's warm greetings and questions. "Here I am—a little older, and *much* dirtier than when you last saw me!" He glanced down laughingly at his travel-stained garments.

"And *much* wiser," said Laidlaw, with a smile, as he bustled about the platform for porters and gave his chief the latest scientific news.

At last, they came down to practical considerations.

"And your luggage—where is that? You must have tons of it, I suppose?" said Laidlaw.

"Hardly anything," Professor Ebor answered. "Nothing, in fact, but what you see."

"Nothing but this hand-bag?" laughed the other, thinking he was joking.

"And a small portmanteau in the van," was the quiet reply. "I have no other luggage."

"You have no other luggage?" repeated Laidlaw, turning sharply to see if he were in earnest.

"Why should I need more?" the professor added simply.

Something in the man's face, or voice, or manner—the doctor hardly knew which—suddenly struck him as strange. There was a change in him, a change so profound—so little on the surface, that is—that at first, he had not become aware of it. For a moment it was as though an utterly alien personality stood before him in that noisy, bustling throng. Here, in all the homely, friendly turmoil of a Charing Cross crowd, a curious feeling of cold passed over his heart, touching his life with icy finger, so that he actually trembled and felt afraid.

He looked up quickly at his friend, his mind working with startled and unwelcome thoughts.

"Only this?" he repeated, indicating the bag. "But where's all the stuff you went away with? And—have you brought nothing home—no treasures?"

"This is all I have," the other said briefly. The pale smile that went with the words caused the doctor a second indescribable sensation of uneasiness. Something was very wrong, something was very queer; he wondered now that he had not noticed it sooner.

"The rest follows, of course, by slow freight," he added tactfully and as naturally as possible. "But come, sir, you must be tired and in want of food after your long journey. I'll get a taxi at once, and we can see about the other luggage afterwards."

It seemed to him he hardly knew quite what he was saying; the change in his friend had come upon him so suddenly and now grew upon him more and more distressingly. Yet he could not make out exactly in what it consisted. A terrible suspicion began to take shape in his mind, troubling him dreadfully.

"I am neither very tired, nor in need of food, thank you," the professor said quietly. "And this is all I have. There is no luggage to follow."

I have brought home nothing—nothing but what you see."

His words conveyed finality. They got into a taxi, tipped the porter, who had been staring in amazement at the venerable figure of the scientist, and were conveyed slowly and noisily to the house in the north of London where the laboratory was, the scene of their labours of years.

And the whole way Professor Ebor uttered no word, nor did Dr. Laidlaw find the courage to ask a single question.

It was only late that night, before he took his departure, as the two men were standing before the fire in the study—that study where they had discussed so many problems of vital and absorbing interest—that Dr. Laidlaw at last found strength to come to the point with direct questions. The professor had been giving him a superficial and desultory account of his travels, of his journeys by camel, of his encampments among the mountains and in the desert, and of his explorations among the buried temples, and, deeper, into the waste of the prehistoric sands, when suddenly the doctor came to the desired point with a kind of nervous rush, almost like a frightened boy.

"And you found——" he began stammering, looking hard at the other's dreadfully altered face, from which every line of hope and cheerfulness seemed to have been obliterated as a sponge wipes markings from a slate—"you found——"

"I found," replied the other, in a solemn voice, and it was the voice of the mystic rather than the man of science—"I found what I went to seek. The vision never once failed me. It led me straight to the place like a star in the heavens. I found—the Tablets of the Gods."

Dr. Laidlaw caught his breath, and steadied himself on the back of a chair. The words fell like particles of ice upon his heart. For the first time the professor had uttered the well-known phrase without the glow of light and wonder in his face that always accompanied it.

"You have—brought them?" he faltered.

"I have brought them home," said the other, in a voice with a ring like iron; "and I have—deciphered them."

Profound despair, the bloom of outer darkness, the dead sound of a hopeless soul freezing in the utter cold of space seemed to fill in the pauses between the brief sentences. A silence followed, during which Dr. Laidlaw saw nothing but the white face before him alternately fade and return. And it was like the face of a dead man.

"They are, alas, indestructible," he heard the voice continue, with its even, metallic ring.

"Indestructible," Laidlaw repeated mechanically, hardly knowing what he was saying.

Again a silence of several minutes passed, during which, with a creeping cold about his heart, he stood and stared into the eyes of the man he had known and loved so long—aye, and worshipped, too; the man who had first opened his own eyes when they were blind, and had led him to the gates of knowledge, and no little distance along the difficult path beyond; the man who, in another direction, had passed on the strength of his faith into the hearts of thousands by his books.

"I may see them?" he asked at last, in a low voice he hardly recognized as his own. "You will let me know—their message?"

Professor Ebor kept his eyes fixedly upon his assistant's face as he answered, with a smile that was more like the grin of death than a living human smile.

"When I am gone," he whispered; "when I have passed away. Then you shall find them and read the translation I have made. And then, too, in your turn, you must try, with the latest resources of science at your disposal to aid you, to compass their utter destruction." He paused a moment, and his face grew pale as the face of a corpse. "Until that time," he added presently, without looking up, "I must ask you not to refer to the subject again—and to keep my confidence meanwhile—*ab—so—lute—ly*."

3

A year passed slowly by, and at the end of it Dr. Laidlaw had found it necessary to sever his working connexion with his friend and one-time leader. Professor Ebor was no longer the same man. The light had gone out of his life; the laboratory was closed; he no longer put pen to paper or applied his mind to a single problem. In the short space of a few months, he had passed from a hale and hearty man of late middle life to the condition of old age—a man collapsed and on the edge of dissolution. Death, it was plain, lay waiting for him in the shadows of any day—and he knew it.

To describe faithfully the nature of this profound alteration in his character and temperament is not easy, but Dr. Laidlaw summed it up to himself in three words: *Loss of Hope*. The splendid mental powers remained indeed undimmed, but the incentive to use them—to use them for the help of others—had gone. The character still held to its fine and unselfish habits of years, but the far goal to which they had been the leading strings had faded away. The desire for knowledge—

knowledge for its own sake—had died, and the passionate hope which hitherto had animated with tireless energy the heart and brain of this splendidly equipped intellect had suffered total eclipse. The central fires had gone out. Nothing was worth doing, thinking, working for. There *was* nothing to work for any longer!

The professor's first step was to recall as many of his books as possible; his second to close his laboratory and stop all research. He gave no explanation; he invited no questions. His whole personality crumbled away, so to speak, till his daily life became a mere mechanical process of clothing the body, feeding the body, keeping it in good health so as to avoid physical discomfort, and, above all, doing nothing that could interfere with sleep. The professor did everything he could to lengthen the hours of sleep, and therefore of forgetfulness.

It was all clear enough to Dr. Laidlaw. A weaker man, he knew, would have sought to lose himself in one form or another of sensual indulgence—sleeping-draughts, drink, the first pleasures that came to hand. Self-destruction would have been the method of a little bolder type; and deliberate evil-doing, poisoning with his awful knowledge all he could, the means of still another kind of man. Mark Ebor was none of these. He held himself under fine control, facing silently and without complaint the terrible facts he honestly believed himself to have been unfortunate enough to discover. Even to his intimate friend and assistant, Dr. Laidlaw, he vouchsafed no word of true explanation or lament. He went straight forward to the end, knowing well that the end was not very far away.

And death came very quietly one day to him, as he was sitting in the arm-chair of the study, directly facing the doors of the laboratory—the doors that no longer opened. Dr. Laidlaw, by happy chance, was with him at the time, and just able to reach his side in response to the sudden painful efforts for breath; just in time, too, to catch the murmured words that fell from the pallid lips like a message from the other side of the grave.

"Read them, if you must; and, if you can—destroy. But"—his voice sank so low that Dr. Laidlaw only just caught the dying syllables— "but—never, never—give them to the world."

And like a grey bundle of dust loosely gathered up in an old garment the professor sank back into his chair and expired.

But this was only the death of the body. His spirit had died two years before.

The estate of the dead man was small and uncomplicated, and Dr. Laidlaw, as sole executor and residuary legatee, had no difficulty in settling it up. A month after the funeral he was sitting alone in his upstairs library, the last sad duties completed, and his mind full of poignant memories and regrets for the loss of a friend he had revered and loved, and to whom his debt was so incalculably great. The last two years, indeed, had been for him terrible. To watch the swift decay of the greatest combination of heart and brain he had ever known, and to realise he was powerless to help, was a source of profound grief to him that would remain to the end of his days.

At the same time an insatiable curiosity possessed him. The study of dementia was, of course, outside his special province as a specialist, but he knew enough of it to understand how small a matter might be the actual cause of how great an illusion, and he had been devoured from the very beginning by a ceaseless and increasing anxiety to know what the professor had found in the sands of "Chaldea," what these precious Tablets of the Gods might be, and particularly—for this was the real cause that had sapped the man's sanity and hope—what the inscription was that he had believed to have deciphered thereon.

The curious feature of it all to his own mind was, that whereas his friend had dreamed of finding a message of glorious hope and comfort, he had apparently found (so far as he had found anything intelligible at all, and not invented the whole thing in his dementia) that the secret of the world, and the meaning of life and death, was of so terrible a nature that it robbed the heart of courage and the soul of hope. What, then, could be the contents of the little brown parcel the professor had bequeathed to him with his pregnant dying sentences?

Actually, his hand was trembling as he turned to the writing-table and began slowly to unfasten a small old-fashioned desk on which the small gilt initials "M.E." stood forth as a melancholy memento. He put the key into the lock and half turned it. Then, suddenly, he stopped and looked about him. Was that a sound at the back of the room? It was just as though someone had laughed and then tried to smother the laugh with a cough. A slight shiver ran over him as he stood listening.

"This is absurd," he said aloud; "too absurd for belief—that I should be so nervous! It's the effect of curiosity unduly prolonged." He smiled a little sadly and his eyes wandered to the blue summer sky and the plane trees swaying in the wind below his window. "It's the reaction," he continued. "The curiosity of two years to be quenched in a single moment! The nervous tension, of course, must be considerable."

He turned back to the brown desk and opened it without further delay. His hand was firm now, and he took out the paper parcel that lay inside without a tremor. It was heavy. A moment later there lay on the table before him a couple of weather-worn plaques of grey stone—they looked like stone, although they felt like metal—on which he saw markings of a curious character that might have been the mere tracings of natural forces through the ages, or, equally well, the half-obliterated hieroglyphics cut upon their surface in past centuries by the more or less untutored hand of a common scribe.

He lifted each stone in turn and examined it carefully. It seemed to him that a faint glow of heat passed from the substance into his skin, and he put them down again suddenly, as with a gesture of uneasiness.

"A very clever, or a very imaginative man," he said to himself, "who could squeeze the secrets of life and death from such broken lines as those!"

Then he turned to a yellow envelope lying beside them in the desk, with the single word on the outside in the writing of the professor—the word *Translation*.

"Now," he thought, taking it up with a sudden violence to conceal his nervousness, "now for the great solution. Now to learn the meaning of the worlds, and why mankind was made, and why discipline is worthwhile, and sacrifice and pain the true law of advancement."

There was the shadow of a sneer in his voice, and yet something in him shivered at the same time. He held the envelope as though weighing it in his hand, his mind pondering many things. Then curiosity won the day, and he suddenly tore it open with the gesture of an actor who tears open a letter on the stage, knowing there is no real writing inside at all.

A page of finely written script in the late scientist's handwriting lay before him. He read it through from beginning to end, missing no word, uttering each syllable distinctly under his breath as he read.

The pallor of his face grew ghastly as he neared the end. He began to shake all over as with ague. His breath came heavily in gasps. He still gripped the sheet of paper, however, and deliberately, as by an intense effort of will, read it through a second time from beginning to end. And this time, as the last syllable dropped from his lips, the whole face of the man flamed with a sudden and terrible anger. His skin became deep, deep red, and he clenched his teeth. With all the strength of his vigorous soul he was struggling to keep control of himself.

For perhaps five minutes he stood there beside the table without stirring a muscle. He might have been carved out of stone. His eyes were shut, and only the heaving of the chest betrayed the fact that he was a living being. Then, with a strange quietness, he lit a match and applied it to the sheet of paper he held in his hand. The ashes fell slowly about him, piece by piece, and he blew them from the window-sill into the air, his eyes following them as they floated away on the summer wind that breathed so warmly over the world.

He turned back slowly into the room. Although his actions and movements were absolutely steady and controlled, it was clear that he was on the edge of violent action. A hurricane might burst upon the still room any moment. His muscles were tense and rigid. Then, suddenly, he whitened, collapsed, and sank backwards into a chair, like a tumbled bundle of inert matter. He had fainted.

In less than half an hour he recovered consciousness and sat up. As before, he made no sound. Not a syllable passed his lips. He rose quietly and looked about the room.

Then he did a curious thing.

Taking a heavy stick from the rack in the corner he approached the mantelpiece, and with a heavy shattering blow he smashed the clock to pieces. The glass fell in shivering atoms.

"Cease your lying voice for ever," he said, in a curiously still, even tone. "There is no such thing as *time!*"

He took the watch from his pocket, swung it round several times by the long gold chain, smashed it into smithereens against the wall with a single blow, and then walked into his laboratory next door, and hung its broken body on the bones of the skeleton in the corner of the room.

"Let one damned mockery hang upon another," he said smiling oddly. "Delusions, both of you, and cruel as false!"

He slowly moved back to the front room. He stopped opposite the bookcase where stood in a row the *Scriptures of the World*, choicely bound and exquisitely printed, the late professor's most treasured possession, and next to them several books signed "Pilgrim."

One by one he took them from the shelf and hurled them through the open window.

"A devil's dreams! A devil's foolish dreams!" he cried, with a vicious laugh.

Presently he stopped from sheer exhaustion. He turned his eyes slowly to the wall opposite, where hung a weird array of Eastern swords and daggers, scimitars and spears, the collections of many journeys. He crossed the room and ran his finger along the edge. His mind seemed to waver.

"No," he muttered presently; "not that way. There are easier and better ways than that."

He took his hat and passed downstairs into the street.

5

It was five o'clock, and the June sun lay hot upon the pavement. He felt the metal door-knob burn the palm of his hand.

"Ah, Laidlaw, this is well met," cried a voice at his elbow; "I was in the act of coming to see you. I've a case that will interest you, and besides, I remembered that you flavoured your tea with orange leaves!—and I admit——"

It was Alexis Stephen, the great hypnotic doctor.

"I've had no tea today," Laidlaw said, in a dazed manner, after staring for a moment as though the other had struck him in the face. A new idea had entered his mind.

"What's the matter?" asked Dr. Stephen quickly. "Something's wrong with you. It's this sudden heat, or overwork. Come, man, let's go inside."

A sudden light broke upon the face of the younger man, the light of a heaven-sent inspiration. He looked into his friend's face, and told a direct lie.

"Odd," he said, "I myself was just coming to see you. I have something of great importance to test your confidence with. But in *your* house, please," as Stephen urged him towards his own door—"in your house. It's only round the corner, and I—I cannot go back there—to my rooms—till I have told you."

"I'm your patient—for the moment," he added stammeringly as soon as they were seated in the privacy of the hypnotist's sanctum, "and I want—er——"

"My dear Laidlaw," interrupted the other, in that soothing voice of command which had suggested to many a suffering soul that the cure for its pain lay in the powers of its own reawakened will, "I am always at your service, as you know. You have only to tell me what I can do for you, and I will do it." He showed every desire to help him out. His manner was indescribably tactful and direct.

Dr. Laidlaw looked up into his face.

"I surrender my will to you," he said, already calmed by the other's healing presence, "and I want you to treat me hypnotically—and at once. I want you to suggest to me"—his voice became very tense—"that I shall forget—forget till I die—everything that has occurred to me during the last two hours; till I die, mind," he added, with solemn emphasis, "till I die."

He floundered and stammered like a frightened boy. Alexis Stephen looked at him fixedly without speaking.

"And further," Laidlaw continued, "I want you to ask me no questions. I wish to forget for ever something I have recently discovered—something so terrible and yet so obvious that I can hardly understand why it is not patent to every mind in the world—for I have had a moment of absolute *clear vision*—of merciless clairvoyance. But I want no one else in the whole world to know what it is—least of all, old friend, yourself."

He talked in utter confusion, and hardly knew what he was saying. But the pain on his face and the anguish in his voice were an instant passport to the other's heart.

"Nothing is easier," replied Dr. Stephen, after a hesitation so slight that the other probably did not even notice it. "Come into my other room where we shall not be disturbed. I can heal you. Your memory of the last two hours shall be wiped out as though it had never been. You can trust me absolutely."

"I know I can," Laidlaw said simply, as he followed him in.

6

An hour later they passed back into the front room again. The sun was already behind the houses opposite, and the shadows began to gather.

"I went off easily?" Laidlaw asked.

"You were a little obstinate at first. But though you came in like a lion, you went out like a lamb. I let you sleep a bit afterwards."

Dr. Stephen kept his eyes rather steadily upon his friend's face.

"What were you doing by the fire before you came here?" he asked, pausing, in a casual tone, as he lit a cigarette and handed the case to his patient.

"I? Let me see. Oh, I know; I was worrying my way through poor old Ebor's papers and things. I'm his executor, you know. Then I got weary and came out for a whiff of air." He spoke lightly and with perfect naturalness. Obviously, he was telling the truth. "I prefer specimens to papers," he laughed cheerily.

"I know, I know," said Dr. Stephen, holding a lighted match for the cigarette. His face wore an expression of content. The experiment had been a complete success. The memory of the last two hours was wiped out utterly. Laidlaw was already chatting gaily and easily about a dozen other things that interested him. Together they went out into the street, and at his door Dr. Stephen left him with a joke and a wry face that made his friend laugh heartily.

"Don't dine on the professor's old papers by mistake," he cried, as he vanished down the street.

Dr. Laidlaw went up to his study at the top of the house. Half way down he met his housekeeper, Mrs. Fewings. She was flustered and excited, and her face was very red and perspiring.

"There've been burglars here," she cried excitedly, "or something funny! All your things is just anyhow, sir. I found everything all about everywhere!" She was very confused. In this orderly and very precise establishment it was unusual to find a thing out of place.

"Oh, my specimens!" cried the doctor, dashing up the rest of the stairs at top speed. "Have they been touched or——"

He flew to the door of the laboratory. Mrs. Fewings panted up heavily behind him.

"The labatry ain't been touched," she explained, breathlessly, "but they smashed the libry clock and they've 'ung your gold watch, sir, on the skelinton's hands. And the books that weren't no value they flung out er the window just like so much rubbish. They must have been wild drunk, Dr. Laidlaw, sir!"

The young scientist made a hurried examination of the rooms. Nothing of value was missing. He began to wonder what kind of burglars they were. He looked up sharply at Mrs. Fewings standing in the doorway. For a moment he seemed to cast about in his mind for something.

"Odd," he said at length. "I only left here an hour ago and everything was all right then."

"Was it, sir? Yes, sir." She glanced sharply at him. Her room looked out upon the courtyard, and she must have seen the books come crashing down, and also have heard her master leave the house a few minutes later.

"And what's this rubbish the brutes have left?" he cried, taking up two slabs of worn grey stone, on the writing-table. "Bath brick, or something, I do declare."

He looked very sharply again at the confused and troubled house-keeper.

"Throw them on the dust heap, Mrs. Fewings, and—and let me know if anything is missing in the house, and I will notify the police this evening."

When she left the room, he went into the laboratory and took his watch off the skeleton's fingers. His face wore a troubled expression, but after a moment's thought it cleared again. His memory was a complete blank.

"I suppose I left it on the writing-table when I went out to take the air," he said. And there was no one present to contradict him.

He crossed to the window and blew carelessly some ashes of burned paper from the sill, and stood watching them as they floated away lazily over the tops of the trees.

The Other Wing

1

It used to puzzle him that, after dark, someone *would* look in round the edge of the bedroom door, and withdraw again too rapidly for him to see the face. When the nurse had gone away with the candle this happened: "Goodnight, Master Tim," she said usually, shading the light with one hand to protect his eyes; "dream of me and I'll dream of you." She went out slowly. The sharp-edged shadow of the door ran across the ceiling like a train. There came a whispered colloquy in the corridor outside, about himself, of course, and—he was alone.

He heard her steps going deeper and deeper into the bosom of the old country house; they were audible for a moment on the stone flooring of the hall; and sometimes the dull thump of the baize door into the servants' quarters just reached him, too—then silence. But it was only when the last sound, as well as the last sign of her had vanished, that the face emerged from its hiding-place and flashed in upon him round the corner. As a rule, too, it came just as he was saying, "Now I'll go to sleep. I won't think any longer. Goodnight, Master Tim, and happy dreams." He loved to say this to himself; it brought a sense of companionship, as though there were two persons speaking.

The room was on the top of the old house, a big, high-ceilinged room, and his bed against the wall had an iron railing round it; he felt very safe and protected in it. The curtains at the other end of the room were drawn. He lay watching the firelight dancing on the heavy folds, and their pattern, showing a spaniel chasing a long-tailed bird towards a bushy tree, interested and amused him. It was repeated over and over again. He counted the number of dogs, and the number of birds, and the number of trees, but could never make them agree. There was a plan somewhere in that pattern; if only he could discover it, the dogs and birds and trees would "come out right." Hundreds and hundreds of times he had played this game, for the plan in the pattern made it

153

possible to take sides, and the bird and dog were against him.

They always won, however; Tim usually fell asleep just when the advantage was on his own side. The curtains hung steadily enough most of the time, but it seemed to him once or twice that they stirred—hiding a dog or bird on purpose to prevent his winning. For instance, he had eleven birds and eleven trees, and, fixing them in his mind by saying, "that's eleven birds and eleven trees, but only ten dogs," his eyes darted back to find the eleventh dog, when—the curtain moved and threw all his calculations into confusion again. The eleventh dog was hidden. He did not quite like the movement; it gave him questionable feelings, rather, for the curtain did not move of itself. Yet, usually, he was too intent upon counting the dogs to feel positive alarm.

Opposite to him was the fireplace, full of red and yellow coals; and, lying with his head sideways on the pillow, he could see directly in between the bars. When the coals settled with a soft and powdery crash, he turned his eyes from the curtains to the grate, trying to discover exactly which bits had fallen. So long as the glow was there the sound seemed pleasant enough, but sometimes he awoke later in the night, the room huge with darkness, the fire almost out—and the sound was not so pleasant then. It startled him. The coals did not fall of themselves. It seemed that someone poked them cautiously. The shadows were very thick before the bars. As with the curtains, moreover, the morning aspect of the extinguished fire, the ice-cold cinders that made a clinking sound like tin, caused no emotion whatever in his soul.

And it was usually while he lay waiting for sleep, tired both of the curtain and the coal games, on the point, indeed, of saying, "I'll go to sleep now," that the puzzling thing took place. He would be staring drowsily at the dying fire, perhaps counting the stockings and flannel garments that hung along the high fender-rail when, suddenly, a person looked in with lightning swiftness through the door and vanished again before he could possibly turn his head to see. The appearance and disappearance were accomplished with amazing rapidity always.

It was a head and shoulders that looked in, and the movement combined the speed, the lightness and the silence of a shadow. Only it was not a shadow. A hand held the edge of the door. The face shot round, saw him, and withdrew like lightning. It was utterly beyond him to imagine anything more quick and clever. It darted. He heard no sound. It went. But—it had seen him, looked him all over, examined him, noted what he was doing with that lightning glance. It wanted to know if he were awake still, or asleep. And though it went off, it still watched him from a distance; it waited somewhere; it knew all about him. *Where* it waited no one could ever guess. It came probably, he felt, from beyond the house, possibly from the roof, but most likely from the garden or the sky. Yet, though strange, it was not terrible. It was a kindly and protective figure, he felt. And when it happened, he never called for help, because the occurrence simply took his voice away.

"It comes from the Nightmare Passage," he decided; "but it's *not* a nightmare." It puzzled him.

Sometimes, moreover, it came more than once in a single night. He was pretty sure—not *quite* positive—that it occupied his room as soon as he was properly asleep. It took possession, sitting perhaps before the dying fire, standing upright behind the heavy curtains, or even lying down in the empty bed his brother used when he was home from school. Perhaps it played the curtain game, perhaps it poked the coals; it knew, at any rate, where the eleventh dog had lain concealed. It certainly came in and out; certainly, too, it did not wish to be seen. For, more than once, on waking suddenly in the midnight blackness, Tim knew it was standing close beside his bed and bending over him.

He felt, rather than heard, its presence. It glided quietly away. It moved with marvellous softness, yet he was positive it moved. He felt the difference, so to speak. It had been near him, now it was gone. It came back, too—just as he was falling into sleep again. Its midnight coming and going, however, stood out sharply different from its first shy, tentative approach. For in the firelight, it came alone; whereas in the black and silent hours, it had with it—others.

And it was then he made up his mind that its swift and quiet movements were due to the fact that it had wings. It flew. And the others that came with it in the darkness were "its little ones." He also made up his mind that all were friendly, comforting, protective, and that while positively *not* a Nightmare, it yet came somehow along the Nightmare Passage before it reached him. "

You see, it's like this," he explained to the nurse: "The big one comes to visit me alone, but it only brings its little ones when I'm *quite* asleep."

"Then the quicker you get to sleep the better, isn't it, Master Tim?"

He replied: "Rather! I always do. Only I wonder where they come *from!*" He spoke, however, as though he had an inkling.

But the nurse was so dull about it that he gave her up and tried his father. "Of course," replied this busy but affectionate parent; "it's either nobody at all, or else it's Sleep coming to carry you away to the land of dreams." He made the statement kindly but somewhat briskly, for he was worried just then about the extra taxes on his land, and the effort to fix his mind on Tim's fanciful world was beyond him at the moment. He lifted the boy on to his knee, kissed and patted him as though he were a favourite dog, and planted him on the rug again with a flying sweep. "Run and ask your mother," he added; "she knows all that kind of thing. Then come back and tell me all about it—another time."

Tim found his mother in an armchair before the fire of another room; she was knitting and reading at the same time—a wonderful thing the boy could never understand. She raised her head as he came in, pushed her glasses on to her forehead, and held her arms out. He told her everything, ending up with what his father said.

"You see, it's *not* Jackman, or Thompson, or anyone like that," he exclaimed. "It's someone real."

"But nice," she assured him, "someone who comes to take care of you and see that you're all safe and cosy."

"Oh, yes, I know that. But——"

"I think your father's right," she added quickly. "It's Sleep, I'm sure, who pops in round the door like that. Sleep *has* got wings, I've always heard."

"Then the other thing—the little ones?" he asked. "Are they just sorts of dozes, you think?"

Mother did not answer for a moment. She turned down the page of her book, closed it slowly, put it on the table beside her. More slowly still she put her knitting away, arranging the wool and needles with some deliberation.

"Perhaps," she said, drawing the boy closer to her and looking into his big eyes of wonder, "they're dreams!"

Tim felt a thrill run through him as she said it. He stepped back a foot or so and clapped his hands softly. "Dreams!" he whispered with enthusiasm and belief; "of course! I never thought of that."

His mother, having proved her sagacity, then made a mistake. She noted her success, but instead of leaving it there, she elaborated and explained. As Tim expressed it, she "went on about it." Therefore, he did not listen. He followed his train of thought alone. And presently, he interrupted her long sentences with a conclusion of his own:

"Then I know where She hides," he announced with a touch of

awe. "Where She lives, I mean." And without waiting to be asked, he imparted the information: "It's in the Other Wing."

"Ah!" said his mother, taken by surprise. "How clever of you, Tim!"—and thus confirmed it.

Thenceforward this was established in his life—that Sleep and her attendant Dreams hid during the daytime in that unused portion of the great Elizabethan mansion called the Other Wing. This other wing was unoccupied, its corridors untrodden, its windows shuttered and its rooms all closed. At various places green baize doors led into it, but no one ever opened them. For many years this part had been shut up; and for the children, properly speaking, it was out of bounds. They never mentioned it as a possible place, at any rate; in hide-and-seek it was not considered, even; there was a hint of the inaccessible about the Other Wing. Shadows, dust, and silence had it to themselves.

But Tim, having ideas of his own about everything, possessed special information about the Other Wing. He believed it *was* inhabited. Who occupied the immense series of empty rooms, who trod the spacious corridors, who passed to and fro behind the shuttered windows, he had not known exactly. He had called these occupants "they," and the most important among them was "The Ruler." The Ruler of the Other Wing was a kind of deity, powerful, far away, ever present yet never seen.

And about this Ruler he had a wonderful conception for a little boy; he connected her, somehow, with deep thoughts of his own, the deepest of all. When he made up adventures to the moon, to the stars, or to the bottom of the sea, adventures that he lived inside himself, as it were—to reach them he must invariably pass through the chambers of the Other Wing. Those corridors and halls, the Nightmare Passage among them, lay along the route; they were the first stage of the journey.

Once the green baize doors swung to behind him and the long dim passage stretched ahead, he was well on his way into the adventure of the moment; the Nightmare Passage once passed, he was safe from capture; but once the shutters of a window had been flung open, he was free of the gigantic world that lay beyond. For then light poured in and he could see his way.

The conception, for a child, was curious. It established a correspondence between the mysterious chambers of the Other Wing and the occupied, but unguessed chambers of his Inner Being. Through these chambers, through these darkened corridors, along a passage, sometimes dangerous, or at least of questionable repute, he must pass to find all adventures that were *real*. The light—when he pierced far enough to take the shutters down—was discovery. Tim did not actually think, much less say, all this. He was aware of it, however. He felt it. The Other Wing was inside himself as well as through the green baize doors. His inner map of wonder included both of them.

But now, for the first time in his life, he knew who lived there and who the Ruler was. A shutter had fallen of its own accord; light poured in; he made a guess, and Mother had confirmed it. Sleep and her Little Ones, the host of dreams, were the daylight occupants. They stole out when the darkness fell. All adventures in life began and ended by a dream—discoverable by first passing through the Other Wing.

2

And, having settled this, his one desire now was to travel over the map upon journeys of exploration and discovery. The map inside himself he knew already, but the map of the Other Wing he had not seen. His mind knew it, he had a clear mental picture of rooms and halls and passages, but his feet had never trod the silent floors where dust and shadows hid the flock of dreams by day. The mighty chambers where Sleep ruled, he longed to stand in, to see the Ruler face to face. He made up his mind to get into the Other Wing.

To accomplish this was difficult; but Tim was a determined youngster, and he meant to try; he meant, also, to succeed. He deliberated. At night he could not possibly manage it; in any case, the Ruler and her host all left it after dark, to fly about the world; the Wing would be empty, and the emptiness would frighten him. Therefore, he must make a daylight visit; and it was a daylight visit he decided on. He deliberated more. There were rules and risks involved: it meant going out of bounds, the danger of being seen, the certainty of being questioned by some idle and inquisitive grown-up: "Where in the world have you been all this time"—and so forth. These things he thought out carefully, and though he arrived at no solution, he felt satisfied that it would be all right. That is, he recognised the risks. To be prepared was half the battle, for nothing then could take him by surprise.

The notion that he might slip in from the garden was soon abandoned; the red bricks showed no openings; there was no door; from the courtyard, also, entrance was impracticable; even on tiptoe he could barely reach the broad windowsills of stone. When playing alone, or walking with the French governess, he examined every outside possibility. None offered. The shutters, supposing he could reach them, were thick and solid.

Meanwhile, when opportunity offered, he stood against the outside walls and listened, his ear pressed against the tight red bricks; the towers and gables of the Wing rose overhead; he heard the wind go whispering along the eaves; he imagined tiptoe movements and a sound of wings inside. Sleep and her Little Ones were busily preparing for their journeys after dark; they hid, but they did not sleep; in this unused Wing, vaster alone than any other country house he had ever seen, Sleep taught and trained her flock of feathered Dreams.

It was very wonderful. They probably supplied the entire county. But more wonderful still was the thought that the Ruler herself should take the trouble to come to his particular room and personally watch over him all night long. That was amazing. And it flashed across his imaginative, inquiring mind: "Perhaps they take me with them! The moment I'm asleep! That's why she comes to see me!"

Yet his chief preoccupation was, how Sleep got out. Through the green baize doors, of course! By a process of elimination, he arrived at a conclusion: he, too, must enter through a green baize door and risk detection.

Of late, the lightning visits had ceased. The silent, darting figure had not peeped in and vanished as it used to do. He fell asleep too quickly now, almost before Jackman reached the hall, and long before the fire began to die. Also, the dogs and birds upon the curtains always matched the trees exactly, and he won the curtain game quite easily; there was never a dog or bird too many; the curtain never stirred. It had been thus ever since his talk with Mother and Father.

And so, he came to make a second discovery: His parents did not really believe in his Figure. She kept away on that account. They doubted her; she hid. Here was still another incentive to go and find her out. He ached for her, she was so kind, she gave herself so much trouble—just for his little self in the big and lonely bedroom. Yet his parents spoke of her as though she were of no account. He longed to see her, face to face, and tell her that *he* believed in her and loved her. For he was positive she would like to hear it. She cared. Though he had fallen asleep of late too quickly for him to see her flash in at the door, he had known nicer dreams than ever in his life before—travelling dreams. And it was she who sent them. More—he was sure she took him out with her.

One evening, in the dusk of a March day, his opportunity came;

and only just in time, for his brother Jack was expected home from school on the morrow, and with Jack in the other bed, no Figure would ever care to show itself. Also, it was Easter, and after Easter, though Tim was not aware of it at the time, he was to say goodbye finally to governesses and become a day-boarder at a preparatory school for Wellington. The opportunity offered itself so naturally, moreover, that Tim took it without hesitation. It never occurred to him to question, much less to refuse it. The thing was obviously meant to be. For he found himself unexpectedly in front of a green baize door; and the green baize door was—swinging! Somebody, therefore, had just passed through it.

It had come about in this wise. Father, away in Scotland, at Inglemuir, the shooting place, was expected back next morning; Mother had driven over to the church upon some Easter business or other; and the governess had been allowed her holiday at home in France. Tim, therefore, had the run of the house, and in the hour between tea and bed-time he made good use of it. Fully able to defy such second-rate obstacles as nurses and butlers, he explored all manner of forbidden places with ardent thoroughness, arriving finally in the sacred precincts of his father's study.

This wonderful room was the very heart and centre of the whole big house; he had been birched here long ago; here, too, his father had told him with a grave yet smiling face: "You've got a new companion, Tim, a little sister; you must be very kind to her." Also, it was the place where all the money was kept. What he called "father's jolly smell" was strong in it—papers, tobacco, books, flavoured by hunting crops and gunpowder.

At first, he felt awed, standing motionless just inside the door; but presently, recovering equilibrium, he moved cautiously on tiptoe towards the gigantic desk where important papers were piled in untidy patches. These he did not touch; but beside them his quick eye noted the jagged piece of iron shell his father brought home from his Crimean campaign and now used as a letter-weight. It was difficult to lift, however. He climbed into the comfortable chair and swung round and round. It was a swivel-chair, and he sank down among the cushions in it, staring at the strange things on the great desk before him, as if fascinated.

Next, he turned away and saw the stick-rack in the corner—this, he knew, he was allowed to touch. He had played with these sticks before. There were twenty, perhaps, all told, with curious carved handles,

160

brought from every corner of the world; many of them cut by his father's own hand in queer and distant places. And, among them, Tim fixed his eye upon a cane with an ivory handle, a slender, polished cane that he had always coveted tremendously. It was the kind he meant to use when he was a man. It bent, it quivered, and when he swished it through the air it trembled like a riding-whip, and made a whistling noise. Yet it was very strong in spite of its elastic qualities. A family treasure, it was also an old-fashioned relic; it had been his grandfather's walking stick. Something of another century clung visibly about it still. It had dignity and grace and leisure in its very aspect. And it suddenly occurred to him: "How grandpapa must miss it! Wouldn't he just love to have it back again!"

How it happened exactly, Tim did not know, but a few minutes later he found himself walking about the deserted halls and passages of the house with the air of an elderly gentleman of a hundred years ago, proud as a courtier, flourishing the stick like an Eighteenth Century dandy in the Mall. That the cane reached to his shoulder made no difference; he held it accordingly, swaggering on his way. He was off upon an adventure. He dived down through the byways of the Other Wing, inside himself, as though the stick transported him to the days of the old gentleman who had used it in another century.

It may seem strange to those who dwell in smaller houses, but in this rambling Elizabethan mansion there were whole sections that, even to Tim, were strange and unfamiliar. In his mind the map of the Other Wing was clearer by far than the geography of the part he travelled daily. He came to passages and dim-lit halls, long corridors of stone beyond the Picture Gallery; narrow, wainscoted connecting-channels with four steps down and a little later two steps up; deserted chambers with arches guarding them—all hung with the soft March twilight and all bewilderingly unrecognised.

With a sense of adventure born of naughtiness he went carelessly along, farther and farther into the heart of this unfamiliar country, swinging the cane, one thumb stuck into the arm-pit of his blue serge suit, whistling softly to himself, excited yet keenly on the alert—and suddenly found himself opposite a door that checked all further advance. It was a green baize door. And it was swinging.

He stopped abruptly, facing it. He stared, he gripped his cane more tightly, he held his breath. "The Other Wing!" he gasped in a swallowed whisper. It was an entrance, but an entrance he had never seen before. He thought he knew every door by heart; but this one was new. He stood motionless for several minutes, watching it; the door had two halves, but one half only was swinging, each swing shorter than the one before; he heard the little puffs of air it made; it settled finally, the last movements very short and rapid; it stopped. And the boy's heart, after similar rapid strokes, stopped also—for a moment.

"Someone's just gone through," he gulped. And even as he said it he knew who the someone was. The conviction just dropped into him. "It's Grandfather; he knows I've got his stick. He wants it!" On the heels of this flashed instantly another amazing certainty. "He sleeps in there. He's having dreams. That's what being dead means."

His first impulse, then, took the form of, "I must let Father know; it'll make him burst for joy"; but his second was for himself—to finish his adventure. And it was this, naturally enough, that gained the day. He could tell his father later. His first duty was plainly to go through the door into the Other Wing. He must give the stick back to its owner. He must *hand* it back.

The test of will and character came now. Tim had imagination, and so knew the meaning of fear; but there was nothing craven in him. He could howl and scream and stamp like any other person of his age when the occasion called for such behaviour, but such occasions were due to temper roused by a thwarted will, and the histrionics were half "pretended" to produce a calculated effect. There was no one to thwart his will at present. He also knew how to be afraid of Nothing, to be afraid without ostensible cause, that is—which was merely "nerves." He could have "the shudders" with the best of them.

But, when a real thing faced him, Tim's character emerged to meet it. He would clench his hands, brace his muscles, set his teeth—and wish to heaven he was bigger. But he would not flinch. Being imaginative, he lived the worst a dozen times before it happened, yet in the final crash he stood up like a man. He had that highest pluck—the courage of a sensitive temperament. And at this particular juncture, somewhat ticklish for a boy of eight or nine, it did not fail him. He lifted the cane and pushed the swinging door wide open. Then he walked through it—into the Other Wing.

3

The green baize door swung to behind him; he was even sufficiently master of himself to turn and close it with a steady hand, because he did not care to hear the series of muffled thuds its lessening swings would cause. But he realised clearly his position, knew he was

162

doing a tremendous thing.

Holding the cane between fingers very tightly clenched, he advanced bravely along the corridor that stretched before him. And all fear left him from that moment, replaced, it seemed, by a mild and exquisite surprise. His footsteps made no sound, he walked on air; instead of darkness, or the twilight he expected, a diffused and gentle light that seemed like the silver on the lawn when a half-moon sails a cloudless sky, lay everywhere. He knew his way, moreover, knew exactly where he was and whither he was going. The corridor was as familiar to him as the floor of his own bedroom; he recognised the shape and length of it; it agreed exactly with the map he had constructed long ago. Though he had never, to the best of his knowledge, entered it before, he knew with intimacy its every detail.

And thus, the surprise he felt was mild and far from disconcerting. "I'm here again!" was the kind of thought he had. It was *how* he got here that caused the faint surprise, apparently. He no longer swaggered, however, but walked carefully, and half on tiptoe, holding the ivory handle of the cane with a kind of affectionate respect.

And as he advanced, the light closed softly up behind him, obliterating the way by which he had come. But this he did not know, because he did not look behind him. He only looked in front, where the corridor stretched its silvery length towards the great chamber where he knew the cane must be surrendered. The person who had preceded him down this ancient corridor, passing through the green baize door just before he reached it, this person, his father's father, now stood in that great chamber, waiting to receive his own. Tim knew it as surely as he knew he breathed. At the far end he even made out the larger patch of silvery light which marked its gaping doorway.

There was another thing he knew as well—that this corridor he moved along between rooms with fast-closed doors, was the Nightmare Corridor; often and often he had traversed it; each room was occupied. "This is the Nightmare Passage," he whispered to himself, "but I know the Ruler—it doesn't matter. None of them can get out or do anything." He heard them, none the less, inside, as he passed by he heard them scratching to get out. The feeling of security made him reckless; he took unnecessary risks; he brushed the panels as he passed. And the love of keen sensation for its own sake, the desire to feel "an awful thrill," tempted him once so sharply that he raised his stick and poked a fast-shut door with it!

He was not prepared for the result, but he gained the sensation and the thrill. For the door opened with instant swiftness half an inch, a hand emerged, caught the stick and tried to draw it in. Tim sprang back as if he had been struck. He pulled at the ivory handle with all his strength, but his strength was less than nothing. He tried to shout, but his voice had gone. A terror of the moon came over him, for he was unable to loosen his hold of the handle; his fingers had become a part of it. An appalling weakness turned him helpless.

He was dragged inch by inch towards the fearful door. The end of the stick was already through the narrow, crack. He could not see the hand that pulled, but he knew it was terrific. He understood now why the world was strange, why horses galloped furiously, and why trains whistled as they raced through stations. All the comedy and terror of nightmare gripped his heart with pincers made of ice. The dispro-portion was abominable. The final collapse rushed over him when, without a sign of warning, the door slammed silently, and between the jamb and the wall the cane was crushed as flat as if it were a bulrush. So irresistible was the force behind the door that the solid stick just went flat as a stalk of a bulrush.

He looked at it. It *was* a bulrush.

He did not laugh; the absurdity was so distressingly unnatural. The horror of finding a bulrush where he had expected a polished cane—this hideous and appalling detail held the nameless horror of the nightmare. It betrayed him utterly. Why had he not always known really that the stick was not a stick, but a thin and hollow reed. . .?

Then the cane was safely in his hand, unbroken. He stood looking at it. The Nightmare was in full swing. He heard another door open-ing behind his back, a door he had not touched. There was just time to see a hand thrusting and waving dreadfully, familiarly, at him through the narrow crack—just time to realise that this was another Night-mare acting in atrocious concert with the first, when he saw closely beside him, towering to the ceiling, the protective, kindly Figure that visited his bedroom. In the turning movement he made to meet the attack, he became aware of her. And his terror passed. It was a night-mare terror merely. The infinite horror vanished. Only the comedy remained. He smiled.

He saw her dimly only, she was so vast, but he saw her, the Ruler of the Other Wing at last, and knew that he was safe again. He gazed with a tremendous love and wonder, trying to see her clearly; but the face was hidden far aloft and seemed to melt into the sky beyond the roof. He discerned that she was larger than the Night, only far,

far softer, with wings that folded above him more tenderly even than his mother's arms; that there were points of light like stars among the feathers, and that she was vast enough to cover millions and millions of people all at once. Moreover, she did not fade or go, so far as he could see, but spread herself in such a way that he lost sight of her. She spread over the entire Wing. . . .

And Tim remembered that this was all quite natural really. He had often and often been down this corridor before; the Nightmare Corridor was no new experience it had to be faced as usual. Once knowing what hid inside the rooms, he was bound to tempt them out. They drew, enticed, attracted him; this was their power. It was their special strength that they could suck him helplessly towards them, and that he was obliged to go. He understood exactly why he was tempted to tap with the cane upon their awful doors, but, having done so, he had accepted the challenge and could now continue his journey quietly and safely. The Ruler of the Other Wing had taken him in charge.

A delicious sense of carelessness came on him. There was softness as of water in the solid things about him, nothing that could hurt or bruise. Holding the cane firmly by its ivory handle, he went forward along the corridor, walking as on air.

The end was quickly reached: He stood upon the threshold of the mighty chamber where he knew the owner of the cane was waiting: the long corridor lay behind him, in front he saw the spacious dimensions of a lofty hall that gave him the feeling of being in the Crystal Palace, Euston Station, or St. Paul's. High, narrow windows, cut deeply into the wall, stood in a row upon the other side; an enormous open fireplace of burning logs was on his right; thick tapestries hung from the ceiling to the floor of stone; and in the centre of the chamber was a massive table of dark, shining wood, great chairs with carved stiff backs set here and there beside it. And in the biggest of these throne-like chairs there sat a figure looking at him gravely—the figure of an old, old man.

Yet there was no surprise in the boy's fast-beating heart; there was a thrill of pleasure and excitement only, a feeling of satisfaction. He had known quite well the figure would be there, known also it would look like this exactly. He stepped forward on to the floor of stone without a trace of fear or trembling, holding the precious cane in two hands now before him, as though to present it to its owner. He felt proud and pleased. He had run risks for this.

And the figure rose quietly to meet him, advancing in a stately manner over the hard stone floor. The eyes looked gravely, sweetly down at him, the aquiline nose stood out. Tim knew him perfectly: the knee-breeches of shining satin, the gleaming buckles on the shoes, the neat dark stockings, the lace and ruffles about neck and wrists, the coloured waistcoat opening so widely—all the details of the picture over father's mantelpiece, where it hung between two Crimean bayonets, were reproduced in life before his eyes at last. Only the polished cane with the ivory handle was not there.

Tim went three steps nearer to the advancing figure and held out both his hands with the cane laid crosswise on them.

"I've brought it, Grandfather," he said, in a faint but clear and steady tone; "here it is."

And the other stooped a little, put out three fingers half concealed by falling lace, and took it by the ivory handle. He made a courtly bow to Tim. He smiled, but though there was pleasure, it was a grave, sad smile. He spoke then: the voice was slow and very deep. There was a delicate softness in it, the suave politeness of an older day.

"Thank you," he said; "I value it. It was given to me by my grandfather. I forgot it when I——" His voice grew indistinct a little.

"Yes?" said Tim.

"When I—left," the old gentleman repeated.

"Oh," said Tim, thinking how beautiful and kind the gracious figure was.

The old man ran his slender fingers carefully along the cane, feeling the polished surface with satisfaction. He lingered specially over the smoothness of the ivory handle. He was evidently very pleased.

"I was not quite myself—er—at the moment," he went on gently; "my memory failed me somewhat." He sighed, as though an immense relief was in him.

"*I* forget things, too—sometimes," Tim mentioned sympathetically. He simply loved his grandfather. He hoped—for a moment— he would be lifted up and kissed. "I'm *awfully* glad I brought it," he faltered—"that you've got it again."

The other turned his kind grey eyes upon him; the smile on his face was full of gratitude as he looked down.

"Thank you, my boy. I am truly and deeply indebted to you. You courted danger for my sake. Others have tried before, but the Nightmare Passage—er——" He broke off. He tapped the stick firmly on the stone flooring, as though to test it. Bending a trifle, he put his weight upon it. "Ah!" he exclaimed with a short sigh of relief, "I can

166

now———"

His voice again grew indistinct; Tim did not catch the words.

"Yes?" he asked again, aware for the first time that a touch of awe was in his heart.

"—get about again," the other continued very low. "Without my cane," he added, the voice failing with each word the old lips uttered, "I could not . . . possibly . . . allow myself . . . to be seen. It was indeed . . . deplorable . . . unpardonable of me . . . to forget in such a way. Zounds, sir . . .! I—I . . ."

His voice sank away suddenly into a sound of wind. He straightened up, tapping the iron ferrule of his cane on the stones in a series of loud knocks. Tim felt a strange sensation creep into his legs. The queer words frightened him a little.

The old man took a step towards him. He still smiled, but there was a new meaning in the smile. A sudden earnestness had replaced the courtly, leisurely manner. The next words seemed to blow down upon the boy from above, as though a cold wind brought them from the sky outside.

Yet the words, he knew, were kindly meant, and very sensible. It was only the abrupt change that startled him. Grandfather, after all, was but a man! The distant sound recalled something in him to that outside world from which the cold wind blew.

"My eternal thanks to you." he heard, while the voice and face and figure seemed to withdraw deeper and deeper into the heart of the mighty chamber. "I shall not forget your kindness and your courage. It is a debt I can, fortunately, one day repay . . . But now you had best return and with dispatch. For your head and arm lie heavily on the table, the documents are scattered, there is a cushion fallen . . . and my son is in the house . . . Farewell! You had best leave me quickly. See! *She* stands behind you, waiting. Go with her! Go now . . .!"

The entire scene had vanished even before the final words were uttered. Tim felt empty space about him. A vast, shadowy Figure bore him through it as with mighty wings. He flew, he rushed, he remembered nothing more—until he heard another voice and felt a heavy hand upon his shoulder.

"Tim, you rascal! What are you doing in my study? And in the dark, like this!"

He looked up into his father's face without a word. He felt dazed. The next minute his father had caught him up and kissed him.

"Ragamuffin! How did you guess I was coming back tonight?" He shook him playfully and kissed his tumbling hair. "And you've been asleep, too, into the bargain. Well—how's everything at home—eh? Jack's coming back from school tomorrow, you know, and . . ."

4

Jack came home, indeed, the following day, and when the Easter holidays were over, the governess stayed abroad and Tim went off to adventures of another kind in the preparatory school for Wellington. Life slipped rapidly along with him; he grew into a man; his mother and his father died; Jack followed them within a little space; Tim inherited, married, settled down into his great possessions—and opened up the Other Wing. The dreams of imaginative boyhood all had faded; perhaps he had merely put them away, or perhaps he had forgotten them. At any rate, he never spoke of such things now, and when his Irish wife mentioned her belief that the old country house possessed a family ghost, even declaring that she had met an Eighteenth Century figure of a man in the corridors, "an old, old man who bends down upon a stick"—Tim only laughed and said:

"That's as it ought to be! And if these awful land-taxes force us to sell some day, a respectable ghost will increase the market value."

But one night he woke and heard a tapping on the floor. He sat up in bed and listened. There was a chilly feeling down his back. Belief had long since gone out of him; he felt uncannily afraid. The sound came nearer and nearer; there were light footsteps with it. The door opened—it opened a little wider, that is, for it already stood ajar—and there upon the threshold stood a figure that it seemed he knew. He saw the face as with all the vivid sharpness of reality.

There was a smile upon it, but a smile of warning and alarm. The arm was raised. Tim saw the slender hand, lace falling down upon the long, thin fingers, and in them, tightly gripped, a polished cane. Shaking the cane twice to and fro in the air, the face thrust forward, spoke certain words, and—vanished. But the words were inaudible; for, though the lips distinctly moved, no sound, apparently, came from them.

And Tim sprang out of bed. The room was full of darkness. He turned the light on. The door, he saw, was shut as usual. He had, of course, been dreaming. But he noticed a curious odour in the air. He sniffed it once or twice—then grasped the truth. It was a smell of burning!

Fortunately, he awoke just in time . . .

168

He was acclaimed a hero for his promptitude. After many days, when the damage was repaired, and nerves had settled down once more into the calm routine of country life, he told the story to his wife—the entire story. He told the adventure of his imaginative boyhood with it. She asked to see the old family cane. And it was this request of hers that brought back to memory a detail Tim had entirely forgotten all these years. He remembered it suddenly again—the loss of the cane, the hubbub his father kicked up about it, the endless, futile search. For the stick had never been found, and Tim, who was questioned very closely concerning it, swore with all his might that he had not the smallest notion where it was. Which was, of course, the truth.

The Prayer

There was a glitter in the eye of O'Malley when they met. "I've got it!" he said under his breath, holding out a tiny phial with the ominous red label.

"Got what?" asked Jones, as though he didn't know. Both were medical students; both of a speculative and adventurous turn of mind as well; the Irishman, however, ever the leader in mischief.

"The stuff!" was the reply. "The recipe the Hindu gave me. Your night's free, isn't it? Mine, too. We'll try it. Eh?"

They eyed the little bottle with its shouting label—Poison. Jones took it up, fingered it, drew the cork, sniffed it. "Ugh!" he exclaimed. "it's got an awful smell. Don't think I could swallow that!"

"You don't swallow it," answered O'Malley impatiently. "You sniff it up through the nose-just a drop. It goes down the throat that way."

"Irish swallowing, eh?" laughed Jones uneasily. "It looks wicked to me." He played with the bottle, till the other snatched it away.

"Look out, man! Begad, there's enough there to kill a Cabinet Minister, or a horse. It's the real stuff, I tell you. I told him it was for a psychical experiment. You remember the talk we had that night—"

"Oh, I remember well enough. But it's not worth while in my opinion. It will only make us sick." He said it almost angrily. "Besides we've got enough hallucinations in life already without inducing others—"

O'Malley glanced up quickly. "Nothing of the sort," he snapped. "You're backing out. You swore you'd try it with me if I got it. The effect—"

"Well, what is the effect?"

The Irishman looked keenly at him. He answered very low. Evidently, he said something he really believed. There was gravity, almost solemnity, in his voice and manner.

"Opens the inner sight," he whispered darkly. "Makes you sensi-

171

tive to thoughts and thought-forces." He paused a moment, staring hard into the other's eyes. For instance," he added slowly, earnestly, "if somebody's thinking hard about *you*, I should twig it. See? I should *see* the thought-stream getting at you—influencing you—making you do this and that. The air is full of loose and wandering thoughts from other minds. I should see these thoughts hovering about your mind like flies trying to settle. Understand? The cause of a sudden change of mood in a man, an inspiration, a helping thought—a temptation—!"

"Bosh!"

"Are you afraid?"

"No. But it's a poisonous doctrine—that such experiments are worthwhile even if—if—"

But O'Malley knew his pal. . . . They took the prescribed dose together, laughing, scoffing, hoping. Then they went out to dine. "We must eat very little," explained the Irishman. "The stomach must be comparatively empty. And drink nothing at all."

"What a bore!" said Jones, who was always hungry, and usually thirsty. The prescribed hour passed between the taking of the dose and dinner. They felt nothing more than what Jones described as a "beastly uncomfortable sort of inner heat."

★★★★★★★★★★★★

Opposite them, at a table alone, sat a small man, over-dressed according to their standards, and wearing diamond rings. His face had a curious mixture of refinement and wickedness—like a man naturally sensitive whom circumstances, indulgence, or some special temptation had led astray. He did not notice their somewhat close attention because, in his turn, he was closely watching—somebody else. He ate and drank soberly, but drew his dinner out. The "somebody else" he watched, obviously enough, was a country couple, up probably for the festivities due to the presence of a foreign potentate in town.

They were bewildered by big London. They carried hand-bags. From time to time the old man fingered his breast-pocket. He looked about him nervously. The be-ringed man was kind to them, lent them his newspaper, passed the salt, gave them scraps of favoured, kind, and sympathetic conversation. He was very gentle with them.

"Feel anything yet?" asked O'Malley for the tenth time, noticing a curious, passing look on his companion's face. "I don't feel a blessed thing meself! I believe that chemist fooled me, gave me diluted stuff or something—" He stopped short, caught by the other's eye. They had been dining very sparingly, much to the disgust of the waiter, who wanted their table for more remunerative customers.

"I do feel something, yes," was the quiet reply. "Or, rather, I *see* something. It's odd; but I really do"

"What? Out with it! Tell me!"

"A sort of wavy line of gold," said Jones calmly, "gold and shining. And sometimes it's white. It flits about that fellow's head—that fellow over there." He indicated the man with the rings. "Almost as if—it were trying to get into him—"

"Bosh!" said O'Malley, who was ever the last to believe in the success of his own experiments. You swear it?"

The other's face convinced him, and a thrill went down his Irish spine.

"Hush," said Jones in a lower tone, "don't shout. I see it right enough. It's like a little wavy stream of light. It's going all about his head and eyes. By gad, it's lovely, though—it's like a flower now, a floating blossom—and now a strip of thin soft gold. It's got him! By George, I tell you, it's got him—!"

"Got him?" echoed the Irishman, genuinely impressed.

"Got *into* him, I meant. It's disappeared—gone clean into his head. Look!"

O'Malley looked hard, but saw nothing. "Me boy!" he cried, "the stuff *was* real. It's working. Watch it. I do believe you've seen a thought—a thought from somebody else—a wandering thought. It's got into his mind. It may affect his actions, movements, decisions. Good Lord! The stuff was not diluted, after all. You've seen a thought-force!" He was tremendously excited. Jones, however, was too absorbed in what he saw to feel excitement. Whether it was due to the drug or not, he knew he saw a real thing.

"Wonder if it's a good one or a bad one!" whispered the Irishman "Wonder what sort of mind it comes from! Where? How far away?" He wondered a number of things. He chattered below his breath like a dying gramophone. But his companion just sat, staring in rapt silence.

"What are *you* doing here?" said a voice from the table behind them quietly. And O'Malley, turning—Jones was too preoccupied—recognised a plain-clothes detective whom he chanced to know from having been associated with him in a recent poisoning case.

"Nothing particular; just having dinner," he answered. "And you?"

The detective made no secret of his object. "Watching the crowds for their own safety," he said, "that's all. London's full of prey just now—all up from the country, with their bags in their hands, their money in their breast-pockets, and good-natured folks ready every-where to help 'em, and help themselves at the same time." He laughed, nodding towards the man with the rings.

"All the crooks are on the job," he added significantly. "There's an old friend of ours. He doesn't know *me*, but I know him right enough. He's usually made up as a clergyman; and tonight, he's after that old couple at the nex' table, or my name ain't Joe Leary! Don't stare, or he'll notice." He turned his head the other way.

O'Malley, however, was far too interested in hoping for a psychi-cal experience of his own, and in watching the "alleged phenomena" of his companion, to feel much interest in a mere detective's hunt for pickpockets. He turned towards his friend again. "What's up now?" he asked, with his back to the detective; "see anything more?"

"It's perfectly wonderful," whispered Jones softly. "It's out again. I can see the gold thread, all shining and alive, clean down in the man's mind and heart, then out, then in again. It's making him different—I swear it is. By George, it's like a blessed chemical experiment. I can't explain it as I see it, but he's getting sort of bright within—golden like the thread." Jones was wrought up, excited, moved. It was impossible to doubt his earnestness. He described a thing he really saw. O'Malley listened with envy and resentment.

"Blast it all!" he exclaimed. "I see nothing. I didn't take enough!" And he drew the little phial out of his pocket.

"Look! He's *changed!*" exclaimed Jones, interrupting the move-ment so suddenly that O'Malley dropped the phial and it smashed to atoms against the iron edge of the umbrella-stand. "His thought's altered. He's going out. The gold has spread all through him—!"

"By gosh!" put in O'Malley, so loud that people stared, "it's helped him—made him a better man—turned him from evil. It's that blessed wandering thought! Follow it, follow it! Quick!" And in the general confusion that came with the paying of bills, cleaning up the broken glass, and the rest, the "crook" slipped out into the crowd and was lost, the detective murmured something about "wonder what made him leave so good a trail!" and the Irishman filled in the pauses with hur-ried, nervous sentences—"Keep your eye on the line of gold! We'll follow it! We'll trace it to its source. Never mind the tip! Hurry, hurry! Don't lose it!"

But Jones was already out, drawn by the power of his obvious con-viction. They went into the street. Regardless of the blaze of lights and blur of shadows, the noise of traffic and the rush of the crowds, they followed what Jones described as the "line of wavy gold."

"Don't lose it! For Heaven's sake, don't lose it!" O'Malley cried, dodging with difficulty after the disappearing figure. "It's a genuine thought-force from another mind. Follow it! Trace it! We'll track it to its source—some noble thinker somewhere—some gracious woman —some exalted, golden source, at any rate!" He was wholly caught away now by the splendour of the experiment's success. A thought that could make a criminal change his mind must issue from a radiant well of rare and purest thinking. He remembered the Hindu's words: "You will *see* thoughts in colour—bad ones, lurid and streaked—good ones, sweet and shining, like a line of golden light—and if you follow, you may trace them to the mind that sent them out."

"It goes so fast!" Jones called back, "I can hardly keep up. It's in the air, just over the heads of the crowd. It leaves a trail like a meteor. Come on, come on!"

"Take a taxi," shouted the Irishman. "It'll escape us!" They laughed, and panted, dodged past the stream of people, crossed the street.

"Shut up!" answered Jones. "Don't talk so much. I lose it when you talk. It's in my mind. I really see it, but your chatter blurs it Come on, come on!"

★★★★★★★★★★★★

And so, they came at last to the region of mean streets, where the traffic was less, the shadows deeper, the lights dim, streets that visiting emperors do not change. No match-sellers, bootlace venders, or "dreadful shadows proffering toys," blocked their way on the pavement edge, because here were none to buy.

"It's changed from gold to white," Jones whispered breathlessly. "It shines now—by gad, it shines—like a bit of escaped sunrise. And others have joined it. Can't you see 'em ? Why, they're like a network. They're rays—rays of glory. And—hullo!—I see where they come from now! It's that house over there. Look, man, look! They're streaming like a river of light out of that high window, that little attic window up there"—he pointed to a dingy house standing black against the murk of the sky. They come out in a big stream, and then separate in all directions. It's simply wonderful!"

O'Malley gasped and panted. He said nothing. Jones, the phlegmatic, heavy Jones, had got a real vision, whereas he who always imagined "visions" got nothing. He followed the lead. Jones, he understood, was taking his instinct where it led him. He would not interfere.

And the instinct led him to the door. They stopped dead, hesitating for the first time. "Better not go in, you know," said O'Malley, breaking the decision he had just made. Jones looked up at him, slightly bewildered. "I've lost it," he whispered, "lost the line—" A taxi-cab drew up with a rattling thunder just in front and a man got out, came up to the door and stood beside them. It was the crook.

For a second or two the three men eyed each other. Clearly the new arrival did not recognise them. "Pardon, gentlemen," he said, pushing past to pull the bell. They saw his rings. The taxi boomed away down the little dark street that knew more of coal-carts than of motors. "You're coming in?" the man asked, as the door opened and he stepped inside. O'Malley, usually so quick-witted, found no word to say, but Jones had a question ready. The Irishman never understood how he asked it, and got the answer, too, without giving offence. The instinct guided him in choice of words and tone and gesture—somehow or other. He asked who lived upstairs in the front attic room, and the man, as he quietly closed the door upon them, gave the information—"My father."

And, for the rest, all they ever learnt-by a little diligent inquiry up and down the street, engineered by Jones—was that the old man, bedridden for a dozen years, was never seen, and that an occasional district-visitor, or such like, were his only callers. But they all agreed that he was good. "They do say he lies there praying day and night— jest praying for the world." It was the grocer at the corner who told them that.

The Tradition

The noises outside the little flat at first were very disconcerting after living in the country. They made sleep difficult. At the cottage in Sussex where the family had lived, night brought deep, comfortable silence, unless the wind was high, when the pine trees round the duck-pond made a sound like surf, or if the gale was from the southwest, the orchard roared a bit unpleasantly.

But in London it was very different; sleep was easier in the daytime than at night. For after nightfall the rumble of the traffic became spasmodic instead of continuous; the motor-horns startled like warnings of alarm; after comparative silence the furious rushing of a taxi-cab touched the nerves. From dinner till eleven o'clock the streets subsided gradually; then came the army from theatres, parties, and late dinners, hurrying home to bed. The motor-horns during this hour were lively and incessant, like bugles of a regiment moving into battle. The parents rarely retired until this attack was over. If quick about it, sleep was possible then before the flying of the night-birds—an uncertain squadron—screamed half the street awake again. But these finally disposed of, a delightful hush settled down upon the neighbourhood, profounder far than any peace of the countryside. The deep rumble of the produce wagons, coming in to the big London markets from the farms—generally about three a.m.—held no disturbing quality.

But sometimes in the stillness of very early morning, when streets were empty and pavements all deserted, there was a sound of another kind that was startling and unwelcome. For it was ominous. It came with a clattering violence that made nerves quiver and forced the heart to pause and listen. A strange resonance was in it, a volume of sound, moreover, that was hardly justified by its cause. For it was hoofs. A horse swept hurrying up the deserted street, and was close upon the building in a moment. It was audible suddenly, no gradual approach from a distance, but as though it turned a corner from soft ground that

177

muffled the hoofs, on to the echoing, hard paving that emphasised the dreadful clatter. Nor did it die away again when once the house was reached. It ceased as abruptly as it came. The hoofs did not go away.

It was the mother who heard them first, and drew her husband's attention to their disagreeable quality.

"It is the mail-vans, dear," he answered. "They go at four a. m. to catch the early trains into the country."

She looked up sharply, as though something in his tone surprised her.

"But there's no sound of wheels," she said. And then, as he did not reply, she added gravely, "You have heard it too, John. I can tell."

"I have," he said. "I have heard it—twice."

And they looked at one another searchingly, each trying to read the other's mind. She did not question him; he did not propose writing to complain in a newspaper; both understood something that neither of them understood.

"I heard it first," she then said softly, "the night before Jack got the fever. And as I listened, I heard him crying. But when I went in to see he was asleep. The noise stopped just outside the building." There was a shadow in her eyes as she said this, and a hush crept in between her words. "I did not hear it *go*." She said this almost beneath her breath.

He looked a moment at the ground; then, coming towards her, he took her in his arms and kissed her. And she clung very tightly to him.

"Sometimes," he said in a quiet voice, "a mounted policeman passes down the street, I think."

"It is a horse," she answered. But whether it was a question or mere corroboration he did not ask, for at that moment the doctor arrived, and the question of little Jack's health became the paramount matter of immediate interest. The great man's verdict was uncommonly disquieting.

All that night they sat up in the sick room. It was strangely still, as though by one accord the traffic avoided the house where a little boy hung between life and death. The motor-horns even had a muffled sound, and heavy drays and wagons used the wide streets; there were fewer taxicabs about, or else they flew by noiselessly. Yet no straw was down; the expense prohibited that. And towards morning, very early, the mother decided to watch alone. She had been a trained nurse before her marriage, accustomed when she was younger to long vigils. "You go down, dear, and get a little sleep," she urged in a whisper. "He's quiet now. At five o'clock I'll come for you to take my place."

"You'll fetch me at once," he whispered, "if——" then hesitated as though breath failed him. A moment he stood there staring from her face to the bed. "If you hear anything," he finished. She nodded, and he went downstairs to his study, not to his bedroom. He left the door ajar. He sat in darkness, listening. Mother, he knew, was listening, too, beside the bed. His heart was very full, for he did not believe the boy could live till morning. The picture of the room was all the time before his eyes—the shaded lamp, the table with the medicines, the little wasted figure beneath the blankets, and mother close beside it, listening. He sat alert, ready to fly upstairs at the smallest cry.

But no sound broke the stillness; the entire neighbourhood was silent; all London slept. He heard the clock strike three in the dining-room at the end of the corridor. It was still enough for that. There was not even the heavy rumble of a single produce wagon, though usually they passed about this time on their way to Smithfield and Covent Garden markets. He waited, far too anxious to close his eyes. . . .At four o'clock he would go up and relieve her vigil. Four, he knew, was the time when life sinks to its lowest ebb. . . .Then, in the middle of his reflections, thought stopped dead, and it seemed his heart stopped too.

Far away, but coming nearer with extraordinary rapidity, a sharp, clear sound broke out of the surrounding stillness—a horse's hoofs. At first it was so distant that it might have been almost on the high roads of the country, but the amazing speed with which it came closer, and the sudden increase of the beating sound, was such, that by the time he turned his head it seemed to have entered the street outside. It was within a hundred yards of the building. The next second it was before the very door. And something in him blenched. He knew a moment's complete paralysis.

The abrupt cessation of the heavy clatter was strangest of all. It came like lightning, it struck, it paused. It did not go away again. Yet the sound of it was still beating in his ears as he dashed upstairs three steps at a time. It seemed in the house as well, on the stairs behind him, in the little passage-way, *inside the very bedroom*. It was an appalling sound. Yet he entered a room that was quiet, orderly, and calm. It was silent. Beside the bed his wife sat, holding Jack's hand and stroking it. She was soothing him; her face was very peaceful. No sound but her gentle whisper was audible.

He controlled himself by a tremendous effort, but his face betrayed his consternation and distress. "Hush," she said beneath her breath; "he's sleeping much more calmly now. The crisis, bless God, is over, I do believe. I dared not leave him."

He saw in a moment that she was right, and an untenable relief passed over him. He sat down beside her, very cold, yet perspiring with heat.

"You heard——?" he asked after a pause.

"Nothing," she replied quickly, "except his pitiful, wild words when the delirium was on him. It's passed. It lasted but a moment, or I'd have called you."

He stared closely into her tired eyes. "And his words?" he asked in a whisper. Whereupon she told him quietly that the little chap had sat up with wide-opened eyes and talked excitedly about a "great, great horse" he heard, but that was not "coming for him." "He laughed and said he would not go with it because he 'was not ready yet.' Some scrap of talk he had overheard from us," she added, "when we discussed the traffic once. . . ."

"But you heard nothing?" he repeated almost impatiently.

No, she had heard nothing. After all, then, he *had* dozed a moment in his chair. . . .

Four weeks later Jack, entirely convalescent, was playing a restricted game of hide-and-seek with his sister in the flat. It was really a forbidden joy, owing to noise and risk of breakages, but he had unusual privileges after his grave illness. It was dusk. The lamps in the street were being lit. "Quietly, remember; your mother's resting in her room," were the father's orders. She had just returned from a week by the sea, recuperating from the strain of nursing for so many nights. The traffic rolled and boomed along the streets below.

"Jack! Do come on and hide. It's your turn. I hid last."

But the boy was standing spellbound by the window, staring hard at something on the pavement. Sybil called and tugged in vain. Tears threatened. Jack would not budge. He declared he saw something.

"Oh, you're always seeing something. I wish you'd go and hide. It's only because you can't think of a good place, really."

"Look!" he cried in a voice of wonder. And as he said it his father rose quickly from his chair before the fire.

"Look!" the child repeated with delight and excitement. "It's a great big horse. And it's perfectly white all over." His sister joined him at the window. "Where? Where? I can't see it. Oh, *do* show me!"

Their father was standing close behind them now. "I heard it," he was whispering, but so low the children did not notice him. His face was the colour of chalk.

"Straight in front of our door, stupid! Can't you see it? Oh, I do wish it had come for me. It's *such* a beauty!" And he clapped his hands with pleasure and excitement. "Quick, quick! It's going away again!"

But while the children stood half-squabbling by the window, their father leaned over a sofa in the adjoining room above a figure whose heart in sleep had quietly stopped its beating. The great white horse had come. But this time he had not only heard its wonderful arrival. He had also heard it go. It seemed he heard the awful hoofs beat down the sky, far, far away, and very swiftly, dying into silence, finally up among the stars.

The Whisperers

To be too impressionable is as much a source of weakness as to be hyper-sensitive: so many messages come flooding in upon one another that confusion is the result; the mind chokes, imagination grows congested.

Jones, as an imaginative writing man, was well aware of this, yet could not always prevent for if he dulled his mind to one impression, he ran the risk of blunting it to all. To guard his main idea, and picket its safe conduct through the seethe of additions that instantly flocked to join it, was a psychological puzzle that sometimes overtaxed his powers of critical selection. He prepared for it, however. An editor would ask him for a story—"about five thousand words, you know"; and Jones would answer, "I'll send it you with pleasure—when it comes." He knew his difficulty too well to promise more.

Ideas were never lacking, but their length of treatment belonged to machinery he could not coerce. They were alive; they refused to come to heel to suit mere editors. Midway in a tale that started crystal clear and definite in its original germ, would pour a flood of new impressions that either smothered the first conception, or developed it beyond recognition. Often a short story exfoliated in this bursting way beyond his power to stop it. He began one, never knowing where it would lead him. It was ever an adventure. Like Jack the Giant Killer's beanstalk it grew secretly in the night, fed by everything he read, saw felt, or heard. Jones was too impressionable; he received too many impressions, and too easily.

For this reason, when working at a definite, short idea, he preferred an empty room, without pictures, furniture, books, or anything suggestive, and with a skylight that shut out scenery—just ink, blank paper, and the clear picture in his mind. His own interior, unstimulated by the geysers of external life, he made some pretence of regulating; though even under these favourable conditions the matter was not too easy, so prolifically does a sensitive mind engender.

His experience in the empty room of the carpenter's house was a curious case in point—in the little Jura village where his cousin lived to educate his children.

"We're all in a pension above the Post Office here," the cousin wrote, "but just now the house is full, and besides is rather noisy. I've taken an attic room for you at the carpenter's near the forest. Some things of mine have been stored there all the winter, but I moved the cases out this morning. was There's a bed, writing-table, wash-hand-stand, sofa, and a skylight window—otherwise empty, as I know you prefer it. You can have your meals with us," etc.

And this just suited Jones, who had six weeks' work on hand for which he needed empty solitude. His "idea" slight and very tender; accretions would easily smother clear presentment; its treatment must be delicate, simple, unconfused.

The room really was an attic, but large, wide, high. He heard the wind rush past the skylight when he went to bed. When the cupboard was open, he heard the wind there too, washing the outer walls and tiles. From his pillow he saw a patch of stars peep down upon him. Jones knew the mountains and the woods were close, but he could not see them. Better still, he could not smell them. And he went to bed dead tired, full of his theme for work next morning.

He saw it to the end. He could almost have promised five thousand words. With the dawn he would be up and "at it," for he usually woke very early, his mind surcharged, as though subconsciousness had matured the material in sleep. Cold bath, a cup of tea, and then—his writing-table; and the quicker he could reach the writing-table the richer was the content of imaginative thought. What had puzzled him the night before was invariably cleared up in the morning. Only illness could interfere with the process and routine of it.

But this time it was otherwise. He woke, and instantly realised, with a shock of surprise and disappointment, that his mind was-groping. It was—groping for his little lost idea. There was nothing physically wrong with him; he felt rested, fresh, clear-headed; but his brain was searching, searching, moreover, in a crowd. Trying to seize hold of the train it had relinquished several hours ago, it caught at an evasive, empty shell. The idea had utterly changed; or rather it seemed smothered by a host of new impressions that came pouring in upon it—new modes of treatment, points of view, in fact development. In the light of these extensions and novel aspects, his original idea had altered beyond recognition. The germ had marvellously exfoliated, so that a whole volume could alone express it. An army of fresh suggestions clamoured for expression. His subconsciousness had grown thick with life; it surged—active, crowded, tumultuous.

And the darkness puzzled him. He remembered the absence of accustomed windows, but it was only when the candle-light brought close the face of his watch, with two o'clock upon it, that he heard the sound of confused whispering in the corners of the room, and realised with a little twinge of fear that those who whispered had just been standing beside his very bed. The room was full.

Though the candle-light proclaimed it empty—bare walls, bare floor, five pieces of unimaginative furniture, and fifty stars peeping through the skylight—it was undeniably thronged with living people whose minds had called him out of heavy sleep. The whispers, of course, died off into the wind that swept the roof and skylight; but the Whisperers remained. They had been trying to get at him; waking suddenly, he had caught them in the very act. . . . And all had brought new interpretations with them; his thought had fundamentally altered; the original idea was snowed under; new images brimmed his mind, and his brain was working as it worked under the high pressure of creative moments.

Jones sat up, trembling a little, and stared about him into the empty room that yet was densely packed with these invisible Whisperers. And he realised this astonishing thing—that he was the object of their deliberate assault, and that scores of other minds, deep, powerful, very active minds, were thundering and beating upon the doors of his imagination.

The onset of them was terrific and bewildering, the attack of aggressive ideas obliterating his original story beneath a flood of new suggestions. Inspiration had become suddenly torrential yet so vast as to be unwieldy, incoherent, useless. It was like the tempest of images that fever brings. His first conception seemed no longer "delicate," but petty. It had turned unreal and tiny, compared with this enormous choice of treatment extension, development, that now overwhelmed his throbbing brain.

Fear caught vividly at him, as he searched the empty attic-room in vain for explanation. There was absolutely nothing to produce this tempest of new impressions. People seemed talking to him all together, jumbled somewhat, but insistently. It was obsession, rather than inspiration; and so bitingly, dreadfully real.

"Who are you all?" his mind whispered to blank walls and vacant corners.

Back from the shouting floor and ceiling came the chorus of images that stormed and clamoured for expression. Jones lay still and listened; he let them come. There was nothing else to do. He lay fearful, negative, receptive. It was all too big for him to manage, set to some scale of high achievement that submerged his own small powers. It came, too, in a series of impressions, all separate, yet all somehow interwoven.

In vain he tried to sort them out and sift them. As well sort out waves upon an agitated sea. They were too self-assertive for direction or control. Like wild animals, hungry, thirsty, ravening, they rushed from every side and fastened on his mind.

Yet he perceived them in a certain sequence. For, first, the unfurnished attic-chamber was full of human passion, of love and hate, revenge and wicked cunning, of jealousy, courage, cowardice, of every vital human emotion ever longed for, enjoyed, or frustrated, all clamouring for—expression.

Flaming across and through these, incongruously threaded in and out, ran next a yearning softness of incredible beauty that sighed in the empty spaces of his heart, pleading for impossible fulfilment.

And, after these, carrying both one and other upon their surface, huge questions flashed and dived and thundered in a patterned, wild entanglement, calling to be unravelled and made straight. Moreover, with every set came a new suggested treatment of the little clear idea he had taken to bed with him five hours before.

Jones adopted each in turn. Imagination writhed and twisted beneath the stress of all these potential modes of expression he must choose between. His small idea exfoliated into many volumes, work enough to fill a dozen lives. It was most gorgeously exhilarating, though so hopelessly unmanageable. He felt like many minds in one. . . .

Then came another chain of impressions, violent, yet steady owing to their depth; the voices, questions, pleadings turned to pictures; and he saw, struggling through the deeps of him, enormous quantities of people, passing along like rivers, massed, herded, swayed here and there by some outstanding figure of command who directed them like flowing water. They shrieked, and fought, and battled, then sank out of sight, huddled and destroyed in—blood.

And their places were taken instantly by white crowds with shining eyes, and yearning in their faces, who climbed precipitous heights towards some Radiance that kept ever out of sight, like sunrise behind mountains that clouds then swallow. . . . The pelt and thunder of images was destructive in its torrent; his little, first idea was drowned and wrecked. . . . . . . Jones sank back exhausted, utterly dismayed. He gave up all attempt to make selection.

The driving storm swept through him, on and on, now waxing, now waning, but never growing less, and apparently endless as the sky. It rushed in circles, like the turning of a giant wheel. All the activities that human minds have ever battled with since thought began came booming, crashing, straining for expression against the imaginative stuff whereof his mind was built. The walls began to yield and settle. It was like the chaos that madness brings. He did not struggle against it; he let it come, lying open and receptive, pliant and plastic to every detail of the vast invasion.

And the only time he attempted a complete obedience, reaching out for the pencil and notebook that lay beside his bed, he desisted instantly again, sinking back upon his pillows with a kind of frightened laughter. For the tempest seemed then to knock him down and bruise his very brain. Inextricable confusion caught him. He might as well have tried to make notes of the entire Alexandrian Library in half an hour.

Then, most singular of all, as he felt the sleep of exhaustion fall upon his tired nerves, he heard that deep, prodigious sound. All that had preceded, it gathered marvellously in, mothering it with a sweetness that seemed to his imagination like some harmonious, geometrical skein including all the activities men's minds have ever known. Faintly he realised it only, discerned from infinitely far away. Into the streams of apparent contradiction that warred so strenuously about him, it seemed to bring some hint of unifying, harmonious explanation. . . And, here and there, as sleep buried him, he imagined that chords lay threaded along strings of cadences, breaking sometimes even into melody—music that rose everywhere from life and wove Thought into a homogeneous Whole. . . . .

Sleep well? "his cousin inquired, when he appeared very late next day for *déjeuner.* "Think you'l be able to work in that room all right?"

"I slept, yes, thanks," said Jones. "No doubt I shall work there right enough—when I'm rested. By the bye," he asked presently, "what has the attic been used for lately? What's been in it, I mean?"

"Books, only books," was the reply. "I've stored my 'library' there for months, without a chance of using it. I move about so much, you see. Five hundred books were taken out just before you came. I often think," he added lightly, "that when books are unopened like that for long, the minds that wrote them must get restless and—"

"What sort of books were they?" Jones interrupted.

"Fiction, poetry, philosophy, history, religion, music. I've got two hundred books on music alone."

The Wings of Horus

Binovitch had the bird in him somewhere: in his features, certainly, with his piercing eye and hawk-like nose; in his movements, with his quick way of flitting, hopping, darting; in the way he perched on the edge of a chair; in the manner he pecked at his food; in his twittering, high-pitched voice as well; and, above all, in his mind. He skimmed all subjects and picked their heart out neatly, as a bird skims lawn or air to snatch its prey, He had the bird's-eye view of everything. He loved birds and understood them instinctively; could imitate their whistling notes with astonishing accuracy. Their one quality he had not was poise and balance. He was a nervous little man; he was neurasthenic. And he was in Egypt by doctor's orders.

Such imaginative, unnecessary ideas he had! Such uncommon beliefs!

"The old Egyptians," he said laughingly, yet with a touch of solemn conviction in his manner, "were a great people. Their consciousness was different from ours. The bird idea, for instance, conveyed a sense of deity to them—of bird deity, that is: they had sacred birds—hawks, ibis, and so forth—and worshiped them." And he put his tongue out as though to say with challenge, "Ha, ha!"

"They also worshiped cats and crocodiles and cows," grinned Palazov. Binovitch seemed to dart across the table at his adversary. His eyes flashed: his nose pecked the air. Almost one could imagine the beating of his angry wings.

"Because everything alive," he half screamed, "was a symbol of some spiritual power to them. Your mind is as literal as a dictionary and as incoherent. Pages of ink without connected meaning! Verb always in the infinitive! If you were an old Egyptian, you—you—" he flashed and spluttered, his tongue shot out again, his keen eyes blazed—"you might take all those words and spin them into a great interpretation of life, a cosmic romance, as they did. Instead, you get the bitter, dead taste of ink in your mouth, and spit it over us like that"—he made a quick movement of his whole body as a bird that shakes itself—"in empty phrases."

Khilkoff ordered another bottle of champagne, while Vera, his sister, said half nervously, "Let's go for a drive; it's moonlight." There was enthusiasm at once. Another of the party called the headwaiter and told him to pack food and drink in baskets. It was only eleven o'clock. They would drive out into the desert, have a meal at two in the morning, tell stories, sing, and see the dawn.

It was in one of those cosmopolitan hotels in Egypt which attract the ordinary tourists as well as those who are doing a "cure," and all these Russians were ill with one thing or another. All were ordered out for their health, and all were the despair of their doctors. They were as unmanageable as a bazaar and as incoherent. Excess and bed were their routine. They lived, but none of them got better. Equally, none of them got angry. They talked in this strange personal way without a shred of malice or offense.

The English, French, and Germans in the hotel watched them with remote amazement, referring to them as "that Russian lot." Their energy was elemental. They never stopped. They merely disappeared when the pace became too fast, then reappeared again after a day or two, and resumed their "living" as before. Binovitch, despite his neurasthenia, was the life of the party. He was also a special patient of Dr. Plitzinger, the famous psychiatrist, who took a peculiar interest in his case. It was not surprising. Binovitch was a man of unusual ability and of genuine, deep culture. But there was something more about him that stimulated curiosity. There was this striking originality. He said and did surprising things.

"I could fly if I wanted to," he said once when the airmen came to astonish the natives with their biplanes over the desert, "but without all that machinery and noise. It's only a question of believing and understanding—"

"Show us!" they cried. "Let's see you fly!"

"He's got it! He's off again! One of his impossible moments."

These occasions when Binovitch let himself go always proved wildly entertaining. He said monstrously incredible things as though he really did believe them. They loved his madness, for it gave them new sensations.

"It's only levitation, after all, this flying," he exclaimed, shooting out his tongue between the words, as his habit was when excited; "and what is levitation but a power of the air? None of you can hang an orange in space for a second, with all your scientific knowledge; but the moon is always levitated perfectly. And the stars. D'you think they swing on wires? What raised the enormous stones of ancient Egypt? D'you really believe it was heaped-up sand and ropes and clumsy leverage and all our weary and laborious mechanical contrivances? Bah! It was levitation. It was the powers of the air. Believe in those powers, and gravity becomes a mere nursery trick—true where it is, but true nowhere else. To know the fourth dimension is to step out of a locked room and appear instantly on the roof or in another country altogether. To know the powers of the air, similarly, is to annihilate what you call weight—and fly."

"Show us, show us!" they cried, roaring with delighted laughter.

"It's a question of belief," he repeated, his tongue appearing and disappearing like a pointed shadow. "It's in the heart; the power of the air gets into your whole being. Why should I show you? Why should I ask my deity to persuade your scoffing little minds by any miracle? For it *is* deity, I tell you, and nothing else. I *know* it. Follow one idea like that, as I follow my bird idea—follow it with the impetus and undeviating concentration of a projectile—and you arrive at power. You know deity—the bird idea of deity, that is. *They* knew that. The old Egyptians knew it."

"Oh, show us, show us!" they shouted impatiently, wearied of his nonsense-talk. "Get up and fly! Levitate yourself, as they did! Become a star!"

Binovitch turned suddenly very pale, and an odd light shone in his keen brown eyes. He rose slowly from the edge of the chair where he was perched. Something about him changed. There was silence instantly.

"I *will* show you" he said calmly, to their intense amazement; "not to convince your disbelief, but to prove it to myself. For the powers of the air are with me here. I believe. And Horus, great falcon-headed symbol, is my patron god."

The suppressed energy in his voice and manner was indescribable. There was a sense of lifting, upheaving power about him. He raised his arms; his face turned upward; he inflated his lungs with a deep, long breath, and his voice broke into a kind of singing cry, half-prayer, half-chant:

"*O Horus,*

191

Bright-eyed deity of wind,

Feather my soul (Russian untranslatable. The phrase means, "Give my life wings.")

Through earth's thick air.
To know thy awful swiftness—"

He broke off suddenly. He climbed lightly and swiftly upon the nearest table—it was in a deserted cardroom, after a game in which he had lost more pounds than there are days in the year—and leaped into the air. He hovered a second, spread his arms and legs in space, appeared to float a moment, then buckled, rushed down and forward, and dropped in a heap upon the floor, while everyone roared with laughter.

But the laughter died out quickly, for there was something in his wild performance that was peculiar and unusual. It was uncanny, not quite natural. His body had seemed, as with Mordkin and Nijinski, literally to hang upon the air a moment. For a second he gave the distressing impression of overcoming gravity. There was a touch in it of that faint horror which appals by its very vagueness. He picked himself up unhurt, and his face was as grave as a portrait in the academy, but with a new expression in it that everybody noticed with this strange, half-shocked amazement. And it was this expression that extinguished the claps of laughter as wind that takes away the sound of bells. Like many ugly men, he was an inimitable actor, and his facial repertory was endless and incredible. But this was neither acting nor clever manipulation of expressive features. There was something in his curious Russian physiognomy that made the heart beat slower. And that was why the laughter died away so suddenly.

"You ought to have flown farther," cried someone. It expressed what all had felt.

"Icarus didn't drink champagne," another replied, with a laugh; but nobody laughed with him.

"You went too near to Vera" said Palazov, "and passion melted the wax." But his face twitched oddly as he said if. There was something he did not understand, and so heartily disliked.

The strange expression on the features deepened. It was arresting in a disagreeable, almost in a horrible, way. The talk stopped dead; all stared; there was a feeling of dismay in everybody's heart, yet unexplained. Some lowered their eyes, or else looked stupidly elsewhere; but the women of the party felt a kind of fascination. Vera, in particular, could not move her sight away. The joking reference to his passionate admiration for her passed unnoticed. There was a general and individual sense of shock. And a chorus of whispers rose instantly;

"Look at Binovitch! What's happened to his face?"

"He's changed—he's changing!"

"God! Why he looks like a—bird!"

But no one laughed. Instead, they chose the names of birds—hawk, eagle, even owl. The figure of a man leaning against the edge of the door, watching them closely, they did not notice. He had been passing down the corridor, had looked in unobserved, and then had paused. He had seen the whole performance. He watched Binovitch narrowly, now with calm, discerning eyes. It was Dr. Plitzinger, the great psychiatrist.

For Binovitch had picked himself up from the floor in a way that was oddly self-possessed, and precluded the least possibility of the ludicrous. He looked neither foolish nor abashed. He looked surprised, but also, he looked half angry and half frightened. As someone had said, he "ought to have flown farther," That was the incredible impression his acrobatics had produced—incredible, yet somehow actual. This uncanny idea prevailed, as at a *séance* where nothing genuine is expected to happen, and something genuine, after all, does happen. There was no pretence in this: Binovitch had flown.

And now he stood there, white in the face—with terror and with anger white. He looked extraordinary, this little, neurasthenic Russian, but he looked at the same time half terrific. Another thing, not commonly experienced by men, was in him, breaking out of him, affecting *directly* the minds of his companions. His mouth opened; blood and fury shone in his blazing eyes; his tongue shot out like an ant-eater's, though even in that the comic had no place. His arms were spread like flapping wings, and his voice rose dreadfully:

"He failed me, he failed me!" he tried to bellow, "Horus, my falcon-headed deity, my power of the air, deserted me! Hell take him! hell burn his wings and blast his piercing sight! Hell scorch him into dust for his false prophecies! I curse him—I curse Horus!"

The voice that should have roared across the silent room emitted, instead, this high-pitched, birdlike scream. The added touch of sound, the reality it lent, was ghastly. Yet it was marvellously done and acted. The entire thing was a bit of instantaneous inspiration—his voice, his words, his gestures, his whole wild appearance. Only—here was the reality that caused the sense of shock—the expression on his altered features was genuine. *That* was not assumed. There was something new and alien in him, something cold and difficult to human life, something alert and swift and cruel, of another element than earth. A strange, rapacious grandeur had leaped upon the struggling features. The face looked hawk-like.

And he came forward suddenly and sharply toward Vera, whose fixed, staring eyes had never once ceased watching him with a kind of anxious and devouring pain in them. She was both drawn and beaten back. Binovitch advanced on tiptoe. No doubt he still was acting, still pretending this mad nonsense that he worshiped Horus, the falcon-headed deity of forgotten days, and that Horus had failed him in his hour of need; but somehow there was just a hint of too much reality in the way he moved and looked.

The girl, a little creature, with fluffy golden hair, opened her lips; her cigarette fell to the floor; she shrank back; she looked for a moment like some smaller, coloured bird trying to escape from a great pursuing hawk; she screamed. Binovitch, his arms wide, his bird-like face thrust forward, had swooped upon her. He leaped. Almost he caught her.

No one could say exactly what happened. Play, become suddenly and unexpectedly too real, contuses the emotions. The change of key was swift. From fun to terror is a dislocating jolt upon the mind. Someone—it was Khilkoff, the brother—upset a chair; everybody spoke, at once; everybody stood up. An unaccountable feeling of disaster was in the air, as with those drinkers' quarrels that blaze out from nothing, and end in a pistol-shot and death, no one able to explain clearly how it came about. It was the silent, watching figure in the doorway who saved the situation.

Before anyone had noticed his approach, there he was among the group, laughing, talking, applauding—between Binovitch and Vera. He was vigorously patting his patient on the back, and his voice rose easily above the general clamour. He was a strong, quiet personality; even in his laughter there was authority. And his laughter now was the only sound in the room, as though by his mere presence peace and harmony were restored. Confidence came with him. The noise subsided; Vera was in her chair again. Khilkoff poured out a glass of wine, for the great man.

"The *Czar!*" said Plitzinger, sipping his champagne, while all stood up, delighted with his compliment and tact. "And to your opening night with the Russian ballet," he added quickly a second toast, "or to your first performance at the Moscow Théâtre des Arts!" Smiling significantly, he glanced at Binovitch; he clinked glasses with him. Their arms were already linked, but it was Palazov who noticed that the doctor's fingers seemed rather tight upon the creased black coat. All drank, looking with laughter, yet with a touch of respect toward Binovitch, who stood there dwarfed beside the stalwart German, and suddenly as meek and subdued as any mole. Apparently, the abrupt change of key had taken his mind successfully off something else.

"Of course—'The Fire-Bird,'" exclaimed the little man, mentioning the famous Russian ballet. "The very thing!" he exclaimed. "For *us*," he added, looking with devouring eyes at Vera, He was greatly pleased. He began talking vociferously about dancing and the rationale of dancing. They told him he was an undiscovered master. He was delighted. He winked at Vera and touched her glass again with his. "We'll make our *début* together," he cried. "We'll begin at Covent Garden, in London. I'll design the dresses and the posters 'The Hawk and the Dove!' *Magnifique*! I in dark grey, and you in blue and gold! Ah, dancing, you know, is sacred. The little self is lost, absorbed. It is ecstasy, it is divine. And dancing in air—the passion of the birds and stars—ah! they are the movements of the gods. You know deity that way—by living it."

He went on and on. His entire being had shifted with a leap upon this new subject. The idea of realising divinity by dancing it absorbed him. The party discussed it with him as though nothing else existed in the world, all sitting now and talking eagerly together. Vera took the cigarette he offered her, lighting it from his own; their fingers touched; he was as harmless and normal as a retired diplomat in a drawing-room. But it was Plitzinger whose subtle manoeuvring had accomplished the change so cleverly, and it was Plitzinger who presently suggested a game of billiards, and led him off, full now of a fresh enthusiasm for cannons, balls, and pockets, into another room. They departed arm in arm, laughing and talking together.

Their departure, it seemed, made no great difference. Vera's eyes watched him out of sight, then turned to listen to Baron Minski, who was describing with gusto how he caught wolves alive for coursing purposes. The speed and power of the wolf, he said, was impossible to realise; the force of their awful leap, the strength of their teeth, which could bite through metal stirrup-fastenings. He showed a scar on his arm and another on his lip. He was telling truth, and everybody listened with deep interest. The narrative lasted perhaps ten minutes or more, when Minski abruptly stopped. He had come to an end; he looked about him; he saw his glass, and emptied it. There was a general pause.

Another subject did not at once present itself. Sighs were heard; several fidgeted; fresh cigarettes were lighted. But there was no sign of boredom, for where one or two Russians are gathered together there is always life. They produce gaiety and enthusiasm as wind produces waves. Like great children, they plunge whole-heartedly into whatever interest presents itself at the moment. There is a kind of uncouth gambolling in their way of taking life. It seems as if they are always fighting that deep, underlying, national sadness which creeps into their very blood.

"Midnight!" then exclaimed Palazov, abruptly, looking at his watch; and the others fell instantly to talking about that watch, admiring it and asking questions. For the moment that very ordinary timepiece became the centre of observation. Palazov mentioned the price. "It never stops," he said proudly, "not even under water." He looked up at everybody, challenging admiration. And he told how, at a country house, he made a bet that he would swim to a certain island in the lake, and won the bet. He and a girl were the winners, but as it was a horse, they had bet, he got nothing out of it for himself, giving the horse to her. It was a genuine grievance in him. One felt he could have cried as he spoke of it. "But the watch went all the time," he said delightedly, holding the gun-metal object in his hand to show, "and I was twelve minutes in the water with my clothes on."

Yet this fragmentary talk was nothing but pretence. The sound of clicking billiard-balls was audible from the room at the end of the corridor. There was another pause. The pause, however, was intentional. It was not vacuity of mind or absence of ideas that caused it. There was another subject, an unfinished subject that each member of the group was still considering. Only no one cared to begin about it till at last, unable to resist the strain any longer, Palazov turned to Khilkoff, who was saying he would take a "whisky-soda," as the champagne was too sweet, and whispered something beneath his breath; whereupon Khilkoff, forgetting his drink, glanced at his sister, shrugged his shoulders, and made a curious grimace, "He's all right now,"—his reply was just audible—"he's with Plitzinger." He cocked his head sidewise to indicate that the clicking of the billiard-balls still was going on.

The subject was out: all turned their heads; voices hummed and buzzed; questions were asked and answered or half answered; eyebrows were raised, shoulders shrugged, hands spread out expressively. There came into the atmosphere a feeling of presentiment, of mystery, or things half understood; primitive, buried instinct stirred a little, the kind of racial dread of vague emotions that might gain the upper hand if encouraged. They shrank from looking something in the face, while yet this unwelcome influence drew closer round them all. They discussed Binovitch and his astonishing performance. Pretty little Vera listened with large and troubled eyes, though saying nothing. The Arab waiter had put out the lights in the corridor, and only a cluster burned now above their heads, leaving their faces in shadow. In the distance the clicking of the billiard-balls still continued.

"It was not play; it was real," exclaimed Minski, vehemently. "I can catch wolves," he blurted; "but birds—ugh!—and human birds!" He was half inarticulate. He had witnessed something he could not understand, and it had touched instinctive terror in him, "It was the way he leaped that put the wolf first into my mind, only it was not a wolf at all." The others agreed and disagreed.

"It was play at first, but it was reality at the end," another whispered; "and it was no animal he mimicked, but a bird of prey at that!"

Vera thrilled. In the Russian woman hides that touch of savagery which loves to be caught, mastered, swept helplessly away, captured utterly and deliciously by the one strong enough to do it thoroughly. She left her chair and sat down beside an older woman in the party, who took her arm quietly at once. Her little face wore a perplexed expression, mournful, yet somehow wild. It was clear that Binovitch was not indifferent to her.

"It's become an *idée fixe* with him," this older woman said. "The bird idea lives in his mind. He lives it in his imagination. Ever since that time at Edfu, when he pretended to worship the great stone falcons outside the temple—the Horus figures—he's been full of it." She stopped. The way Binovitch had behaved at Edfu was better left unmentioned at the moment, perhaps. A slight shiver ran round the listening group, each one waiting for someone else to focus their emotion, and so explain it by saying the convincing thing. Only no one ventured. Then Vera abruptly gave a little jump.

"Hark!" she exclaimed, in a *staccato* whisper, speaking for the first time. She sat bolt upright. She was listening. "Hark!" she repeated. "There it is again, but nearer than before. It's coming closer. I hear it." She trembled. Her voice, her manner, above all her great staring eyes, startled everybody. No one spoke for several seconds; all listened.

The clicking of the billiard-balls had ceased. The halls and corridors lay in darkness, and gloom was over the big hotel. Everybody else was in bed.

"Hear what?" asked the older woman, soothingly, yet with a perceptible quaver in her voice, too. She was aware that the girl's arm shook upon her own.

"Do you not hear it, too?" the girl whispered.

All listened without speaking. All watched her paling face. Something wonderful, yet half terrible, seemed in the air about them. There was a dull murmur, audible, faint, remote, its direction hard to tell. It had come suddenly from nowhere. They shivered. That strange racial thrill again passed into the group, unwelcome, unexplained. It was aboriginal; it belonged to the unconscious primitive mind, half childish, half terrifying,

"*What* do you hear?" her brother asked angrily—the irritable anger of nervous fear.

"When he came at me," she answered very low, "I heard it first I hear it now again. He's coming."

And at that minute, out or the dark mouth of the corridor, emerged two human figures, Plitzinger and Binovitch Their game was over; they were going up to bed. They passed the open door of the card-room. But Binovitch was being half dragged, half restrained, for he was apparently attempting to run down the passage with flying, dancing leaps. He bounded. It was like a huge bird trying to rise for flight, while his companion kept him down, by force upon the earth.

As they entered the strip of light, Plitzinger changed his own position, placing himself swiftly between his companion and the group in the dark corner of the room. He hurried Binovitch along as though he sheltered him from view. They passed into the shadows down the passage. They disappeared. And everyone looked significantly, questioningly, at his neighbour, though at first saying no word. It seemed a curious disturbance of the air had followed them.

Vera was the first to open her lips. "You heard it *then*," she said breathlessly, her face whiter than the ceiling.

"Damn!" exclaimed her brother, furiously. "It was wind against the outside walls—wind in the desert. The sand is driving."

Vera looked at him. She shrank closer against the side of the older woman, whose arm was tight about her.

"It was *not* wind," she whispered simply. She paused. All waited uneasily for the completion of her sentence. They stared into her face like peasants who expected a miracle.

"Wings," she whispered. "It was the sound of enormous wings."

★★★★★★★★★★★★

And at four o'clock in the morning, when they all returned exhausted from their excursion into the desert, little Binovitch was sleeping soundly and peacefully in his bed. They passed his door on tiptoe. But he did not hear them. He was dreaming. His spirit was at Edfu, experiencing with that ancient deity who was master of all flying life those strange enjoyments upon which his troubled heart was passionately set. Safe with that mighty falcon whose powers his lips had scorned a few hours before, his soul, released in vivid dream, went sweetly flying.

It was amazing, it was gorgeous, he skimmed the Nile at lightning speed. Dashing down headlong from the height of the great Pyramid, he chased with faultless accuracy a little dove that sought vainly to hide from his terrific pursuit beneath the palm-trees. For what he loved must worship where he worshiped, and the majesty of those tremendous effigies had fired his imagination to the creative point where expression was imperative.

Then suddenly, at the very moment of delicious capture, the dream turned horrible, becoming awful with the nightmare touch. The sky lost all its blue and sunshine. Far, far below him the little dove enticed him into nameless depths, so that he flew faster and faster, yet never fast enough to overtake it. Behind him came a great thing down the air, black, hovering, with gigantic wings outstretched. It had terrific eyes, and the beating of its feathers stole his wind away. It followed him, crowding space. He was aware of a colossal beak, curved like a simitar and pointed wickedly like a tooth of iron. He dropped. He faltered. He tried to scream.

Through empty space he fell, caught by the neck. The huge falcon was upon him. The talons were in his heart. And in sleep he remembered then that he had cursed He recalled his reckless language. The curse of the ignorant is meaningless; that of the worshiper is real. This attack was on his soul. He had invoked it. He realised next, with a touch of ghastly horror, that the dove he chased was, after all, the bait that had lured him purposely to destruction, and awoke with a suffocating terror upon him, and his entire body bathed in icy perspiration. Outside the open window he heard a sound of wings retreating with powerful strokes into the surrounding darkness of the sky.

The nightmare made its impression upon Binovitch's impressionable and dramatic temperament. It aggravated his tendencies. He related it next day to Mme, de Drühn, the friend of Vera, telling it with that somewhat boisterous laughter some minds use to disguise less kind emotions. But he received no encouragement. The mood of the previous night was not recoverable; it was already ancient history. Russians never make the hand mistake of repeating a sensation till it is exhausted; they hurry on to novelties. Life flashes and rushes with them, never standing still for exposures before the cameras of their minds. Mme. de Drühn, however, took the trouble to mention the matter to Plitzinger, for Plitzinger, like Froud of Vienna, held that dreams revealed subconscious tendencies which sooner or later must betray themselves in action.

"Thank you for telling me," he smiled politely, "but I have already heard it from him." He watched her eyes a moment, really examining her soul. "Binovitch, you see," he continued, apparently satisfied with what he saw, "I regard as that rare phenomenon—a genius without an outlet. His spirit, intensely creative, finds no adequate expression. His power of production is enormous and prolific; yet he accomplishes nothing." He paused an instant. "Binovitch, therefore, is in danger of poisoning—himself." He looked steadily into her face, as a man who weighs how much he may confide. "Now," he continued, "*if* we can find an outlet for him, a field wherein his bursting imaginative genius can produce results—above all, *visible* results,"—he shrugged his shoulders—"the man is saved. Otherwise"—he looked extraordinarily impressive—"there is bound to be sooner or later—"

"Madness?" she asked very quietly.

"An explosion, let us say," he replied gravely, "For instance, take this Horus obsession of his, quite wrong archaeologically though it is. *Au fond* it is megalomania of a most unusual kind. His passionate interest, his love, his worship of birds, wholesome enough in itself, finds no satisfying outlet. A man who *really* loves birds neither keeps them in cages nor shoots them nor stuffs them. What, then, can he do? The commonplace bird-lover observes them through glasses, studies their habits, then writes a book about them. But a man like Binovitch, overflowing with this intense creative power of mind and imagination, is not content with that. He wants to know them from within.

"He wants to feel what they feel, to live their life. He wants to *become* them. You follow me? Not quite. Well, he seeks to be identified with the object of his sacred, passionate admiration. All genius seeks to know the thing itself from its own point of view. It desires union. That tendency, unrecognised by himself, perhaps, and therefore subconscious, hides in his very soul," He paused a moment. "And the sudden sight of those majestic figures at Edfu—that crystallisation of his *idée fixe* in granite—took hold of this excess in him, so to speak—and is now focusing it toward some definite act. Binovitch sometimes—feels himself a bird! You noticed what occurred last night?"

She nodded; a slight shiver passed over her.

"A most curious performance," she murmured; "an exhibition I never want to see again,"

"The most curious part," replied the doctor, coolly, "was its truth."

"Its truth!" she exclaimed beneath her breath. She was frightened by something in his voice and by the uncommon gravity in his eyes. It seemed to arrest her intelligence. She felt upon the edge of things beyond her. "You mean that Binovitch did for a moment—hang—in the air?" The other verb, the right one, she could not bring herself to use.

The great man's face was enigmatical. He talked to her sympathy, perhaps, rather than to her mind.

"Real genius," he said smilingly, "is as rare as talent, even great talent, is common. It means that the personality, if only for one second, becomes everything; becomes the universe; becomes the soul of the world. It gets the flash. It is identified with the universal life. Being everything and everywhere, all is possible to it—in that second of vivid realisation. It can brood with the crystal, grow with the plant, leap with the animal, fly with the bird; genius unifies all three. That is the meaning of 'creative,' It is faith. Knowing it, you can pass through fire and not be burned, walk on water and not sink, move a mountain, fly. Because you *are* fire, water, earth, air. Genius, you see, is madness in the magnificent sense of being superhuman. Binovitch has it."

He broke off abruptly, seeing he was not understood. Some great enthusiasm in him he deliberately suppressed.

"The point is," he resumed, speaking more carefully, "that we must try to lead this passionate constructive genius of the man into some human channel that will absorb it, and therefore render it harmless."

"He loves Vera," the woman said, bewildered, yet seizing this point correctly.

"But would he marry her?" asked Plitzinger at once.

"He is already married."

The doctor looked steadily at her a moment, hesitating whether he should utter all his thought.

"In that case," he said slowly after a pause, "it is better he or she should leave."

His tone and manner were exceedingly impressive.

"You mean there's danger?" she asked,

"I mean, rather," he replied earnestly, "that this great creative flood in him, so curiously focused now upon his Horus-falcon-bird idea, may result in some act of violence—"

"Which would be madness," she said, looking hard at him.

"Which would be disastrous," he corrected her. And then he added slowly, "Because in the mental moment of immense creation he might overlook material laws."

★★★★★★★★★★★★

The costume ball two nights later was a great success. Palazov was a Bedouin, and Khilkoff an Apache; Mme, de Drühn wore a national head-dress; Minski looked almost natural as Don Quixote; and the entire Russian "set" was cleverly, if somewhat extravagantly, dressed. But Binovitch and Vera were the most successful of all the two hundred dancers who took part. Another figure, a big man dressed as a Pierrot, also claimed exceptional attention, for though the costume was commonplace enough, there was something of dignity in his appearance that drew the eyes of all upon him. But he wore a mask, and his identity was not discoverable.

It was Binovitch and Vera, however, who must have won the prize, if prize there had been, for they not only looked their parts, but acted them as well. The former in his dark grey feathered tunic, and his falcon mask, complete even to the brown hooked beak and tufted talons, looked fierce and splendid. The disguise was so admirable, yet so entirely natural, that it was uncommonly seductive. Vera, in blue and gold, a charming head-dress of a dove upon her loosened hair, and a pair of little dove-pale wings fluttering from her shoulders, her tiny twinkling feet and slender ankles well visible, too, was equally successful and admired. Her large and timid eyes, her flitting movements, her light and dainty way of dancing—all added touches that made the picture perfect.

How Binovitch contrived his dress remained a mystery, for the layers of wings upon his back were real; the large black kites that haunt the Nile, soaring in their hundreds over Cairo and the bleak Mokattam Hills, had furnished them. He had procured them none knew how. They measured four feet across from tip to tip; they swished and rustled as he swept along; they were true falcons' wings. He danced with *Nautch*-girls and Egyptian princesses and Rumanian Gipsies; he danced well, with beauty, grace, and lightness.

But with Vera he did not dance at all; with her he simply flew. A kind of passionate abandon was in him as he skimmed the floor with her in a way that made everybody turn to watch them. They seemed to leave the ground together. It was delightful, an amazing sight; but it was peculiar. The strangeness of it was on many lips. Somehow its queer extravagance communicated itself to the entire ballroom. They became the centre of observation. There were whispers.

"There's that extraordinary bird-man! Look! He goes by like a hawk. And he's always after that dove-girl. How marvellously he does it! It's rather awful. Who is he? I don't envy *her*."

People stood aside when he rushed past. They got out of his way. He seemed forever pursuing Vera, even when dancing with another partner. Word passed from mouth to mouth. A kind of telepathic interest was established everywhere. It was a shade too real sometimes, something unduly earnest in the chasing wildness, something unpleasant. There was even alarm.

"It's rowdy; I'd rather not see it; it's quite disgraceful," was heard. "*I* think it's horrible; you can see she's terrified,"

And once there was a little scene, trivial enough, yet betraying this reality that many noticed and disliked. Binovitch came up to claim a dance, program clutched in his great tufted claws, and at the same moment the big Pierrot appeared abruptly round the corner with a similar claim. Those who saw it assert he had been waiting, and came on purpose, and that there was something protective and authoritative in his bearing. The misunderstanding was ordinary enough—both men had written her name against the dance—but "No, 13, Tango" also included the supper interval, and neither Hawk nor Pierrot would give way. They were very obstinate. Both men wanted her. It was awkward,

"The Dove shall decide between us," smiled the Hawk, politely, yet his taloned fingers working nervously. Pierrot, however, more experienced in the ways of dealing with women, or more bold, said suavely:

"I am ready to abide by her decision"—his voice poorly cloaked this aggravating authority, as though he had the right to her—"only I engaged this dance before his Majesty Horus appeared upon the scene at all, and therefore it is clear that Pierrot has the right of way."

At once, with a masterful air, he took her off. There was no withstanding him. He meant to have her and he got her. She yielded meekly. They vanished among the maze of coloured dancers, leaving the Hawk, disconsolate and vanquished, amid the titters of the

203

onlookers. His swiftness, as against this steady power, was of no avail.

It was then that the singular phenomenon was witnessed first. Those who saw it affirm that he changed absolutely into the part he played. It was dreadful; it was wicked. A frightened whisper ran about the rooms and corridors:

"An extraordinary thing is in the air!"

Some shrank away, while others nocked to see. There were those who swore that a curious, rushing sound was audible, the atmosphere visibly disturbed and shaken; that a shadow fell upon the spot the couple had vacated; that a cry was heard, a high, wild, searching cry: "Horus! brightest deity of wind," it began, then died away. One man was positive that the windows had been opened and that something had flown in. It was the obvious explanation. The thing spread horribly. As in a fire-panic, there was consternation and excitement. Confusion caught the feet of all the dancers. The music fumbled and lost time. The leading pair of tango-dancers halted and looked round, it seemed that everybody pressed back, hiding, shuffling, eager to see, yet more eager not to be seen, as though something dangerous, hostile, terrible, had broken loose. In rows against the wall, they stood. For a great space had made itself in the middle of the ballroom, and into this empty space appeared suddenly the Pierrot and the Dove.

It was like a challenge. A sound of applause, half voices, halt clapping of gloved hands, was heard. The couple danced exquisitely into the arena. All stared. There was an impression that a set piece had been prepared, and that this was its beginning. The music again took heart, Pierrot was strong and dignified, no whit nonplussed by this abrupt publicity. The Dove, though faltering, was deliciously obedient. They danced together like a single outline. She was captured utterly. And to the man who needed her the sight was naturally agonizing the protective way the Pierrot held her, the right and strength of it, the mastery, the complete possession.

"He's got her!" someone breathed too loud, uttering the thought of all. "Good thing it's not the Hawk!"

And, to the absolute amazement of the throng, this sight was then apparent. A figure dropped through space. That high, shrill cry again was heard;

"Feather my soul . . . to know thy awful swiftness!"

Its singing loveliness touched the heart, its appealing, passionate sweetness was marvellous, as from the gallery this figure of a man, dressed as a strong, dark bird, shot down with splendid grace and ease.

The feathers, swept; the wings spread out as sails that take the wind. Like a hawk that darts with unerring power and aim upon its prey, this thing of mighty wings rushed down into the empty space where the two danced. Observed by all, he entered, swooping beautifully, stretching his wings like any eagle. He dropped. He fixed his point of landing with consummate skill close beside the astonished dancers. He landed.

It happened with such swiftness it brought the dazzle and blindness as when lightning strikes. People in different parts of the room saw different details; a few saw nothing at all after the first startling shock, closing their eyes, or holding their arms before their faces as in self-protection. The touch of panic fear caught the room. The nameless thing that all the evening had been vaguely felt was come. It had suddenly materialised.

For this incredible thing occurred in the full blaze of light upon the open floor. Binovitch, grown in some sense formidable, opened his dark, big wings about the girl. The long grey feathers moved, causing powerful drafts of wind that made a rushing sound. An aspect of the terrible was in him, like an emanation. The great beaked head was poised to strike, the tufted claws were raised like fingers that shut and opened, and the whole presentiment of his amazing figure focused in an attitude of attack that was magnificent and terrible. No one who saw it doubted.

Yet there were those who swore that it was not Binovitch at all. but that another outline, monstrous and shadowy, towered above him, draping his lesser proportions with two colossal wings of darkness. That some touch of strange divinity lay in it may be claimed, however confused the wild descriptions afterward. For many lowered their heads and bowed their shoulders. There was awe. There was also terror. The onlookers swayed as though some power passed over them through the air.

A sound of wings was certainly in the room.

Then someone screamed; a shriek broke high and clear; and emotion, ordinary, human emotion, unaccustomed to terrific things, swept loose. The Hawk and Vera flew. Beaten back against the wall as by a stroke of whirlwind, the Pierrot staggered. He watched them go. Out of the lighted room they flew, out of the crowded human atmosphere, out of the heat and artificial light, the walled-in, airless halls that were a cage. All this they left behind. They seemed things of wind and air, made free happily of another element. Earth held them not. Toward the open night they raced with this extraordinary lightness as of birds, down the long corridor and on to the southern terrace, where great coloured curtains were hung suspended from the columns. A moment they were visible. Then the fringe of one huge curtain, lifted by the wind, showed their dark outline for a second against the starry sky. There was a cry, a leap. The curtain flapped again and closed. They vanished. And into the ballroom swept the cold draft of night air from the desert.

But three figures instantly were close upon their heels. The throng of half clawed, half-stupefied onlookers, it seemed, projected them as though by some explosive force. The general mass held back, but, like projectiles, these three flung themselves after the fugitives down the corridor at high speed—the Apache, Don Quixote, and, last of them, the Pierrot. For Khilkoff, the brother, and Karon Minski, the man who caught wolves alive, had been for some time keenly on the watch, while Dr. Plitzinger, reading the symptoms clearly, never far away, had been faithfully observant of every movement.

His mask tossed aside, the great psychiatrist was now recognised by all. They reached the parapet just as the curtain flapped back heavily into place; the next second all three were out of sight behind it. Khilkoff was first, however, urged forward at frantic speed by the warning words the duct or had whispered as they ran. Some thirty yards beyond the terrace was the brink of the crumbling cliff on which the great hotel was built, and there was a drop of sixty feet to the desert floor below. Only a low stone wall marked the edge.

Accounts varied, Khilkoff, it seems, arrived in time—in the nick of time—to seize his sister, virtually hovering on the brink. He heard the loose stones strike the sand below. There was no struggle, though it appears she did not thank him for his interference at first. In a sense she was beside—outside—herself. And he did a characteristic thing: he not only brought her back into the ballroom, but he *danced* her back. It was admirable. Nothing could have calmed the general excitement better.

The pair of them danced in together as though nothing was amiss. Accustomed to the strenuous practice of his Cossack regiment, this young cavalry officer's muscles were equal to the semi-dead weight in his arms. At most the onlookers thought her tired, perhaps. Confidence, was restored—such is the psychology of a crowd—and in the middle of a thrilling Viennese waltz, he easily smuggled her out of the room, administered brandy, and got her up to bed.

The absence of the Hawk, meanwhile, was hardly noticed; comments were made and then forgotten; it was Vera in whom the strange, anxious sympathy had centred. And, with her obvious safely, the moment of primitive, childish panic passed away. Don Quixote, too, was presently seen dancing gaily as though nothing untoward had happened; supper intervened; the incident was over; it had melted into the general wildness of the evening's irresponsibility. The fact that Pierrot did not appear again was noticed by no single person.

But Dr. Plitzinger was otherwise engaged, his heart and mind and soul all deeply exercised. A death-certificate is not always made out quite so simply as the public thinks. That Binovitch had died of suffocation in his swift descent through merely sixty feet of air was not conceivable; yet that his body lay so neatly placed upon the desert after such a fall was stranger still. It was not crumpled, it was not torn; no single bone was broken, no muscle wrenched; there was no bruise. There was no indenture in the sand. The figure lay side wise as though in sleep, no sign of violence visible anywhere, the dark wings folded as a great bird folds them when it creeps away to die in loneliness. Beneath the Horus mask the face was smiling. It seemed he had floated into death upon the element he loved.

And only Vera saw the enormous wings that, hovering invitingly above the dark abyss, bore him so softly into another world. Plitzinger, that is, saw them, too, but he said firmly that they belonged to the big black falcons that haunt the Mokattam Hills and roost upon these ridges, close beside the hotel, at night. Both he and Vera, however, agreed on one thing: the high, sharp cry in the air above them, wild and plaintive, was certainly the black kite's cry—the note, of the falcon that passionately seeks its mate. It was the pause of a second, when she stood to listen, that made her rescue possible. A moment later and she, too, would have flown to death with Binovitch.

Transition

John Mudbury was on his way home from the shops, his arms full of Christmas presents. It was after six o'clock and the streets were very crowded. He was an ordinary man, lived in an ordinary suburban flat, with an ordinary wife and four ordinary children. *He* did not think them ordinary, but everybody else did. He had ordinary presents for each one, a cheap blotter for his wife, a cheap air-gun for the eldest boy, and so forth. He was over fifty, bald, in an office, decent in mind and habits, of uncertain opinions, uncertain politics, and uncertain religion.

Yet he considered himself a decided, positive gentleman, quite unaware that the morning newspaper determined his opinions for the day. He just lived—from day to day. Physically, he was fit enough, except for a weak heart (which never troubled him); and his summer holiday was bad golf, while the children bathed and his wife read *Garvice* on the sands. Like the majority of men, he dreamed idly of the past, muddled away the present, and guessed vaguely—after imaginative reading on occasions—at the future.

"I'd like to survive all right," he said, "provided it's better than this," surveying his wife and children and thinking of his daily toil. "Otherwise——!" and he shrugged his shoulders as a brave man should.

He went to church regularly. But nothing in church *convinced* him that he did survive, just as nothing in church enticed him into hoping that he would. On the other hand, nothing in life persuaded him that he didn't, wouldn't, couldn't. "I'm an Evolutionist," he loved to say to thoughtful cronies (over a glass), having never heard that Darwinism had been questioned. . . .

And so, he came home gaily, happily, with his bunch of Christmas presents "for the wife and little ones," stroking himself upon their keen enjoyment and excitement. The night before he had taken "the wife" to see *Magic* at a select London theatre where the Intellectuals went—and had been extraordinarily stirred. He had gone question-ingly, yet expecting something out of the common. "It's *not* musical," he warned her, "nor farce, nor comedy, so to speak"; and in answer to her question as to what the Critics had said, he had wriggled, sighed, and put his gaudy necktie straight four times in quick succession. For no "Man in the Street," with any claim to self-respect, could be ex-pected to understand what the Critics had said, even if he understood the Play. And John had answered truthfully: "Oh, they just said things. But the theatre's always full—and that's the only test."

And just now, as he crossed the crowded Circus to catch his 'bus, it chanced that his mind (having glimpsed an advertisement) was full of this particular Play, or, rather, of the effect it had produced upon him at the time. For it had *thrilled* him—inexplicably: with its mar-vellous speculative hint, its big audacity, its alert and spiritual beauty. . . .Thought plunged to find something—plunged after this bizarre suggestion of a bigger universe, after this quasi-jocular suggestion that man is not the only—then dashed full-tilt against a sentence that memory thrust beneath his nose: "Science does *not* exhaust the Uni-verse"—and at the same time dashed full-tilt against destruction of another kind as well. . . .!

How it happened, he never exactly knew. He saw a Monster glar-ing at him with eyes of blazing fire. It was horrible! It rushed upon him. He dodged....Another Monster met him round the corner. Both came at him simultaneously. . . .He dodged again—a leap that might have cleared a hurdle easily, but was too late. Between the pair of them—his heart literally in his gullet—he was mercilessly caught. . Bones crunched. . . .There was a soft sensation, icy cold and hot as fire. Horns and voices roared. Battering-rams he saw, and a carapace of iron. . . .Then dazzling light. . . . "Always *face* the traffic!" he remem-bered with a frantic yell—and, by some extraordinary luck, escaped miraculously on to the opposite pavement. . . .

There was no doubt about it. By the skin of his teeth he had dodged a rather ugly death. . . . .he felt for his presents—all were safe. And then, instead of congratulating himself and taking breath, he hurried homewards—*on foot*, which proved that his mind had lost control a bit!—thinking only how disappointed the wife and children would have been if—if anything had happened. . . .Another thing he realised, oddly enough, was that he no longer really *loved* his wife, but had only great affection for her. What made him think of that, Heaven only knows, but he *did* think of it. He was an honest man without pretence. This came as a discovery somehow. He turned a moment, and saw the crowd gathered about the entangled taxicabs, policemen's helmets gleaming in the lights of the shop windows. . . .then hurried on again, his thoughts full of the joy his presents would give. . . . of the scampering children. . . .and of his wife—bless her silly heart!—eyeing the mysterious parcels. . . .

And, though he never could explain *how*, he presently stood at the door of the jail-like building that contained his flat, having walked the whole three miles! His thoughts had been so busy and absorbed that he had hardly noticed the length of weary trudge. . . . "Besides," he reflected, thinking of the narrow escape, "I've had a nasty shock. It was a d——d near thing, now I come to think of it. . . ." He did feel a bit shaky and bewildered. . . .Yet, at the same time, he felt extraordinarily jolly and light-hearted. . . .

He counted his Christmas parcels. . . .hugged himself in anticipatory joy. . . .and let himself in swiftly with his latchkey. "I'm late," he realised, "but when she sees the brown-paper parcels, she'll forget to say a word. God bless the old faithful soul." And he softly used the key a second time and entered his flat on tiptoe. . . .In his mind was the master impulse of that afternoon—the pleasure these Christmas presents would give his wife and children. . . .

He heard a noise. He hung up hat and coat in the pokey vestibule (they never called it "hall") and moved softly towards the parlour door, holding the packages behind him. Only of them he thought, not of himself—of his family, that is, not of the packages. Pushing the door cunningly ajar, he peeped in slyly. To his amazement, the room was full of people! He withdrew quickly, wondering what it meant. A party? And without his knowing about it! Extraordinary! . . . .Keen disappointment came over him. But, as he stepped back, the vestibule, he saw, was full of people too.

He was uncommonly surprised, yet somehow not surprised at all. People were congratulating him. There was a perfect mob of them. Moreover, he knew them all—vaguely remembered them, at least. And they all knew him.

"Isn't it a game?" laughed someone, patting him on the back. "*They* haven't the least idea. . . .!"

And the speaker—it was old John Palmer, the bookkeeper at the office—emphasised the "they."

"Not the least idea," he answered with a smile, saying something he didn't understand, yet knew was right.

His face, apparently, showed the utter bewilderment he felt. The shock of the collision had been greater than he realised evidently. His mind was wandering. . . .Possibly! Only the odd thing was—he had never felt so clear-headed in his life. Ten thousand things grew simple suddenly. But, how thickly these people pressed about him, and how—familiarly!

"My parcels," he said, joyously pushing his way across the throng. "These are Christmas presents I've bought for them." He nodded toward the room. "I've saved for weeks—stopped cigars and billiards and—and several other good things—to buy them."

"Good man!" said Palmer with a happy laugh. "It's the heart that counts."

Mudbury looked at him. Palmer had said an amazing truth, only—people would hardly understand and believe him. . . .Would they?

"Eh?" he asked, feeling stuffed and stupid, muddled somewhere between two meanings, one of which was gorgeous and the other stupid beyond belief.

"If you *please*, Mr. Mudbury, step inside. They are expecting you," said a kindly, pompous voice. And, turning sharply, he met the gentle, foolish eyes of Sir James Epiphany, a director of the Bank where he worked.

The effect of the voice was instantaneous from long habit.

"They are?" he smiled from his heart, and advanced as from the custom of many years. Oh, how happy and gay he felt! His affection for his wife was real. Romance, indeed, had gone, but he needed her—and she needed him. And the children—Milly, Bill, and Jean—he deeply loved them. Life *was* worth living indeed!

In the room was a crowd, but—an astounding silence. John Mudbury looked round him. He advanced towards his wife, who sat in the corner arm-chair with Milly on her knee. A lot of people talked and moved about. Momentarily the crowd increased. He stood in front of them—in front of Milly and his wife. And he spoke—holding out his packages. "It's Christmas Eve," he whispered shyly, "and I've—brought you something—something for everybody. Look!" He held the packages before their eyes.

"Of course, of course," said a voice behind him, "but you may hold them out like that for a century. They'll *never* see them!"

"Of course, they won't. But I love to do the old, sweet thing," replied John Mudbury—then wondered with a gasp of stark amazement why he said it.

"*I* think——" whispered Milly, staring round her.

"Well, *what* do you think?" her mother asked sharply. "You're always thinking something queer."

"I think," the child continued dreamily, "that Daddy's already here." She paused, then added with a child's impossible conviction, "I'm sure he is. I *feel* him."

There was an extraordinary laugh. Sir James Epiphany laughed. The others—the whole crowd of them—also turned their heads and smiled. But the mother, thrusting the child away from her, rose up suddenly with a violent start. Her face had turned to chalk. She stretched her arms out—into the air before her. She gasped and shivered. There was an awful anguish in her eyes.

"Look!" repeated John, "these are the presents that I brought."

But his voice apparently was soundless. And, with a spasm of icy pain, he remembered that Palmer and Sir James—some years ago— had died.

"It's magic," he cried, "but—I love you, Jinny—I love you—and— and I have always been true to you—as true as steel. We need each other—oh, can't you see—we go on together—you and I—for ever and ever——"

"*Think*," interrupted an exquisitely tender voice, "don't shout! *They* can't hear you—now." And, turning, John Mudbury met the eyes of Everard Minturn, their President of the year before. Minturn had gone down with the *Titanic*.

He dropped his parcels then. His heart gave an enormous leap of joy.

He saw her face—the face of his wife—look through him.

But the child gazed straight into his eyes. She *saw* him.

The next thing he knew was that he heard something tinkling. . . .far, far away. It sounded miles below him—inside him—he was sounding himself—all utterly bewildering—like a bell. It *was* a bell.

Milly stooped down and picked the parcels up. Her face shone with happiness and laughter. . . .

But a man came in soon after, a man with a ridiculous, solemn face, a pencil, and a notebook. He wore a dark blue helmet. Behind him came a string of other men. They carried something. . . .something. . . .he could not see exactly what it was. But when he pressed forward through the laughing throng to gaze upon it, he dimly made out two eyes, a nose, a chin, a deep red smear, and a pair of folded hands upon an overcoat. A woman's form fell down upon them then, and. .

. .he heard. . . .soft sounds of children weeping strangely. . . .and other sounds. . . .sounds as of familiar voices. . . .laughing. . . .laughing gaily.

"They'll join us presently. It goes like a flash. . . ."

And, turning with great happiness in his heart, he saw that Sir James had said it, holding Palmer by the arm as with some natural yet unexpected love of sympathetic friendship.

"Come on," said Palmer, smiling like a man who accepts a gift in universal fellowship, "let's help 'em. They'll never understand. . . .Still, we can always try."

The entire throng moved up with laughter and amusement. It was a moment of hearty, genuine life at last. Delight and Joy and Peace were everywhere.

Then John Mudbury realised the truth—that he was *dead*.

Two in One

Some idle talker, playing with half-truths, had once told him that he was too self-centred to fall into love out of himself; he was unwilling to lose himself in another; and that was the reason he had never married. But Le Maitre was not really more of an egoist than is necessary to make a useful man. A too selfless person is ever ineffective. The suggestion, nevertheless, had remained to distress, for he was no great philosopher—merely a writer of successful tales—tales of wild Nature chiefly; the "human interest" (a publisher's term) was weak; the great divine enigma of an undeveloped soul—certainly of a lover's or a woman's soul—had never claimed his attention enough, perhaps. He was somewhat too much detached from human life. Nature had laid so powerful a spell upon his heart...

"I hope she won't be late," ran the practical thought across his mind as he waited that early Sunday morning in the Great Central Station and reflected that it was the cleanest, brightest, and most airy terminus of all London. He had promised her the whole day out—a promise somewhat long neglected. He was not conscious of doing an unselfish act, yet on the whole, probably, he would rather—or just as soon—have been alone.

The air was fragrant, and the sunshine blazed in soft white patches on the line. The maddening loveliness of an exceptional spring danced everywhere into his heart. Yes, he rather wished he were going off into the fields and woods alone, instead of with her. Only—she was really a dear person, more, far more now, than secretary and typist; more, even, than the devoted girl who had nursed him through that illness. A friend she was; the years of their working together had made her that; and she was wise and gentle. Oh, yes; it would be delightful to have her with him. How she would enjoy the long sunny day!

Then he saw her coming towards him through the station. In a patch of sunshine she came, as though the light produced her—came suddenly from the middle of a group of men in flannels carrying golf-sticks. And he smiled his welcome a little paternally, trying to kill the selfish thought that he would rather have been alone. Soft things fluttered about her. The big hat was becoming. She was dressed in brown, he believed.

He bought a Sunday paper. "I must buy one too," she laughed. She chose one with pictures, chose it at random rather. He had never heard its name even. And in a first-class carriage alone—he meant to do it really well—they raced through a world of sunshine and brilliant fields to Amersham. She was very happy. She tried every seat in turn; the blazing sheets of yellow—such a spring for buttercups there had never been—drew her from side to side. She put her head out, and nearly lost her big hat, and that soft fluttering thing she wore streamed behind her like the colour of escaping flowers. She opened both windows. The very carriage held the perfume of May that floated over the whole countryside.

He was very nice to her, but read his paper—though always ready with a smile and answer when she asked for them. She teased and laughed and chattered. The luncheon packages engaged her serious attention. Never for a moment was she still, trying every corner in turn, putting her feet up, and bouncing to enjoy the softness of the first-class cushions. "You'll be sitting in the rack next," he suggested. But her head was out of the window again and she did not hear him. She was radiant as a child. His paper interested him—book reviews or something.

"I've asked you that three times, you know, already," he heard her laughing opposite. And with a touch of shame, he tossed the paper through the window.

"There! I'd quite forgotten her again!" he thought, with a touch of shame. "I must pull myself together." For it was true. He had for the moment—more than once—forgotten her existence, just as though he really *were* alone.

Together they strolled down through the beech wood towards Amersham, he for ever dropping the luncheon packages, which she picked up again and tried to stuff into his pockets. For she refused to carry anything at all. "It's *my* day out, not yours, remember! *I* do no work today!" And he caught her happiness, pausing to watch her while she picked flowers and leaves and all the rest, and disentangling without the least impatience that soft fluttering thing she wore when it caught in thorns, and even talking with her about this wild spring glory as though she were just the companion that he needed out of all the world. He no longer felt quite so conscious of her objective presence as at first. In the train, for instance, he had felt so vividly aware that she was there.

Alternately he had forgotten and remembered her presence. Now it was better. They were more together, as it were. "I wish I were alone," he thought once more as the beauty of the spring called to him tumultuously and he longed to lie and dream it all, unhampered by another's presence. Then, even while thinking it, he realised that he was—alone. It was curious.

This happened even in their first wood when they went downhill into Amersham. As they left it and passed again into the open it came. And on its heels, as he watched her moving here and there, light-footed as a child or nymph, there came this other instinctive thought—"I wish I were ten years younger than I am!"—the first time in all his life, probably, that such a thought had ever bothered him. Apparently, he said it aloud, laughingly, as he watched her dancing movements. For she turned and ran up to his side quickly, her little face quite grave beneath the big hat's rim. "You *are!*" That answer struck him as rather wonderful. Who was she after all . . .?

And in Amersham they hired from the Griffin a rickety old cart, drawn by a still more rickety horse, to drive them to Penn's Woods. She, with her own money, bought stone-bottle ginger-beer—two bottles. It made her day complete to have those bottles, though unless they had driven, she would have done without them. The street was deserted, drenched in blazing sunshine. Rooks were cawing in the elms behind the church. Not a soul was about as they crawled away from the houses and passed upwards between hedges smothered in cow-parsley over the hill. She had kept her picture-paper. It lay on her lap all the way. She never opened it or turned a single page; but she held it in her lap. They drove in silence.

The old man on the box was like a faded, weather-beaten farmer dressed in somebody else's cast-off Sunday coat. He flicked the horse with a tattered whip. Sometimes he grunted. Plover rose from the fields, cuckoos called, butterflies danced sideways past the carriage, eyeing them . . . and, as they passed through Penn Street, Le Maitre started suddenly and said something. For, again, he had quite forgotten she was there. "What a selfish beast I am! Why can't I forget myself and my own feelings, and look after her and make her feel amused and happy? It's *her* day out, not mine!" This, somehow, was the way he put it to himself, just as any ordinary man would have put it. But, when he turned to look at her, he received a shock. Here was something new and unexpected. With a thud it dropped down into his mind—*crash!*

For at the sound of his voice she looked up confused and startled into his face. She had forgotten *him!* For the first time in all the years together, years of work, of semi-official attention to his least desire, yet of personal devotion as well, because she respected him and thought him wonderful—she had forgotten *he* was there. She had forgotten his existence beside her as a separate person. She, too, had been—alone.

It was here, perhaps, he first realised this singular thing that set this day apart from every other day that he had ever known. In reality, of course, it had come far sooner—begun with the exquisite spring dawn before either of them was awake, had tentatively fluttered about his soul even while he stood waiting for her in the station, come softly nearer all the way in the train, dropped threads of its golden web about him, especially in that first beech wood, then moved with its swifter yet unhurried rush—until, here, now, in this startling moment, he realised it fully. Thus steal those changes o'er the sky, perhaps, that the day itself knows at sunrise, but that unobservant folk do not notice till the sun bursts out with fuller explanation, and they say, "The weather's changed; how delightful! how unexpected!" Le Maitre had never been observant very—of people.

And then in this deep, lonely valley, too full of sunshine to hold anything else, it seemed, they stopped where the beech woods trooped to the edge of the white road. No wind was here; it was still and silent; the leaves glittered, motionless. They entered the thick trees together, she carrying the ginger-beer bottles *and* that picture-paper. He noticed that: the way she held it, almost clutched still unopened. Her face, he saw, was pale. Or was it merely the contrast of the shade? The trees were very big and wonderful. No birds sang, the network of dazzling sunshine-patches in the gloom bewildered a little.

At first, they did not talk at all, and then in hushed voices. But it was only when they were some way into the wood, and she had put down the bottles—though not the paper—to pick a flower or spray of leaves, that he traced the singular secret thrill to its source and understood why he had felt—no, not uneasy, but so strangely moved. For he had asked the sleepy driver of the way, and how they might best reach Beaconsfield across these Penn Woods, and the old's man's mumbled answer took no note of—her:

"It's a bit rough, maybe, on t'other side, stony like and steep, but that ain't nothing for a gentleman-when he's alone . . .!"

The words disturbed him with a sense of darkness, yet of wonder. As though the old man had not noticed her; almost as though he had seen only one person—himself.

They lunched among heather and bracken just beside a pool of sunshine. In front lay a copse of pines, with little beeches in between. The roof was thick just there, the stillness haunting. All the country-side, it seemed, this Sunday noon, had gone to sleep, he and she alone left out of the deep, soft dream. He watched those pines, mother-ing the slim young beeches, the brilliant fresh green of whose lower branches, he thought, were like little platforms of level sunlight amid the general gloom—patches that had left the ground to yet it escape by the upper air and had then been caught.

"Look," he heard, "they make one think of laughter crept in una-wares among a lot of solemn monks—or of children lost among grave elder beings whose ways are dull and sombre!" It was his own thought continued was she, lying there beside him, who had said it. . . .

And all that wonderful afternoon she had this curious way of pick-ing the thoughts out of his mind and putting them into words for him. "Look," she said again later, "you can always tell whether the wind loves a tree or not by the way it blows the branches. If it loves them, it tries to draw them out to go away with it. The others it merely shakes carelessly as it passes!" It was the very thought in his own mind, too. Indeed, he had been on the point of saying it, but had desisted, feeling she would not understand—with the half wish—though far less strong than before—that he were alone to enjoy it all in his own indulgent way. Then, even more swiftly, came that other strange sensation that he *was* alone all the time; more—that he was for the first time in his life most wonderfully complete and happy, all sense of isolation gone.

He turned quickly the instant she had said it. But not quickly enough. By the look in her great grey eyes, by the expression on the face where the discarded hat no longer hid it, he read the same amazing enigma he had half divined before. She, too, was—alone. She had forgotten him again—forgotten his presence—radiant and happy without him, enjoying herself in her own way. She had merely uttered her delightful thought aloud, as if speaking to herself!

How the afternoon, with its long sunny hours, passed so quickly away, he never understood, nor how they made their way eventually to Beaconsfield through other woods and over other meadows. He remembers only that the whole time he kept forgetting that she was with him, and then suddenly remembering it again. And once on the grass, when they rested to drink the cold tea from his rather musty flask, he lit his pipe, and after a bit he—dozed.

He actually slept; for ten minutes at her side, yes, he slept. He heard her laughing at him, but the laughter was faint and very far away; it might just as well have been the wind in the cow-parsley that said, "If you sleep, I shall change you—change you while you sleep!" And for some minutes after he woke again, it hardly seemed queer to him that he did not see her, for when he noticed her coming towards him from the hedgerow, her arms full of flowers and things, he only thought, "Oh, there she is"—as though her absence, or his own absence in sleep, were not quite the common absences of the world.

And he remembered that on the walk to the village her shoe hurt her, and he offered to carry her, and that then she took her shoe off and ran along the grass beside the lane the whole way. But it was at the inn where they had their supper that the oddest thing of all occurred, for the deaf and rather stupid servant girl would insist on laying the table on the lawn for—one.

"Oh, expectin' someone, are yer?" she said at last. "Is that it?" and so brought plates and knives for two. The girl never once looked at his companion—almost as though she did not see her and seemed unaware of her presence. Le Maitre began to feel that he was dreaming. This was a dream-country, where the people had curious sight. He remembered the driver. . .

In the dusk they made their way to the station. They spoke no word. He kept losing sight of her. Once or twice, he forgot who he But the whole amazing thing blazed into him most strongly, showing how it had seized upon his mind, when he stood before the ticket-window and hesitated—for a second—how many tickets he should buy. He stammered at length for two first-class, but he was absurdly flustered for a second. It had actually occurred to him that they needed only one ticket . . .

And suddenly in the train he understood—and his heart came up in his throat. They were alone. He turned to her where she lay in the corner, feet up, weary, crumpled among the leaves and flowers she had gathered. Like a hedgerow flower she looked, tired by the sunshine and the wind. In one hand was the picture-paper, still unopened and unread, symbol of everyday reality. She was dozing certainly, if not actually asleep. So, he woke her with a touch, calling her name aloud.

There were no words at first. He looked at her, coming up very close to do so, and she looked back at him—straight into his eyes—just as she did at home when they were working and he was explaining something important. And then her own eyes dropped, and a deep blush spread over all her face.

"I wasn't asleep—really," she said, as he took her at last into his arms; "I was wondering—when—you'd find out—"

"Come to myself, you mean?" he asked tremblingly.

"Well," she hesitated, as soon as she got breath, "that I *am* yourself—and that you are me. Of course, we're really only one. I knew it years—oh, years and years ago . . ."

Up and Down

His vagueness, apparently, is only on the surface of his mind; down at the centre the pulses of life throb with unusual vigour and decision. And I think the explanation of his puzzled expression and dazed manner—to say nothing of his idiotic replies—when addressed upon ordinary topics is due to the fact that he prefers to live in that hot and very active centre. He dislikes being called out of it.

Down there his creative imagination is for ever at work: he sees clearly, thinks hard, acts even splendidly. But the moment you speak to him about trivial things the mists gather about his eyes, his voice hesitates, his hands make futile gestures, and he screws up his face into an expression of puzzled alarm. Up he comes to the best of his ability, but it is clear he is vexed at being disturbed.

"Oh yes, I think so—very," he replied the other day as we met on our way to the Club and I asked if he had enjoyed his holiday.

"Awful amount of rain, though, wasn't there?"

"Was there, now? Yes, there must have been, of course. It *was* a wet summer."

He looked at me as though I were a comparative stranger, although our intimacy is of years' standing, and our talks on life, literature, and all the rest are a chief pleasure to each of us. We had not met for some months. I wanted to pierce through to that hot centre where the real man lived, and to find out what the real man had been doing during the interval. He came up but slowly, however.

"You went to the mountains as usual, suppose?" he asked, with his mind obviously elsewhere. He hopped along the pavement with his quick, birdlike motion.

"Mountains, yes. And you?"

He made no reply. From his face I could tell he had come about half-way up, but was already on the way down again. Once he got back to that centre of his I should get nothing out of him at all.

"And you?" I repeated louder. "Abroad, I suppose, somewhere?"

"Well—er—not exactly," he mumbled. "That is to say—I—er— went to Switzerland somewhere—Austria, I mean—down there on the way towards Italy *beyond Boxen, you know.*" He ended the sentence very loud indeed, with quite absurd emphasis, as his way is when he knows he hasn't been listening. "I found a quiet inn out of the tourist track and did a rare lot of work there too." His face cleared and the brown eyes began to glow a little. It was like seeing the sun through opening mists. "Come in, and I'll tell you about it," he added, in an eager whisper, as we reached the Club doors.

At the same moment, however, the porter came down the steps and touched his hat, and my vague friend, recognising a face he felt he ought to know, stopped to ask him how he was, and whether So-and-so was back yet; and while the porter replied briefly and respectfully, I saw to my dismay the mists settle down again upon the other's face. A moment later the porter touched his hat again and moved off down the street. My friend looked round at me as though I had but just arrived upon the scene.

"Here we are," he observed gently, "at the Club. I think I shall go in. What are *you* going to do?"

"I'm coming in too," I said.

"Good," he murmured; "let's go in together, then," his thoughts working away busily at something deep within him.

On our way to the hat-racks, and all up the winding stairs, he mumbled away about the wet summer, and tourists, and his little mountain inn, but never a word of the work I was so anxious to hear about, and he so anxious really to tell. In the reading-room I manoeuvred to get two armchairs side by side before he could seize the heap of papers, he smothered his lap with, but never read.

"And where have *you* been all the summer?" he asked, crossing his little legs and speaking in a voice loud enough to have been heard in the street. "Somewhere in the mountains, I suppose, as usual?"

"You were going to tell me about the work you got through up in your lonely inn," I insisted sharply. "Was it a play, or a novel, or criticism, or what?"

He looked so small and lost in the big armchair that I felt quite ashamed of myself for speaking so violently. He turned round on the slippery leather and offered me a cigarette. The glow came back to his face.

"Well," he said, "as a matter of fact it was both. That is, I was preparing a stage version of my new novel." All the mist had gone now; he was alive at the centre, and thoroughly awake. He snapped his case to and put it away before I had taken my cigarette. But, of course, he did not notice that, and held out a lighted match to my lips as though there was something there to light.

"No, thanks," I said quickly, fearful that if I asked again for the cigarette the mists would instantly gather once more and the real man disappear.

"Won't you *really*, though?" he said, blowing the match out and forgetting to light his own cigarette at the same time. "I did the whole scenario, and most of the first act. There was nothing else to do. It rained all the time, and the place was quiet as the grave—"

A waiter brought him several letters on a tray. He took them automatically. The face clouded a bit.

"What'll you have?" he asked absentmindedly, acting automatically upon the presence of the waiter.

"Nothing, thanks."

"Nor will I, then. Oh yes, I will, though—I'll have some dry ginger ale. Here, waiter! Bring me a small dry ginger ale."

The waiter, with the force of habit, bent his head questioningly for my order too.

"*You* said—?" asked my exasperating friend. He was right down in the mists now, and I knew I should never get him up again this side of lunch.

"I said nothing, thanks."

"Nothing, then, for this gentleman," he continued, gazing up at the waiter as though he were some monster seen for the first time, "and for me—a dry ginger ale, please."

"Yes, sir," said the man, moving off.

"Small," the other called after him.

"Yes—sir—small."

"And a slice of lemon in it."

The waiter inclined his head respectfully from the door. The other turned to me, searching in his perturbed mind—I could tell it by the way his eyes worked—for the trail of his vanished conversation. Before he got it, however, he slithered round again on the leather seat towards the door.

"A bit of ice too, don't forget!"

The waiter's head peeped round the corner, and from the movement of his lips I gathered he repeated the remark about the bit of ice.

"I *did* say 'dry'?" my friend asked, looking anxiously at me; "didn't I?"

"You did."

"And a bit of lemon?"

"And a slice of lemon."

"And what are *you* going to have, then? Upon my word, old man, I forgot to ask you." He looked so distressed that it was impossible to show impatience.

"Nothing, thanks. You asked me, you know."

A pause fell between us. I gave it up. He would talk when he wanted to, but there was no forcing him. It struck me suddenly that he had a rather fagged and weary look for a man who had been spending several weeks at a mountain inn with work he loved. The pity and affection his presence always wakes in me ran a neck-and-neck race. At that "centre" of his, I knew full well, he was ever devising plans for the helping of others, quite as much as creating those 11 remarkable things that issued periodically, ill-understood by a sensation-loving public, from the press. A sharp telepathic suspicion flashed through my mind, but before there was time to give it expression in words, up came the waiter with a long glass of ginger ale fizzing on a tray.

He handed it to my vague friend, and my vague friend took it and handed it to me.

"But it's yours, my dear chap," I suggested.

He looked puzzled for a second, and then his face cleared. "I forget what *you* ordered," he observed softly, looking interrogatively at the waiter and at me. We informed him simultaneously, "Nothing," and the waiter respectfully mentioned the price of the drink. My friend's left hand plunged into his trousers pocket, while his right carried the glass to his lips. Perhaps his left hand did not know what his right was about, or perhaps his mind was too far away to direct the motions of either with safety.

Anyhow, the result was deplorable. He swallowed an uncomfortable gulp of air-bubbles and ginger—and choked—over me, over the waiter and tray, over his beard and clothes. The floating lump of ice bobbed up and hit his nose. I never saw a man look so surprised and distressed in my life. I took the glass from him, and when his left hand finally emerged with money, he handed it first vaguely to me as though I were the waiter—for which there was no real excuse, since we were not in evening dress.

When, at length, order was restored and he was sipping quietly at

226

the remains of the fizzing liquid, he looked up at me over the brim of his glass and remarked, with more concentration on the actual present than he had yet shown:

"By the way, you know, I'm going away tomorrow—going abroad for my holiday. Taking a lot of work with me, too—"

"But you've only just come back!" I expostulated, with a feeling very like anger in my heart.

He shook his head with decision. Evidently that choking had choked him into the living present. He was really "up" this time, and not likely to go down again.

"No, no," he replied; "I've been here all the summer in town looking after old Podger—"

"Old Podger!" I remembered a dirty, down-at-heel old man I once met at my friend's rooms—a poet who had "smothered his splendid talent" in drink, and who was always at starvation's door. "What in the world was the matter with Podger?"

"D. T. I've been nursing him through it. The poor devil nearly went under this time. I've got him into a home down in the country at last, but all August he was—well, we thought he was gone."

All August! So that was how my friend's summer had been spent. With never a word of thanks probably at that!

"But your mountain inn beyond Bozen! You said—"

" Did I? I must be wool-gathering," he laughed, with that beautifully tender smile that comes sometimes to his delicate, dreamy face. "That was last year. I spent my holidays last year up there. How stupid of me to get so absurdly muddled!" He plunged his nose into the empty glass, waiting for the last drop to trickle out, with his neck at an angle that betrayed the collar to be undone and the tie sadly frayed at the edges.

"But—all the work you said you did up there—the scenario and the first act and—and—"

He turned upon me with such sudden energy that I fairly jumped. Then, in a voice that mumbled the first half of his sentence, but shouted the end like a German officer giving instructions involving life or death, I heard:

"But, my dear good fellow, you don't half listen to what I say! All that work, as I told you just now, is what I expect and mean to do when I get up there. *Now*—have you got it clear at last?"

He looked me up and down with great energy. By biting the inner side of my lip, I kept my face grave. Later we went down to lunch together, and I heard details of the weeks of unselfish devotion he had lavished upon "old Podger." I would give a great deal to possess some of the driving power for good that throbs and thrills at the real centre of my old friend with the vague manner and the absent-minded surface. But he is a singular contradiction, and almost always misunderstood. I should like to know, too, what Podger thinks.

Violence

"But what seems so odd to me, so horribly pathetic, is that such people don't resist," said Leidall, suddenly entering the conversation. The intensity of his tone startled everybody; it was so passionate, yet with a beseeching touch that made the women feel uncomfortable a little. "As a rule, I'm told, they submit willingly, almost as though—"

He hesitated, grew confused, and dropped his glance to the floor; and a "smartly dressed woman eager to be heard, seized the opening." "Oh, come now," she laughed; "one always hears of a man being *put* into a strait waistcoat. I'm sure he doesn't slip it on as if he were going to a dance!" And she looked flippantly at Leidall, whose casual manners she resented. "People are *put* under restraint. It's not in human nature to accept it—healthy human nature, that is?"

But for some reason no one took her question up. "That is so, I believe, yes," a polite voice murmured, while the group at tea in the Dover Street Club turned with one accord to Leidall as to one whose interesting sentence still remained unfinished. He had hardly spoken before, and a silent man is ever credited with wisdom.

"As though—you were just saying, Mr. Leidall?" a quiet little man in a dark corner helped him.

"As though, I meant, a man in that condition of mind is not insane—all through," Leidall continued stammeringly; "but that some wise portion of him watches the proceeding with gratitude, and welcomes the protection against himself. It seems awfully pathetic. Still," again hesitating and fumbling in his speech—"er—it seems queer to me that he should yield quietly to enforced restraint—the waistcoat, handcuffs, and the rest." He looked round hurriedly, half suspiciously, at the faces in the circle, then dropped his eyes again to the floor. He sighed, leaning back in his chair. "I cannot understand it," he added, as no one spoke, but in a very low voice, and almost to himself. "One would expect them to struggle furiously."

Someone had mentioned that remarkable, book, *The Mind that Found Itself*, and the conversation had slipped into this serious vein. The women did not like it. What kept it alive was the fact that the silent Leidall, with his handsome, melancholy face, had suddenly wakened into speech, and that the little man opposite to him, half invisible in his dark corner, was assistant to one of London's great hypnotic doctors, who could, and he would, tell, interesting and terrible things. No one cared to ask the direct question, but all hoped for revelations, possibly about people they actually knew. It was a very ordinary tea-party indeed. And this little man now spoke, though hardly in the desired vein. He addressed his remarks to Leidall across the disappointed lady.

"I think, probably, your explanation is the true one," he said gently, "for madness in its commoner forms is merely want of proportion; the mind gets out of right and proper relations with its environment. The majority of madmen are mad on one thing only, while the rest of them is as sane as myself—or you."

The words fell into the silence. Leidall bowed his agreement, saying no actual word. The ladies fidgeted. Someone made a jocular remark to the effect that most of the world was mad anyhow, and the conversation shifted with relief into a lighter vein—the scandal in the family of a politician. Everybody talked at once. Cigarettes were lit. The corner soon became excited and even uproarious. The tea-party was a great success, and the offended lady, no longer ignored, led all the skirmishes—towards herself. She was in her element. Only Leidall and the little invisible man in the corner took small part in it; and presently, seizing the opportunity when some new arrivals joined the group.

Leidall rose to say his *adieux*, and slipped away, his departure scarcely noticed. Dr. Hancock followed him a minute later. The two men met in the hall; Leidall already had his hat and coat on. "I'm going West, Mr. Leidall. If that's your way too, and you feel inclined for the walk we might go together." Leidall turned with a start. His glance took in the other with avidity—a keenly-searching, hungry glance. He hesitated for an imperceptible moment, then made a movement towards him, half inviting, while a curious shadow dropped across his face and vanished. It was both pathetic and terrible. The lips trembled. He seemed to say, God bless you; *do* come with me!" But no words were audible.

"It's a pleasant evening for a walk," added Dr. Hancock gently; "clean and dry under foot for a change. I'll get my hat and join you in a second." And there was a hint, the merest flavour of authority in his voice.

That touch of authority was his mistake. Instantly Leidall's hesitation passed. "I'm sorry," he said abruptly, but I'm afraid I must take a taxi. I have an appointment at the Club and I'm late already."

"Oh, I see," the other replied, with a kindly smile; "then I mustn't keep you. But if you ever have a free evening, won't you look me up, or come and dine? You'll find my telephone number in the book. I should like to talk with you about—those things we mentioned at tea." Leidall thanked him politely and went out. The memory of the little man's kindly sympathy and understanding eyes went with him.

"Who was that man? "someone asked, the moment Leidall had left the tea-table. "Surely he's not the Leidall who wrote that awful book some years ago?"

"Yes—the *Gulf of Darkness.* Did you read it?"

They discussed it and its author for five minutes, deciding by a large majority that it was the book of a madman. Silent, rude men like that always had a screw loose somewhere, they agreed. Silence was invariably morbid.

"And did you notice Dr. Hancock? He never took his eyes off him. That's why he followed him out like that. I wonder if *he* thought anything!"

"I know Hancock well," said the lady of the wounded vanity. "I'll ask him and find out." They chattered on, somebody mentioned a *risqué* play, and talk switched into other fields, and in due course the tea-party came to an end.

And Leidall, meanwhile, made his way towards the Park on foot. for he had not taken a taxi after all. The suggestion of the other man, perhaps, had worked upon him. He was very open to suggestion. With hands deep in his overcoat pockets, and head sunk forward between his shoulders, he walked briskly, entering the Park at one of the smaller gates. He made his way across the wet turf, avoiding the paths and people. The February sky was shining in the west; beautiful clouds floated over the houses; they looked like the shore-line of some radiant strand his childhood once had known. He sighed; thought dived and searched within; self-analysis, that old, implacable demon, lifted its voice; introspection took the reins again as usual. There seemed a strain upon the mind he could not dispel.

Thought circled poignantly. He knew it was unhealthy, morbid, a sign of these many years of difficulty and stress that had marked him so deeply, but for the life of him he could not escape from the hideous spell that held him. The same old thoughts bored their way into his mind like burning wires, tracing the same unanswerable questions. From this torture, waking or sleeping there was no escape. Had a companion been with him it might have been different. If, for instance. Dr. Hancock——

He was angry with himself for having refused—furious; it was that vile, false pride his long loneliness had fostered. The man was sympathetic to him, friendly, marvellously understanding; he could have talked freely with him, and found relief. His intuition had picked out the little doctor as a man in ten thousand. Why had he so curtly declined his gentle invitation? Dr. Hancock *knew*; he guessed his awful secret. But how? In what had he betrayed himself?

The weary self-questioning began again, till he sighed and groaned from sheer exhaustion. He *must* find people, companionship, someone to talk to. The Club—it crossed his tortured mind for a second—was impossible; there was a conspiracy among the members against him. He had left his usual haunts everywhere for the same reason—his restaurants, where he had his lonely meals; his music hall, where he tried sometimes to forget himself; his favourite walks, where the very policemen knew and eyed him. And, coming to the bridge across the Serpentine just then, he paused and leaned over the edge, watching a bubble rise to the surface.

"I suppose there *are* fish in the Serpentine?" he said to a man a few feet away.

They talked a moment—the other was evidently a clerk on his way home—and then the stranger edged off and continued his walk, looking back once or twice at the sad-faced man who had addressed him. It's ridiculous, that with all our science we can't live under water as the fish do," reflected Leidall, and moved on round the other bank of the water, where he watched a flight of duck whirl down from the darkening air and settle with a long, mournful splash beside the bushy island.

"Or that, for all our pride of mechanism in a mechanical age, we cannot really fly." But these attempts to escape from self were never very successful. Another part of him looked on and mocked. He returned ever to the endless introspection and self-analysis, and in the deepest moment of it—ran into a big, motionless figure that blocked his way. It was the Park policeman, the one who always eyed him. He sheered off suddenly towards the trees, while the man, recognising him, touched his cap respectfully. "It's a pleasant evening, sir; turned quite mild again."

Leidall mumbled some reply or other, and hurried on to hide himself among the shadows of the trees. The policeman stood and watched him, till the darkness swallowed him. "He knows too!" groaned the wretched man. And every bench was occupied; every face turned to watch him; there were even figures behind the trees. He dared not go into the street, for the very taxi-drivers were against him. If he gave an address, he would not be driven to it; the man would *know*, and take him elsewhere. And something in his heart, sick with anguish, weary with the endless battle, suddenly yielded.

"There *are* fish in the Serpentine," he remembered the stranger had said. "And," he added to himself, with a wave of delicious comfort, "they lead secret, hidden lives that no one can disturb." His mind cleared surprisingly. In the water he could find peace and rest and healing. Good Lord! How easy it all was! Yet he had never thought of it before. He turned sharply to retrace his steps, but in that very second the clouds descended upon his thought again, his mind darkened, he hesitated. Could he get out again when he had had enough? Would he rise to the surface? A battle began over these questions. He ran quickly, then stood still again to think the matter out. Darkness shrouded him.

He heard the wind rush laughing through the trees. The picture of the whirring duck flashed back a moment, and he decided that the best way was by air, and not by water. He would *fly* into the place of rest, not sink or merely float; and he remembered the view from his bedroom window, high over old smoky London town, with a drop of eighty feet on to the pavements. Yes, that was the best way. He waited a moment, trying to think it all out clearly, but one moment the fish had it, and the next the birds. It was really impossible to decide. Was there no one who could help him, no one in all this enormous town who was sufficiently on his side to advise him on the point? Some clear-headed, experienced, kindly man?

And the face of Dr. Hancock flashed before his vision. He saw the gentle eyes and sympathetic smile, remembered the soothing voice and the offer of companionship he had refused. Of course, there was one serious drawback: Hancock *knew*. But he was far too tactful, too sweet and good a man to let that influence his judgment, or to betray in any way at all that he did know.

Leidall found it in him to decide. Facing the entire hostile world, he hailed a taxi from the nearest gate upon the street, looked up the address in a chemist's telephone-book, and reached the door in a condition of delight and relief. Yes, Dr. Hancock was at home. Leidall sent his name in. A few minutes later the two men were chatting pleasantly together, almost like old friends, so keen was the little man's intuitive sympathy and tact. Only Hancock, patient listener though he proved himself to be, was uncommonly full of words. Leidall explained the matter very clearly. "Now, what is your decision. Dr. Hancock? Is it to be the way of the fish or the way of the duck?"

And, while Hancock began his answer with slow, well-chosen words, a new idea, better than either leaped with a flash into his listener's mind. It was an inspiration. For where could he find a better hiding-place from all his troubles than—inside Hancock himself? The man was kindly; he surely would not object. Leidall this time did not hesitate a second. He was tall and broad; Hancock was small; yet he was sure there would be room. He sprang upon him like a wild animal. He felt the warm, thin throat yield and bend between his great hands . . . then darkness, peace and rest, a nothingness that surely was the oblivion he had so long prayed for. He had accomplished his desire. He had secreted himself for ever from persecution—inside the kindliest little man he had ever met—inside Hancock. . . .

He opened his eyes and looked about him into a room he did not know. The walls were soft and dimly coloured. It was very silent. Cushions were everywhere. Peaceful it was, and out of the world. Overhead was a skylight, and one window, opposite the door, was heavily barred. Delicious! No one could get in. He was sitting in a deep comfortable chair. He felt rested and happy. There was a click, and he saw a tiny window in the door drop down, as though worked by a sliding panel. Then the door opened noiselessly, and in came a little man with smiling face and soft brown eyes—Dr. Hancock.

Leidall's first feeling was amazement. "Then I didn't get into him properly after all! Or I've slipped out again, perhaps! The dear, good fellow!" And he rose to greet him. He put his hand out, and found that the other came with it in some inexplicable fashion. Movement was cramped. "Ah, then I've had a stroke," he thought, as Hancock pressed him, ever so gently, back into the big chair.

"Do not get up," he said soothingly but with authority; "sit where you are and rest. You must take it very easy for a bit; like all clever men who have overworked—"

"I'll get in the moment he turns," thought Leidall. "I did it badly before. It must be through the back of his head, of course, where the spine runs up into the brain," and he waited till Hancock should turn. But Hancock never turned. He kept his face towards him all the time, while he chatted, moving gradually nearer to the door. On Leidall's face was the smile of an innocent child, but there lay a hideous cunning behind that smile, and the eyes were terrible.

"Are those bars firm and strong," asked Leidall, "so that no one can get in? "He pointed craftily, and the doctor, caught for a second unawares, turned his head. That instant Leidall was upon him with a roar, then sank back powerless into the chair, unable to move his arms more than a few inches in any direction. Hancock stepped up quietly and made him comfortable again with cushions.

And something in Leidall's soul turned round and looked another way. His mind became clear as daylight for a moment. The effort perhaps had caused the sudden change from darkness to great light. A memory rushed over him. "Good God!" he cried. "I am violent. I was going to do you an injury—you, who are so sweet and good to me!" He trembled dreadfully, and burst into tears. "For the sake of Heaven," he implored, looking up, ashamed and keenly penitent, "put me under restraint. Fasten my hands before I try it again." He held both hands out willingly, beseechingly, then looked down, following the direction of the other's kind brown eyes. His wrists, he saw, already wore steel handcuffs, and a strait waistcoat was across his chest and arms and shoulders.

Wayfarers

I missed the train at Evian, and, after infinite trouble, discovered a motor that would take me, ice-axe and all, to Geneva. By hurrying, the connection might be just possible. I telegraphed to Haddon to meet me at the station, and lay back comfortably, dreaming of the precipices of Haute Savoie. We made good time; the roads were excellent, traffic of the slightest, when—*crash!* There was an instant's excruciating pain, the sun went out like a snuffed candle, and I fell into something as soft as a bed of flowers and as yielding to my weight as warm water . . . .

It was *very* warm. There was a perfume of flowers. My eyes opened, focused vividly upon a detailed picture for a moment, then closed again. There was no context—at least, none that I could recall—for the scene, though familiar as home, brought nothing that I definitely remembered. Broken away from any sequence, unattached to any past, unaware even of my own identity, I simply saw this picture as a camera snaps it off from the world, a scene apart, with meaning only for those who knew the context:

The warm, soft thing I lay in was a bed—big, deep, comfortable, and the perfume came from flowers that stood beside it on a little table. It was in a stately, ancient chamber, with lofty ceiling and immense open fireplace of stone; old-fashioned pictures—familiar portraits and engravings I knew intimately—hung upon the walls; the floor was bare, with dignified, carved furniture of oak and mahogany, huge chairs and massive cupboards. And there were latticed windows set within deep embrasures of grey stone, where clambering roses patterned the sunshine that cast their moving shadows on the polished boards. With the perfume of the flowers there mingled, too, that delicate, elusive odour of age—of wood, of musty tapestries in spacious halls and corridors, and of chambers long unopened to the sun and air.

By the door that stood ajar far away at the end of the room—very far away it seemed—an old lady, wearing a little cap of silk embroidery, was whispering to a man of stern, uncompromising figure, who, as he listened, bent down to her with a grave and even solemn face. A wide stone corridor was just visible through the crack of the open door behind her.

The picture flashed, and vanished. The numerous details I took in because they were well known to me already. That I could not supply the context was merely a trick of the mind, the kind of trick that dreams play. Darkness swamped vision again. I sank back into the warm, soft, comfortable bed of delicious oblivion. There was not the slightest desire to know; sleep and soft forgetfulness were all I craved.

But a little later—or was it a very great deal later?—when I opened my eyes again, there was a thin trail of memory. I remembered my name and age. I remembered vaguely, as though from some unpleasant dream, that I was on the way to meet a climbing friend in the Alps of Haute Savoie, and that there was need to hurry and be very active. Something had gone wrong, it seemed. There had been a stupid, violent disaster, pain in it somewhere, an accident. Where were my belongings? Where, for instance, was my precious ice-axe—tried old instrument on which my life and safety depended? A rush of jumbled questions poured across my mind. The effort to sort them hurt atrociously. . . .

A figure stood beside my bed. It was the same old lady I had seen a moment ago—or was it a month ago, even last year perhaps? And this time she was alone. Yet, though familiar to me as my own right hand, I could not for the life of me attract her name. Searching for it brought the pain again. Instead, I asked an easier question; it seemed the most important somehow, though a feeling of shame came with it, as though I knew I was talking nonsense:

'My ice-axe—is it safe? It should have stood any ordinary strain. It's ash. . . .' My voice failed absurdly, caught away by a whisper halfway down my throat. What *was* I talking about? There was vile confusion somewhere.

She smiled tenderly, sweetly, as she placed her small, cool hand upon my forehead. Her touch calmed me as it always did, and the pain retreated a little.

'All your things are safe,' she answered, in a voice so soft beneath the distant ceiling it was like a bird's note singing in the sky. 'And *you* are also safe. There is no danger now. The bullet has been taken out and all is going well. Only you must be patient, and lie very still, and rest.' And then she added the morsel of delicious comfort she knew quite well I waited for: 'Marion is near you all day long, and most of the night besides. She rarely leaves you. She is in and out all day.'

I stared, thirsting for more. Memory put certain pieces in their place again. I heard them click together as they joined. But they only tried to join. There were several pieces missing. They must have been lost in the disaster. The pattern was too ridiculous.

'I ought to tel—telegraph——' I began, seizing at a fragment that poked its end up, then plunged out of sight again before I could read more of it. The pieces fell apart; they would not hold together without these missing fragments. Anger flamed up in me.

'They're badly made,' I said, with a petulance I was secretly ashamed of; 'you have chosen the wrong pieces! I'm not a child—to be treated——' A shock of heat tore through me, led by a point of iron, with blasting pain.

'Sleep, my poor dear Félix, sleep,' she murmured soothingly, while her tiny hand stroked my forehead, just in time to prevent that pointed, hot thing entering my heart. 'Sleep again now, and a little later you shall tell me their names, and I will send on horseback quickly——'

'Telegraph——' I tried to say, but the word went lost before I could pronounce it. It was a nonsense word, caught up from dreams. Thought fluttered and went out.

'I will send,' she whispered, 'in the quickest possible way. You shall explain to Marion. Sleep first a little longer; promise me to lie quite still and sleep. When you wake again, she will come to you at once.'

She sat down gently on the edge of the enormous bed, so that I saw her outline against the window where the roses clambered to come in. She bent over me—or was it a rose that bent in the wind across the stone embrasure? I saw her clear blue eyes—or was it two raindrops upon a withered rose-leaf that mirrored the summer sky?

'Thank you,' my voice murmured with intense relief, as everything sank away and the old-world garden seemed to enter by the latticed windows. For there was a power in her way that made obedience sweet, and her little hand, besides, cushioned the attack of that cruel iron point so that I hardly felt its entrance. Before the fierce heat could reach me, darkness again put out the world. . . .

Then, after a prodigious interval, my eyes once more opened to the stately, old-world chamber that I knew so well; and this time I found myself alone. In my brain was a stinging, splitting sensation, as though Memory shook her pieces together with angry violence, pieces, moreover, made of clashing metal. A degrading nausea almost

239

vanquished me. Against my feet was a heated metal body, too heavy for me to move, and bandages were tight round my neck and the back of my head. Dimly, it came back to me that hands had been about me hours ago, soft, ministering hands that I loved. Their perfume lingered still. Faces and names fled in swift procession past me, yet without my making any attempt to bid them stay. I asked myself no questions. Effort of any sort was utterly beyond me. I lay and watched and waited, helpless and strangely weak.

One or two things alone were clear. They came, too, without the effort to think them:

There had been a disaster; they had carried me into the nearest house; and—the mountain heights, so keenly longed for, were suddenly denied me. I was being cared for by kind people somewhere far from the world's high routes. They were familiar people, yet for the moment I had lost the name. But it was the bitterness of losing my holiday climbing that chiefly savaged me, so that strong desire returned upon itself unfulfilled. And, knowing the danger of frustrated yearnings, and the curious states of mind they may engender, my tumbling brain registered a decision automatically:

'Keep careful watch upon yourself,' it whispered.

For I saw the peaks that towered above the world, and felt the wind rise from the hidden valleys. The perfume of lonely ridges came to me, and I saw the snow against the blue-black sky. Yet I could not reach them. I lay, instead, broken and useless upon my back, in a soft, deep, comfortable bed. And I loathed the thought. A dull and evil fury rose within me. Where was Haddon? He would get me out of it if anyone could. And where was my dear, old trusted ice-axe? Above all, who were these gentle, old-world people who cared for me? . . . . And, with this last thought, came some fairy touch of sweetness so delicious that I was conscious of sudden resignation—more, even of delight and joy.

This joy and anger ran races for possession of my mind, and I knew not which to follow: both seemed real, and both seemed true. The cruel confusion was an added torture. Two sets of places and people seemed to mingle.

'Keep a careful watch upon yourself,' repeated the automatic caution.

Then, with returning, blissful darkness, came another thing—a tiny point of wonder, where light entered in. I thought of a woman. . . .It was a vehement, commanding thought; and though at first it was very close and real—as much of Today as Haddon and my precious ice-axe—the next second it was leagues away in another world somewhere. Yet, before the confusion twisted it all askew, I knew her; I remembered clearly even where she lived; that I knew her husband, too—had stayed with them in—in Scotland—yes, in Scotland. Yet no word in this life had ever crossed my lips, for she was not free to come. Neither of us, with eyes or lips or gesture, had ever betrayed a hint to the other of our deeply hidden secret. And, although for me she was *the* woman, my great yearning—long, long ago it was, in early youth—had been sternly put aside and buried with all the vigour nature gave me. Her husband was my friend as well.

Only, now, the shock had somehow strained the prison bars, and the yearning escaped for a moment full-fledged, and vehement with passion long denied. The inhibition was destroyed. The knowledge swept deliciously upon me that we had the right to be together, because we always *were* together. I had the right to ask for her.

My mind was certainly a mere field of confused, ungoverned images. No thinking was possible, for it hurt too vilely. But this one memory stood out with violence. I distinctly remember that I called to her to come, and that she had the right to come because my need was so peremptory. To the one most loved of all this life had brought me, yet to whom I had never spoken because she was in another's keeping, I called for help, and called, I verily believe, aloud:

'Please come!' Then, close upon its heels, the automatic warning again: 'Keep close watch upon yourself. . . .!'

It was as though one great yearning had loosed the other that was even greater, and had set it free.

Disappearing consciousness then followed the cry for an incalculable distance. Down into subterraneans within myself that were positively frightening it plunged away. But the cry was real; the yearning appeal held authority in it as of command. Love gave the right, supplied the power as well. For it seemed to me a tiny answer came, but from so far away that it was scarcely audible. And names were nowhere in it, either in answer or appeal.

'I am always here. I have never, never left you!'

★★★★★★★★★★★★

The unconsciousness that followed was not complete, apparently. There was a memory of effort in it, of struggle, and, as it were, of searching. Someone was trying to get at me. I tossed in a troubled sea upon a piece of wreckage that another swimmer also fought to reach. Huge waves of transparent green now brought this figure nearer, now concealed it, but it came steadily on, holding out a rope. My exhaustion was too great for me to respond, yet this swimmer swept up nearer, brought by enormous rollers that threatened to engulf us both. The rope was for my safety, too. I saw hands outstretched. In the deep water I saw the outline of the body, and once I even saw the face. But for a second, merely.

The wave that bore it crashed with a horrible roar that smothered us both and swept me from my piece of wreckage. In the violent flood of water, the rope whipped against my feeble hands. I grasped it. A sense of divine security at once came over me—an intolerable sweetness of utter bliss and comfort, then blackness and suffocation as of the grave. The white-hot point of iron struck me. It beat audibly against my heart. I heard the knocking. The pain brought me up to the surface, and the knocking of my dreams was in reality a knocking on the door. Someone was gently tapping.

Such was the confusion of images in my pain-racked mind, that I expected to see the old lady enter, bringing ropes and ice-axes, and followed by Haddon, my mountaineering friend; for I thought that I had fallen down a deep crevasse and had waited hours for help in the cold, blue darkness of the ice. I was too weak to answer, and the knocking for that matter was not repeated. I did not even hear the opening of the door, so softly did she move into the room. I only knew that before I actually saw her, this wave of intolerable sweetness drenched me once again with bliss and peace and comfort, my pain retreated, and I closed my eyes, knowing I should feel that cool and soothing hand upon my forehead.

The same minute I did feel it. There was a perfume of old gardens in the air. I opened my eyes to look the gratitude I could not utter, and saw, close against me—not the old lady, but the young and lovely face my worship had long made familiar. With lips that smiled their yearning and eyes of brown that held tears of sympathy, she sat down beside me on the bed. The warmth and fragrance of her atmosphere enveloped me. I sank away into a garden where spring melts magically into summer. Her arms were round my neck. Her face dropped down, so that I felt her hair upon my cheek and eyes. And then, whispering my name twice over, she kissed me on the lips.

'Marion,' I murmured.

'Hush! Mother sends you this,' she answered softly. 'You are to take it all; she made it with her own hands. But *I* bring it to you. You must be quite obedient, please.'

She tried to rise, but I held her against my breast.

'Kiss me again and I'll promise obedience always,' I strove to say. But my voice refused so long a sentence, and anyhow her lips were on my own before I could have finished it. Slowly, very carefully, she disentangled herself, and my arms sank back upon the coverlet. I sighed in happiness. A moment longer she stood beside my bed, gazing down with love and deep anxiety into my face.

'And when all is eaten, all, mind, *all*,' she smiled, 'you are to sleep until the doctor comes this afternoon. You are much better. Soon you shall get up. Only, remember,' shaking her finger with a sweet pretence of looking stern, 'I shall exact complete obedience. You must yield your will utterly to mine. You are in my heart, and my heart must be kept very warm and happy.'

Her eyes were tender as her mother's, and I loved the authority and strength that were so real in her. I remembered how it was this strength that had sealed the contract her beauty first drew up for me to sign. She bent down once more to arrange my pillows.

'What happened to—to the motor?' I asked hesitatingly, for my thoughts *would* not regulate themselves. The mind presented such incongruous fragments.

'The—what?' she asked, evidently puzzled. The word seemed strange to her. 'What is that?' she repeated, anxiety in her eyes.

I made an effort to tell her, but I could not. Explanation was suddenly impossible. The whole idea dived away out of sight. It utterly evaded me. I had again invented a word that was without meaning. I was talking nonsense. In its place my dream came up. I tried to tell her how I had dreamed of climbing dangerous heights with a stranger, and had spoken another language with him than my own—English, was it?—at any rate, not my native French.

'Darling,' she whispered close into my ear, 'the bad dreams will not come back. You are safe here, quite safe.' She put her little hand like a flower on my forehead and drew it softly down the cheek. 'Your wound is already healing. They took the bullet out four days ago. I have got it,' she added with a touch of shy embarrassment, and kissed me tenderly upon my eyes.

'How long have you been away from me?' I asked, feeling exhaustion coming back.

'Never once for more than ten minutes,' was the reply. 'I watched with you all night. Only this morning, while mother took my place, I slept a little. But, hush!' she said, with dear authority again; 'you are not to talk so much. You must eat what I have brought, then sleep again. You must rest and sleep. Goodbye, goodbye, my love. I shall come back in an hour, and I shall always be within reach of your dear voice.'

Her tall, slim figure, dressed in the grey I loved, crossed silently to the door. She gave me one more look—there was all the tenderness of passionate love in it—and then was gone.

I followed instructions meekly, and when a delicious sleep stole over me soon afterwards, I had forgotten utterly the ugly dream that I was climbing dangerous heights with another man, forgotten as well everything else, except that it seemed so many days since my love had come to me, and that my bullet wound would after all be healed in time for our wedding on the day so long, so eagerly waited for.

And when, several hours later, her mother came in with the doctor—his face less grave and solemn this time—the news that I might get up next day and lie a little in the garden, did more to heal me than a thousand bandages or twice that quantity of medical instructions.

I watched them as they stood a moment by the open door. They went out very slowly together, speaking in whispers. But the only thing I caught was the mother's voice, talking brokenly of the great wars. Napoleon, the doctor was saying in a low, hushed tone, was in full retreat from Moscow, though the news had only just come through. They passed into the corridor then, and there was a sound of weeping as the old lady murmured something about her son and the cruelty of Heaven. 'Both will be taken from me,' she was sobbing softly, while he stooped to comfort her; 'one in marriage, and the other in death.' They closed the door then, and I heard no more.

Convalescence seemed to follow very quickly then, for I was utterly obedient as I had promised, and never spoke of what could excite me to my own detriment—the wars and my own unfortunate part in them. We talked instead of our love, our already too-long engagement, and of the sweet dream of happiness that life held waiting for us in the future. And, indeed, I was sufficiently weary of the world to prefer repose to much activity, for my body was almost incessantly in pain, and this old garden where we lay between high walls of stone, aloof from the busy world and very peaceful, was far more to my taste just then than wars and fighting.

The orchards were in blossom, and the winds of spring showered their rain of petals upon the long, new grass. We lay, half in sunshine, half in shade, beneath the poplars that lined the avenue towards the lake, and behind us rose the ancient grey stone towers where the jackdaws nested in the ivy and the pigeons cooed and fluttered from the woods beyond.

There was loveliness everywhere, but there was sadness too, for though we both knew that the wars had taken her brother whence there is no return, and that only her aged, failing mother's life stood between ourselves and the stately property, there hid a sadness yet deeper than either of these thoughts in both our hearts. And it was, I think, the sadness that comes with spring. For spring, with her lavish, short-lived promises of eternal beauty, is ever a symbol of passing human happiness, incomplete and always unfulfilled. Promises made on earth are playthings, after all, for children. Even while we make them so solemnly, we seem to know they are not meant to hold. They are made, as spring is made, with a glory of soft, radiant blossoms that pass away before there is time to realise them. And yet they come again with the return of spring, as unashamed and glorious as if Time had utterly forgotten.

And this sadness was in her too. I mean it was part of her and she was part of it. Not that our love could change to pass or die, but that its sweet, so-long-desired accomplishment must hold away, and, like the spring, must melt and vanish before it had been fully known. I did not speak of it. I well understood that the depression of a broken body can influence the spirit with its poisonous melancholy, but it must have betrayed itself in my words and gestures, even in my manner too. At any rate, she was aware of it. I think, if truth be told, she felt it too. It seemed so painfully inevitable.

My recovery, meanwhile, was rapid, and from spending an hour or two in the garden, I soon came to spend the entire day. For the spring came on with a rush, and the warmth increased deliciously. While the cuckoos called to one another in the great beech-woods behind the *château*, we sat and talked and sometimes had our simple meals or coffee there together, and I particularly recall the occasion when solid food was first permitted me and she gave me a delicate young *bondelle*, fresh caught that very morning in the lake. There were leaves of sweet, crisp lettuce with it, and she picked the bones out for me with her own white hands.

The day was radiant, with a sky of cloudless blue, soft airs stirred the poplar crests; the little waves fell on the pebbly beach not fifty metres away, and the orchard floor was carpeted with flowers that seemed to have caught from heaven's stars the patterns of their yellow blossoms. The bees droned peacefully among the fruit trees; the air was full of musical deep hummings. My former vigour stirred delightfully in my blood, and I knew no pain, beyond occasional dull twinges in the head that came with a rush of temporary darkness over my mind. The scar was healed, however, and the hair had grown over it again. This temporary darkness alarmed her more than it alarmed me. There were grave complications, apparently, that I did not know of.

But the deep-lying sadness in me seemed independent of the glorious weather, due to causes so intangible, so far off that I never could dispel them by arguing them away. For I could not discover what they actually were. There was a vague, distressing sense of restlessness that I ought to have been elsewhere and otherwise, that we were together for a few days only, and that these few days I had snatched unlawfully from stern, imperative duties. These duties were immediate, but neglected. In a sense I had no right to this springtide of bliss her presence brought me. I was playing truant somehow, somewhere. It was *not* my absence from the regiment; that I know. It was infinitely deeper, set to some enormous scale that vaguely frightened me, while it deepened the sweetness of the stolen joy.

Like a child, I sought to pin the sunny hours against the sky and make them stay. They passed with such a mocking swiftness, snatched momentarily from some big oblivion. The twilights swallowed our days together before they had been properly tasted, and on looking back, each afternoon of happiness seemed to have been a mere moment in a flying dream. And I must have somehow betrayed the aching mood, for Marion turned of a sudden and gazed into my face with yearning and anxiety in the sweet brown eyes.

'What is it, dearest?' I asked, 'and why do your eyes bring questions?'

'You sighed,' she answered, smiling a little sadly; 'and sighed so deeply. You are in pain again. The darkness, perhaps, is over you?' And her hand stole out to meet my own. 'You are in pain?'

'Not physical pain,' I said, 'and not *the* darkness either. I see *you* clearly,' and would have told her more, as I carried her soft fingers to my lips, had I not divined from the expression in her eyes that she read my heart and knew all my strange, mysterious forebodings in herself.

'I know,' she whispered before I could find speech, 'for I feel it too. It is the shadow of separation that oppresses you—yet of no common, measurable separation you can understand. Is it not that?'

Leaning over then, I took her close into my arms, since words in that moment were mere foolishness. I held her so that she could not get away; but even while I did so it was like trying to hold the spring, or fasten the flying hour with a fierce desire. All slipped from me, and my arms caught at the sunshine and the wind.

'We have both felt it all these weeks,' she said bravely, as soon as I had released her, 'and we both have struggled to conceal it. But now——' she hesitated for a second, and with so exquisite a tenderness that I would have caught her to me again but for my anxiety to hear her further words—'now that you are well, we may speak plainly to each other, and so lessen our pain by sharing it.' And then she added, still more softly: 'You feel there is "something" that shall take you from me—yet what it is you cannot discover nor divine. Tell me, Félix—all your thought, that I in turn may tell you mine.'

Her voice floated about me in the sunny air. I stared at her, striving to focus the dear face more clearly for my sight. A shower of apple blossoms fell about us, and her words seemed floating past me like those passing petals of white. They drifted away. I followed them with difficulty and confusion. With the wind, I fancied, a veil of indefinable change slipped across her face and eyes.

'Yet nothing that could alter feeling,' I answered; for she had expressed my own thought completely. 'Nor anything that either of us can control. Only—perhaps, that everything must fade and pass away, just as this glory of the spring must fade and pass away——'

'Yet leaving its sweetness in us,' she caught me up passionately, 'and to come again, my beloved, to come again in every subsequent life, each time with an added sweetness in it too!' Her little face showed suddenly the courage of a lion in its eyes. Her heart was ever braver than my own, a vigorous, fighting soul. She spoke of lives, I prattled of days and hours merely.

A touch of shame stole over me. But that delicate, swift change in her spread too. With a thrill of ominous warning, I noticed how it rose and grew about her. From within, outwards, it seemed to pass—like a shadow of great blue distance. Shadow was somewhere in it, so that she dimmed a little before my very eyes. The dreadful yearning searched and shook me, for I could not understand it, try as I would. She seemed going from me—drifting like her words and like the apple blossoms.

'But when we shall no longer be here to know it,' I made answer quickly, yet as calmly as I could, 'and when we shall have passed to some other place—to other conditions—where we shall not recognise the joy and wonder. When barriers of mist shall have rolled between us—our love and passion so made-over that we shall not know each other'—the words rushed out feverishly, half beyond control—'and perhaps shall not even dare to speak to each other of our deep desire——'

I broke off abruptly, conscious that I was speaking out of some unfamiliar place where I floundered, helpless among strange conditions. I was saying things I hardly understood myself. Her bigger, deeper mood spoke through me, perhaps.

Her darling face came back again; she moved close within reach once more.

'Hush, hush!' she whispered, terror and love both battling in her eyes. 'It is the truth, perhaps, but you must not say such things. To speak them brings them closer. A chain is about our hearts, a chain of fashioning lives without number, but do not seek to draw upon it with anxiety or fear. To do so can only cause the pain of wrong entanglement, and interrupt the natural running of the iron links.' And she placed her hand swiftly upon my mouth, as though divining that the bleak attack of anguish was again upon me with its throbbing rush of darkness.

But for once I was disobedient and resisted. The physical pain, I realised vividly, was linked closely with this spiritual torture. One caused the other somehow. The disordered brain received, though brokenly, some hints of darker and unusual knowledge. It had stammered forth in me, but through her it flowed easily and clear. I saw the change move more swiftly then across her face. Some ancient look passed into both her eyes.

And it was inevitable; I must speak out, regardless of mere bodily well-being.

'We shall have to face them someday,' I cried, although the effort hurt abominably, 'then why not now?' And I drew her hand down and kissed it passionately over and over again. 'We are not children, to hide our faces among shadows and pretend we are invisible. At least we have the Present—the Moment that is here and now. We stand side by side in the heart of this deep spring day. This sunshine and these flowers, this wind across the lake, this sky of blue and this singing of the birds—all, all are ours *now*. Let us use the moment that Time gives, and so strengthen the chain you speak of that shall bring us again together times without number. We shall then, perhaps, remember. Oh, my heart, think what that would mean—to remember!'

Exhaustion caught me, and I sank back among my cushions. But

Marion rose up suddenly and stood beside me. And as she did so, another Sky dropped softly down upon us both, and I smelt again the incense of old, old gardens that brought long-forgotten perfumes, incredibly sweet, but with it an ache of far-off, passionate remembrance that was pain. This great ache of distance swept over me like a wave.

I know not what grand change then was wrought upon her beauty, so that I saw her defiant and erect, commanding Fate because she understood it. She towered over me, but it was her soul that towered. The rush of internal darkness in me blotted out all else. The familiar, present sky grew dim, the sunshine faded, the lake and flowers and poplars dipped away. Conditions a thousand times more vivid took their place. She stood out, clear and shining in the glory of an undressed soul, brave and confident with an eternal love that separation strengthened but could never, never change. The deep sadness I abruptly realised, was very little removed from joy—because, somehow, it was the condition of joy. I could not explain it more than that.

And her voice, when she spoke, was firm with a note of steel in it; intense, yet devoid of the wasting anger that passion brings. She was determined beyond Death itself, upon a foundation sure and lasting as the stars. The heart in her was calm, because she *knew*. She was magnificent.

'We are together—always,' she said, her voice rich with the knowledge of some unfathomable experience, 'for separation is temporary merely, forging new links in the ancient chain of lives that binds our hearts eternally together.' She looked like one who has conquered the adversity Time brings, by accepting it. 'You speak of the Present as though our souls were already fitted now to bid it stay, needing no further fashioning. Looking only to the Future, you forget our ample Past that has made us what we are. Yet our Past is here and now, beside us at this very moment. Into the hollow cups of weeks and months, of years and centuries, Time pours its flood beneath our eyes. Time is our schoolroom. . . . Are you so soon afraid? Does not separation achieve that which companionship never could accomplish? And how shall we dare eternity together if we cannot be strong in separation first?'

I listened while a flood of memories broke up through film upon film and layer upon layer that had long covered them.

'This Present that we seem to hold between our hands,' she went on in that earnest, distant voice, '*is* our moment of sweet remembrance that you speak of, of renewal, perhaps, too, of reconciliation—a fleeting instant when we may kiss again and say goodbye, but with strengthened hope and courage revived. But we may not stay together finally—we *cannot*—until long discipline and pain shall have perfected sympathy and schooled our love by searching, difficult tests, that it may last for ever.'

I stretched my arms out dumbly to take her in. Her face shone down upon me, bathed in an older, fiercer sunlight. The change in her seemed in an instant then complete. Some big, soft wind blew both of us ten thousand miles away. The centuries gathered us back together.

'Look, rather, to the Past,' she whispered grandly, 'where first we knew the sweet opening of our love. Remember, if you can, how the pain and separation have made it so worthwhile to continue. And be braver thence.'

She turned her eyes more fully upon my own, so that their light persuaded me utterly away with her. An immense new happiness broke over me. I listened, and with the stirrings of an ampler courage. It seemed I followed her down an interminable vista of remembrance till I was happy with her among the flowers and fields of our earliest pre-existence.

Her voice came to me with the singing of birds and the hum of summer insects.

'Have you so soon forgotten,' she sighed, 'when we knew together the perfume of the hanging Babylonian Gardens, or when the Hesperides were so soft to us in the dawn of the world? And do you not remember,' with a little rise of passion in her voice, 'the sweet plantations of Chaldea, and how we tasted the odour of many a drooping flower in the gardens of Alcinous and Adonis, when the bees of olden time picked out the honey for our eating? It is the fragrance of those first hours we knew together that still lies in our hearts to-day, sweetening our love to this apparent suddenness. Hence comes the full, deep happiness we gather so easily Today. . . . The breast of every ancient forest is torn with storms and lightning. . . . that's why it is so soft and full of little gardens. You have forgotten too easily the glades of Lebanon, where we whispered our earliest secrets while the big winds drove their chariots down those earlier skies. . . .'

There rose an indescribable tempest of remembrance in my heart as I strove to bring the pictures into focus; but words failed me, and the hand I eagerly stretched out to touch her own, met only sunshine and the rain of apple blossoms.

'The myrrh and frankincense,' she continued in a sighing voice that seemed to come with the wind from invisible caverns in the sky, 'the grapes and pomegranates—have they all passed from you, with the train of apes and peacocks, the tigers and the ibis, and the hordes of dark-faced slaves? And this little sun that plays so lightly here upon our woods of beech and pine—does it bring back nothing of the old-time scorching when the olive slopes, the figs and ripening cornfields heard our vows and watched our love mature?... Our spread encampment in the Desert—do not these sands upon our little beach revive its lonely majesty for you, and have you forgotten the gleaming towers of Semiramis....or, in Sardis, those strange lilies that first tempted our souls to their divine disclosure....?'

Conscious of a violent struggle between pain and joy, both too deep for me to understand, I rose to seize her in my arms. But the effort dimmed the flying pictures. The wind that bore her voice down the stupendous vista fled back into the caverns whence it came. And the pain caught me in a vice of agony so searching that I could not move a muscle. My tongue lay dry against my lips. I could not frame a word of any sentence....

Her voice presently came back to me, but fainter, like a whisper from the stars. The light dimmed everywhere; I saw no more the vivid, shining scenery she had summoned. A mournful dusk instead crept down upon the world she had momentarily revived.

'....we may not stay together,' I heard her little whisper, 'until long discipline shall have perfected sympathy, and schooled our love to last. For this love of ours *is* for ever, and the pain that tries it is the furnace that fashions precious stones....'

Again, I stretched my arms out. Her face shone a moment longer in that forgotten fiercer sunlight, then faded very swiftly. The change, like a veil, passed over it. From the place of prodigious distance where she had been, she swept down towards me with such dizzy speed. As she was Today I saw her again, more and more.

'Pain and separation, then, are welcome,' I tried to stammer, 'and we will desire them'—but my thought got no further into expression than the first two words. Aching blotted out coherent utterance.

She bent down very close against my face. Her fragrance was about my lips. But her voice ran off like a faint thrill of music, far, far away. I caught the final words, dying away as wind dies in high branches of a wood. And they reached me this time through the droning of bees and of waves that murmured close at hand upon the shore.

'....for our love is of the soul, and our souls are moulded in Eternity. It is not yet, it is not now, our perfect consummation. Nor shall

251

our next time of meeting know it. We shall not even speak. . . . For I shall not be free. . . .' was what I heard. She paused.

'You mean we shall not know each other?' I cried, in an anguish of spirit that mastered the lesser physical pain.

I barely caught her answer:

'My discipline then will be in another's keeping—yet only that I may come back to you. . . .more perfect. . . .in the end. . . .'

The bees and waves then cushioned her whisper with their humming. The trail of a deeper silence led them far away. The rush of temporary darkness passed and lifted. I opened my eyes. My love sat close beside me in the shadow of the poplars. One hand held both my own, while with the other she arranged my pillows and stroked my aching head. The world dropped back into a tiny scale once more.

'You have had the pain again,' Marion murmured anxiously, 'but it is better now. It is passing.' She kissed my cheek. 'You must come in....'

But I would not let her go. I held her to me with all the strength that was in me. 'I had it, but it's gone again. An awful darkness came with it,' I whispered in the little ear that was so close against my mouth. 'I've been dreaming,' I told her, as memory dipped away, 'dreaming of you and me—together somewhere—in old gardens, or forests—where the sun was——'

But she would not let me finish. I think, in any case, I could not have said more, for thought evaded me, and any language of coherent description was in the same instant beyond my power. Exhaustion came upon me, that vile, compelling nausea with it.

'The sun here is too strong for you, dear love,' I heard her saying, 'and you must rest more. We have been doing too much these last few days. You must have more repose.' She rose to help me move indoors.

'I have been unconscious then?' I asked, in the feeble whisper that was all I could manage.

'For a little while. You slept, while I watched over you.'

'But I was away from you! Oh, how could you let me sleep, when our time together is so short?'

She soothed me instantly in the way she knew we both loved so. I clung to her until she released herself again.

'Not away from me,' she smiled, 'for I was with you in your dreaming.'

'Of course, of course you were'; but already I knew not exactly why I said it, nor caught the deep meaning that struggled up into my words from such unfathomable distance.

'Come,' she added, with her sweet authority again, 'we must go in now. Give me your arm, and I will send out for the cushions. Lean on me. I am going to put you back to bed.'

'But I shall sleep again,' I said petulantly, 'and we shall be separated.'

'We shall dream together,' she replied, as she helped me slowly and painfully towards the old grey walls of the *château*.

2

Half an hour later I slept deeply, peacefully, upon my bed in the big stately chamber where the roses watched beside the latticed windows.

And to say I dreamed again is not correct, for it can only be expressed by saying that I saw and knew. The figures round the bed were actual, and in life. Nothing could be more real than the whisper of the doctor's voice—that solemn, grave-faced man who was so tall—as he said, sternly yet brokenly, to someone: 'You must say goodbye; and you had better say it *now*.' Nor could anything be more definite and sure, more charged with the actuality of living, than the figure of Marion, as she stooped over me to obey the terrible command. For I saw her face float down towards me like a star, and a shower of pale spring blossoms rained upon me with her hair. The perfume of old, old gardens rose about me as she slipped to her knees beside the bed and kissed my lips—so softly it was like the breath of wind from lake and orchard, and so lingeringly it was as though the blossoms lay upon my mouth and grew into flowers that she planted there.

'Goodbye, my love; be brave. It is only separation.'

'It is death,' I tried to say, but could only feebly stir my lips against her own.

I drew her breath of flowers into my mouth. . . .and there came then the darkness which is final.

★★★★★★★★★★★★

The voices grew louder. I heard a man struggling with an unfamiliar language. Turning restlessly, I opened my eyes—upon a little, stuffy room, with white walls whereon no pictures hung. It was very hot. A woman was standing beside the bed, and the bed was very short. I stretched, and my feet kicked against the boarding at the end.

'Yes, he *is* awake,' the woman said in French. 'Will you come in? The doctor said you might see him when he woke. I think he'll know you.' She spoke in French. I just knew enough to understand.

And of course, I knew him. It was Haddon. I heard him thanking her for all her kindness, as he blundered in. His French, if anything, was worse than my own. I felt inclined to laugh. I did laugh.

'By Jove! old man, this is bad luck, isn't it? You've had a narrow shave. This good lady telegraphed——'

'Have you got my ice-axe? Is it all right?' I asked. I remembered clearly the motor accident—everything.

'The ice-axe is right enough,' he laughed, looking cheerfully at the woman, 'but what about yourself? Feel bad still? Any pain, I mean?'

'Oh, I feel all right,' I answered, searching for the pain of broken bones, but finding none. 'What happened? I was stunned, I suppose?'

'Bit stunned, yes,' said Haddon. 'You got a nasty knock on the head, it seems. The point of the axe ran into you, or something.'

'Was that all?'

He nodded. 'But I'm afraid it's knocked our climbing on the head. Shocking bad luck, isn't it?'

'I telegraphed last night,' the kind woman was explaining.

'But I couldn't get here till this morning,' Haddon said. 'The telegram didn't find me till midnight, you see.' And he turned to thank the woman in his voluble, dreadful French. She kept a little *pension* on the shores of the lake. It was the nearest house, and they had carried me in there and got the doctor to me all within the hour. It proved slight enough, apart from the shock. It was not even concussion. I had merely been stunned. Sleep had cured me, as it seemed.

'Jolly little place,' said Haddon, as he moved me that afternoon to Geneva, whence, after a few days' rest, we went on into the Alps of Haute Savoie, 'and lucky the old body was so kind and quick. Odd, wasn't it?' He glanced at me.

Something in his voice betrayed he hid another thought. I saw nothing 'odd' in it at all, only very tiresome.

'What's its name?' I asked, taking a shot at a venture.

He hesitated a second. Haddon, the climber, was not skilled in the delicacies of tact.

'Don't know its present name,' he answered, looking away from me across the lake, 'but it stands on the site of an old *château*—destroyed a hundred years ago—the Château de Bellerive.'

And then I understood my old friend's absurd confusion. For Bellerive chanced also to be the name of a married woman I knew in Scotland—at least, it was her maiden name, and she was of French extraction.

254

Wind

It is a curious reflection, though of course an obvious one, that wind in itself is—silent; and that only from the friction against objects set in its path comes the multiform music instantly associated with its name. The fact, too, that so potent a force should be both silent and invisible readily explains its common use as a simile, and a beautiful one, for Spirit. Like flame, that other exquisite simile of spirit, how clean it licks, how mysteriously it moves, how swiftly it penetrates! And so subtly linked are they that the one almost seems to produce the other—the swift hot winds that beat about a conflagration; the tongues of fire that follow a fanning draught—"the wind that blew the stars to flame!" True inspiration seems certainly born of this marriage of wind and fire.

How singular—have you ever thought?—would be the impressions of a man to whom the motion of air, as wind, was unknown, when first he witnessed the phenomenon of a twenty-knot breeze. Imagine a people that knew not wind—how they would tremble to see the tree-tops bend; to hear the roar, the whispers, the sweet singing of all Nature about them for the first time; to know the sounds and movements of the myriad objects that but for wind would be silent and motionless from one year's end to another! To me, it has always seemed that such a revelation might be far more wonderful than the first torrent of light that beats upon the eyes of a man who has been blind.

And so, one comes to a further suggestive reflection: that objects all possess their own particular sound or voice that the winds love to set free; their essential note—that specific set of vibrations lying buried in their form—of which, as some curious doctrines of the old magic assert, their forms, indeed, are the visible expression. In this region—pondering the relation between sound and shape—the imagination may wander till it grows dizzy, for it leads very soon to the still more wonderful world where sound and colour spin their puzzling web, and the spiritual phenomena of music cry for further explanation. But, for the moment, let only the sound of wind be in our ears; for in wind, I think, there is a sweetness and a variety of music that no instruments invented by men have yet succeeded in approaching so far as sheer thrill and beauty are concerned.

Each lover of Nature knows, of course, the special voice of wind that most appeals to him—the sighing of pines, the shouting of oaks, the murmur of grasses, the whirring over a bare hillside, or the whistling about the corners of the streets—the variety is endless; and there can be no great interest in obtruding one's own predilection. Only, to know this music thoroughly, to catch all the overtones and undertones that make it so wonderful, and to absorb its essential thrill and power, you must listen, not for minutes, but for hours. If you want to learn the secrets of the things themselves, betrayed in the varying response they give back to the winds that sweep or caress them, lie leisurely for hours at a time and—listen.

How, from the high desolation of mountain peaks it blows out— terror, yet from the sea of bearded grain calls with soft whispering sounds such as children use for their tales of mystery; from old buildings—the melancholy of all dead human passion, yet from the rigging of ships the abandon of wild and passionate adventure: wind, clapping its mighty hands among the flapping sails, or running with weary little feet among the ruined towers of broken habitations; sighing with long, gentle music over English lawns, or rushing, full of dreams, across vast prairies over-seas; kissing a garden into music, or blundering blind-eyed through dark London squares; racing with thoughts of ice down precipices and dropping, as through spaces of sleep, into little corners of oblivion in waste lands of loneliness and desolation, or sighing with almost human melody through the keyhole and down the farmhouse chimney.

From the curtained softness of the summer sky these viewless winds sift silently into the heart, to wake yearnings infinite. From some high attic window, perhaps, where you stand and watch, listen to that wind of sighs that rises, almost articulate with the pains and sorrows, the half-caught joys, too, from that crowded human world beneath the sea of roofs and tiles. Winds of desire, winds of hope, winds of fear and love. Ah! winds of all the spirit's life and moods . . . and, finally, the wind of Death!

And wind down a wet and deserted London street, shouting its whistling song, its song of the triumphant desolation that has cleared the way for it of human obstruction—how it sings the music of magnificent poverty, of heavy luxury, and then of the loneliness bred by both! And you see some solitary figure battling forwards, and hear that curious whistling it makes over the dripping umbrella. Ah! how *that* wind summons pictures of courage in isolation, and of singing in a wilderness! "The wind bloweth where it listeth, and thou hearest the sound thereof, yet canst not tell whence it cometh nor whither it goeth" for wind is, indeed, of the nature of spirit, and its music, crowded with suggestion, as some. times, too, with memory and association, is, in the true sense, magical.

"Where is thy soul? Thou liest i' the wind and rain," says the poetess to the "Beloved Dead"; and in another passage the sound of wind brings back for her the phantom face of the departed: "But who shall drive a mournful face from the sad winds about my door?" Shelley, more than any other, perhaps, loved wind and wind-voices, and has the most marvellous and subtle descriptions of it in his work. Though he so often speaks of the "viewless wind," one cannot help thinking that in his imagination lay some mental picture of wind—in the terms of sight. He *saw* the wind. For him it had colour as well as shape. He saw bright sylphs—spirits of air—which "star the winds with points of coloured light, as they rain through them," and enchanted shapes of wandering mist" that for his inner vision were "snow-white and swift as wind nursed among lilies near a brimming stream."

And, alone among poets so far as I know, he had that delightful conception of solid, smooth surfaces of wind upon which it is possible to run and dance and sleep. His verse is alive with spirits "trampling the wind"; "trampling the slant winds on high with golden-sandalled feet"; or climbing the hills of wind that run up into the highest peaks of heaven. The "Witch of Atlas" not only rode "singing through the shoreless air," but also "ran upon the platforms of the wind, and laughed to hear the fireballs roar behind." And it is the Chorus in *Prometheus Unbound* that so exquisitely "weaves the dance on the floor of the breeze."

But for less gifted mortals there are certain effects of wind that seem to me to approach uncommonly close to actual sight, or at least to a point where one may imagine what wind *ought* to look like. Watch the gusts of a northwest wind as they fall in rapid succession upon a standing field of high barley, beating the surface into long curved shadows that bring to mind Shelley's "kindling within the strings of the waved air, Æolian modulations." One can see the velvet touch of those soft, vast paws, and the immense stretch of the invisible footsteps that press the long stalks down and as suddenly sweep away and set them free again. And with the changing angle of the myriad yellow heads the colour also changes, till gradually there swims upon the mind the impression of some huge and shadowy image that flies above the field—some personal deity of wind, some *djin* of air. One almost sees the spirit of the wind. . .

It is fascinating, too, to stand opposite a slope of wooded mountains, near enough to distinguish the individual swing of each separate tree, yet far enough to note how the forest as a whole blows all one way—the way of the wind. Also—to hear the chord of sound as a whole, yet mark the different notes that pour out of the various trees composing it. In some such way—one wonders, perhaps—the Spirit of God moves over the surface of men's minds, each swinging apparently its own individual way, yet when seen in proper perspective, all moving the one way—*to Him*. And the voices of all these separate little stray winds—who shall describe them? Creep with me now out of the house among these Jura vineyards, and come up into the pine forests that encircle the village. Put your ear against that bosom of the soft dark woods where the wind is born and listen! Find the words if you can——!